Cosella
Wayne

Jews and Judaism: History and Culture

Cosella Wayne
Or, Will and Destiny

CORA WILBURN

Edited by JONATHAN D. SARNA

THE UNIVERSITY OF ALABAMA PRESS
Tuscaloosa

The University of Alabama Press
Tuscaloosa, Alabama 35487-0380
uapress.ua.edu

Inquiries about reproducing material from this work should be addressed to the
University of Alabama Press.

Typeface: Caslon

Cover image: "Cora Wilburn"; courtesy of Moran Barak
Cover design: Michele Myatt Quinn

Library of Congress Cataloging-in-Publication Data

Names: Wilburn, Cora, 1824 -1906, author. | Sarna, Jonathan D., editor.
Title: Cosella Wayne : or, will and destiny / Cora Wilburn ;
edited by Jonathan D. Sarna.
Description: Tuscaloosa : The University of Alabama Press, 2019. | Series: Jews
and Judaism: history and culture | Includes bibliographical references.
Identifiers: LCCN 2019010539| ISBN 9780817320348 (cloth) |
ISBN 9780817359560 (pbk.) | ISBN 9780817392611 (e book)
Subjects: LCSH: Jewish women --Fiction. | Jews --United States --History
--19th century --Fiction. | GSAFD: Historical fiction
Classification: LCC PS3309.W485 C57 2019 | DDC 813/.3 --dc23
LC record available at https://lccn.loc.gov/2019010539

To Talya and Ethan,
In appreciation and with love:
"You will know that all is well in your tent" (Job 5:24).

CORA WILBURN

Contents

Acknowledgments

I stand deeply indebted to the Israel Institute for Advanced Studies (on the campus of the Hebrew University) for affording me the time to pursue my research on Cora Wilburn. Had Moshe Rosman not invited me to join the IIAS group that he created devoted to "Jewish Women's Cultural Capital," my scattered notes on Cora Wilburn might never have yielded this volume. All of my IIAS colleagues expressed interest in my work. Thanks to Elisheva Baumgarten, Ruth Karras, Frances Malino, Renee Levine Melammed, Claudia Rosenzweig, and Oded Zinger for listening to me; special thanks to Paola Tartakoff and Shira Wolosky for their insights and suggestions.

I presented an early draft of the introduction to *Cosella Wayne* before the North American Religions Colloquium at the Harvard Divinity School. Comments by Ann D. Braude, David F. Holland, and others there resulted in significant improvements. Elizabeth E. Imber, Pamela S. Nadell, and Dalia Wassner assisted in areas of their expertise when I queried them, graciously taking time away from their work to assist me in mine. Thanks too to Rachel Gordan, Lori Harrison-Kahan, Kathryn Hellerstein, and Sasha Senderovich, who joined me on a panel at the American Jewish Historical Society's Scholars' Conference where Cora Wilburn was discussed.

My colleagues at the Jacob Rader Marcus Center of the American Jewish Archives played an essential role in this project. Kevin Proffitt located Cora Wilburn's diary, had it scanned, and sent me other documents as well; Dana Herman displayed great interest in this project and showed me the original of the Wilburn diary; and Executive Director Gary P. Zola, my friend of four decades, permitted me to publish selections from that diary here. Brandeis students Tamar Shachaf Schneider and Devon Kennedy provided invaluable research assistance, locating many Cora Wilburn items that might otherwise have eluded me. In Jerusalem, Elisheva Hyams expertly typed the text of *Cosella Wayne* and commented intelligently upon the novel, reinforcing my sense that contemporary readers would appreciate it. Thanks too to Carolyn Hessel and Peter W. Bernstein for their faith in this project.

My wife, Ruth Langer, suspects that I have spent more time with Cora Wilburn than with her over these past few years. Yet she has actually been essential to all of my work, doing what she can to keep me healthy and offering encouragement and sage wisdom at key moments.

This volume affords me an opportunity to welcome two wonderful new members to our family, our daughter-in-law, Talya Housman, and our son-in-law, Ethan Schwartz. Both appreciate the life of the mind and have added immeasurably to our lives as well. In dedicating this book to them, I pray that they and their spouses, our children Aaron and Leah, may proceed "from strength to strength."

Editor's Introduction

Cora Wilburn's *Cosella Wayne* (1860) is both the first novel written and published in English by an American Jewish woman writer and the first coming-of-age novel to depict Jews in the United States. Published serially in the Spiritualist journal *Banner of Light*—the same journal that featured articles by the first African American woman writer, Harriet E. Adams Wilson, author of *Our Nig* (1859)[1]—*Cosella Wayne* transforms what we know about the history of early American Jewish literature and adds an important new name to the pantheon of nineteenth-century Jewish women writers. It is, as well, an important Spiritualist source, shedding light on that religious movement's pre–Civil War origins and ideology. Likewise, it is a valuable source for reconstructing nineteenth-century Jewish women's history on five continents. It is the only nineteenth-century American Jewish literary source to recount a relationship between an abusive Jewish father and a rebellious, molested daughter. It is also unique in portraying such themes as an unmarried Jewish woman's descent into poverty, her forlorn years as a starving orphaned seamstress, her apostasy and return to Judaism, and her quest to be both Jewish and a Spiritualist at the same time. The fact that the novel may now be supplemented by Cora Wilburn's recently rediscovered diary (1844–1848), selections from which are reprinted in the appendix, only adds to its significance. That, and hundreds of pages of Wilburn's nonfiction and fiction writings, available online, help to situate *Cosella Wayne* within the life and times of one of nineteenth-century American Jewry's least-known and yet most prolific female authors.

Cora Wilburn: A Brief Biography

Cora Wilburn was born on December 1, 1824.[2] Her original first name was Henrietta, and her family name was probably Pulfermacher ("Powdermaker"). She listed her birthplace, at different times, as either Germany or

France; most likely she was born in Alsace.[3] Fluent in German, with some knowledge of French, Spanish, and Yiddish, she nevertheless wrote the surviving volume of her diary (1844–1848) in English; that, presumably, was her mother tongue.[4] If, based on the evidence in the diary, we read her novel as thinly veiled autobiography, her birth mother lived and was buried in England.

Cora Wilburn's father, whom she despised and whose name she subsequently discarded, was an unscrupulous gem merchant and con man, as well as an abusive father and husband. He remarried following the untimely death of his first wife but maintained his criminal ways. In 1837 the *London Gazette* listed him as an insolvent debtor and prisoner named "Moss Pulfermacher," a self-described "agent for foreign houses in the West Indies, and for Spaniards on the Spanish Main."[5] Six years later, the *Maulmain Chronicle* (Burma), in a cautionary article reprinted in the *Sydney Morning Herald*, portrayed the same man as "Moritz Pulfermacher." Under the headline "Tricks of a Traveller," it described how, opulently attired and in the company of his wife and daughter, he claimed to be both a captain in the Prussian cavalry and a naturalized Englishman. He held himself forth as a "rich diamond merchant" and swindled a sea captain and others by taking loans that he did not repay and by supplying them, in pledge, "false stones," "counterfeit gold," and "German" [faux] silver. Next, according to the exposé, he proceeded under various guises to Muscat (Oman) and to Bushire (Iran), where again he affected "affluent circumstances." This time, he paraded as "an American Jew named Moritz Jackson"—precisely the same last name that his daughter subsequently used when she immigrated to America. He also allegedly impersonated Sir Moses Montefiore! Even in an age when "self-fashioning" was something of a social norm, and Jews, in particular, changed their ways and their names in quest of social and economic mobility, the case of "Moritz Jackson" seemed extreme. The *Maulmain Chronicle* warned readers to beware, and revealed that the con man was en route to "Khorasau" [Curaçao?] to ensnare new victims.[6]

Ultimately, "Moritz" settled some two hundred miles away from Curaçao, in the Venezuelan port of La Guaira, near Caracas, where the "Jackson" family took up residence in 1844. By then, he had dragged his long-suffering wife and teen-aged daughter, in her words, "nearly over the world"[7]— forever seeking to escape creditors and victims. World travelers, especially Jewish ones, were few and far between in the first half of the nineteenth century. Sea travel, prior to the advent of oceangoing steamboats, was risky, wearying, and expensive. Cora Wilburn thus knew the wide world better than almost any other author of her day. Her writings would eventually include elaborate descriptions of the places she visited, not just England and

Germany but also such exotic locations as Singapore, Burma, India, Australia, Hawaii, and Venezuela.[8]

The surviving volume of Cora Wilburn's diary—written while she was still Henrietta—commenced upon her arrival in La Guaira, Venezuela. It began on February 28, 1844, and painted a grim picture of her Jewish family, far different from the idealized Jewish family that so many nineteenth-century Jewish writers and artists celebrated.

"I had not been home long yesterday but it began anew," she reported cryptically on March 1, 1844. A week later she explained that she and her father "had again a most tremendous row, as usual for nothing. . . . The brandy bottle was applied and so began his cursing and bellowing; it continued till near morning." Within months the situation at home deteriorated further; her father, perhaps fearing that discovery was near, turned violent. "Yesterday the looking glass was broken," she reported to her diary in May. "Today after 15 glasses, butter glasses, were broken . . . he began to take a knife up to my [step]mother so we both left the house."

In *Cosella Wayne*, Wilburn elaborated on the abuse that she suffered at the hands of her father, through the voice of an alter ego, her central character. Her novel described the threats, the screams, the assaults, and the beatings that Cosella endured. The tension at home likewise took a physical toll on Cosella's stepmother. Her health declined and she could no longer keep house. Finally, on June 29, 1844, according to Cora Wilburn's diary, her stepmother "departed this life for a better. God gave her a calm and peaceful end." Following this death, according to both the diary and the novel, conditions only became worse. Enraged that his daughter not only refused to assist him in his crimes but also spurned the (much older) man whom he selected to be her husband, her father threatened her physically (with a pistol, according to the novel) and drove her from the house.

In 1845 "Moritz Jackson" né Pulfermacher died; rumors abounded that he had been murdered. Fifteen years later, in *Cosella Wayne*, Wilburn imagined the tortures he suffered as he lay dying, the "winged and horrible demons, wild birds of prey with outstretched sable wings" that perched upon her father's "laboring breast, croaked hoarsely in his ear, and snatched his trembling fingers from his eyes!" This, she suggested, was his deserved punishment, retribution for his damning sins: "From the open book in her hand, he read, in blood-red letters, there inscribed, the record of her wrongs; the manifold and pardonless sins committed against her life; and, at the close of each page was written the ever recurring, fearful word, "Retribution!"[9]

The orphaned Henrietta (as she still was known) lost everything upon her father's death. Whatever of value he may have owned was stolen. "My little fortune is irrevocably lost!" she reported to her diary in anguish. "Alas I am a being doomed to misfortune." Eventually, she sold what was left of her jewelry for "295 dollars."[10] Her days as a "gentlewoman," raised in a home with servants and the visible accoutrements of wealth, ended abruptly. She found herself practically penniless.[11]

Adrift in the world, and taken in by sympathetic Catholic neighbors in La Guaira, Henrietta succumbed to pressure from those around her and, on June 24, 1846, converted to Catholicism. "I had repented before it began," she subsequently admitted to her diary, "but it was now too late, my word had been given." She attributed manifold misfortunes to this act of apostasy, describing it as "an event that has called upon me the just anger of a most just God." Despairing of "the fatal day I changed my pure and holy religion for a false one," she vowed, eighteen months later, to return, "although alone, friendless and penniless, to my religion, to my God!" In halting Yiddish, she wrote prayerfully in her diary to the "Dear God of Israel," beseeching him to "save her" and to enfold her again "within his sacred love." She considered hers to have been an almost unpardonable act of betrayal. Apostasy, like bastardy, was a sin one could never live down.[12] Nevertheless, and more often than a recent history of "radical assimilation" realizes, conversion could be a two-way street, permitting apostates like Henrietta to return home, or, as in *Cosella Wayne*, to seek out a neutral in-between space where multiple faiths might harmoniously coexist.[13]

In hopes of improving her situation and returning to her people, and buoyed by the traditional belief that fellow Jews would embrace and uplift one of their own, Henrietta spent $40 of her remaining funds and took to sea for a final time, hoping to make a fresh start as a Jew in Philadelphia, about which she had read. She spent three weeks at sea on the *Euphemia*, arrived in New York on September 30, 1848,[14] and reached Philadelphia that same night. Over the ensuing days, she bitterly recalled, her faith in a Jewish moral economy based on mutual assistance was cruelly shattered. "Went to the houses of my brethren, was but ill received alas!" she reported to her diary. Philadelphia's Jews offered her only menial labor. She poured out her deep feelings of disappointment in one of her final diary entries: "Ye who worship the God my soul adores, the High & Holy One of Israel, wherefore meet me with the cold look of indifference, and the haughtiness of superior wealth? Does no voice tell ye that within that orphan's breast lie hid the purest hopes and ambition the most Holy?"[15]

Henrietta found herself reduced to menial servitude in Philadelphia. Other descriptions of the female Jewish poor in Philadelphia, aside from hers, stemmed from the ladies bountiful who aided them, such as the aristocratic philanthropist Rebecca Gratz.[16] In *Cosella Wayne*, by contrast, Wilburn gave voice to the poor themselves, allowing us to see class relations among Jewish women through the eyes of those who toiled to survive. The novel poignantly describes Cosella's four years of penury:

> Through all the various grades of discipline that poverty enforces has Cosella passed; for some weeks "companion to a lady," that misnomer for ceaseless drudge; then assisting in the care of children; then laboring with the needle for the stores; then watching by the sick, deprived of weeks of rest, of night after night of sleep; then, in despair returning to the hated needle; and sometimes compelled to spend days of utter listlessness, when there was no work to be obtained, and consequently no bread to eat. She would then go and offer her services at places where she had been employed before in order to obtain a meal. Sometimes, with a few pennies saved, she would buy a loaf of bread and a draught of milk, and seek a lodging for the night. At last, she rented the small room in a retired part of the city, and for a while bore up bravely against the ills that beset her. She sold her few remaining books in order to obtain food; she lived for many days without a fire that inclement winter; and her scanty garments bore the marks of time, the shoes upon her feet were worn, the poetry, beauty, and refinement of life was gone (228).

Cora Wilburn was far from alone in her poverty. Early women's rights advocates frequently compared the conditions of women to those of black slaves. Victorian social protest literature likewise abounded with "seamstress narratives" that bemoaned their subjects' unhappy plight. Women writers in particular evoked seamstresses in their writings, partly out of a sense of sisterly empathy and partly in the hope that concern for seamstresses would inspire women to embrace other social justice causes as well.[17]

In Wilburn's case, the conditions under which she recalled working were appalling—long hours, limited pay, low respect. "'Here, *you!*' is a usual form of address," she recounted, "and to find fault with the large stitches necessarily taken in the coarse garments, is a common everyday occurrence. A seat is not offered to her; and 'you must come for your money next week,' is often repeated; then if the poor toiler urges her needs, she is gruffly answered with—'We can't help that; we have no change at present,' and perhaps, too, there will be no work cut out for the ensuing week" (p. 227). Writing for readers who likely employed seamstresses and servants of their own, she sought sympathy by describing the seamstress's plight from personal experience.

A strong Jewish element also permeated this tale of woe. Cora Wilburn's sketches, supposedly "from life," reveal aspects of the Philadelphia Jewish community that its elite might rather have seen suppressed. She tells one story, for example, about "Mrs. Na— [Nathan?], a wealthy lady, one of the daughters of Israel," in whose Philadelphia home Cosella sewed for three weeks. Repeatedly, Wilburn writes, she was "admonished to sew faster, and told that 'girls who made their living must not talk of exercise and such things—they had only to attend to their duties.'" Tormented by the family's rude, spoiled children, she looks forward with anticipation to concluding her job, only to discover that the wealthy "Mrs. Na——" has shortchanged her, paying her twenty-five cents less per week than originally agreed upon. When she gently points this out, she is ordered from the house. Her response, powerful and prophetic, reflects the lofty egalitarian values and unvarnished language that Cora Wilburn herself would consistently espouse. "You may wrong the orphan and the stranger, but you will be none the richer, none the happier! . . . Your religion is a sham, your lives hypocrisy! I scorn, I shrink from association with such as you!" (pp. 210–211).[18]

Jews in standard seamstress narratives, when they appeared at all, did so as wealthy, male, industrial capitalists who took financial advantage of unorganized women workers. Wilburn turned that trope upside down: her central Jewish character (modeled on herself) was poor, female, and an unfortunate victim of circumstance. Standard seamstress narratives also focused on the industrial arena—the factories and the mills. Wilburn focused on the domestic arena, the private homes where she herself had toiled. Finally, most seamstress narratives depicted needlework as a dead end, a life-defining fate. Wilburn's own story belied that. She nevertheless continued to champion those less fortunate than herself, giving voice to women who might otherwise have been invisible.[19]

After four years of mind-numbing toil (1848–1852), Henrietta Jackson broke free of her hated needle. Aided by Christian friends, she became a professional writer and began life anew. She would from now on be known only by her nom de plume, Cora Wilburn, which soon became her legal name, listed in official censuses and also on her death certificate. Like her father, who often took on new names to hide from pursuers, she apparently hoped that by changing her name she would change her fortune. In Cosella Wayne, name changes form a recurring trope, as if to underscore human beings' ability to refashion themselves at will. The change of name, in her case, did not remake her into a woman of leisure. To keep "the demon of want from the door," she still found herself having to work "from early dawn to midnight."[20] Still, the new career and name enabled her to labor in a "respectable" profession. Writing was one of the few occupations that a woman of her day could take up with pride.

As a writer Cora Wilburn aligned herself for some seventeen years (1852–

1869) with the fast-growing but controversial Spiritualist movement, which held that the spirits of the departed lived on in a distinct "spirit world" from which they continued to communicate with human beings. Nourished by the same upstate New York soil as the women's rights movement, Spiritualists advocated women's rights and treated women on a par with men in their practices, policies, and ideologies.[21] Wilburn herself did not become a professional medium or "trance lecturer," as the movement's best-known women did. Spiritualists like Cora L. V. Hatch (Scott) and Victoria Woodhull became wealthy through their lectures, books, séances, and well-publicized theatrics. Grieving relatives, especially during the Civil War, paid handsomely to communicate with lost loved ones through a professional medium. Audiences, meanwhile, thronged to performances where a skillful practitioner interacted with the spirit world; it was the equivalent of a modern-day circus or magic show.[22] Wilburn, though, reached people mostly through her voluminous writings. "I do not," she explained "feel myself adapted for public speaking."[23] She published regularly in Spiritualist magazines such as *Banner of Light* and the *Agitator*.

Wilburn was one of a comparatively small number of Jews who identified with Spiritualism.[24] In her case, she never denied her Jewish heritage (in fact, in *Cosella Wayne* she celebrated it), but much like Jews who would later participate in such movements as Unitarianism, Ethical Culture, Christian Science, and Buddhism, she insisted that her liberal Spiritualist faith required her only "to be true and pure," and "to live the life that is approved of God and angels."[25] In a series boldly entitled "My Religion," she went so far as to portray the "human soul" as a more reliable guide for human beings than the Bible. "I have never reaped any benefit from the teachings of the Old Testament," she declared, and "in later years, when I turned from the materialism of the Jewish faith, to the search for light in Christianity, the New Testament failed to inspire me." As a religious seeker, she placed her faith, instead, in "Nature's God," proclaiming that "we need no Bible and no Creed."[26] The specifics of her austere way of life—a mélange of the religion-inspired health reforms so prominent in her day—appear in the concluding chapter of *Jasmine*, another of her autobiographical novels:

[W]e preach and practice reform in the minutest departments of life, allowing no swines's flesh to pass our portals; using very seldom and very sparingly any animal food; living upon the nutritious grains, the plentiful vegetables and healthful fruits of our providing generous mother, Nature. We make use of no condiments, no stimulating drinks; no greasy dishes find favor in our sight. We have abolished pies; and in their place use wholesome, savory, simple puddings. We have no nightmare dreams from the use of late and hearty suppers; we are not pursued by demons or other terrible visitations by night, nor do we awaken torpid and unrefreshed from a seven hour sleep: For there is not a feather bed in the house to cause a feverish unrest. We do not fear the night air; preferring it to the hermetical sealing up of bedrooms so much in vogue. We hail the life-giving atmosphere by night or by day. Our house is sweet and fragrant at all times for no breath of tobacco or alcohol has ever polluted its walls. I admit no gentlemen who smoke or chew tobacco. I am called a *fanatic*, for this and other reforms I cling to. No matter, so I obey the dictates of my conscience. We strive for the exercise of temperance in food as well as in drink; in sleep as well as in labor; for moderation in speech and expectation, in reproof and endeavor. In all our intercourse with the world.[27]

Wilburn's productivity during these years was astonishing. Serialized novels, lengthy translations from German and French, colorful short stories, pointed nonfiction essays, and hundreds of poems flowed from her inexhaustible pen. No nineteenth-century American Jewish woman wrote more.

These writings reveal Wilburn to have been a staunch advocate for social justice—a forgotten foremother of twentieth-century liberal Jewish activism. She spoke out boldly against African American slavery before and during the Civil War. In addition, as early as 1860 other forms of social injustice ("all forms of slavery") likewise drew from her sharp rebuke:

I protest . . . against the sale of my black brother and sister, and their subjection to unholy bondage; against the education and sale of maidens for the marriage altar; against the tyranny of unjust laws; and against the slavery of labor, as it is enjoined in our northern cities, in our factories, in our households; against the monstrous systems of extortion practiced by the aristocratic drones of our land toward the defenseless poor; the hard-heartedness of landlords, the tasking of the wretched seamstress, the burdening of orphans and widows with the double weight of humiliation and toil, the contemptuous treatment of dependents, the starvation wages that force young women into the paths of degradation; against all of these outrages perpetrated in this christian land, under legal sanction and authority, my soul protests![28]

Wilburn's "outspoken speech and writings" outraged some Spiritualists, notwithstanding the movement's general engagement with activist causes.[29] Critics did not share her politics, much less her high-minded views on the evils of worldliness and the importance of altruism. Her insistence that "true Spiritualists deny the outer distinction of clothing, fine surroundings and caste," and that they "spend hours of their most valuable time ministering to the poor, the ignorant, the sick"[30] distanced her from more materialistic-minded colleagues and did nothing to promote her long-term reputation. As she herself later recalled, some Spiritualists "vowed an implacable animosity toward me, because with unsparing tongue and pen I revealed their worthlessness." She was labeled a "half-believer," a "skeptic," an "exclusive." "Because I opposed immoral doctrines, and yet labored for a righteous freedom," she explained, "those of the very household of faith reviled me."[31] Much of the literature on Spiritualism would later efface her name completely.[32]

In 1868 Wilburn gathered funds sufficient to publish a small book of her poems entitled *The Spiritual Significance of Gems*. She had learned about gems in her father's house, but where he used the precious stones to profit and deceive, she looked upon them as spiritual preceptors, each imbuing its wearer with a moral lesson ("Sapphire—Trust in Heaven"; "Diamond— Spiritual Purity"; "Chrysolite—Holiness"; and so forth). *The Spiritual Significance of Gems*, like most published volumes of poetry, brought its author neither fame nor fortune. Yet the volume was noticed by the *American Israelite*, the Reform Jewish newspaper founded by Rabbi Isaac Mayer Wise, and, significantly, it identified Wilburn as a Jew. "The poems . . . teem with kind and affectionate expressions and noble aspirations for the happiness of man," it reported, even as it grieved at Wilburn's belief "in the dread superstitions of spiritualism." "We are sorry," it wrote, "to see so gifted a daughter of Zion being deluded by the heathen demonology of prostrating imposters."[33]

Notwithstanding the Spiritualist teachings reflected in her poems, Cora Wilburn, by the time her book appeared, had grown disenchanted with the Spiritualist movement. Investigators had shown that the mysterious "rapping" sounds that once held believers like Wilburn in thrall were nothing more than noise produced by the vigorous cracking of toe joints. Other Spiritualist "demonstrations" likewise turned out to be reproducible tricks, rather than manifestations of a "spirit world" beyond ordinary perception. Internal controversies too weakened the movement, particularly well-publicized battles concerning the issue of "free love." To Wilburn, an advocate of sexual purity, and herself (as she put it) an "old maid," free love meant no more than equality and freedom for women: "Let woman be free; and she will be what God ordained and Nature desired, a beautiful loving being, full of holy sympathies and boundless aspirations."[34] For others, though, and particularly for the outspoken Spiritualist radical, Victoria

Woodhull, free love meant exactly that: "sexual freedom for all people—freedom for the monogamist to practice monogamy, for the varietist [polyamorist] to be a varietist still, for the promiscuous to remain promiscuous."[35]

With Spiritualism on the wane, Wilburn drifted into the new Free Religious Association that aimed to emancipate religion from dogmatic traditions and to "promote the interests of pure religion." A wide variety of religious liberals joined this new association, many of them (like Ralph Waldo Emerson) of Unitarian background, some of them Spiritualists, and a few, like Rabbi Isaac Mayer Wise, notable Reform Jews.[36] Thanks to these latter, Wilburn became aware of a form of Judaism that embraced the liberal and progressive causes that she held dear. This discovery further distanced her from her Spiritualist past and brought her back to her people.

"Urged by the strongest convictions of right and duty, I have returned to the faith I was born and educated in, namely the Jewish religion," she announced to readers of the Spiritualist *Banner of Light* on November 13, 1869. She explained that she now identified with its "progressive ranks," not its "so-called Orthodox standard," and that Reform Judaism accepted "all enlightenment, and welcomes every truth tending to exalt the material and the spiritual life of our aspiring humanity." She promised to continue to labor for the "pure, the true, the beautiful" to the best of her "humble capacities," but would henceforward do so as an identifying Jew.[37]

Wilburn was almost forty-five years old when she made this announcement. Middle age was catching up with her, and her health and productivity had greatly declined. Finding herself with few friends and, significantly, "without one kindred tie in this world," she looked to live her remaining days in a small cottage in Maine.[38] New York's Temple Emanu-El, the leading Reform Jewish congregation in the United States, provided her with half the sum needed to purchase the cottage, and generous supporters from the Free Religious Association proffered additional assistance. Maine became her home for several years.

By 1877, though, she was living in Lynn, Massachusetts, and writing more and more for Jewish publications like the *Philadelphia Jewish Record* and B'nai B'rith's *Menorah*. She no longer produced much in the way of fiction or critical essays; instead, the bulk of her writing consisted of poetry. Visitors found her increasingly bitter and reclusive. "Were I not bound by woman's fate, that keeps / Me here inactive, while man grandly reaps, / I would, in Israel's sweet and holy name, / Help to enkindle the world's freedom-flame," one of her poems exclaimed.[39] Her age, her sex, her ill health, her poverty—all precluded her from doing more to advance the great social causes that she cherished. Instead, she spent most of her time caring for beloved animals (a lifelong passion),[40] reading widely, and writing poetry.

Jewish themes suffused her work during these final decades of her life. She published poems entitled "After Yom Kippur," "Israel's Power," and "The Mission of Israel," as well as ones honoring or memorializing Jewish worthies, such as Emma Lazarus, Amy Levy, Henrietta Szold, Sabato Morais, Alfred T. Jones, Baron Maurice de Hirsch, and Benjamin F. Peixotto. Her most celebrated Jewish poem was "Israel to the World in Greeting," written for the Jewish Women's Congress in Chicago in 1893, forerunner of the National Council of Jewish Women. "Greeting to Israel still in captive chains!" she sang out. "Greeting to all in Freedom's wide domains! / Not Toleration, but Fraternal Love, / Be the New Era's olive-bearing dove!"[41] If not poetry of the caliber that Emma Lazarus produced, the fact that this poem was commissioned and that it subsequently appeared in the pages of the Women's Congress's published proceedings suggests that contemporaries admired it and looked up to Wilburn as a Jewish poet laureate.

Wilburn in her old age optimistically believed that she was witnessing "the dawn of the Woman's Era." She encouraged young women of promise, like Henrietta Szold, and she gloried in the fact that "the women of Israel are coming to the fore in rostrum, pulpit and other places of public usefulness."[42] She recognized that she herself had suffered for being a woman and hoped that a new generation of women would succeed where she had not.

Thanks to a long letter that she sent to her friend Rabbi Bernhard Felsenthal of Chicago, we know that she was supported by the Jewish community during her declining years. The banker Jacob H. Schiff sent her a monthly check of ten dollars ("and he knows me only by reputation"), and the Hebrew Benevolent Society of Boston, headed by Jacob Hecht, granted her eight dollars a month, which she took, though she found it "dreadful" to be on the receiving end of "public charity." She also received occasional commissions for poems and cared for beloved pets.[43]

Overall, though, hers was a reclusive and bitter retirement, for, as she put it, "I am homeless, almost friendless, sick, uncared for as I deserve to be." She feared being "looked down upon" but was too poor to live among "our people," the Jewish community of Boston. Nevertheless, she assured Rabbi Felsenthal that she remained true to her faith: "I observe the Shabbes [Sabbath] conscientiously; the Pessach [Passover] and the holy days. I keep Yom Kippur as would the most rigidly orthodox."[44]

Cora Wilburn died at home in Duxbury, Massachusetts, on December 4, 1906.[45] She had just turned eighty-two. Notice of her death flew across the

Associated Press wires and soon appeared in newspapers across the United States, from Boston to Honolulu. Fifteen days later, in deference to her express wishes rooted in late nineteenth-century environmental values (albeit in violation of Jewish law), she was cremated; reputedly, she was "the first person of Jewish faith" ever cremated in Boston.[46]

Cosella Wayne: Or Will and Destiny

Wilburn's novel *Cosella Wayne*, with its significant subtitle, *Will and Destiny*, recounts the story of the title character, who bears the same initials as Cora Wilburn herself. It appeared weekly in serial form in the *Banner of Light*, beginning on March 31, 1860, and concluding on July 7, 1860. The novel never appeared as a book and went unmentioned, so far as I can tell, in Jewish newspapers. Studies of nineteenth-century American Jewish literature ignore it completely.

Following a common formula, *Cosella Wayne* opens upon a death scene. Lea, a Jewess, lies dying in childbirth in her parental home in England. Her regal Iberian-born mother, Hannah Montepesoa, quickly arranges for the surviving Jewish baby, whom Lea has named Cosella, to be abducted. The goal is to thwart what destiny seemingly demands: that Cosella be raised by Lea's non-Jewish husband, Percival Wayne, a saintly Christian, described in a manner reminiscent of the storied founder of Spiritualism, Emanuel Swedenborg (1688–1772). While family members intimate to Percival that his wife and daughter have tragically died, Cosella is being abducted by the wicked Jewish gem merchant Manasseh Moshem and his long-suffering wife, Shina,[47] closely modeled on the author's real father and stepmother. Manasseh proceeds to cart his little family around the world to escape Percival, who, having heard that his daughter yet lives, never abandons efforts to locate and recover her. England, Germany, Australia, India, Venezuela—the novel richly describes each location, as well as its Jews, including extraordinary ethnographic descriptions of Jewish rituals and sacred spaces. Almost uniquely for a nineteenth-century Jewish woman, the writer Cora Wilburn knew each location at first hand, thanks to her tempestuous upbringing and her parents' roving lives.

Cosella Wayne paints a disturbing portrait of a patriarchal and dysfunctional nineteenth-century Jewish family. Manasseh, an abusive, alcoholic man, terrorizes his wife and beats his daughter. He insists that he is the lord and master of his family and expects the family's women to bow to his will. He treats his daughter as property, attempting to marry her off in return for a large dowry, ridiculing her desire to marry only for love, and responding in fury to her efforts to thwart him. Family tensions, recounted from Cosella's point of view, extraordinary displays of female independence, and a celebration of strong-minded women form the novel's central tropes.

Family tensions, of course, animated many autobiographical and fictional works composed by nineteenth-century Jews. As modernization took hold and traditional Jewish societies collapsed under the weight of legal emancipation and cultural enlightenment, young Jews across Europe (and beyond) broke with ancestral traditions and parental ways. They adopted new modes of life inspired by vernacular works that they read and non-Jews whom they came to admire. Literary accounts of these developments often cast women ("the young Jewess") as the central agents of change, depicted, as in *Cosella Wayne*, much more positively than Jewish men. The result was the well-known literary stereotype of "bad Jew, good Jewess." Nadia Valman's account of the "Jewess" in nineteenth-century British literary culture explores this gendered trope and, broadly speaking, applies to *Cosella Wayne* as well: "The Jewess embodied the theological and intellectual problem of the Jews and enabled a range of possible responses to it. Characterised by attractiveness and pathos, she was the vehicle of literary debate about the Jews articulated not only through argument but also through affect. In diametric contrast to her narrow, patriarchal and unfeeling Jewish family, the Jewess personified the capability of Jews for enlightenment and self-transformation."[48]

Marriage, in particular, sparked generational tensions between "good" daughters and "bad" fathers. Young mid-nineteenth-century Jews "fell in love with love," to borrow Naomi Seidman's felicitous phrase. They spurned old-fashioned "arranged marriages" and espoused new romantic ideals of love and companionate marriage.[49] "I feel that it is sinful, wicked, to live with those we love not" (99), Cosella Wayne thunders to her father when he seeks to marry her off to a wealthy and much older widowed Jewish merchant. Similar scenes played out in many a Jewish autobiography and novel.

What distinguishes *Cosella Wayne*, as its conclusion makes clear, is that its central characters *never* marry. Indeed, the novel advocates "fraternal union" and reports that Cosella "turned with soul-abhorrence from the proffered loves of earth" and "from all that bore the stamp of earth's desire" (262–63). Elsewhere, Wilburn went so far as to advocate "liberty from the bondage of the passions . . . from the environments of gross, debasing sensualism," and she criticized those who considered love dependent on "physical gratification."[50] Having grown up with an abusive father and amidst a loveless parental marriage, she criticized marital chains and heartily sympathized with the Spiritualist critique of the institution as a whole.[51] Indeed, her name appeared on a list of prestigious women writers said by a contributor to the *Banner of Light* to "*revel* in the rose-lands of single bless-edness." No precise equivalent to the Christian cult of single blessedness emerged in the nineteenth-century Jewish community, but growing num-bers of Jewish women, especially in Philadelphia, did, happily or not, re-main single. Some Spiritualists (akin to Shakers) found such aversion to marriage highly praiseworthy. "Ladies," the contributor to the *Banner of Light* concluded, "continue reveling!"[52]

Beyond family tensions, *Cosella Wayne* frankly explores—and critiques—Judaism and Christianity, finding strengths and weaknesses in both tradi-tions, and good and bad people in both as well. Unlike the Jewish "middle-brow literature" that began to be produced in her day, especially in Germany, Wilburn's writing was not primarily directed toward Jews looking to navi-gate between tradition and modernity.[53] Nor did it follow the formula of missionary literature produced by apostate Jews to strengthen the faith of Christians.[54] Instead a certain hybridity characterizes *Cosella Wayne*—akin to the hybrid literature famously produced by crypto-Jews and their descendants (Cosella herself claims Iberian descent in the novel's open-ing chapter). The novel crosses boundaries, imagines an ecumenical space where Jews and Christians intermarry, embraces multiple faith traditions, and addresses above all seekers and fellow Spiritualists; it is not specifically Jewish or Christian.

In the novel, Manasseh, portrayed as a Shylock-type traditional Jew, the embodiment of pharisaical dogmatism and material ambition,[55] despises all Christians ("A bitter, relentless, unsparing enmity against the Christian race held entire possession of him" [13]), and takes satisfaction in wreaking ven-geance upon them. He hypocritically employs the language of nineteenth-century liberals ("we are a persecuted race, deprived of home and country; what is there too vile to be brought up against us?" [49]) to deflect at-tention from his own monstrous crimes. Cosella, meanwhile, finds herself drawn to Christian neighbors, falls in love with a Christian boy, discovers beauty in Christian imagery, and ultimately, after her mother dies and her father assaults her, escapes to the home of a Catholic neighbor in Vene-zuela and undergoes conversion. Yet hers is far from the usual nineteenth-century tale of a beautiful young Jewess's conversion to truth. Instead, the once-beloved Hispanic Catholic "mother" who sponsors Cosella turns out to be an adulteress, while Cosella herself comes quickly to question the tenets of the new faith that she has adopted:

Religious scruples arose; conflicts of reason with traditionary teach-ings. Which was the path to heaven? Was it the faith professed by her mother's people, to the last upheld even by the scattered, persecuted tribes of Israel? Was it the Christian faith, with all its panoply of church and form? Was it right for man to make unto himself embodiments of things unseen, and worship them in lieu of the divine realities? Was Jesus of Nazareth indeed the very God? And was that God a spirit, infinite and all-pervading; or was he some grand, incomprehensible personality, dwelling afar in space where time is not? *And heaven?*—was it a place of never-ending day, where Jehovah sat enthroned in kingly pomp, where a blaze of glory veiled the Father's countenance, and the occupation of the angels was to sing and glorify him alone? And that mystery of the Godhead—the Christian, the Catholic Trinity—could the human intellect accept it and the human heart approve? (180–81)

Cosella Wayne, in short, lives on the seam between Judaism and Christianity, attracted to both and uncertain about both. She is among the earliest characters in an English-language Jewish novel to explore that ambivalence, probably because her creator, Cora Wilburn, was among the first writers to live out that ambivalence in real life.

For all of her ambivalence, Cora Wilburn displayed substantial sympathy for Jewish rituals. However much she criticized individual Jews, like Manasseh, she praised Judaism. Indeed, *Cosella Wayne* provides thick descriptions of the Sabbath, the Day of Atonement (Yom Kippur), and Passover, among other rituals, sometimes offering a distinctive woman's perspective, as well as translations of selected Hebrew texts, generally borrowed from Isaac Leeser's prayer book, *The Book of Daily Prayers for Every Day of the Year According to the Custom of the German and Polish Jews (Sidur Divre Tsadikim)*, originally published in 1848. German Polish customs, not Western Sephardic ones, are most often portrayed in the novel, such as the Friday night parental blessing for a daughter, offered in this case only by Cosella's mother (18),[56] and a German Jewish custom for men to wear a "conical cap" on the Day of Atonement, perhaps recalling the *Judenhut* ("Jew's hat") that distinguished Central European Jews in the Middle Ages.[57] Where Christian volumes depicting Judaism, such as the American Sunday-School Union's *The Jew at Home and Abroad* (1845), interspersed ethnographic descriptions of Yom Kippur rites with negative editorial remarks ("How little they know of pardon!"),[58] such was not the case with *Cosella Wayne*. The novel's portrayal of Yom Kippur looks to defend Jews, going out of its way to mention, for example, that Jews "pray, too, for the earthly and Christian rulers set before them, for the prosperity of their adopted country, for the welfare of all" (32).

The heroine of *Cosella Wayne* sees her life change, in the novel, upon the death (murder?) of her father, along with the theft of all of his money and property. Plunged unexpectedly into poverty, orphaned and without any living relatives, Cosella bravely migrates on her own to Philadelphia, hoping to forge ties with that city's famed Jewish community, and to start her life anew. Her humorous portrayal of Philadelphia's immigrant Jews, her unforgettable depiction of life as an impoverished Jewish seamstress in that city, and her heartbreaking encounter with hunger and privation— all reflect, we now know, real-life experiences. In the end, just as she verges upon death, destiny inevitably triumphs. Thanks to her Spiritual protectors, Cosella is found, rescued, and reunited with Percival Wayne. "She overcame the earthly obstacles and gained the spiritual summit of her loftiest aspirations" (265).

Spiritualism and Judaism

Cosella's quest for the "spiritual summit," and the other Spiritualist motifs and teachings that suffuse Cosella Wayne, distinguishes it from other American Jewish novels and may today puzzle and alienate some readers. From a historian's perspective, however, the confluence of Jewish and Spiritualist motifs actually magnifies the novel's significance. As we have already seen, the Spiritualist Movement, influenced by Swedenborgian thought, emerged from the fertile religious soil of the so-called Burned-Over District of Western and Central New York State. Like other religious movements that took root there in the 1840s, such as Mormonism, Adventism, and Shakerism, it spread rapidly. Within a decade, hundreds of thousands of Americans had come to believe that individuals live on as spirits after their passing, that spirits serve as "guiding stars" for their relatives on earth, that a skillful "medium" might open up communications between human beings and those in the "spirit realm," and that seemingly deceased parents, spouses, and children might, in this way, be heard from again. Cora Wilburn, who as an orphan with no living relatives was understandably attracted to these ideas, became a devoted Spiritualist in Philadelphia in the early 1850s. Through Cosella Wayne she gave expression to Spiritualism as she understood and espoused it during the movement's early years, prior to its explosive growth during the Civil War.

Revealingly, Wilburn portrayed her mother and stepmother as Jews in the novel, and her "real" father as a Spiritualist, as if to claim both religious traditions at once as part of her patrimony. "Destiny" eventually reunited her with her Spiritualist father in the story, but there is no mention of any "conversion" to his faith—Spiritualism, indeed, knows of no such ritual. Instead, akin to others at that time, Wilburn, in the 1850s, considered Spiritualism to be a reflection of natural science—its mysterious "rappings" no more improbable than the Morse code messages transmitted via telegraph.[59] Her own Spiritual experiences ("we have heard the melodies of the spirit land; we have beheld its paradisean scenes; we have felt the touch of spirit hands; and we have received messages of love immortal from the dear ones gone before"[60]) reassured her that the "spirit world" was real. She understood that others too needed "the evidence of their own senses to convince them" and felt sure that it would "come in its time and place."[61] In the meanwhile, she maintained an interest in Judaism, evident not only in *Cosella Wayne* but in some of her other writings, and she emphatically made clear that, while attracted to aspects of Christianity, she had *not* accepted Jesus as her savior. "I cannot accept of any theological or spiritual Trinity," she proclaimed. "My God is One, sole and Eternal, whose breath of life pervades all forms."[62] Taking advantage of Spiritualism's opposition to all sects and creeds ("We are earnestly laboring to pulverize all sectarian creeds and to fraternize the spiritual affections of mankind"[63]), she sought to inhabit multiple religious worlds at once.

A key aspect of Spiritualism, for Cora Wilburn, entailed the disciplining of the soul. "The agony of discipline" (265), in her words, provided an explanation for the multiple traumas that she had experienced, including her abusive father, her stepmother's death, and her descent into poverty. "I look upon every trial as a means of discipline, as upon some healthful, though bitter medicine, necessary for the cure of the soul," she explained in one of her novels.[64] In a philosophical article entitled "Spiritual Discipline," published in the same year as *Cosella Wayne*, she explained "that discipline is holy; that sorrow is an angel message; [and] that patience and humility are spiritual aids that purify the soul from earthliness." "Peace, rest, joy, knowledge," she concluded, "all shall be attained by the divine process of spiritual discipline."[65]

Another key aspect of Spiritualism that attracted Cora Wilburn was its fervid embrace of women's rights. The pioneers of the women's rights movement, Elizabeth Cady Stanton and Susan B. Anthony, recognized in the 1880s that "the only religious sect in the world . . . that has recognized the equality of women is the Spiritualists," and that it did more than any other movement "to give woman an equal career with man."[66] Beginning already in the 1850s, Wilburn as a Spiritualist worked to advance these goals. "Allow us to unfold in knowledge, do not close upon us the gates of science, let us trace the path of progression, give us liberty of speech and action, and woman's true unperverted nature will burst forth in all its native brilliancy," she proclaimed in one of her first articles in the *Woman's Advocate*. "Let woman be free; and she will be what God ordained and Nature desired, a beautiful loving being, full of holy sympathies and boundless aspirations."[67] One of her early novels in the *Banner of Light* called upon woman "to battle nobly for the right to wield her prerogative of power and example by enforcing the law of equity that places man and woman on the like footing in the eyes of society, as well as in the sight of God."[68] Following the Emancipation Proclamation, she joined other women's rights advocates in linking freedom for slaves in the South with freedom for women in the North ("We have no right to free the slaves abroad, and keep the women of our cities in the grasp of forced labor."[69]) She also, as we have seen, advocated marriage reform, and looked to a future where "woman will hold her divinely legitimate place as the central power, ordained by Nature, coequal with her brother man."[70] In her case (but not, we now know, in all cases), Spiritualism and women's rights marched hand in hand.[71]

As for Judaism and Spiritualism, most contemporary Jews considered it impossible for them to march hand in hand. "We deem it our duty to warn our readers against the new superstition which is just now spreading over the land, under the name of 'spiritual manifestations' or 'spiritual rappings,'" the *Occident*, published by the traditionalist Jewish leader Isaac Leeser in Philadelphia, exhorted just about the time that Cora Wilburn began her Spiritualist career.[72] A Reform Jewish newspaper, Isaac Mayer Wise's *Israelite*, published in Cincinnati, proved no more sympathetic, lambasting Spiritualism as "a species of Divination," strictly forbidden by the laws of the Torah.[73] Even in the novel, Cosella recalls how one "young lady of the Jewish persuasion," hearing of her affinity for Spiritualism, suggests that she has been "bitten by a mad dog," and that another acquaintance "sent her a message that, as she had become a Spiritualist, she should no more darken her doors" (233). Still, in the novel as in life, Cora Wilburn never completely severed ties with Jews. The fact that news of her return "to the faith I was born and educated in, namely the Jewish religion," appeared first in the Spiritualist *Banner of Light* implies as much. Likewise, the fact that she defined her new Progressive Jewish faith as one that "accepts of all enlightenment" and "welcomes every truth tending to exalt the material and the spiritual life of our aspiring humanity" indicates that, at least to her mind, Spiritualism's central values—its focus on spirituality, its quest for social justice, and its gender egalitarianism—harmonized with Reform Judaism as she had come to understand it. Indeed, Spiritualism's long-term influence on Progressive Judaism may turn out to be more significant than heretofore recognized.

How *Cosella Wayne* and Cora Wilburn's Diary Were Discovered

I discovered *Cosella Wayne* while pursuing research at the Israel Institute for Advanced Studies in Jerusalem in 2016–17. I had proposed to study the "unknown" American Jewish woman writer, Cora Wilburn. Over the years, I had encountered Wilburn's poems in various late nineteenth-century Jewish periodicals. I also found an intriguing letter Wilburn wrote to a young Henrietta Szold (later the founder of Hadassah), extolling her "efforts in behalf of our unfortunate Jewish brethren of Russia."[74] I read the early twentieth-century writer and immigration rights activist Mary Antin's sad account of her own visit to Wilburn ("the most interesting woman I know, in many respects"), secluded in her old age, who had become, according to Antin, "a hater of the world and individuals."[75] I learned that Wilburn wrote for Spiritual publications from Ann Braude's *Radical Spirits*. Finally, thanks to the newly available online edition of the Boston *Jewish Advocate*, I found an article-length biographical retrospect on Wilburn's life and career, published in the issue of February 23, 1912. I sensed from the many brief obituaries to Wilburn published upon her death in 1906 that there must be more to her story. In preparation for my year at the institute—where I would be part of a research group focusing on "Jewish Women's Cultural Capital"—two Brandeis students and I scoured the internet.

What we discovered astonished me: hundreds of pages of small-print prose and poetry by Wilburn spread over a wide range of journals, most of them not Jewish at all, and extending over half a century. I had no time to read all this material prior to departing, so I assembled it all in two large loose-leaf notebooks and dispatched it by FedEx to the Israel Institute for Advanced Studies in Jerusalem.

Day after day, beginning in September 2016, I sat in my office on the campus of the Hebrew University and read Cora Wilburn's voluminous writings chronologically, starting with her 1855 essay "Free Love," and continuing through fiction, nonfiction, and poetry. In due course, I reached her serialized novel, *Cosella Wayne*, which began on the front page of the March 31, 1860, issue of *The Banner of Light: A Weekly Journal of Romance Literature and General Intelligence*.

The novel immediately captured my attention, for its central characters were Jews. It soon dawned on me that nothing resembling this novel exists in the (meager) canon of nineteenth-century American Jewish fiction. It anticipates central themes of American Jewish writing: intermarriage, generational tension, family dysfunction, Jewish–Christian relations, immigration, poverty, the place of women in Jewish life, the rise of romantic love, and the tension between destiny and free will. It provides thick descriptions of Jewish rituals as well as of Jewish communities around the world, and it introduces readers to Jewish texts little available at that time in English, such as the Ethics of the Fathers. It casts light on the early decades of Spiritualism, today appreciated for its openness toward women and advocacy for liberal political causes, such as abolitionism and women's rights. Finally, it dates back further than any previously known Jewish novel published in the United States with an American theme.

Standard accounts consider Nathan Mayer's Civil War novel *Differences*, published in 1867, to be "the first novel of literary value to treat of American Jews seriously, realistically, and at length."[76] *Cosella Wayne*, set in the 1840s and published in 1860, predates *Differences* by seven years. The first novel authored by an American Jewish woman, according to most accounts, is Emma Wolfe's novel of intermarriage, *Other Things Being Equal*, published in 1892.[77] *Cosella Wayne* revises this chronology and demonstrates that the very *first* American Jewish novelist of consequence was a woman, Cora Wilburn.

The only full-length biographical article that I found concerning Cora Wilburn, published in the *Jewish Advocate* by a Boston rabbi named Menachem M. Eichler, who knew her, included quotations from a diary that Wilburn kept. Might that diary survive? I wondered. I searched in all of the obvious places as well as some obscure ones, like local historical societies in Massachusetts and Rabbi Eichler's Temple Ohabei Shalom in Boston, but without success. Then I chanced upon a handwritten letter to historian Jacob Rader Marcus, founder of the American Jewish Archives in Cincinnati, from Sadie R. Cohen (d. 1959), widow of Judge A. K. Cohen of Boston. It thanked Marcus for letting her know that "the papers of the diary of Cora Wilburn have been received with the minutes of the Beth El Synagogue." The diaries of little-known women, in those days, were not catalogued separately at the American Jewish Archives (or most other archival institutions), but archivist Kevin Proffitt, with this clue, had no trouble locating the long-overlooked item. "Found it!" he wrote to me in a gleeful email, and he soon sent me a scanned copy.

Thanks to this diary, which covers the precise time period of the novel and was clearly its central source, we can now fill in many blanks concerning Cora Wilburn, particularly her tumultuous life from age twenty to twenty-four, when both of her parents died and she immigrated alone to Philadelphia. Selections from the diary appear here as an appendix to the novel.

Why Was Cora Wilburn Forgotten?

Following Cora Wilburn's death, *The Standard Book of Jewish Verse* (1917), the largest and most comprehensive volume of Jewish poetry published to that time in the United States, anthologized three of her poems, and some were also included in liturgies and other works. But only one critical treatment of her writing is known to have appeared: the aforementioned study of her life and work by Rabbi Menachem M. Eichler of Temple Ohabei Shalom in Boston, delivered before the American Jewish Historical Society in 1912 and thereafter published in Boston's *Jewish Advocate*. "Cora Wilburn was not a great poet," he pronounced. "Many of her verses are 'prosy,' others are obscure and almost unintelligible on account of loose construction and poor grammar. She betrays a want of early training in composition. Her technique is poor. But here and there is a divine flash and a truly poetical thought beautifully expressed. Eloquently she sings the praise of the God of Israel. There is so much religious fervor, spiritual intensity and humanitarianism in her poems that they deserve [to] be rescued from oblivion. A little obscure niche," he concluded, "should be assigned in the Temple of American Jewish Literature to this humble singer whose life was an unending tragedy."[78]

Eichler's evaluation offers a partial explanation for the historical amnesia surrounding Cora Wilburn. The quality of much of her poetry, he argued, did not warrant her being remembered. But Eichler himself had managed to overlook most of her prose, including *Cosella Wayne*, as well as other novels, short stories, and essays, most of them published in Spiritualist publications during the most creative period of her life. Why was that too forgotten?

One reason, of course, is that she had no living relatives. Unlike Jewish women writers like Emma Lazarus and Anzia Yezierska, she had no loving siblings or proud descendants to collect and preserve her writings, keep her name alive, and encourage posterity to remember her works.

A different way of approaching historical amnesia, drawing upon the insights of Ali Behdad, relates cultural forgetfulness to ideological consolidation. According to this view, forgetfulness is "convenient." It "improves" history by obliterating knowledge of the past that conflicts with messages that a country or group seeks to project about itself in the present.[79] Cora Wilburn, we have seen, transgressed in numerous ways that would have troubled Jews. They would, one suspects, have been glad to forget her dysfunctional and abusive Jewish family, her conversion to Catholicism, her affinity for Spiritualism, her criticism of the Bible, her revelations concerning Philadelphia's less-than-charitable Jewish elite, even much of her strident social activism. The fact that she remained single did not help, either, even if a long list of well-known Jews of her day likewise failed to marry. Nor would Jews have wanted to perpetuate her criticism of large families and marital norms ("Give us fewer children, and let them be noble specimens of manhood—pure and loving ideals of womanhood. Let us have soul unions, not marriages of convenience or passion"[80]). Her lack of active involvement in any synagogue or other Jewish institution damaged her reputation as well.

Wilburn, in short, failed to live up either to the ideals of Judaism or to the ideals of "true womanhood" common in her day. Even modesty, which Shira Wolosky has shown to have been so central to women's voice during that time, characterized Cora Wilburn writings and demeanor only in part.[81] While, akin to many women poets, she took no personal credit for her poetic abilities, maintaining that she wrote "almost without any mental effort on my part," and that poems came to her and all she did was transcribe them "with ease and rapidity,"[82] she also celebrated in her novels strongly assertive and immodest women. Cosella Wayne, for example, spoke aggressively to her father and to her godmother, talked back to her employers, and displayed extraordinary independence. Jasmine, another character based on the author's life, was even more assertive. Wilburn herself explained at one point that "Jasmine talks plainly . . . and strongly, even as I feel. Let no false shame deter any honest, true-hearted woman, in this age, from using speech and pen in behalf of the oppressed."[83] Speaking through Jasmine's voice, she likewise explained that she "became known, but never popular; for, always preferring truth to expediency, I shocked the prejudices of many by my outspoken speech and writings."[84] No wonder that contemporaries failed to perpetuate her memory!

Finally, one suspects that Cora Wilburn was forgotten because unlike so many other nineteenth-century American Jewish writers who "present[ed] their adopted nation as a glorious land brimming with promise,"[85] she dissented. Slavery, the mistreatment of Native Americans, the inequality of women, the gap between rich and poor—these and other national afflictions caused her to criticize her adopted countrymen, even as she cherished "this dear land of conquering peace and plenty."[86] With the outbreak of the Civil War, she boldly attacked not only the South but also her fellow northerners: "Our free soil has been polluted by the footprints of the slave-catcher; our heartstones, as well as our legislative halls, have been desecrated by the apologists of 'that sum of all villainies—Slavery.'"[87] Later, in 1893, she interrupted her long celebratory poem delivered at the Jewish Women's Congress to remind her middle- and upper-class Jewish audience that even in America social problems abounded:

Though safe beneath the Starry Flag *we* dwell
Dare we assert that with us all is well?
While homeless brothers may not seek their bread,
On native soil; but cringe mid phantoms dread
Of famine, Murder, Pillage, women slain!

Are *we* so deadened to another's pain,
In arms of luxury lulled, that willingly,
We shackle *here* the soul of Liberty?[88]

American Jewish history has generally been unkind to individuals who failed to live up to the community's (shifting) ideals. Subversives, the independent-minded, the transgressors—women in particular—have been banished from cultural memory. That, more than anything else, may account for the forgetting of Cora Wilburn—until now.

Notes

1. Harriet E. Wilson, *Our Nig; or Sketches from the Life of a Free Black*, ed. Henry Louis Gates and Richard J. Ellis, expanded ed. (New York: Vintage, 2011), appendix 1, 2, iii–xc. Both *Our Nig* and *Cosella Wayne* build their plots upon "a hybrid mix of events," some actually experienced and some invented or changed (*Our Nig*, xxvii). Wilson, like Wilburn, experienced the loss of her mother at a young age, faced severe maltreatment, became a religious seeker, took up Spiritualism, and published in the *Banner of Light*.

2. While some obituaries for Wilburn listed 1830 or 1831 as the year of her birth, the death certificate (available on Ancestry.com and in the American Jewish Archives) properly lists her as eighty-two years of age in 1906; see also for her correct dates M. M. Eichler, "Cora Wilburn," *Jewish Advocate*, February 23, 1912, 6. Wilburn's handwritten diary suggests that she herself may have been uncertain about her age or sought in her twenties to make herself younger.

3. The 1870 Manuscript Census from Lincolnville in Waldo County, Maine (p. 14), and the 1880 Manuscript Census from Lynn in Essex County, Massachusetts (p. 25) both list her birthplace as France. The 1900 Manuscript Census, from Duxbury in Plymouth County, lists her birthplace as France but her parents' birthplaces as Germany. All of this census information is available on Ancestry.com.

4. Cora Wilburn Diary, SC-12996, American Jewish Archives, Cincinnati, OH. For the Yiddish entry, see August 22, 1848; and for a translation from German, *Banner of Light* (August 28, 1858), 1, first of many translations.

5. *London Gazette* (London: 1837), part I, 801.

6. "Tricks of a Traveller," *Sydney Morning Herald* (March 30, 1843), 4; Cora Wilburn portrayed her father as a swindler of wealthy gentiles in *Banner of Light* (May 19, 1860), 1.

7. Cora Wilburn to Henrietta Szold (January 5, 1891), reprinted in Alexandra Lee Levin, *The Szolds of Lombard Street* (Philadelphia: Jewish Publication Society, 1960), 259–260.

8. For Singapore, see Cora Wilburn Diary, March 22, 1844; for Burma, her memoir of how her dog saved her life there in 1839 in *Our Dumb Animals* (November 1878), 46; for Hawaii, see Cora Wilburn, "Dreams of the Hawaiian Islands in

Northern Wintertime," *Jewish Messenger*, April 9, 1897, 1; and for Venezuela, see Cora Wilburn Diary, which recounts her time in La Guayra (today La Guaira), 1844–1848.

9. *Banner of Light*, June 2, 1860, 1.

10. Cora Wilburn Diary, June 16, 1845; January 4, 1846; February 1847; see also the reference to the death of her parents in *Our Dumb Animals* (February 1879), 79. If she sold her jewels for American dollars, her $295 would have been worth the equivalent of about $7,700 in 2016 dollars.

11. She describes herself as "born and bred a gentlewoman" in her letter to Rabbi Bernard Felsenthal (June 2, 1885), Bernhard Felsenthal papers; P-21; Box 1; Folder 5; American Jewish Historical Society, New York, NY, and Boston, MA.

12. Cora Wilburn Diary, June 24, 1846; December 23, 1847; see her fictionalized account in *Cosella Wayne*, 161.

13. Todd M. Endelman, *Leaving the Jewish Fold: Conversion and Radical Assimilation in Modern Jewish History* (Princeton: Princeton University Press, 2015), believes that "few converts returned to Judaism (355)," but there are actually more examples than he credits. Famous ones include the biblical scholar Arnold B. Ehrlich, as well as Rabbis Samuel Freuder, Henry Gersoni, Samuel H. Markowitz, and Jacob Mayer; see Jacob Kabakoff, "New Light on Arnold Bagomil Ehrlich," *American Jewish Archives* 36 (1984): 204; Dana Evan Kaplan, "Rabbi Samuel Freuder as a Christian Missionary: American Protestant Premillennialism and an Apostate Returner, 1891–1924," *American Jewish Archives Journal* 50 (1998): 41–74; Jacob Kabakoff, *Pioneers of American Hebrew Literature* (Tel Aviv: Yavneh, 1966), 79–130, esp. 81 [in Hebrew]; Samuel H. Markowitz, "Autobiography," *American Jewish Archives* 24 (1972): 128–59, esp. 136; Isaac Fein, *The Making of an American Jewish Community: The History of Baltimore Jewry from 1773–1920* (Philadelphia: Jewish Publication Society, 1971), 111–12; Endelman, *Leaving the Fold*, 284–85. For a somewhat different understanding of conversion in the American setting than Endelman provides, see Lincoln A. Mullen, *The Chance of Salvation: A History of Conversion* (Cambridge: Harvard University Press, 2017), esp. 173–220.

14. Cora Wilburn Diary, September 9–30, 1848. The U.S. Government Passenger and Immigration lists available on Ancestry.com, claim that the *Euphemia* arrived in New York on September 3, 1848 with a passenger named "Henretty Jackson" on board, but this seems to be an error for September 30th; Ancestry.com. New York, Passenger and Immigration Lists 1820–1850. *Registers of Vessels Arriving at the Port of New York from Foreign Ports, 1789–1919. Microfilm Publication M237 rolls 1–95 National Archives, Washington DC.*

15. Cora Wilburn Diary, October 5, 1848.

16. See the many reports in the *Occident*, such as *Occident* 2 (1845): 454–459.

17. Lynn M. Alexander, "The Seamstress in Victorian Literature," *Tulsa Studies in Women's Literature* 18 (Spring 1999): 29–38; Lynn M. Alexander, *Women, Work and Representation: Needlewomen in Victorian Art and Literature* (Athens: Ohio State University Press, 2003); Beth Harris, *Famine and Fashion: Needlewomen in*

the Nineteenth Century (Burlington, VT:Ashgate, 2005); on the radicalism of Spiritualists, see more broadly Ann Braude, *Radical Spirits: Spiritualism and Women's Rights in Nineteenth-Century America* (2nd ed., Bloomington: Indiana University Press, 2001).

18. See also Cora Wilburn, "The Pride of Station; or The Experiences of a Seamstress," *Banner of Light*, February 20, 1858, 2; Cora Wilburn, "The Wrongs of Needle-Women," *Banner of Light*, December 24, 1864, 3; *Banner of Light*, November 25, 1865, 1; and Jonathan D. Sarna, "Jewish Women without Money: The Case of Cora Wilburn," *Nashim* 32 (2018): 23–37.

19. The best study of the changing role of Jews in the clothing trade is Adam D. Mendelsohn, *The Rag Race* (New York: New York University Press, 2015), esp. 50–90.

20. *Banner of Light*, December 2, 1865, 1.

21. On women and Spiritualism, see Braude, *Radical Spirits*, esp. 3. This, of course, helps to explain why both the first Jewish American woman writer and the first African American woman writer published in the Spiritualist *Banner of Light*.

22. David Walker, "The Humbug in American Religion: Ritual Theories of Nineteenth-Century Spiritualism," *Religion and American Culture* 23 (Winter 2013): 30–74.

23. *Banner of Light*, January 2, 1864, 4.

24. Mark A. Lause, *Free Spirits: Spiritualism, Republicanism and Radicalism in the Civil War Era* (Champaign: University of Illinois Press, 2016), 23–43. The Jewish women's rights agitator Ernestine Rose and a German Jew named Maximilian Leopold Langenschwarz were other Jews who appeared at Spiritualist gatherings.

25. *Agitator*, April 1, 1860, 98.

26. Cora Wilburn, "My Religion," *Agitator*, April 1, 1860. See her earlier articles in this series in the issues of December 15, 1859, January 1, February 1, and March 1, 1860.

27. Cora Wilburn, "Jasmine, or the Discipline of Life," *Banner of Light* (December 26, 1863), 2; see James C. Whorton, *Crusaders for Fitness: The History of American Health Reformers* (Princeton: Princeton University Press, 1982).

28. *Agitator* March 1, 1860.

29. "They led so-called ultraist wings of the movements for the abolition of slavery, for the reform of marriage, for children's rights, and for religious freedom, and they actively supported socialism, labor reform, vegetarianism, dress reform, health reform, temperance, and antisabbatarianism, to name a few of their favorite causes [Braude, *Radical Spirits*, 3.]"

30. *Agitator*, February 1, 1860, pp. 70–71.

31. *Banner of Light*, December 5, 1863, 1.

32. Emma Hardinge, *Modern American Spiritualism: A Twenty Years' Record of the Communion between Earth and the World of Spirits* (New York: The Author, 1870) is one of many volumes that omits Wilburn's name.

33. Cora Wilburn, *The Spiritual Significance of Gems* (Hopedale, MA: The Au-

thor, 1868); *American Israelite*, February 21, 1868, 4. The *Israelite* mistakenly called her "Clara" instead of "Cora."

34. Cora Wilburn, "Free Love," *Age of Progress* 2, no. 10 (December 15, 1855).

35. Madeline S. Stern (ed.), *The Victoria Woodhull Reader* (Weston, MA: M&S Press, 1974), 120. Woodhull later recanted these views, but see Wilburn's letter to Frances E. Abbott in the *Index* 10 (January 2, 1879), 9, where she attacks Woodhull and proclaims, "The abominations of 'free love' have driven many earnest souls out of the ranks of Spiritualism." Wilburn strongly opposed forcing women into marriages with those they did not love, and shared the "chainless marriage" ideas of Spiritualist Hannah Brown, editor of the *Agitator*, but opposed libertinism. See, for background, John Spurock, "The Free Love Network in America, 1850 to 1860," *Journal of Social History* 21 (Summer 1988): 765–779.

36. Sydney E. Ahlstrom and Robert B. Mullen, *The Scientific Theist: A Life of Francis Ellingwood Abbot* (Macon, GA: Mercer University Press, 1987), 72–80; Benny Kraut, "Frances E. Abbott: Perceptions of a Nineteenth-Century Religious Radical on Jews and Judaism," *Studies in the American Jewish Experience* (Cincinnati, 1981), 90–113; Benny Kraut, "Judaism Triumphant: Isaac Mayer Wise on Unitarianism and Liberal Christianity," *AJS Review* 7/8 (1982/3): 179–230.

37. *Banner of Light*, November 13, 1869, 3.

38. *Index* 2 (August 26, 1871), 270.

39. Cora Wilburn, "Possibilities," *Philadelphia Jewish Record*, July 6, 1877.

40. Love of animals, dogs in particular, suffuses her writings; see, for example, her descriptions of Jaspe and Topaz in *Cosella Wayne*, 88, 234. In the 1870s Wilburn wrote articles for the journal *Our Dumb Animals*, which underscored her love of animals; see especially "The Story of Linda," *Our Dumb Animals* (February 1879), 79: "Ever since I can remember, my life has been gladdened, cheered, and solaced by the companionship and affection of animals." She credited dogs with saving her life and with keeping her company in her loneliness [see *Banner of Light* October 17, 1863, and December 23, 1865]. In an 1885 letter to Rabbi Bernhard Felsenthal, she reported that since she was "unable to obtain writing to do," she "tried to rear and sell dogs," and that she kept "a dog, two cats, and three canaries." She unsuccessfully sought his assistance in obtaining work at what became known as the Gifford Cat Shelter [Cora Wilburn to Bernhard Felsenthal (June 2, 1885), Bernhard Felsenthal papers; P-21; Box 1; Folder 5; American Jewish Historical Society, New York, NY]. Dogs did not generally appear in so positive a light in nineteenth-century Jewish literature; see Phillip Ackerman-Lieberman and Rakefet Zalashik, *A Jew's Best Friend? The Image of the Dog throughout Jewish History* (Sussex: Sussex Academic Press, 2013); and Susan M. Kahn, "New Jewish Kinship—with Dogs," *AJS Perspectives*, spring 2011, http://perspectives.ajsnet.org/the-secular-issue-spring-2011/new-jewish-kinship-with-dogs/.

41. "Israel to the World in Greeting," in *Papers of the Jewish Women's Congress...* (Philadelphia: Jewish Publication Society, 1894), 131–32. Wilburn did not herself travel to Chicago. The poem was read by Lillie Herschfield of the New York branch of the Council of Jewish Women; see *American Hebrew* (September 15, 1893), 626.

42. Cora Wilburn to Henrietta Szold (January 5, 1891), reprinted in Levin, *Szolds of Lombard Street*, 259–60.

43. Cora Wilburn to Bernhard Felsenthal (June 2, 1885), Bernhard Felsenthal papers; P-21; Box 1; Folder 5; American Jewish Historical Society, New York, NY, and Boston, MA. It was difficult to live on $18 a month—the equivalent of just under $500 in 2016 dollars. On the monthly check from Schiff, see also Sadie R. Cohen to Jacob R. Marcus (n.d.) concerning Wilburn, in the American Jewish Archives.

44. Wilburn to Felsenthal (June 2, 1885).

45. *Boston Daily Globe*, December 5, 1906; *American Israelite*, December 20, 1906, 3; the death certificate is available online at Ancestry.com and in the American Jewish Archives.

46. The cremation certificate and Sadie R. Cohen's undated comment about the cremation (on the back of the document) are reposited in the American Jewish Archives. Sabato Morais, the Sephardic minister of Congregation Mikveh Israel in Philadelphia, who knew Wilburn, had come to favor cremation as early as 1897 but wrote to his son-in-law that "the fear of shocking the Jewish community made me reconsider the determination of being cremated." [Arthur Kiron, "Dust and Ashes: The Funeral and Forgetting of Sabato Morais," *American Jewish History* 84 (September 1996): 176.] On the growing popularity of cremation in the United States, including among liberal Jews, see Stephen R. Prothero, *Purified by Fire: A History of Cremation in America* (Berkeley: University of California Press, 2001), esp. 137.

47. Although the name Shina is generally Asian or Bulgarian (short for Anastasia), in this case it seems more likely a variant for the common Yiddish name Shayna, meaning "beautiful." In some Yiddish dialects, "ay" is pronounced as if it were a long "i" as in "pie"; see Max Weinreich, *History of the Yiddish Language* (Chicago: University of Chicago Press, 1980), 17–18.

48. Nadia Valman, *The Jewess in Nineteenth-Century British Literary Culture* (Cambridge: Cambridge University Press, 2007), 7; Nadia Valman, "Bad Jews/ Good Jewess: Gender and Semitic Discourse in Nineteenth-Century England," *Philosemitism in History*, ed. Jonathan Karp and Adam Sutcliffe (Cambridge: Cambridge University Press, 2011), 149–69; see also Louis Mayo, *The Ambivalent Image: Nineteenth-Century America's Perception of the Jew* (Cranbury, NJ: Associated University Presses, 1988), esp. 72–76.

49. Naomi Seidman, *The Marriage Plot, or How Jews Fell in Love with Love and with Literature* (Stanford: Stanford University Press, 2016).

50. Cora Wilburn, "My Religion," *Agitator*, March 1, 1860, 82.

51. For the Spiritualist critique of marriage, see Braude, *Radical Spirits*, 117–41; and Spurock, "Free Love Network in America, 1850 to 1860," 765–79.

52. J. M. Peebles, "Why," *Banner of Light*, February 25, 1865, 3 (italics added). On single blessedness, see Sally L. Kitch, *Chaste Liberation: Celibacy and Female Cultural Status* (Urbana: University of Illinois Press, 1989); Charles Rosenberg, *No Other Gods* (Baltimore: Johns Hopkins University Press, 1978), 71–88; Lee Chambers-Schiller, *Liberty a Better Husband: Single Women in America* (New Haven:

Yale University Press, 1987). On the many unmarried Jews in Philadelphia, see Dianne Ashton, "Crossing Boundaries: The Career of Mary M. Cohen," *American Jewish History* 83 (June 1995): 154; Jonathan D. Sarna, "The Making of an American Jewish Culture," *When Judaism Was the Capital of Jewish America*, ed. Murray Friedman (Philadelphia: Balch Institute, 1993), 154 n. 17; and Jonathan D. Sarna, "Louisa B. Hart: An Orthodox Jewish Woman's Voice from the Civil War Era," in *You Arose a Mother in Israel: A Festschrift in Honor of Blu Greenberg*, ed. Devorah Zlochower (New York: Jewish Orthodox Feminist Alliance, 2017), 96.

53. Jonathan M. Hess, *Middlebrow Literature and the Making of German-Jewish Identity* (Stanford: Stanford University Press, 2010), esp. 1–29.

54. Yaakov Ariel, *Evangelizing the Chosen People* (Chapel Hill: University of North Carolina Press, 2000), 73; Michael Ragussis, *Figures of Conversion: "The Jewish Question" and English National Identity* (Durham, NC: Duke University Press, 1995); Valman, *Jewess in Nineteenth-Century British Literary Culture*, 51–84.

55. Compare Nadia Valman's discussion of Grace Aguilar's *The Perez Family* (1843) in her "Victorian Jewish Women Novelists," in *Jewish Women Writers in Britain* (Detroit: Wayne State University Press, 2014), 12–18.

56. On this blessing and its history, see Ruth Langer, "The *Minhag* of Parents' Blessing Their Children," in *The Modern Child and Jewish Law*, ed. Walter Jacob (Pittsburgh: Freehof Institute for Progressive Halakhah, 2016), 187–202.

57. For a picture of the conical cap in the early modern era, see Alfred Rubens, *A History of Jewish Costume* (London: Vallentine, Mitchell, 1967), 99 (illus. 130); and for a related discussion of the Jewish hat in Venice, see Benjamin Ravid, "From Yellow to Red: On the Distinguishing Head-Covering of the Jews of Venice," *Jewish History* 6 (1992): 179–210. I have not found a religious source for the custom of wearing the conical cap on Yom Kippur, but perhaps it recalls the priestly headgear mentioned in Exodus 28:40.

58. *The Jew at Home and Abroad* (Philadelphia: American Sunday-School Union, 1845), 86. For "ethnographies" of Judaism in the early modern period, see Elisheva Carlebach, *Divided Souls: Converts from Judaism in Germany, 1500–1750* (New Haven: Yale University Press, 2001), 170–221.

59. Spiritualist mediums, historian Robert S. Cox observes, operated "like the wires of a telegraph over which forces could act at a distance and through which impressions were conveyed to the senses." *Body and Soul: A Sympathetic History of American Spiritualism* (Charlottesville: University of Virginia Press, 2003), 7, cf. 17.

60. *Banner of Light*, November 21, 1857, 8.

61. *Banner of Light*, January 1, 1859, 8.

62. Wilburn, "My Religion," *Agitator*, December 15, 1859.

63. From the masthead of *Herald of Progress*; see April 5, 1862, 1.

64. Cora Wilburn, "Jasmine, or the Discipline of Life," *Banner of Light*, October 17, 1863, chapter 7.

65. Cora Wilburn, "Spiritual Discipline," *Rising Tide*, August 1, 1860, 1.

66. Elizabeth Cady Stanton, Susan B. Anthony, and Matilda Joslin Gage, eds. *History of Women Suffrage* (Rochester: 1881, 1886), 2: 922; 3: 530.

67. Cora Wilburn, "Free Love," *Age of Progress* (December 15, 1855), 157–58; the article was "written for the *Women's Advocate.*"

68. Cora Wilburn, "Pearl Nevins," *Banner of Light*, May 15, 1858, 2.

69. *Banner of Light*, December 24, 1864, 3.

70. *Banner of Light*, September 3, 1864, 3.

71. Braude, *Radical Spirits*, esp. 3; for a critique, see Cox, *Body and Soul*, 17–18; Lynn L. Sharp, "Women in Spiritism: Using the Beyond to Construct the Here and Now," *Proceedings of the Annual Meeting of the Western Society for French History* 21 (1994): 161–68; Alex Owen, *The Darkened Room: Women, Power and Spiritualism in Late Victorian England* (Philadelphia: University of Pennsylvania Press, 1990).

72. "Superstition," *Occident* (May 1, 1853), 37.

73. "Spiritualism—Its Antiquity," *Israelite* (September 5, 1856), 69. Wise cited Leviticus 20:27 and Deuteronomy 18:10–12 as his prooftexts.

74. Cora Wilburn to Henrietta Szold (January 5, 1891) reprinted in Levin, *Szolds of Lombard Street*, 259–60.

75. Mary Antin to Israel Zangwill (May 2, 1900), reprinted in *Selected Letters of Mary Antin*, ed. Evelyn Salz (Syracuse: Syracuse University Press, 2000), 26–27.

76. Louis Harap, *The Image of the Jew in American Literature: From Early Republic to Mass Immigration* (Philadelphia: Jewish Publication Society, 1974), 275.

77. Emma Wolf, *Other Things Being Equal*, ed. with an introduction by Barbara Cantalupo (Detroit: Wayne State University Press, 2002 [1st ed., 1892]).

78. M. M. Eichler, "Cora Wilburn," *Jewish Advocate* (February 23, 1912), 6. Eichler's biographical account, while informed by her diary, is replete with errors.

79. Ali Behdad, *A Forgetful Nation: On Immigration and Cultural Identity in the United States* (Durham, NC: Duke University Press, 2005).

80. Cora Wilburn, "Maternity," *Banner of Light*, August 22, 1863.

81. Shira Wolosky, "Modest Claims," in Sacvan Bercovitch (ed.), *The Cambridge History of American Literature*, Volume 4, *Nineteenth-Century Poetry 1800–1910* (Cambridge: Cambridge University Press, 2004), 155–99.

82. Wilburn, *Spiritual Significance of Gems*, 5.

83. Cora Wilburn, "Jasmine, or the Discipline of Life," *Banner of Light* (November 28, 1863), 2.

84. Cora Wilburn, "Jasmine, or the Discipline of Life," *Banner of Light* (December 5, 1863), 2.

85. Julian Levinson, "Encountering the Idea of America," *The Cambridge History of American Jewish Literature*, ed. Hana Wirth-Nesher (Cambridge: Cambridge University Press, 2016), 21. Levinson somewhat exaggerates the cult of patriotism among nineteenth-century American Jews and ignores the many subversives, like Samuel B. H. Judah and Ernestine Rose, who spoke in a different vein. For this countertradition, see Jonathan D. Sarna, "Subversive Jews and American Culture: Notes on the Leonard Milberg Collection of Early American Judaica," in Adam Mendelsohn, ed., *By Dawn's Early Light: Jewish Contributions to American Culture from the Nation's Founding to the Civil War* (Princeton: Princeton University Library, 2016), 189–204.

86. Cora Wilburn, "Israel's Power," reprinted in Henry Abarbanel, *English School and Family Reader, for the Use of Israelites*. (New York: Roger and Sherwood, 1883), 185.

87. Cora Wilburn, "A Woman's Thoughts upon the War," *Herald of Progress*, July 27, 1861, 3.

88. Wilburn, "Israel to the World in Greeting," 131.

A Note on the Text

Cosella Wayne originally appeared as a serial in the popular Spiritualist weekly *Banner of Light: A Weekly Journal of Romance Literature and General Intelligence*, from March 31st to July 7, 1860. The novel was subsequently forgotten and rediscovered by the editor as part of a larger inquiry into the life and works of its author, Cora Wilburn. For this edition, obvious typographical errors found in the original have been silently corrected, and punctuation somewhat modernized. Readers interested in consulting the original text may find it online at the website of the International Association for the Preservation of Spiritualist and Occult Periodicals, where weekly issues of *Banner of Light* are preserved (http://www.iapsop.com/archive /materials/banner_of_light/), and in the online American Antiquarian Society Historical Periodicals Collection.

Cosella Wayne

Or, Will and Destiny

To my inspirers in the worlds of soul this humble tribute of a grateful heart, blest with immortal certainties, is dedicated.

To those of earth who love and suffer, labor and aspire; to the freed and the enslaved; to the mourner and the outcast, in love, this work is dedicated. And to my friend, O. S. P. of Kentucky, the heart-pages and soul-records of this life-history are dedicated, an offering of spirit unto spirit, by Cora Wilburn.

Introduction

Day dawned. Within a curtained room,
Filled to faintness with perfume,
A lady lay at point of doom.
Day closed. A child had seen the light;
But for the lady, fair and bright,
She rested in undreaming night.

—Barry Cornwall

Deep snow covered the earth, and a mighty storm was raging. Beneath its fury the stripped trees bent their spectral forms, swaying wildly to and fro, in mingled supplication and defiance toward the power that bowed their sturdy frames. Thick snowflakes fell, intermingled with pattering hail; not a star was visible amid the midnight gloom.

There was desolation, sorrow, bereavement, within a spacious mansion skirting the main road of that retired English village, as there was desolation, storm, and night without. As the shrieking blast hurled the descending snow in whirling eddies around the house, and the hail showers fell upon its closed shutters, there mingled with the midnight's storm voices the prolonged wail of women and the frantic cries of a bereaved heart. The low and piteous wail of a newborn infant was unheard amid the great human anguish and the tempest's passing.

In an elegantly furnished chamber, where a lavish taste presided, an almost eastern luxuriance reigned. Upon a couch of crimson velvet that was piled with rich coverlets and surrounded by hangings of lace and damask reposed the still figure of a young and beautiful woman. Upon her white face the rosy curtains cast a mocking gleam of life, but oh, what rapt repose dwelt on that most seraphic countenance! The long dark lashes, drooping on the colorless cheek, veiled forever from the yearning glances around the life beams of those glorious Oriental eyes. The long, wavy, jet black hair fell in half-loosened massive braids upon the richly embroidered pillow; the sweet lips wore a smile of ineffable serenity; and on the wide intellectual brow there rested a mysterious sign that was a hallowed promise. Upon that lady's brow and lip and cheek, in the attitude of that peaceful lasting slumber, there dwelt the repose and all the rapture of immortality achieved! Its smile of victory rested on that tender face; in meek compliance the white hands were folded across the maternal bosom, and the ready spirit had followed whither the summoning angel led—far, already, beyond the storm and the mourners' reach, speeding away to the land of eternal summer, lovingly upheld by a pure life's influence, pressing untremblingly the unknown pathway. And, as the hapless infant wailed, a lingering angel fondly stroked its little brow and stilled its cries.

Upon the rich velvet carpet crouched a woman's form, writhing in despair, uttering frenzied cries, imploring with quivering livid lips that a miracle might restore the dead to life. Lea, the beautiful young Jewess, the idolized Christian wife, lay in the sleep called death. Hannah, her mother, called upon her in piercing tones to return to life and love. With the shades of night that young spirit had winged its heavenward flight. Amid the midnight's storm and terror that frantic mother wept and prayed. The women looked upon the angel countenance of the departed, and wiped their brimming eyes; and the bereaved infant wailed its untimely cries.

A young Jewess of sweet and timid aspect, of light and girlish figure, tenderly held the child while she gazed with tearful reverence upon the beautiful dead. Bending over the chair, her husband regarded her with a look of half approval, half mockery, and a furtive gleam, strange and full of meaning, shot from his dark piercing eyes as he turned to the crouching figure of the distracted mother.

The women, young and old, were grouped around the luxuriant chamber, gesticulating, weeping and praying, while outside the storm still raged with unabated fury. The light of the silver lamp illumining that chamber of sorrow, swayed and flickered beneath the tempest's might, as the whirling snow caps drifted, and the hail showers fell; and the stout building seemed to rock beneath the storm-wind's mandate. The voices of the night seemed fraught with prophecies of sorrow and desolation, with warning tones of solemn meaning, with weird, threatening utterances, appalling to the guilty soul.

From her humble, supplicatory posture the mother of the dead arose; towering in queenly height; stretching forth her jeweled hands in clasped anguished entreaty; lifting up to heaven her proud implacable face; raising high her voice that had never bent to human will or power. "Father of Israel!" she cried, in such loud heart-rending tones that the women clasped each other's hands and trembled with a sudden fear, "Return me my child! She cannot, she *must not* be dead! Give me back my child, oh mighty Judge, dread God, and on me pour out thy decrees of punishment—let me bear the tortures for her soul! Go, run, call the physician—he must try his skill once more! She cannot be dead! *She* dead!—my beautiful, my only one, my Lea, my treasured idol! She to die an apostate to the faith of Abraham—

the faith in which I nurtured her with so jealous, so watchful a care! *Lost, lost, lost* and through *him*! Oh, curses, curses, bitter curses on his soul that lured my child from her mother's arms!"

Intensest hatred gleamed from the dark eyes of the zealous bigot; the religious fanaticism mingled with the woman's enmity, as with upraised hand she invoked heaven's malediction upon him who had won her child to the abhorred Christian faith. The frame of Hannah shook with an intensity of rage that was deep and lasting as her grief.

"He stole her from my arms, my heart!" she continued in strong excitement as she beat her breast and madly rent her silken robe; "he won her by his smooth false tongue, the unbeliever, and she deserted the God of her fathers to become his wife! Oh, he may thank his false Gods that he is away; for I would kill him—*kill him*—as I hope to reach heaven! Oh, Lea, Lea! My child, my child!" she panted for breath and held her hand to her aching side.

The young woman, who held the infant, approached her timidly, tears trembling in her large, brown eyes.

"Away—take that child away!" she screamed, with averted head and imperious gesture.

The young woman drew back in alarm. Manasseh, her husband, advanced toward the lady; holding his fur cap in his hand, with a deference such as is used to princes, he addressed her; but while bending respectfully before her, there was a mocking gleam in his eye that belied the tender solicitude of his manner.

"Madam, you forget the physician's injunctions; excitement is dangerous to you; permit me to remind you of your health. Dear lady, remember—"

She interrupted him with an impatient exclamation—with a haughty, scornful glance that brought the flush of indignation to his sunburnt cheek.

"Go, all!" she said in a voice of forced calmness; "leave the room. I will call when I need you. You, Manasseh, and you, Shina, remain."

The attendants respectfully withdrew, and in presence of the beautiful sleeping mother the future of the child was disposed of.

Never was the Christian father to behold her—never was he to know of her existence. When he returned, the infant should be far away among strangers. Shina was to be the only mother it should ever know—Manasseh, its father. But she would provide gold—gold that should procure every comfort and luxury for this child she dared not look upon—this daughter of a Christian father—this destroyer of her mother's life!

"The nurse is in waiting downstairs," said the cruel woman. "Go with her to your own dwelling. Be secret and true! My people will not betray me. They have sworn by the sacred tablets. As soon as this child can be removed, you will leave the town—you will hasten to a seaport—you will embark for Germany, France, Italy—I care not whither, so you educate this child in the faith of her fathers. You dare not remain in England; her father—curses upon him!—would find her. You will bring her up in the strict tenets of our faith—make her observe the Sabbath and the fast days—teach her the prayers—let her become a true daughter of the covenant; teach her to abhor, despise, regard with horror the creed of Nazareth. Be true, and the Holy One of Israel will bless you—but *he* shall *never, never* find his child!"

Hannah spoke with panting breath, with hurried utterance, with a changed and breaking voice. The hand so often pressed to her aching side betokened the sharp pangs of physical suffering that rent her frame.

Manasseh solemnly promised obedience to the lady's commands, placing the two fingers of his right hand upon the little silver case containing the sacred formula which the Jewish ordinance commands to be affixed to the door-post, with the name of Jehovah revealed.

Shina tremblingly repeated the oath.

"Call her Cosella; it was Lea's last wish," said Hannah, regarding them with exultant mien in the midst of her grief and pain. "That Christian name!" she continued; "but that the will of the dying may not be disobeyed, let her wish be fulfilled! And now call the watchers. I will to my chamber—we must not leave the dead alone!"

As Manasseh hastened to obey her orders, the proud unfortunate woman leant against the velvet hangings of the couch, and its flowing crimson draperies concealed the anguish, the physical torture that distorted her countenance and racked her breast as with darts of living fire.

The storm passed on and morning dawned upon the snow-covered earth, and great icicles hung from the stripped trees and drooped from the glistening leaves. There was more sorrow, distress and mourning in the stately mansion of the wealthy Jewess; for three hours after midnight she had followed her daughter to the unknown land, stricken down by heart disease, summoned by the angel, while her soul was filled with hatred and revenge.

Her cold, stern features, composed by death, her form arrayed in the spotless linen shroud, they had placed her on a low bed beside the daughter's sumptuous couch. A coverlet of black velvet, richly embroidered, was thrown carelessly over it, and a large wax candle burned at the foot, as did another at the feet of the young and the beautiful.

The wintry sun was faintly struggling through leaden-hued clouds, riders and weary pedestrians were wending their way to the village; but all stopped a while to gaze upon the graceful horseman urging along his fiery steed over the frozen and uneven path. Impelled by love and expectant joy, he alighted at the gateway of the still and solitary mansion, revealing a tall and princely form, a handsome, noble countenance, radiant with the exultant happiness of early manhood. He alighted with a free and bounding step, and knocked loudly and impatiently for admittance at the fast closed portal.

Alas! Alas! There was in his soul no boding fear; no presentiment had warned, no prophetic voices spoken; the blow fell crushingly and at once!

As he entered, there passed him in the wide hall a young woman of modest and timid aspect whose form was enveloped in a large dark mantle. It was Shina, the young Jewess, and a dark handsome man followed bearing a silver casket. She carried, beneath her cloak, the unconscious infant.

And Percival Wayne knew not that his child was carried out into the bleak cold world by stranger hands. Alas! He knew not that his soul's best loved one hovered around him, a spirit, divested of mortality!

With wondering curiosity that strengthened to foreboding fear, he passed along the silent hall and up the deserted stairway. There, at *her* chamber door, he met a weeping, pallid throng of attendants and neighbors; and the shadow of a terrible calamity enfolded his strong, loving heart.

Soon, and he knew his great bereavement; and the trembling, guilty servants shrank from the mightiness of the Christian's grief, and avoided his questioning eye. They showed him a little coffin, whose lid was nailed down, and told him that his child rested within. And he turned away and wept upon the silent bosom of his beloved, and called in wild anguish upon her name, seeing naught but the lifeless form of his heart's divinity.

They were buried the next day, mother and daughter, laid side by side in their own consecrated ground, in the adjoining town of B, and the little coffin lowered in solemn mockery beside them. A last lingering anguished look of love the husband cast upon the spot, and faint and heart-broken, he was turning away from the crowd when a slip of paper was thrust into his hand and the weary mourner read:

Christian, your child lives; she will be brought up a Jewess. You shall never meet with her. She will never know her father's name, and thy accursed faith shall have in her a zealous, bitter enemy. The lost soul of Lea, a mother's dying curse, a child's sworn enmity, are in league against thee. From a true son of Israel and thy sworn foe!

His cup of sorrow was full even to overflowing. With a groan he sank to the ground and was borne senseless to the nearest inn.

The sympathizing eyes of Shina had watched his reading of the fatal missive. In a timid whisper, she inquired of her husband whether it was not sinful to deprive a father of his child?

"Not when that father is an unbeliever," he sternly responded, and Shina wiped her accusing eyes and was silent.

The widowed mother of Lea, the proud and aristocratic Hannah Montepesoa, left no living kindred in her native Portugal, nor in her adopted country, England. A large share of her wealth endowed several benevolent institutions of her nation, and enriched the synagogues of several towns. Her dresses and ornaments were distributed among her women; the male attendants received a handsome legacy. What Manasseh's share of worldly goods amounted to remained a secret. He it was who in a week from the day of the funerals sold the house and furniture. The poor, and the inhabitants of the village, loudly vaunted his extreme liberality. Summoned to the bedside of Percival Wayne, he acquitted himself with consummate tact and ability, until not a doubt remained upon the sufferer's mind that his child lay buried beside the idolized wife, and that the cruel missive that had so rent his heart was an unfeeling taunt and falsehood. While the mourning husband and father lay powerless in the grasp of sorrow and sickness, Manasseh, with Shina his wife, and the Hebrew nurse, left the village forever, bearing with them the hapless infant that was doubly orphaned from its birth. Many weeks afterwards, while Percival Wayne yet lingered faint and suffering at the village inn, a letter was brought to him, dated from a distant seaport. It ran thus:

> Percival Wayne, your daughter lives, and shall be brought up the enemy to your faith. You shall never look upon her face. She shall learn to curse your name as that of a stranger. Your sworn foe!

With a loud cry of grief, the father flung the paper from him, and bowing his throbbing head upon his hands, he wept as only the great and wronged can weep. For weeks he tossed about in the delirium of fever; and when he arose, changed and haggard, he sought his child throughout the kingdom, scattering his wealth with a reckless hand. In vain! He found not his child!

God in his bounty, nature with her beautiful providence, had given to that wandering child a true and loving mother. Even as a spirit, that mother's love was deathless, watchful as an angel's care. The Christian father, with his noble tenderness of heart, his large conscientiousness and reverential love of the true and beautiful, with his benevolent soul and sympathizing nature, would have proved to the motherless one all that the heart of childhood yearns for. But a revengeful woman's plans cast the frail blossom upon uncongenial soil; fanaticism coped successfully against nature's promptings, and overcame the whisperings of tenderness and pity.

Fatherless and motherless, the orphan is cast upon the waters. Will spirits guide and shield her? Will an angel mother beckon upward, and God speak to the lone one's heart? Will circumstances bend the pure soul to their bidding, and necessity stifle the divine whispering of conscience? Will the inherent power of Godlike will, asserting its supremacy, rise superior to the evil promptings of despair, to the temptations of the hour, the might of opportunity, the weakness of tottering faith? We shall see. God is all conquering and the angel hosts are strong.

Heart-broken and desolate, Percival Wayne returns to the world, which he has left for love and sweet home joys. One glorious image forever enshrined in his heart's deepest sanctuary, which no form of earth shall displace thence; one haunting, blessed memory is ever beside him. From the pictured face of Lea, he turns to feel her spirit presence, to feel her breath of welcome, her signal of approach. Ever radiant with their own deep, tender light, her glorious Oriental eyes beam on him with the unspeakable love of yore; her ripe lips unclose with a winning tenderness, her midnight tresses flow unconfined, her soft footfall thrills his soul, her white garments flutter in the doorway. A "peace that passeth understanding" comes o'er his spirit. Will earthly affection bless, and the world smile once more for him?

Come with me, reader, and I will lead thee through many lands, and over many seas, to many sunny places and desert solitudes—not of earth only, but of the heart. Come with me into the mystic realms of thought, and the hidden springs that flow amid strange flowers shall water thy feet and whisper music to thy listening ear. Come and acknowledge that life is beautiful, that virtue is happiness, that sorrows and experiences exalt and purify from earthly dross the spirit. Oh, come! From desk and mart and bench; from the weary journey and the toilsome labor; peruse the life-pages here unrolled, that at the angels' bidding unfold their sunny and their shadowy records. To watch the progress of a human soul, the battling of a woman's heart, the final victory of the angel band—come one, come all!

Look, then, into thine heart, and write!
Yes, into Life's deep stream!
All forms of sorrow and delight,
All solemn voices of the Night,
That can soothe thee, or affright—
Be these henceforth thy theme.

1

A Wandering Childhood

Gaze on, 'tis lovely! childhood's lip and cheek,
Mantling beneath its earnest brow of thought.
Gaze—yet what seest thou in that fair and meek,
And fragile things, as but for sunshine wrought?
Thou seest what grief must nurture for the sky,
What earth must fashion for eternity!

—Hemans

As the swiftly changing scenes of a panorama, as the recurring glories of some bewildering dream, passed sudden glimpses of the surging life of cities, with their cathedral spires and lofty monuments, followed by idyllic scenes of perfect repose and sylvan beauty, sunlit lakes, towering mountains, flowery vales and forest solitudes, athwart the awakening consciousness of a little child. Before the wondering eyes, spread the wide expanse of ocean; and the wild-wood stillness whispered mysteriously, and the rivulet spoke in song. The leaping waterfall, from amid majestic crags, spoke in thunder tones of sublimity, and the blooming vine clad hills of home and rest.

On the child's earliest recollections were impressed lasting images of poetic beauty; an angel stirred the slumbering waters, and the thrilled infant soul responded in ecstatic gratitude for Nature's holy teachings; for the revelations of solitude, the messages of Immortality brought by the wild bird and the singing breeze. The enigma of busy life, as well as the grandeur of solitude, outspread before the childish vision, left their influence upon her heart and memory.

There was, at times, a strange abstraction of manner about this child of seven years; there flitted shadows, as if of thought, upon the open brow, and a melancholy expression lingered upon the mobile lips, as if some great sorrow, mighty and unexpressed, weighed on that yearning heart. Often the lips unclosed, as if in reply to an invisible questioner, who, mayhap, dwelt amid the flowers, floated on the summer's air, or descended on the storm cloud's wing.

Strange Cosella! Wild, yet docile, dreamy, and eager for a knowledge beyond her years, she caused many an affectionate pang, many an undefined apprehension to the tender heart of Shina; while the look with which her adopted father regarded her, was oftener one of malicious triumph than of paternal joy.

The timid, suffering heart of Shina made an idol of this child; she lavished upon her all the hoarded tenderness of an intensely loving nature. Cruelly, repeatedly repulsed by her strange, morose, ambitious husband, her fond affection all thrown back, the childless woman sought, with lavish indulgence, to win the love of the wayward *Cosy*, as she affectionately called her. With sweet, plaintive melodies, she lulled the little one to rest; her soft hand smoothed the shining mass of dark brown curls, and arranged them upon the wide open brow. She it was who taught the orphan her prayers; who spoke to her of God and Heaven in a strangely mingled strain of reverence and superstition; who told her pretty stories, and the names of the angel flowers. She endeavored most judiciously to instill into that molding spirit lessons of goodness, charity, forbearance, but she was ever most unaccountably thwarted by her husband, whom she had learned to fear, to dread, for his sarcasm and pointed contempt of her noble efforts.

Often a superstitious awe almost spell-bounded the timid woman in the presence of the motherless child; for it seemed to her that it held communion with things unseen. In the clear May sunlight, as well as beneath the leaden skies of winter, little Cosy would stretch forth her hands, as if in joyful recognition; and, fixing her eyes on vacancy, would speak unconscious words of tenderness and endearment, with kindling looks and glowing cheeks. When called by Shina, she would start as if awakened from a dream, and shrink, as it were, into herself. The light faded from her face, the usual paleness succeeded the illumined rose tint; sighingly she folded her little hands, and timidly, mournfully, questioningly, she looked around.

When Shina asked her what she had been looking at so intently, she replied with reluctance: "I saw a pretty lady, all dressed in white, with stars, with long, flowing, black hair, and a silver veil; she lives up there, in a flower-garden," said Cosy, pointing to the sky. And Shina shuddered with fear, and prayed to God for pardon, for her guilty husband and herself. She dared not tell Manasseh these strange fancies of the child.

The cheek of Shina, once so blooming, had paled beneath the tyranny and disdain of him to whom she had given herself for life. A few years since, he had knelt at her feet, a humble suitor, and passionately entreated for her love. She left her aged father and her quiet home to share his wandering fortunes; too soon she awoke from the heart dream of life to find the golden seeming fruit of promise turn to bitter ashes on her lips; to find herself unloved and disregarded, her gentle affection returned with scorn and sarcasm, her prayers spurned, her young life doomed to restless wandering! Once only in eight years was she permitted to revisit her native place, to invoke the blessing of the good old father she had left to a menial's care. Alas! They only showed her his final resting place, and she could weep upon his grave, and erect a tombstone to his memory. She returned to her tyrant, to the child that knew no other mother, and thenceforth accepted her lot without struggle for release.

Closer and closer, around her isolated, wounded heart she twined the links that bound her to the child of her adoption, centering her all of love and motherhood upon that unconscious head. But, alas! The sorrow of retribution! Cosella responded not, as that lone heart desired and prayed. She submitted passively to her showered caresses; giving coldly the good-night kiss, the morning embrace; she calmly wiped the tears from Shina's eyes, and toyed with her raven curls, and called her "pretty mother;" but there was no spontaneous outburst of filial love, no sudden clinging of dependence, no childlike intuition that reads the heart's demand and responds so warmly! The yearning childless woman wept, and loved her all the more. Daily, hourly, did Shina suffer for the wrong inflicted on a parent's heart, as she beheld the dark eyes of the child she fairly worshiped turn coldly from her pale face and looks of tender reproach, to fondle a shaggy dog, or caress a favorite bird, or press the wild flowers to her heart and lips, bestowing upon these objects of her affection words of endearment that would have warmed into life and joy the yearning, motherly, deserted soul.

"Oh!" cried Shina with tears, ringing her hands and looking imploringly up to Heaven, "she calls me mother *so* coldly! She loves me not, but that viewless image to which she stretches forth her hands—it answers—what can it be—a spirit! Oh, Father of Israel, her mother's haunting spirit! Yet Lea was so pure, so good—though she married an unbeliever. She comes in robe of stars—she is in Heaven, then! And in her dreams, my Cosy calls upon her mother, not as she calls on *me*; oh, there is so much tenderness in her voice when she smiles in sleep and says the sweet word *mother!*" When Cosella again toyed with those raven curls and looked at those tender eyes, she knew not they were dimmed with shedding bitter tears for her.

For eight years the once blooming and yet lovely Shina had been Manasseh's wife, she knew him not yet fully; and the many traits of his character revealed in that time but increased her awe and fear of him, though in her weak and yielding spirit, the love yet lingered tremblingly, hoping amid tears, praying from amid discouragement. He was a strange being, this husband of hers; commanding, even handsome in person and address; possessed of the knowledge of several languages, unaccountably acquired; for he avowed himself to be of humble parentage; a man of limited means, until his admittance to the friendship of Lea's mother. He was peculiarly self-possessed and gentlemanly in his deportment; a profound Hebrew scholar, most superstitiously observant of the ordinances of his faith; that is, *outwardly* observant of all due form and ceremony. Was he truly religious? Shina asked herself the question, in fear and trembling; for often the prayers were by him recited in so flippant and careless a manner as to give pain to the truly religious feelings of the truthful woman. A bitter, relentless, unsparing enmity against the Christian race held entire possession of him; he nurtured it in violation, not in obedience to the mandates of his faith; for the injunctions of the inspired law-givers of the Jewish nation enjoin the fulfillment of charity and forgiveness, and make it binding upon the souls of the people, as a command from the All-merciful Father, to cherish and succor the orphan and the widow, the stranger and the needy. Charity and forgiveness are solemnly enjoined by the oft misapplied selfishly perverted laws of Moses. The heart of the true Israelite, no less than that of the pious followers of the loving Nazarene, overflows with justice and benevolence, with pity and self-denial.

But I write of one who was a fanatic, who enshrined ambition and worldliness his guiding stars; who perverted holy precepts, and quoted the sacred writings, the traditions of his people, for selfish designs, in bitter mockery of all that is good and true. He stood among his brethren a religious man, observing scrupulously the appointed fast days and penances, the festivals and the Sabbath. He followed "line upon line and precept upon precept," in the fulfillment of outer form and requirement, thinking thereby to lull to rest an accusing conscience, while the heart planned in secret schemes of evil and revenge.

In a retired, pleasantly situated country town, not many miles from the banks of the Rhine, the wanderers rested a few months; rested amid the quiet and security that was as balm to Shina's tortured spirit, which, with its home-longings, was happy where the morose and restless Manasseh fretted. For seven years—since Cosella's birth—they had flitted from place to place, fleeing from the shadow of her father's approach. As if some mocking spirit goaded him on in his restless life, Manasseh often heard the name of Percival Wayne; now spoken of as one from earth departed in the fullness of life and genius; then, as if living, honored and beloved in the present.

Once he heard that the father of Cosella was one of many victims that met with a watery grave in the midst of the broad Atlantic; his name was registered among the lost. And Manasseh rejoiced and gave impious thanks to Heaven. Soon afterwards he heard of him as traveling in Italy—as having rested at the same hotel in Milan, where he, with his wife and child, had sojourned a week before. Then came the rumor that his crushed and mangled body had been found beneath a solitary crag in Switzerland.

Manasseh breathed freer—when chance directed a traveler toward him, who told him of the enemy that haunted his dreams, as living in prosperity in the English metropolis. Manassah ground his teeth and with dire curses journeyed on; ever fleeing from that avenging presence, calling out loudly in his sleep—muttering imprecations on the Christian foe. He heard of the fame of Percival Wayne in the secluded hamlets of Germany, in the famed cities of France, from its gay capital to its wayside villages—he was known as the pale, melancholy traveler, who was so lavish of his wealth to the poor and suffering—who was wasting away in incurable grief for the loss of his beautiful young wife. Ever thus in fear of discovery, assuming various names and disguises, Manasseh sought the world-aparted town of O——, and mingled again with his co-religionists, ever loath to relinquish his hold upon that belief, whose letter he worshipped, whose spirit he practically denied. He was esteemed for his ostentatious piety and virtuous benevolence; a certain display of wealth cast an irresistible charm around him, and frowned into respectful silence the curious few who would have questioned the newcomer. There were certain properties which had unaccountably fallen to his possession, from the sale of which he hoped to realize a fortune; so he told the gentle, unworldly Shina; he was waiting for remittances from England; these received, she was to prepare for a long sea-voyage. They were to leave Europe and the fear of Percival Wayne forever.

Manasseh was lavish of affection upon the child in presence of strangers; when alone with her and Shina his manner was incomprehensible, sneering, sarcastic, repellent; and Cosella feared and shunned him. She evinced a degree of reluctance toward him that was at once gratifying to his feelings and contrary to his cherished plans. But, by degrees, the influences surrounding the child obscured her spiritual vision; and the observance of form and ceremony filled the place of her first spontaneous, simple prayer, thereby thwarting the purposes of the unseen guides that sought to impress that soul for lofty ends. Falsehood and superstition tainted the moral atmosphere around; and from a very child Cosella felt the antagonism of warring elements; the strife of good with evil; felt it in her own soul and in the world without. The holy, unseen influences, the harmonies of Nature, the discords of humanity, the whisperings of inspiration, the eloquence of Nature's silence, the voices of immorality; the taint of wrong, the angel touch of impression, the holy safeguards of intuition, the solemn warnings, the silent premonitions, symbolic dreams, and soul-bursts of heavenly welcoming songs; all, all, neared the orphan child, and left tokens of their influences on the forming heart.

It was the eve of the Jewish Sabbath. In a small but luxuriously appointed room before a table covered with snowy cloth, and richly decked with silver and carved glass dishes, sat Shina, attired with taste and care in a greenish silk dress; a neat lace cap, adorned with pale pink ribbons, concealing the luxuriant tresses which, according to the strict Mosaic law, no married woman may display to the eye of a man. But a few dark ringlets playfully escaped their hiding place, and strayed on down the pale, thoughtful cheek, or fell behind the ear upon the kerchief of Brussels lace that was confined at the throat by a costly diamond breast-pin; a massive gold chain was thrown around her neck, from which was suspended a heavy looking watch, whose cumbrous golden case was set around with small brilliants; it was fastened to her girdle by a thick gold hook, studded with rubies. Her small white hands were covered with rings, and a bracelet, thickly set with rubies, flashed from her waist, just above the lace ruffle that fell over the delicate hand. The simple country folk of that secluded district gazed with reverence upon these signs of affluence, and exaggerated the English people's wealth as something fabulous. The house, too, small as it was, and only rented for a season, gave the same indications of affluent ease that the dress of the strangers revealed. The beautifying hand of Shina had adorned the little room, till it seemed a blessed retreat from the weariness of the world without. The windows opening upon the small but carefully tended garden were draped with white lace curtains, and these were looped up with sprigs of forget-me-not, poor Shina's favorite flower. The little sofa was covered with blue, of a pleasing shade; the alabaster vases, brought from the neighboring city, were filled with fresh and fragrant flowers; the silver cake-basket, with early strawberries peeping from amid their fresh, green leaves. A bouquet of beautifully assorted roses, with a few sprigs of forget-me-nots, was placed in the centre of the table in a crystal vase. An elaborately carved and gilded table, with a marble top, stood beneath a costly mirror, whose frame was veiled by cloud-like folds of lace; there were some rare old pictures in careless attitudes against the wall, in richly gilded modern frames; an old-fashioned musical clock stood in a corner, the jovial face of a round moon with roguish eyes, then quite discernible. A pretty cage so covered with grass and roses that it seemed the flowery prison of some fairy changeling contained a little earthly singing bird—a golden, sweet-voiced canary. A shaggy, surly, but most affectionate terrier, kept watch at the door. And at the window, watching the master's return from the synagogue, stood Lydia Elster, the attendant of Shina and Cosella—a strange, contradictory, superstitious woman, who had come with them from England. She was of English birth, but foreign parentage; remembered not her parents, but had been brought up by an aunt, and had lived as ladies' maid, companion, child-nurse and seamstress, with some of the wealthy Jewish families in London and the country. Manasseh met her in a country town, and his liberal offers of remuneration and apparent wealth quickly decided the mercenary creature to follow their fortunes. She had been with them three years, submitting to their wandering mode of life; looking to "the master" as the only authority; she was repelling to the sensitive Shina; but her queer ways, strange expressions, and ludicrous contortions of countenance amused the child. With her characteristic submission, Shina tolerated this evil with many others.

Cosella stood beside her gentle mother, her dark curls kept from veiling her expressive eyes by a blue ribbon encircling her brow. She was dressed for the Sabbath, in white, with a blue sash, and a necklace of amber was around her throat. Lydia sported a large, flowered, light silk gown, with cap of black lace and flaunting yellow ribbons.

Shina's soft dark eyes, full and tender in their Oriental expression, were cast down upon the prayer-book she held in her hands, the long lashes sweeping the colorless cheek, as a plaintive melody issued from her lips the greeting hymn of the Sabbath that should be read with such reverential joy. There was supplication in her heart, the humility of a stricken spirit in her attitude. It might have been said of her—

> A thousand sad and tender dreams,
> 'Neath those long lashes sleep;
> A native pensiveness that seems
> Too still and sweet to weep.

Such was her habitual expression; but oft, when the bitter waves of suffering rolled all too rudely over that meekly bending spirit, the sweet face became agonized with its intensity of grief and prayer, and she cried aloud to Him who dwells in Peace! An impress of settled resignation dwelt on the lips, but their coral hue alone relieved the whiteness of that perfectly lovely face. She felt herself an accomplice in the cruel deed of keeping from her father's arms the child he sought. She felt this sin, and its daily recurring retribution; but superstitious dread, fear of her bigoted husband, and love of the child that was all of earth to her restrained her from the act of justice, which, had she known where to find Percival Wayne, would still have bound her in trembling silence. Cosella must never become a Christian; her people would spurn and spit upon her could she deliver her to the unbelieving father's care. She dared not incur the anger of Manasseh—and to give up Cosella, oh! she could not live without her! Though he were in the same town she dared not, by word or sign, inform him of his daughter's existence; and every time his death was announced she breathed free and then accused herself of sin.

Shina was repeating the Sabbath hymn, and by her side stood Cosella, her dark eyes riveted upon her mother's pensive face, her lips reverentially following the words. There was a bending forward of her slight figure, a drooping of the head, as if with her, too, the attitude of supplication was not unusual. There was a strange mingling of timidity and boldness, affection and restraint, in her manner. At sight of a glorious sunset, or picturesque view, her eye kindled with enthusiasm, her cheek glowed, her heart throbbed wildly. When Shina spoke ever so tenderly, tearfully even, she remained cold and unmoved. When Manasseh threatened her with punishment her eye flashed defiance, her slight figure towered with pride, and anger quivered in every lineament. The next moment she would fling herself upon the neck of the surly terrier, and weep great tears amid his shaggy coat, and call him her "friend," her "love and dear!"

Shina read, in a low, musical voice, the Hebrew words of greeting to the Sabbath, whose rest and presence is invoked as the coming of a bride; she translated the words into English for the better understanding of her child:

"Come, my beloved! To meet the bride; the presence of the Sabbath let us receive. Come, my beloved, to meet the bride!"

"To meet the Sabbath, come let us go, for it is the fountain of blessing; in the beginning of olden times was it appointed; for, though last in act, yet it was first in the thought of God."

"The thought of God!" repeated Cosella; "God's thoughts must be all good, mother! He is never angry, is he, like father?"

"Hush, darling!" said Shina reprovingly; "you interrupt the prayer, and that is a sin; and you compare man to God, and that is a great sin, dear!"

Cosella looked wonderingly in Shina's face. "You told me we are all God's children," she replied; "one time you tell me God is all good, then you and father say God is angry. Yesterday you told me it was wicked to be angry; then God is wicked sometimes, and father, too!"

Shina trembled with agitation; those clear questioning eyes, the dreadful infidelity of her searching queries! She felt her utter incompetency to reply to the childish monitor. But Lydia came to the rescue.

"Miss Cosy, it is sinfully wicked to go on in that way; it's against the Bible and the law, and the holy prophets of Moses; it's against the Sabbath, and the feast and fast days; it's disobedient and immoralizing, and just like the Christians—as bad as eating pork and ham, and meat and butter, and forbidden things, all together in a mungle. You must not be sinful, Miss Cosy, or you wont go to heaven with your parents, but have to live to all eternity in a place of darkness, and fire, and brimstone, and hobgoblins."

She paused for breath, and Cosella burst into a loud laugh, that, to the startled Shina, seemed the mocking gayety of a lost soul. Without replying, she turned toward the book from which she was reading, and said:

"Go on, mother."

"Oh thou sanctuary of the King! Oh, royal city! Arise, come forth from thy subversion; thou hast dwelt long enough in the vale of tears; for he will now pity thee with kindness—"

"Rouse thyself! Rouse thyself! Arise, and shine for thy light is come. Awake! Awake! Utter a song, for the glory of the Lord is revealed upon thee."

The countenance of Shina glowed with enthusiasm—with momentary faith and deep, religious joy. The promises of the Most High to the mourning city seemed applied to herself; her eye glistened with tears; Cosella shared the faith and the enthusiasm, unknowing why, conscious only of prayer unto the good and loving God!

Shina rose from her chair, and bowing reverently to the right and left, according to the usage, spoke the concluding formula:

"Oh, come in peace, thou who art the crown of thy husband; also with joy and gladness in the midst of the faithful of the beloved people. Come, oh bride! Come, oh bride!"

She sat down, and the child bent before her, invoking her blessing; solemnly, most tenderly, she placed both hands on the orphan's head, and blessed her in the name of the four saintly mothers: Sarah, Rebecca, Rachel and Leah; and silently, yet from the depth of her heart, she prayed that Cosella might learn to love her, even as she was beloved.

Far through the dream-like vista of the past, the haunting footsteps of memory glide along familiar chambers, and in sweet, fragrant resting places; culling there perchance, a cypress flower. In after years, Shina often dreamed of the still home retreat and the Sabbath hymn of long ago; and Cosella turned with wild, vain longing to the little flower-room, to the consecrated hymn, and the fair, pensive face of the loved and true. Memory guarded sacredly the sweet home picture, in all its freshness and beauty to the seeking heart.

2

The Rhine Voyage

It is the Rhine! Our mountain vineyards laving,
I see the bright flood shine!
Sing on the march with every banner waving—
Sing, brothers! 'tis the Rhine!'

—Hemans

The fairy regions of the song-consecrated Rhine! The vine-clad hills, the stately ruins, the towering crags and old baronial castles looming darkly o'er the blue rippling waters! The magical sunshine of that fairy region bathing the blooming hedges and kissing the blushing roses and the lingering violets; the token-flowers that cluster around the sloping banks; the fragrant treasures hiding amid luxuriant grasses; the sweet wildflowers modestly uprearing their timid eyes; the scattered blossoms that line the greenwood path and fill the air with such delicious fragrance! Oh, consecrated Rhine—dreamland of poetic reverie—what mighty inspirations dwell in those storied fanes! Not fraught with the holiness of ages past, but glowing with the violet-breath of summer, the music stirrings of the airs that play amid Eolian harps, that waved amid Elysian tresses, and rested on the golden harp strings of adoring seraphs in the land of souls! Not with the faint repetitions of love-vows spoken by mailed knights of old and titled maidens; not laden with the heart outpourings of the long departed, the long-since blest and reunited, dost thou come, oh summer's breath of life and song! The high heart of youth throbs hopefully exultant now as then, and prophetic voices murmur as the loving hearts of old: "Thine, thine forever!"—and radiant nature smiles, though man's improvements change her forest solitudes to crowded cities, and bring the busy hum of life to the wild-wood shrines once sacred to her worshiping souls alone.

From the deck of one of the first steamers launched on that noble river, the dark, reflective eyes of a child wandered from scene to scene, with a rapidly flushing and paling cheek that betokened one of those sensitive, enthusiastic natures, which is one of God's best gifts; but which the matter of fact denizens of the world deem it a bounden duty to crush out of existence, in obedience to mammon's mandates, or disappointment's stern commands.

White cities were passed, cathedral spires and monuments of lasting fame and beauty; renowned sites, and flower-environed rural residences; forest shades, and vine clad hills; sunlit glens, and fairy islands; ruined battlements, and frowning crags—all passed before the enraptured vision of our own Cosella, who was standing near her mother with throbbing heart and heightened color.

"Mother," she said in a low, earnest tone, "I have dreamt of a river like this, but it was not the Rhine: it was called *Eternity*, mother, the beautiful, blue, shining river! And there were mountains, and the grapes on them were gold and purple; and beautiful roads went up the mountains, and many people were there, walking; and their faces were *so* bright, mother! And I saw the lady with the white dress and silver stars, and she took me by the hand and called me Cosy, and—"

The excited child paused to take breath; again the superstitious tremor shook the frame of Shina.

"My dear Cosy," she began—

"Mrs. Phillips! Why will you not allow that child to stay with her attendant? She is disarranging your dress, and you are completely spoiling her." The loud, imperious tone of her husband's voice startled the gentle woman; she blushed, and glanced hastily around; the passengers could not have heard him; they were all in another part of the vessel.

"You will never manifest the dignity becoming your station," he continued, coming nearer and speaking in a lower key. "Do behave like a lady; you ought to be used to it by this time," he sneered. Tears trembled in the large soft eyes of Shina; her lip quivered, but she made no reply.

"Come here, Ella," he called to the child. She shrank behind Shina's chair. "Come, my dear, come, Ella!" he said mildly and coaxingly. "I wont come by that name; my name is Cosy!" pouted the child. Manasseh cast a threatening look upon his wife, but he approached the little one with smiles. "Your name is Ella, dear; it is foolish to call you Cosy, such a baby name!"

"Have I not expressly forbidden you to call her so?" he said in a low voice, grasping his wife's arm under her shawl. "Call her so again at your peril!" he whispered in her ear. "Can we be too careful? Would you have us discovered? Would you bring ruin, disgrace, imprisonment upon me?"

The face of Shina blanched with fear, and her timid heart contracted with sorrow, as she felt his rude grasp upon her arm. "Oh, Manasseh!" she pleaded with tear-filled eyes.

"Obey me, then," he retorted, and released her arm.

"I don't like you, papa—I don't—go away, go away!" petulantly exclaimed the child. A curious smile played on his lips. "Oh, nonsense, Ella! You must like your father. Come here, I will show you something." He took an ivory case from his pocket and held it before her. She approached him slowly, half in curiosity and half in reluctance. He took a seat beside his wife and drew Cosella on his knee, giving the ivory plaything into her keeping; but his attention was soon diverted from the child to the conversation of three persons who had seated themselves near him, and were speaking in the mother tongue.

The elderly gentleman, whose portly bearing, and natural but easy gravity bespoke the traveling Englishman, was the father of the blue-eyed, sunny-haired maiden at his side, who, a true type of the island beauty that combines perfect feminine grace with healthful glow and strength, bloomed a true summer's rose, in contrast with the pale, drooping Shina. Father and daughter were bound on a pilgrimage of love, for in the churchyard of Mayence reposed the earth form of the wife and mother; and thither they often repaired to pay the tribute of affectionate remembrance.

The third person was a young man with dark complexion, large, soulful eyes of grey, and open brow, around which waved a quantity of dark brown hair; a certain polish and refinement visible in his slightest movement, a certain negligent care in the arrangement of his dress, revealed the graceful Frenchman; while the tender, half mirthful smile that hovered around his lips, and the rich color that momentarily rose to his face, as some fresh point of picturesque scenery broke upon their sight; as curve and bend disclosed the ever varying beauties of the storied Rhine—they gave indications of an enthusiastic nature, of a soul keenly alive to the appreciation of the beautiful and the romantic.

"Last year, Mademoiselle," said the young man, addressing the girl in excellent English that was tinged with a peculiar accent, "I was very much favored with'pleasant company; not so agreeable as the present," he bowed to the lady and smilingly continued, "but very agreeable; in particular there was one *compatriote* of yours, a fine gentleman—beautiful scholar—a learned man—a poet—he was everything! But he was *so* sorrowful, *so triste* always, poor man! He lost a beautiful young wife. We were great friends. I have traveled all over Europe, he too; and we talked over old times till we both laughed and cried. No, I mistake, we both cried together; but he never laughed; he only smiled—*so* sad! He would sigh so deeply, oh, *so* often! And call her name, his dead wife's name! He was such a good, charitable man, was Percival Wayne—"

"Percival Wayne!" cried the Englishman, and "Percival Wayne!" in loud, startled tones cried Manasseh. In a moment he was bending over the child, toying with her curls, speaking low and coaxingly, yet losing not a word of the conversation that so deeply interested him. Shina trembled with undefined apprehension.

"You knew Percival Wayne?" said the sweet voiced English girl. "Oh! Do tell us all about him, please, Monsieur Danvilliers."

"You knew him—you knew my friend?" eagerly questioned the excited Frenchman.

"We knew one Percival Wayne in London," replied the stout Englishman—"just such a one as you describe. Please go on, Monsieur. Perhaps it is someone else, Emma."

"Do you remember the name of his wife?"

"Yes, mademoiselle—it was Lea; and she was a *Juive*. I cannot find the English word just now."

"A Jewess," said Emma. "Yes, father, it is the Mr. Wayne we knew. How many pleasant evenings we spent together! Do you remember, father? He was so much beloved, so universally esteemed; and though many were prejudiced against him on account of his marriage, I know that *we* were not; and we felt deeply for him when he lost his beautiful young wife. He was ill for months; and when he recovered, he was merely the shadow of his former self."

"You knew him! You knew my dear friend! How glad, how very happy I am!" exclaimed the Frenchman, heartily shaking the fair girl's hand, and offering the same joyful demonstration to her father.

"Indeed, we knew and esteemed him," said the portly gentleman. "What was it to us that he married a Jewess? She must have been good, as well as handsome, or *he* would not have chosen her. Why, sir, he could have married the richest lady in the land; but Percival Wayne didn't care for money—that he didn't, sir! But please go on, Monsieur Danvilliers; tell us of our friend."

The light and joyous expression fled from the Frenchman's face, and a moisture gathered in his eyes.

"Alas! I shall make you sad," he replied, and paused.

The cheek of Emma paled, but her father said firmly:

"Go on, go on, my friend. This is a world of changes, we must be prepared for all things. Come, Emma, don't give way. Let us hear the worst."

The slight ivory toy snapped beneath the convulsive grasp of Manasseh; its fragments fell to the deck. A sensation of deadly coldness overspread Shina's trembling frame. Bowing her head to her knees, she vainly struggled for self-control. Yet, seated upon Manasseh's knee, the dark, searching eyes of the child were riveted upon the Frenchman's face, her lips apart, her head bent forward as if in eager listening.

"I will tell you all, as you desire; but I am so sorry to make you feel sad," continued Mr. Danvilliers, speaking low and as with effort. "We traveled together as far as Basle; then we hired a carriage—Monsieur Wayne and myself—and we go through all the beautiful Switzerland, and through Italy—*la belle Italie*; but in Milano my friend was taken very ill. I watched with him for sixteen days and nights. He was not delirious, not wild at all with the fever; but he said he saw the spirit of his wife beckoning to him— that she wore a white dress—that silver stars shone from it. He would hold long conversations with this fancy. I was fearful his reason would depart; but he was quite calm and gentle, and rational on every other point. He sol- emnly declared it was his Lea's spirit; but that, of course, was one *bêtise*— a delusion of the brain.

Well, my friends, he grew weaker and weaker, and I knew that he must die. The doctor said he could not live another week. Then, as my evil fate would have it, I received a letter from my mother, who was at the point of death. What could I do? I loved my mother, and I loved my friend. I left him with tears and sorrow, and I hastened home to find my mother much better. Thank God, she is living still. But my poor friend! As soon as my mother could be removed to the country, I returned to Milano. The land- lord at the hotel told me that my friend recovered a little, but the doctor said he could not live long. He was conveyed to a small village—I forget the name just now. I went there. There was but one miserable hotel in the place—one hut, more like, than like a hotel for a gentleman to live in. The landlord, a little, talkative fellow, told me that he had taken the place a few weeks before, but the last landlord told him that a fine Englishman, a gentleman, died there some weeks before. I described our friend, and the little landlord cried out that was the person and the name. They had buried him privately. I fear that, as he was not known, they treated him disrespect- fully. Some people is all for money. I took the room he occupied, and I as- sure you I cried and I prayed for him. No one seemed to care for him— none knew his name rightly; but I found his grave, in a retired spot, and I put a marble stone upon it. I thought it my duty. He has no relations liv- ing, I took his portrait while he was sick. You know, I am something of an amateur."

Emma was weeping silently. Her father, controlling his emotion, said:

"What a pity! And to die among strangers, in a foreign land! Poor Mr. Wayne! Yes, sir, there's no comfort out of old England. You have beautiful views, and grand scenes, and old curiosities, and you see strange sights; but for genuine comfort, for downright good nursing in sickness, and care in health, give me old England, I say!" And with this patriotic sentiment, the old gentleman gave his gold-headed cane an emphatic thump against the deck.

The Frenchman sat with folded arms, regarding with respectful admiration the lovely Emma, who was wiping way her tears, and gazing pensively upon the vine-covered hills, the changing panorama of the glorious Rhine.

The face of Manasseh was flushed with a fiendish joy. A sensation of faintness, a sickening feeling of dread was upon Shina. With closed eyes and pallid lips she leaned against the skylight.

But the strange, spirit-guarded child! In his deep abstraction, listening so intently to the narration that so deeply interested him, Manasseh had dropped his arm from around her; and when he sought for her again, she stood beside the young Frenchman, a questioning look upon her face, her hand resting on his knee.

"Poor Mr. Wayne! So generous, so noble, so soon called away!" said Emma. How few men are like him—so devoted to a memory! Could you gain no particulars concerning his last moments, Monsieur Danvilliers?"

"I could not get much, I am sorry to say, mademoiselle; but the little talkative landlord told me that his friend, the last landlord, told him that he was always calling on his wife. I asked him if the name was Lea, and he said, 'Oh, yes; *sí, sí, señor*—the last name on his lips was Lea.'"

A soft rose flush mounted to the temples of the listening child. Her head bent forward as with eager listening, or anxious expectation; her dark eyes were upraised to the young man's face with an expression of entreaty that long, long afterwards lingered on his memory. She attracted the attention of all three.

"What a fine little girl!" said the Frenchman, taking her hand and gazing admiringly upon her.

"A sweet child!" said Emma Leslie; "not exactly beautiful, but what an expressive face, what glorious eyes, dear father. Do you not think she has the Jewish type of features?"

"Why, not exactly, my dear;" replied Mr. Leslie. "Her skin is very fair, and her eyes are dark brown, not black—so is her hair; but I don't think she looks Jewish."

"What is your name, darling?" said Emma, stooping towards her, and taking the soft hands within her own.

"Co——" The child met the warning, threatening glance of Manasseh, and replied, casting down her eyes, and blushing, "Ella Phillips; mother calls me Cosy."

"You are a cosy little thing, but you mean rosy, I suppose;" said the gentle Emma, smiling, and stroking her silken curls. "Where is papa and mamma, dear?"

"Over there," said the child pointing.

The dewy, violet eyes of Emma met the dark glances of Manasseh, as he bowed politely and smiled. Instinctively she felt repelled, as pure natures ever must be in presence of the impure, the sordid and debased. Her eyes rested upon the crouching figure of Shina, and a deep womanly pity stole to her heart, and intuition whispered sadly, "She is an unloved wife."

"My little girl is troublesome, I fear," said Mr. Phillips, advancing to the group and looking fondly at the child.

"Not at all, sir—not at all," replied the portly gentleman. "We are very fond of children; is she your only one?"

"She is, sir, my only treasure; I fear that she is delicate, and I travel for the benefit of her health, and that of my wife."

"The little girl appears healthy enough," said the bluff Englishman, "but your good lady does appear pale and suffering."

"Mrs. Phillips is very nervous and excitable; she is always apprehensive of danger for our darling, here. Please excuse my little girl; whenever she hears her own language spoken, she makes free to scrape acquaintance. Good morning, Miss, good morning, gentlemen," and bowing and smiling, he led the child away.

Emma Leslie had been reading his dark face, and the covert sarcasm of his words when he spoke of his wife fell discordantly upon as fine an ear as ever was attuned to the divine harmonies of life and love. He felt those searching eyes upon his face; not for worlds could he have met the questioning glory of those heavenly orbs. She returned not his salutation, but she fondly kissed the child.

Manasseh, looking around him, said to Shina, "Come, my love, rest yourself awhile in the cabin; you are again faint and pale. I will read to you, if you wish; but first call Lydia to take Ella." Shina arose wearily and took his proffered arm; the commiserating glance of Emma rested full upon her face; she felt its influence, and timidly looking up, blushed painfully. She knew by her husband's politeness that he was angry with her; she expected a renewal of the scenes that embittered her life; the deception of passing as a cherished, petted wife before the world, while she was, in reality, a crouching slave, weighed heavily on her heart and conscience.

"I do not like that man," said Emma, with characteristic frankness.

"I agree with mademoiselle entirely," said the Frenchman, with a bow.

"*He* is a Jew, for certain," said Mr. Leslie; "and I think he is a domestic tyrant from the timid manner of his wife. Why, sir! She looks as if she had some sorrow, poor young thing. I don't think she's over twenty-four. The little girl is a pretty child."

"A remarkable child!" said Emma.

The spacious and luxuriantly furnished cabin was deserted; all the passengers were on deck, enjoying the lovely scenery—the breezy fragrance—

listening to the greeting music of the passing boats. The old, steeped in blissful recollections of life's summer time; the young, lulled in enchanted visions that uprose from the vine clad mount and forest denseness, from velvet lawn, and flowery path, to leave their impress of beauty upon the dreaming heart in the angel guise of prophecy.

Manasseh, with flushed face and sternly contracted brow, seated himself upon the velvet cushions of a downy ottoman, and said in loud imperious tones to his trembling wife, "Call the servant to take this child on deck; she need not be a witness to every word I say. Call Lydia!"

Shina went to the door and called the woman.

"Lydia," said "the master," as she appeared; "take Ella on deck, and mind, do not let her go near those English people, and that moustached French dandy! I will not have the child contaminated by intercourse with Christians. I can rely upon you, Lydia; Mrs. Phillips is not so particular. And see here, Lydia; I do wish you would dress more becomingly, and not wear such gaudy things; the flowers on your gown are large enough for a May *bouquet*, and you wear as many ribbons as a country girl of sixteen! Mrs. Phillips, why do you not attend to the dress of your attendant? You look as shabby, and as Jewish, woman, as a rag-picker!"

The angry color mounted to the temples of Lydia, she pushed back her cap, placed her arms akimbo, and commenced:

"If I'm shabby, it's the fault of those I live with that care neither for soul nor body, judge nor judgment; and I ain't ashamed of looking Jewish, and none of *my* folks were ever rag pickers! My great grandfather was a learned Rabbi, and fasted seven days out of three—I mean three days out of seven—and never ate meat in the penitential days, and my grandmother never touched money on the Sabbath, or ate a forbidden thing in her whole long life. Here you are lugging me up and down the world, and I'm compelled to eat all kinds of forbidden eatables and drinkables just to keep body and soul together, and my holy religion is thrown in my face, and I'm told I look Jewish! That's what I want to look like, master Phillips, and madam, and Miss Cosy! I wouldn't change, not to be the King of Prussia's prime minister, nor the lord chancellor's key-bearer. Say, Master Phillips, when is the fast day for the destruction of Jerusalem?"

"Don't torment me with your fasts and feasts—sometime next month— get the almanac and see; and now let me alone and go on deck. I want to speak to Mrs. Phillips."

"If I've said anything disrespectful, or irreligious, or defamatory to my position, please excuse me, master;" said the voluble Lydia, who often committed words to memory without at all noting their signification; the result was she said many curious things, and made sorry blunders with the vernacular. "I never wish to obstrude my unconsequential opinions on those that knows better; but master knows I do grow eloquent when our holy religion is slung about; I can bear a good deal here, but I want to be somebody, and have a good place in *Genadin*."

"I wish you were there, now," muttered Mr. Phillips, as she left the cabin, leading Cosy by the hand.

Shina sat with her hands folded in her lap, her soft, dark eyes swimming in tears. He was dead, the father of Cosella. He could never claim her; she would never know his love and care! Pity mingled with her selfish joy; her child was now her own. Her husband paced the floor, his face flushed and excited, his hands waving about him, triumph in his voice.

"Shina!" he cried, stopping before her, and speaking rapidly, "rejoice, rejoice with me! For he is dead! My worst enemy is no more! This time we are not deceived. That whiskered Frenchman put the tombstone over him—would that it had crushed his soul to atoms! He is dead, the unbeliever! The husband of Lea Montepesoa. Be a true wife, Shina, and rejoice with me, for now we are free to live; to enjoy our wealth. Since that child's birth we have been wanderers from place to place, as if a curse was upon us, to elude *him*, to thwart his efforts. How we have been chased from repose and quiet by the shadow of his approach. Shina—he is *dead! dead!* gone to dust—his soul to perdition! And Cosella is all our own—her fortune is ours; we can live in splendor; we can travel over the wide world and see its wonders, or we can settle here in Germany, in France, or England. We shall be welcome everywhere, for all human souls bow to the power of gold. Honor, fame, rectitude, virtue, love, all can be bought with gold. I know it. Come, Shina, lay aside your troubled looks. You must be pale and sorrowful no more; the dread of discovery is past. *He* is no more—my enemy and yours. We will settle down in some great city, or buy a country seat on the banks of this splendid river. I have changed my name. You were never known in London; we can live there in style. I will deck your little form with silks and satins, and buy the costliest diamonds for you, little wife. You shall have servants in plenty, and pictures, and flowers, and all things that you love; but you must be submissive and never thwart my will. Woman's province is to obey the commands of her lord—never to cavil and resist his power."

Poor Shina had expected reproaches and upbraidings; she drew a long sigh of relief, and her courage rising, with a true and sudden impulse, she said, in low, unfaltering tones, as she placed her hand upon his arm and gazed earnestly into his excited face—

"Is it right to rejoice at his death, Manasseh? Surely, he never injured us. Is it right to dispose of the fortune of his child?"

She had raised the storm; the brow of her husband clouded fearfully; an ireful light shone from his dark, painfully brilliant eyes; the mocking smile disfigured his lip.

"Do you dare to dictate to me?" he cried; "you a weak woman, a paltry, insignificant worm; *you*! The wife is subject to her husband; he makes laws for both; such is our holy law. Dare you rebel? Will you call upon your sinful head the curse of disobedience? Is it not enough that you caused the fall of man—that your sex is in league with evil spirits to waylay and destroy the souls of men? Do you not owe an honorable position, affluence and happiness to me?"

Shina sighed and was silent.

"Your suffering air and pale cheeks," he continued, "are the target for every fool's remarks. That pompous Englishman on deck there noticed how delicate you were. *Beware!* I warn you! I will have no wife to be pitied by strangers. That Christian girl, too, with her blue, piercing eyes; would that I could annihilate the race that for ages has trod upon our necks! Shina, reform your manner before the world, or I swear by the God of our fathers, I will punish you as you deserve! I know how and when to torture you. Be gay, be cheerful; sing, and be happy before the world, or, as I hope for the rebuilding of our holy temple, I will take Cosella from you and you shall never behold her again!"

With a loud cry, thoroughly aroused from her apathetic sorrow, Shina held his arm and wildly exclaimed—

"You would not—you cannot be so cruel to the child—the only thing that loves me. Take *her* away! my life, my soul, my only treasure! Oh, Manasseh! If you have one spark of feeling, leave me my child. I will do all—I will smile, and sing, and laugh, though it be a bitter falsehood."

"Sit down!" he said coldly; "take your arms from around me; we are not rehearsing a love scene, and people may come in and think you crazy. Shina, I command you, call that child Ella; I will it so. *He* is dead—miserably dead and forgotten, and his child is in my power. If his spirit lives, and sees and feels, it shall behold *her* growing up a bitter enemy to his faith; a zealous, nay, even a bigoted Jewess, as her grandmother desired; as I pray to train her, and as I will if I live. *His* spirit shall feel torture to behold his babe, his Cosella, spitting in scorn upon his nation, spurning with holy horror their doctrines. If she grow beautiful and talented, she shall be as a scourge to the unbelievers, an avenger of her nation's wrongs, atoning for the lost soul of her mother!"

There was something so terrible and menacing, so mysteriously threatening in his words, that the trembling Shina veiled her eyes, and turned away in fear. She had often timidly inquired the cause for this bitter hatred, this sworn, undying enmity; but he had repulsed her and told her to wait. Amid her sickening dread and horror arose the impulse to ask him now; to know the full extent of her wretchedness, for a dark shadow pressed on her soul and told her to listen and endure. With wildly beating breast, and choking voice, controlled by a desire she could not resist, Shina asked her husband:

"Why, Manasseh, did you hate Percival Wayne? Did he ever injure you personally?"

With bloodless lips, and frame that trembled convulsively, she awaited his reply.

"Women are inquisitive and troublesome; it needed not the wisdom of the blessed King Solomon to find that out," he sneered. "But I will satisfy your curiosity; I feel just in the mood. Perhaps it will punish you for your arrogance in opposing your opinions to mine, who am your head and lord. Know, then, Shina, that long before I saw you, I loved Lea Montepesoa. Don't start; sit still! I *loved* her, *worshiped* her, as Percival Wayne—cursed be his memory—never could, though he has died of grief for her, and I married and live on. Lea—peace be with her—was, as you know, of a proud, aristocratic family. I was poor then, so I never told my love, for I knew that her mother would have spurned me from the house; she looked for such a high station for that peerless daughter, that Princess of Israel, that lily of the sacred plains; and I know now that she, the departed, would have turned from me contemptuously to give her smiles to that Christian rhyme-maker; but I had a scheme in view, which, if successful, would have insured me wealth for life. I succeeded, but only partially, and I returned to —, and found—destruction, eternal perdition seize him!—Lea had eloped with the Christian! I was mad for several weeks; so was her mother. I traveled to dissipate my grief and rage. I met with you; you were gentle, yielding, the counterpart of Lea; she was proud and immovable, firm and unbending, young and beautiful as she was. I married you, and together we entered the *service* of Hannah Montepesoa. You know the rest. How the intriguing mother won the Christian's consent for the return of Lea to her birthplace that her child might be born there. You know the plans we laid that were all frustrated by Lea's death. Alas! She never would have returned to the religion of her fathers; she had accepted the blasphemous creed of the Nazarenes. When *he* returned from the journey on which *we* sent him, he found his idol a corpse, and her stern mother sleeping in death beside her; and he was told that his babe also was dead. And I gloated over his misery; and he repaid me then, in that chamber of death, for the pangs I had suffered. You know now that it was not only the Christian I hated, but the successful rival, the husband of Lea—peace be to her ashes!"

The head of Shina had drooped upon her breast, the tears were streaming from her veiled eyes, and she sought not to arrest their flow. From her pallid lips issued broken words, unfinished prayers, while great sobs welled from the wounded, loving heart so cruelly betrayed.

"Oh, most wretched!" she moaned. "Father of Israel! Why, oh why? He loved Lea—revenge himself on an innocent child! The dove I dreamed of is a cruel, destroying falcon! Oh, God! Let me die! Let me die! But Cosy—my angel child—my orphan babe—I will cherish—protect—I will—"

Merrily sounded the signal bell of arrival; the boat touched at a landing place. All was bustle and pleasant excitement, but Shina heard it not; she lay in a swoon upon the cabin floor.

3

Foreboding

Over the misty mountains,
Over the sounding sea;
Far through the dreamy distance
Came a white dove to me.

—Mrs. Taylor

It is the great day of Atonement with the Jews. Clad in the habiliments of the grave, the sweeping shroud of linen, with its wide cape edged with lace, the conical cap upon their heads, the worshipers of the ancient law read the accustomed prayers and beat their breasts in penitence. The synagogue is thronged, the gilded chandelier dispenses its rays of artificial light to the broad glare of day, and the voice of the reader rises loud at intervals in the repetition of the sacred formula: "Hear, oh Israel! The Lord thy God, the Lord is One!" and the congregation fervently responded: "Blessed be his holy name forever and ever!"

Occasionally, the sweet, softly murmured chorus of female voices lends its charm to those antique hymns of praise and penitence. The women sit above, in a gallery devoted solely to their use, separated from husbands, fathers and brothers; some, the aged and the matronly, arrayed in the vestment that once shall shroud their lifeless forms; others, the young and gay, wear dresses of pure white, emblematic of the forgiveness of sins, the stainless purity of the day of expiation. Few wear their usual gay clothing; some retain their glittering jewels, their pearls and rings; but the truly pious divest themselves of all outward adornment, and stand in true humility before the Lord. It is a rigid fast day; neither meat nor drink has passed the lips of that prayerful throng since yesterday's sunset; no refreshment will be taken until three stars illuminate the twilight depths of heaven. Israel offers this penance of the body, this humiliation of spirit by the confession of all sin, in place of the burnt offerings, the sacrifices of olden time.

They pray for the restoration of the land by them deemed holy; they weep afresh for the destruction of the sacred temple, for their scattered people and dethroned rulers. They strike their breasts, confessing their sins of commission and omission, and say aloud:

"For all this, oh Lord! King of the Universe grant us remission and pardon for thy name's sake!"

Five times that day, the congregation fall upon their knees in worship to the unseen God, and implore his pardon for the people. They pray, too, for the earthly and Christian rulers set before them, for the prosperity of their adopted country, for the welfare of all.

Trembling with profound humility, with the consciousness of wrong, Shina offers up her supplications, and Cosella prays beside her from the same Hebrew page:

"For the sin we have committed before thee, by false dealing with the neighbor."

Shina beats her breast, and thinks of the wronged Percival Wayne.

"For the sin we have committed before thee with lying lips!"

She weeps more bitterly, for she has stained her lips with falsehood for another's sake. Cosella looks in wonderment upon the gentle face, with its penitential sorrow.

"Thou shalt make restitution!" was the injunction of the law she reverenced; but her spiritual perceptions were obscured; her weak, woman's heart was not endowed with the moral purpose to atone and fulfill. The bold commanding intellect and powerful will of Manasseh bound and subdued her spirit; she felt the whisperings of conscience, the mandates of justice, but she *dared* not be free to act a noble part. She knew that her husband prayed for the repose of Lea's spirit, as well as for that of her mother. From her woman's soul ascended a prayer that was not written in her book of devotions, nor included in the formulas of that great day. She prayed for pardon of herself and husband, not only of the judging God, but of the wronged spirit of the Christian father. Amid the thrilling pathos of the supplicating hymn arose one petition unheard by all:

"Pardon for us sinners, spirit of Percival Wayne!"

All day Shina retained her place in the synagogue, and many praised the fervid piety of the lovely stranger, the graceful obedience of her pretty child. Manasseh called twice during the day for Cosella, but it required much persuasion to induce her to leave her mother's side, even to go out to obtain some food; for it is not incumbent on children to observe the fast. Manasseh took the child to a neighboring restaurant, and placed before her such food as is permitted by the Jewish ordinances. But not a morsel passed his own lips. He then carried Cosella back to her place and took his station among the worshipers.

The September day drew to a close; the departing sunrays illumined the roofs and tree-tops; the evening prayer was begun; and the faint, hungry glances of the worldly minded turned to the slowly moving hands of the massive clock. The twilight deepened, and the last benediction was said; the horn of commemoration was blown twice to announce the consummated sacrifice; the return to worldly cares and duties. Pale and exhausted, much more with weeping and remorse than from want of food, Shina descended with the throng of matrons and maidens and waited at the entrance door for the appearance of Manasseh.

Deeply impressed with the beauty and solemnity of the religious exercises, Cosella was enwrapt in dreams, vague, wild, intangible, of the future and mysterious world.

Manasseh was deep in conversation with a countryman of his; he had just heard a name that caused his heart to bound with a fear that for some time had slumbered; the dark, avenging shadow would not flee from before him; one haunting name pursued him everywhere. Mastering his agitation by a powerful effort, compelling his voice to be firm and calm, he asked, indifferently:

"You say Mr. Wayne, a poet and a gentleman of leisure, passed through this city, this time last year? He was pleased with the synagogue—who could be less, with such a magnificent structure? Germany has the lead in appropriate places of worship for God's chosen people, despite of the despotism of its rulers. But can you describe this Mr. Wayne? I knew a Wayne once—"

"He was tall and slender; very pale, with large expressive blue eyes, and light hair that waved rather than curled; his hands were very white and small; his manner high-bred. In short, he was what the people here call the picture of an English, my lord. He gave a handsome donation to the synagogue—a strange thing for a Christian to do; but he said he gave it for the sake of Lea. Not our father Jacob's wife, I suppose."

Manasseh turned aside his face. Too sure—too true; alas! Was fate in league against him? And the young Frenchman's story—was that all false? Had Percival Wayne arisen from the tomb to haunt him; or was there another of that hated name? But the description was so complete—he was not buried beneath the fragrant sod of Italy; he lived yet to track the footsteps of his child!

Rage and disappointment, akin almost to madness, surged in the bosom of Manasseh; but it was revealed by no outward sign.

"Excuse me, sir; I must join my wife who I see is waiting for me yonder with my little girl," he said politely to his companion, as he bowed and moved away.

It is customary for husbands and wives, friends and relatives, to embrace, in token of continued good-will and expiation of all wrong, on meeting after the close of the services of that great and holy day. As on the New Year, it is a time for reconciliation and forgiveness of all past enmities. Shina extended her hand with a loving, appealing smile. Her husband heeded her not; but bidding her take his arm, and leading Cosella by the hand, they passed the threshold of the house of prayer and silently took their homeward way.

The foreboding heart of Shina felt that some new sorrow had come to disturb her life—to drive them thence from that hospitable German city, further into the bleak and uncongenial world. They arrived at their lodgings, where the voluble and almost famished Lydia awaited them. She had slept throughout the greater portion of the fast day, but at the approach of evening had prepared the supper and set forth the table sumptuously.

"Oh, Mister and Madam and Miss Ella," she began, "I'm so immeasurably pleased with your arrival—just in the nick of time; the fish is browned as well as an ignorant Christian cook could be expected of to do superior things; in my finished manner, of course, there's few can imitate one as is a master in the culinary line; but I made the coffee, and the great prince Mogul of Sardinia and blessed Queen Esther never had a better cup of that same aromatic beverage. Bless my soul, Master Phillips, I'm most dropping down dead with excruciating hunger, I am! My tongue's cleaving to my mouth, so I can scarcely articulate; but I hope I'm unintelligible enough; the blessed holy fast has given me strength. Shall I bring in the coffee?"

"At once, woman! And stop your gibberish. I believe Satan himself has possession of that untiring tongue of yours," cried Manasseh in a loud and angry voice, while Shina took off her child's bonnet and cape, and silently removed her own rich crape shawl and dainty white straw bonnet.

Lydia placed her arms akimbo and launched forth: "Am I a black negro slave or a Hottentot mulatto Caffre, that I'm spoken to as if I was a nonentity and a fifth wheel to the wagon? Am I a useless, lumbering, inimical piece of ignorant silliness to be called a child of Satan? Do I look like a snake that ever tempted anybody to eat what was forbidden by our holy law—the prophets of Moses, Abraham, Isaac and Jacob? My great grandfather was a holy Rabbi, and I'm no bondwoman of Egyptian darkness, nor a heathen ignoramus, nor immoral Ishmaelite! I'm a legitimate Hebrew scholar, and my mother was a saint, in her way. I'm no Sabbath-breaker, or pork-eating idolator of graven images! I'm no violator of feasts and fasts and disturber of families. I'm no mischief monger and satellite; I ain't no shame faced question-asker, or misunderstander either. *There*, Master Phillips, I means no disrespect, nothing incongruous to my servility of obedience. Shall I bring in the coffee?"

Manasseh had regarded her with threatening glances throughout her long harangue; he now filled a large goblet with water, and made an expressive gesture with it toward her. She hastened from the room crying:

"Please, don't, Master Phillips! It's a wicked sin to get angry tonight."

Shina glanced timidly toward her husband; his moody looks were bent to the ground; his brow was clouded. She knew some trouble pressed newly upon him. She ventured the inquiry:

"What has occurred to distress you, Manasseh? May I know?"

He bent down to her ear:

"Send the child away with Lydia," he whispered.

That voluble and now thoroughly subdued individual returned, bringing in the coffee.

"Take Ella with you to your room; she may take supper with you," said Shina.

Glad of this rarely accorded privilege, the strange creature dropped a low curtsey and was about to return her thanks in a lengthy speech when "the master" promptly interrupted her, and bade her begone at once.

"Shina," he said, as soon as the door closed upon the child and her attendant, "I have evil tidings for you! It is decreed that we must cross the ocean, and live in some far distant land. The haunting demon of my life, the Christian foe is *not* dead! He lives. A year ago he visited this place; that was after the time the Frenchman gave as the date of his death. Shina, we must pack up tomorrow; we must leave Germany, England, all Europe for a time. We will to a seaport—from thence wherever God will guide us!"

Percival Wayne still living! The pale face of Shina flushed with a noble joy she dared not reveal.

"Must we wander still further—forever wander?" she murmured.

"Yes, it is the curse of our race—the decree of the Most High!" impiously declared Manasseh.

"You will be happy wherever that child is. If we remain in Europe, his spies may track us; she may be wrested from your arms at any hour."

He calculated well. Impulsively she rose and cried:

"Let us go; let us not waste a moment!" Then, relapsing into thought, the remorse of her selfishness held warfare with her passionate love of that one human thing. She burst into tears.

"Fear not, Shina; the angels of Israel will encompass us; we shall evade the enemy. Better so; for he shall live to know torture in the body before the spirit leaves it. Through that child his infidel soul shall suffer martyrdom. Eat, Shina, eat; you are pale and worn with fasting. I *command* you to eat!" he cried imperatively, as she turned sighingly away.

"Would you incur the danger of sickness with a long sea voyage before us? Strengthen yourself with food, for tomorrow we leave, and soon we depart from Europe."

"It is forever!" cried Shina, wringing her small, jeweled hands. "I shall never behold these hospitable shores again. I shall never again see the blue, lovely Rhine. I shall never look upon my native England—never, oh, never, again!"

There was so much deep earnestness, of heart-felt conviction, in her manner, Manasseh gazed upon her in silence for a while; then he spoke in light bantering tones:

"Pooh, pooh, nonsense! You are timid and nervous. We shall go safely across the sea; and, once fully assured of *his* death, we will return. When Cosella grows a woman, we shall return, for then there will be no danger of discovery; there may be none now—but I feel urged on. I know that Percival Wayne—a thousand curses upon him—suspects me. I would not meet him now; but some ten years hence, I defy him—I challenge him to win! Come, Shina! No more tears; you shall one day return to Europe."

"Never, oh, never! My grave will be in a foreign land," she exclaimed; and the wild gush of sorrow would have its way. She wept long and unrestrainedly.

Drinking a cup of coffee, eating only a slice of bread, Manasseh left his wife without another word of comfort or affection.

Foreboding heart! Too truly the future cast its shadow before thee. The tears of Shina were a parting tribute to the land she would never behold again.

4

The Watcher by the Tomb

I wait thee—I adjure thee! Hast thou known
How I have loved thee—could'st thou dream it all?
Am I not here, with night and death alone,
And fearing not? And hath my spirit's call
O'er thine to sway.

—Mrs. Hemans

In the Jewish cemetery of the town of B——, with darkness and silence around him, stands Percival Wayne beside his Lea's grave. His arms are resting on the pure white marble, his lips moving in prayer, his full heart pounding forth its passion of sorrow and entreaty; for he had not forgotten her who slept beneath; he had not found consolation or oblivion in travel; he wept for Lea still; and as the conviction grew upon him that his child still lived, that she had been wrested from him by guile and treachery, his restlessness know no bounds. He dreamed of that child, so like his Lea; he saw her little hands upraised toward him in entreaty; he saw the glorified form of his beloved, as guardian angel of the wandering child; he beheld, dark and threatening, the form of Manasseh; undefined and evil shapes hovering near him; he beheld his infant clasped to the loving bosom of a tender woman from whose protecting arms the stern Manasseh tore her. Then, in those changing visions, he saw his daughter, a blooming, lovely maiden, endowed with grace and genius, with the power of swaying hearts. She held in her hand the sacred books of the Mosaic law; with her dark, lustrous eyes fixed on her father's face, she kissed the volumes, and, pointing to her feet, with an air of ineffable pride and scorn, she trampled on the cross beneath them.

Again he saw her, in bridal robes of almost regal splendor, a Jewish bride; then she was watching beside a dying bed, and sorrow was impressed upon her lovely face. He saw the ocean, towering in majestic fury, swaying to and fro the bark that held his soul's dearest treasure. In strange, distant lands that child form hovered; over desert sands she fled, on mountain heights she stood; and, ever near her, hovering, shadowy and indistinct, the father's soul beheld the battling influences, angel and demon, striving for the victory.

Often these broken, confused, interrupted dreams left him with a heavy heart; sometimes he was enrapt in delightful hopes; for he dreamed of Lea, a radiant angel, leading her pure child by the hand to where the mourning husband, the longing father stood. The dark forms had vanished, and a bright group of ministering spirits attended the victorious maiden, who fell upon his bosom with a cry of joy! Then Percival Wayne beheld the emblematic cross upon his daughter's breast, and the azure flag she held bore in white letters the one word, "Dawn!" That word alone was visible—the thickly-gathered folds concealed the rest.

With night and darkness around him, he cried unto the ear of Heaven, consigned his child, if true it was she lived, to the Saviour's watchful care. And then, with bended knees and streaming eyes, he demanded of God a boon, such love as his alone could crave—a boon that was not sanctioned by church or creed, but one that mighty love desired, that intuition claimed as its holy right.

"Spirit of my loved departed one, my pure, good, innocent Lea, come to my yearning soul! In sickness and in sorrow thou hast visited me—I know it, though men deem me mad when I say so! Lea, by all the past of love and happiness, by our child, perhaps still living on this earth, by the heaven thou surely dwellest in, I conjure thee, come to me! Speak, smile again! Have I visited this place in vain? Art thou no nearer to me? Father of love and goodness, angels that minister to human sorrow, oh, permit her coming, bring her to me once more!"

He wept for bitterness and disappointment, wept until his eyes were dimmed and heavy, and then his troubled soul grew calm, and the spirit of peace whispered unto him, and faith lit anew her heavenly lamp. Slowly closed those weary eyes, the folded hands dropped by his side, the heavy head sank down upon the tombstone, and the night air played amid his waving hair.

And there, unconscious of the outer world, plunged into deep sleep, or trance, he remained immovable until the golden and crimson east announced the dawn of day. The spirit of his beloved one was with him. The visions of that night must have been gloriously beautiful; for when he left the graveyard his face was radiant, his deep blue eyes were lustrous with an inward and unspeakable joy, his gait was triumphant.

He lingered yet awhile to look upon the sculptured butterfly that, an emblem of immortality, decorated his Lea's grave. He paused to cull a few remaining autumn flowers, to breathe a renewed prayer of forgiveness over the proud mother's resting-place, to read the inscription on the monumental mockery that marked his infant's grave. He dared not look beneath the soil for the evidence of what he feared; the Jewish community would not allow the disinterment; he was compelled to live in doubt and conflict.

As he was passing from the cemetery, a lady entered, followed at some distance by a male attendant. Her veil was thrown back; her golden ringlets shaded a face as fair as ever met the morning's greeting; and Percival Wayne, as he looked upon that seraphic face, started back with a cry of surprise: she was the living image of his departed sister, the Cosella for whom his infant had been named! There are some rare impersonations of that most perfect style of beauty that is all spiritual; creatures of a mould and form celestial; the type of perfect purity, of beautifully-adapted faculties; of affection attuned to the loftiest inspirations of truth and womanhood. Such an one was Solita Mendez, a tropical flower, blending strongly yet harmoniously in her nature the exuberant, wildly-imaginative gifts of the South, with all the refined depth of thought and sentiment, the intellectual grandeur of the hardier North. Sometimes the poet's descriptive pen, the artist's pencil, may fully portray the human loveliness that embodies a rare ideal. But in presence of those choice virginal types, the embodied Psyches, an ancient myth foreshadowed dimly, pen and pencil fail alike; for the music, light and beauty of the perfect face can never be transferred, save to the soul, a promise and a talismanic memory!

Eyes deep and dark and tender, with an Oriental softness in their lustrous depths, contrasted admirably with the exquisite fairness of her complexion, the cheeks lightly breathed upon by a roseate tinge, the pensive, coral-hued lips, the shower of golden ringlets that veiled resplendently the wide, almost massive brow. Her neck was arched with queenly grace; her movements were aerial responses to the melodies within her soul; her figure light and symmetrical; her dainty hand and diminutive foot completed the sylph-like charm. Not a feminine grace was wanting; her voice was low and musical, her pure heart the resting place of angels. She was so like his lost sister, with her strangely-contrasting eyes and hair; but oh, as she came nearer, a thousand times more beautiful!

She lifted her calm, soul-reading eyes, and the roseate tinge upon her cheek deepened, as an expression of tender sympathy overswept her speaking countenance, for she felt that she was in the presence of a mourner. She bent her head in salutation, and looked upon his face again, for upon it rested a strange joy and triumph, blending with a long-cherished grief. He bowed low before her, and the maiden passed on her way.

He met her that day in the saloon of the hotel. She sat between an elderly lady and gentleman—her aunt and uncle. The lady was, like herself, a native to the tropics; her husband, a stout, bluff, merry Englishman. They were making the tour of Europe, with their orphan niece, and would soon return to New Granada, Solita's native land—to her possessions and plantations near the town of Santa Marea.

Percival Wayne lingered a month in B—, visiting daily and nightly the Jewish cemetery. The earnest sympathy of the kind-hearted, matter of fact Mr. Rodgers, the quiet attentions of the señora, the heart-given sympathy of the lovely Solita, exerted a most beneficial influence over the mind and feelings of the constant mourner. Laying aside the usual reserve of ladies of her clime and station, Solita sometimes met him in the graveyard at early dawn. Soon his natural reserve gave way, and he told her the story of his bereavement, of his wrongs and sufferings.

Solita wept for him, and prayed with him beside his Lea's grave. Strange mingling of pure, congenial spirits! On the consecrated Jewish ground, the Catholic maiden and the Protestant prayed to the common Father, the loving God of all! They communed together of all pure and holy things; they spoke reverentially of God and the future, of love eternal, and abiding truth.

Percival deemed himself again by his loved sister's side. He called her Cosella, and she accepted the name. Not a thought of love, of forgetfulness to the dead, entered his soul. Alas! The fervor and worship of a first and lasting love was showered upon him, and he knew it, felt it not!

She passed through all the phases of hope, and doubt, and chilling fear, in that short month. She dreamed of Paradise, and felt the tortures of that fabled purgatory her pure feet might never pass. She saw him wedded to a memory—nay, more, to a spirit, real and tangible; and he stood before her a moral hero, worthy of a true woman's boundless worship, exalted to an angel's place. Other women, deeming him free from earthly ties, would have exerted their powers of fascination. Solita was too pure, too honorable. Renunciation became with her a sacred duty—and duty was the watchword of her angel life.

They stood together by Lea's grave, and the resolve within her bosom had tinged the maiden's cheeks with crimson, had added lustre to her steady gaze. On the morrow, Percival Wayne was to depart. Struggling nobly to overcome the anguish of parting, she said, with a low but unfaltering voice:

"Brother Percival, you leave us tomorrow. I shall soon return to my native country. I have a request to make. Will you give me your miniature? Or is it too much for your adopted sister to demand?"

"My sister Cosella may demand of me all I have the power to give. I feel honored by your vow, your scruples. I shall not the less retain a place in your memory."

"A sister's portrait is an exception. Give it to me, Cosella. I will guard it with Lea's. I have no picture of my own sister."

A flush of joy, radiant and fleeting, passed over that lovely face; and the exchange was agreed upon. Solita said:

"If ever your wanderings lead you to a tropical land, you will visit Santa Marea, will you not? It is what you, accustomed to the grandeur of cities, would call a beautiful village; but it is *so very* beautiful; such a luxuriant garden, it makes me dream of the Paradise of our first parents. Percival Wayne, think not strange of what I am about to say. I feel that your child is living. I know not why, but the conviction forces itself upon me, that *I* shall meet with her. It is indeed improbable; but with God there is naught impossible. I feel it deeply *here*." She placed her hand upon her heart, and upraised her brimming eyes to heaven. "I shall meet your daughter, far, far from here."

For a moment a strange sense of calm, a feeling of security stole over the father's heart. With a beaming smile, he replied:

"My sister Cosella was my angel. Ever since my dear mother died, until she was called away, Cosella was my guide, my teacher, my comforter! Kind Providence, in its overruling love and wisdom, may have sent you, dear lady, to take her place. You may prove my child's guardian angel. God grant it may be so!"

"Percival, I am a Catholic; I believe in the efficacy of prayer, in the intercession of the holy saints. I will pray to the spotless Mother—she will guard your child with her troops of angels! Not a day shall pass, but I will pray to her—to our Lady of Solitude for whom I am named. She is the mother of the orphan, the holy protectress of the wronged and oppressed; never has a prayer been offered up in vain to her—the angel queen of Heaven."

Solita's hands were clasped with an enthusiasm born of holy, fervid faith; she looked the embodiment of that virgin mother she invoked. Percival, gazing upon her, felt a thrill of almost holy awe, a certainty that in some way, she, the stranger from a far distant clime, was connected with his destiny, his all of happiness on earth.

"She who slumbers here," continued Solita, placing her hand upon the cold white marble; "was an enemy to our holy faith, so I am taught to believe; she belonged to the race that placed the crown of thorns upon the Saviour's sacred brow; they pierced his mother's heart with the seven deadly swords! I am young. I cannot reason much upon religion, but I *feel* that God is good, the blessed mother forgiving. You have told me so much of Lea's love and gentleness, her sweet lips acknowledged the Redeemer; she must be, she *is* an angel! And the child of such a mother must be pure and good; the saints will shield her even in the grasp of the infidels. Be patient, and hopeful, Percival; there is joy in store for you. Now please leave me here alone a little while; I much desire it. I will soon come home; see, Manuel is in waiting for me yonder."

He obeyed her commands and reluctantly left her there alone. She sat still and musingly until the gate had closed upon him; then feeling secure from interruption, she threw herself upon her knees and clasped the monument with her white arms, and her heart's nobly borne sorrow found relief in words:

"Would that I could recall thee to life, thou idol of his constant soul! I would behold thee, thou peerless one, without one pang of envious longing. I would feast my eyes upon thy beauty with a deep humility. Perhaps thou art sitting at the Virgin's feet; oh, if so, intercede for me, for him! It was my destiny to love him, my duty is to conceal that love from all human knowledge. The angels will not blame me, for he is so good, so noble! And thou, sovereign mistress of his heart! Thou will forgive. I have thought and dreamed—perhaps they were vague, impious dreams—of a love beyond the grave; of a marriage tie, all angel-like, that was to bind my soul in heaven. Oh, if there be recognition there, thou, Lea, art his own throughout eternity! As mortal and as spirit, thine forever! And my lot through life will be desolate; where is there another like him? I shall be alone, perhaps eternally alone." And the sweet maiden wept; her tears rained on the sculptured marble; for a time the earthly agony claimed its tribute; the unrequited love, pierced deeply that child-like and devoted soul.

"Shall I murmur and repine because of earthly suffering, when thou, sinless and afflicted mother, didst behold the divine one pierced and slain," she said, raising her streaming eyes to Heaven and beating her innocent breast in penitence.

"Mother of Sorrows! Virgin of Solitude! Meekly will I uplift the cross that is so far lighter than mine. To thee I consecrate my life! Thou, Queen of Miracles, will lend thy sovereign aid to restore his child; let it be through me, thy humblest messenger, oh, Lady of good aid!"

The pure enthusiast prayed long and fervently; then with a serene countenance and steady steps, she rejoined Manuel and returned home. She parted from Percival Wayne as from a fondly loved brother; no rising blush or quivering lip betrayed a deeper feeling. He kissed her brow, and she returned the pure embrace calmly as a sister would. She watched his retreating form from the window; she waved her hand in adieu, as the carriage drove off; and when the last faint rumbling of the wheels had ceased, she left the room, and hastened to her chamber to pray for him and for herself.

Mr. Rodgers saw that Solita looked paler than usual for many days; the kind Señora Luisa, that her niece was more attentive than usual to her devotions. But neither of them read the secret so strictly guarded by maiden shame and high-minded delicacy. Solita often wept and struggled with the wild longing that possessed her, to seek for him she loved throughout the world; long pages were filled with the free outpourings of her love and sorrow—pages never destined to meet his eye. But nobly, successfully, she overcame the promptings of weakness; her spirit soared into a purer atmosphere; time brought calm, reflection, submission, to the inevitable decree. Many years passed on, ere again they stood face to face; and in that time the heart of the maiden had grown triumphant in its strength.

On her altar-table, close by the image of the virgin mother and the guardian angel, lay the portrait of Percival Wayne, a cherished and a sacred relic of the past.

Again the father seeks throughout the towns and hamlets of Europe for tidings of his child, and ever fails in obtaining the information that would prove balm to his tortured spirit. He knows not whether the daughter of Lea lives; perhaps the letters sent him were only cruel inventions of a malicious foe.

Solita returned to her native shores, admired by all, beloved by many; her heart is closed to earthly love; an image and a memory are there most sacredly enshrined.

On the high seas, a gallant East Indiaman ploughs her course toward the land of spice groves and golden sands. The majestic freedom of ocean teaches its lessons of sublimity to the listening heart of Cosella: it tells her of immortality—of the life in the world's beyond. From bigoted teachings and narrow creeds that spirit turns instinctively to learn of truth through nature's voices. The brilliant stars, twinkling in the depths of Heaven, first told that child of the "many mansions" of progressive life. The silence of the ocean midnight first taught her soul the voiceless solemnity of prayer and aspiration; the torch of genius was enkindled by angel hands, the lyre of poesy was swept by the wild winds of heaven; and solitude gave forth its manifold inspirations, its holy impressions, its prophetic dreams.

5

The Jewish Betrothal

Strew the bridal path with flowers,
Fill the cups with ruby wine;
Lightly pass life's fleeting hours—
Pleasure and love, fair bride, be thine.

—Old Song

It was the festival of the Passover; the rich plate, the costly china dishes, the crystal goblets foaming with sweet Persian wine were set forth; large cakes of unleavened bread were handed round, and rare Indian vegetables, the customary pilau, the fragrant salads, all partaken of with a blessing, with the loud chanting of hymns, in commemoration of the departure from Egypt.

The master of the house, a snowy bearded, crimson turbaned and richly attired Israelite, sat between his sons, Ezekiel and Asaph, gazing around him with a pious complacency that had in it much of worldly pride. Reuben-ben-Aslan was a wealthy merchant of the "City of Palaces"; his sons were considered among the young men of their race and station perfect paragons of Hebrew learning; his daughter Rifka (the Hebrew for Rebecca) was a perfect type of Oriental loveliness, and long betrothed to a learned Rabbi's son, although the maiden was only fourteen years of age. The mother, Hanucah, so called in commemoration of a certain festival, was a stout and dignified lady, very youthful as yet herself. Near the host sat Manasseh Phillips, as it was his pleasure to be called, and near him was the merchant Soliman Hashem.

The contrast was a striking one. The flowing robes and embroidered girdles of the Orientals, their turbaned heads, the glistening, costly rings upon their fingers; with the sober, English, gentlemanly garb of the stranger. The women sat at the lower end of the hall by themselves, Hanucah doing the honors to her guests, the two wives of the merchant Hashem, the European's wife and child. Rifka silently and gracefully assisted her mother.

The two wives of the merchant Hashem! exclaims the startled reader. But we are telling you of the East, the land of superstition and olden tradition, where the Mosaic dispensation permits to its followers the forming of a second and legal marriage, under certain conditions. Soliman Hashem had married early in life, a lady who had blessed him with three fair daughters; for years his soul was troubled, for to whom should his name and calling descend? He married again, and with his first wife's free consent, and his wishes were fulfilled. The younger wife became the happy mother of a son. Strange, yet true, the two wives lived in perfect harmony; no envious feelings, no disturbing jealousy invaded their mutual home.

The sweet face of Shina beamed with a placid joy. The long sea voyage ended, how happy she is to be with those of her own faith, although their manners and customs are so peculiar! She is richly and tastefully attired, but her jewels are insignificant beside the lavish splendor of the Oriental beauties.

I will describe to you the lady Rifka as she appeared on that festival night.

Her costume was Turkish in form, and was composed of rainbow hued silk and ruby colored velvet, richly embroidered with gold. The snowy muslin folds that veiled her bosom were inwrought with precious gems; three bracelets, richly studded with diamonds and rubies, glistened from each fair, round arm, as the velvet sleeve flew back. Her small ears were pierced in several places, and decked with many earrings, rich and heavy. Rings, thickly set with pearls, rubies, amethyst, topaz and emerald, gleamed from her fingers and *thumbs*; her peaked and spangled slippers were negligently thrust aside, and her little feet were dyed with henna, her finger-nails with the same roseate hue. Kohl stained her eyebrows and marked the drooping, silken lashes, imparting that peculiar expression of softness and languor to the eye—

That makes the maids, whom Kings are proud to call
From fair Circassia's vales, so beautiful

The lovely Rifka wore her own softly waved jet black hair, the youthful and aged matrons of her faith being compelled to wear false tresses. She wore it smoothly parted on the forehead, and surmounted by a double row of valuable gold coins; a crimson turban wound around the gilded network that encased her shapely head, and its long ends fell upon her shoulders in a shower of silver fringe. Gathered into two thick plaits, her long hair fell below her knees, small, musical bells and jingling coins attached to it. Three massive chains formed of golden balls and little fishes with diamond eyes were cast around her neck and descended to her waist, which was clasped by a white Cashmere girdle embroidered with gold and pearls. The sleeves of her velvet robe were looped back by diamond buttons, and above each ankle glittered a massive golden band.

Cosella gazed in wonder and admiration upon the pensive face, the childlike figure, arrayed in all this regal magnificence.

Reuben-ben-Aslan spoke the English language tolerably well; in the intervals of eating and praying, he discussed business and politics with his European brother. The ladies could only converse by signs; they knew no language but their own. To dress, and repeat the prayers allotted them, to implicitly obey their lords and masters was all they had learnt of life; it was all sufficing for these beautiful but sadly neglected women.

The wine and fruits passed around, the concluding blessing chanted, all arose to go to another room where cosy divans were awaiting, and the fragrant hookah was brought in. Two swarthy maidens from Abyssinia fanned the ladies with officious humility.

Reuben and the merchant talked with the stranger, the host acting as interpreter; and the young men listened attentively, but ventured not to join in the conversation of their elders; so strict is the discipline of youth in that land of olden usage. They curiously regarded the little European girl, but addressed to her no word.

The women sat apart, deeming it a mark of respect to their husbands, and maintaining a whispered conversation among themselves. The beautiful Rifka, strangely attracted to the foreign child, held her hand and repeatedly kissed her cheek, murmuring sweet, unintelligible words in Hindostanee.

That night it was arranged that the strangers should remain the inmates of that hospitable home as long as it suited their convenience.

When the night had somewhat advanced, the wives of Soliman Hashem wrapt themselves in the dark silken covering that entirely shrouded their persons, and threw over their faces the thick, black crape veil with its heavy embroidery of gold. Thus concealed from all profane eyes, they descended the stairway to where their palankeens awaited them, first by kindly signs and gesture having invited the English lady and her child to visit them.

That night, when they had been shown to a luxuriously furnished chamber, Manasseh said to his wife:

"I have an idea which, if realized, will insure us comfort and happiness, and secure Cosella to our holy faith forever. I will tell you about it tomorrow."

Poor Lydia, who had been left among the native servants until she was fairly bewildered by their gibberish, was glad to be allowed to sleep in the chamber with Miss Ella. The child laughed heartily at the strange woman's recital of her troubles.

"They obligated me to eat with my five fingers, Miss Ella, indeed they did; I never was so put out of my usual equilibrum of assurance—no, never! I was ready to drop down dead; but I remembered it was the holy Passover, as is constituted in the memory of the rebuilding of the Temple, and return out of captivity of Moses; so I called upon the four holy angels that stand by everybody's bedside every night—Gabriel, Michael, Raphael and Uriel—and I felt my weakness revigorated by the grace of the blessed festival. I don't like unleavened bread, Miss Ella, but I submits to a good deal for our holy religion's sake—the prophets of the law of Moses. But I had to eat with my own five blessed fingers, and no soap to wash them afterwards, only some rose water; and they brought me a pipe—just as if I was an Irish smoker, or heathenish forgetter of what was right. I declare, Miss Ella, I screamed outright when I saw the pipe—it was for all the world like a big snake all coiled up—and they laughed at my reluctance of fright, and pointed their uncivil fingers at me, just like the ignoramus Christians when they say to little boys and girls:—

I had a piece o' pork, and I stuck it on a fork,
And I gave it to a Jew—Jew—Jew!

But ain't the dresses faxinating, Miss Ella?—I means the ladies; the subordinaries is like subordinaries everywhere under the globe; as I am myself a living example of circumstances and evidential conspirations of adversity. One dresses in silks and satins, and another in sackcloth and colors of ashes. I'm a contented human individuality in my own diselevated condition of sphere; but I'm an observatory of nature, Miss Ella, and nothing escapes the perspicacity of my vision. I'm an optical delusionist, my dear; but I'm afraid my language is beyond your comprehension of years. Say your prayers, darling; now turn your head to the East, now bow three times. Blessed angels be around us, the glory of—what is it, Miss Ella—glory of what?—be it above my head. I'm so bewildered in a foreign tongue—foreign land I mean—I forget the blessed, holy prayers!"

Ella laughed, and absently repeated her prayers.

They remained with Reuben-ben-Aslan three months, and then there was another festival, and a merry gathering. Cosella, a child of nine years, was betrothed to the young Asaph, who was seven years her senior. The innocent child, unconscious of the weighty responsibility she was assuming, yielded to Manasseh's commands. Shina's heart was torn with conflicting emotions; the habit of obedience, the *fear* of her husband, battled with her motherly desires for the child's welfare, with her strong reluctance to the proposed union. It had been Manasseh's plan from the first night of their arrival; a plan that fully served his avarice and fanaticism.

Attired in Oriental robes that well became her slender fairy-like figure, Cosella stood before the assembled company, her flowing curls confined by a circlet of gold and pearls, the rose colored bridal veil flung over her face; many jewels glittering on her person. Beside her stood the youthful Asaph, and the venerable Rabbi was reading the betrothal service. A crystal goblet was shivered at their feet, and its fragments collected in token of the betrothal promise. A massive gold ring, with a ruby in the center, was placed on the bride's finger, and the benediction solemnly given. Asaph looked upon the child with admiring eyes; beneath her rosy veil Cosella pondered on the meaning of the strange ceremony, feeling in her unconscious heart neither joy nor fear.

She sat beside her betrothed and her mother at the sumptuous board; her veil was thrown from off her face; with a childlike curiosity she scanned the guests. Several Europeans were there—Christians who were permitted to assist at the feast after witnessing the novel ceremony.

Manasseh was conversing politely with a gentleman from Bombay.

"You have traveled much? Have you ever been in B——, near L——, in England?" asked his companion, fixing on him a scrutinizing glance.

A flush rose to Manasseh's dark cheek. Shina, sitting opposite, paled and trembled.

"I have not been there," he replied calmly. "I have never been in that part of the country. B——, I believe, is in ——shire."

"Yes," said the gentleman, keenly eyeing the inwardly trembling man. "I have a friend there; or rather, he once lived there. I know not where he is at present. Did you ever know a Percival Wayne?"

Slowly, emphatically, the words were spoken; there was a purpose, a meaning in them; but Manasseh was prepared. He answered with polite indifference:

"The name is strange to me; I never heard it before."

Shina had risen from the table, deadly pallor overspreading her face. She murmured:

"I am not well, my child!" and grasping Cosella's hand, she hastened from the room, followed by the closely veiled ladies of the family. A threatening glance from Manasseh's dark eyes followed her. The questioning stranger caught that glance, and interpreted it to himself alone. "He does not follow her," he muttered.

"I was a schoolmate of Percival Wayne," he continued, never taking his keen, grey eyes from Manasseh's face. "I knew him intimately; I was one of his marriage guests. He wedded a lady of your persuasion; her name was Lea Montepesoa"; the face he looked upon paled suddenly—the firm lip trembled slightly. "She died near B—— shortly after the birth of an infant. My business took me to India; circumstances that occurred, letters that have been received"—the stranger spoke with still stronger emphasis—"lead my bereaved friend to suppose that he has been most shockingly, most cruelly deceived, as regards the death of that infant. He believes the child—it was a girl—to have been taken away by a man in the employ of his wife's mother; I received a letter from him some months ago; he thinks of coming to India to search for that child. In Europe he has tried in vain. Without entering upon any discussion of religious views, do you not think it cruel, horrible, revolting, to deprive a father of his child?"

"Monstrous! criminal! unnatural!" cried the hypocrite. "But you must not too hastily believe these things of our people; we are a persecuted race, deprived of home and country; what is there too vile to be brought up against us?" he said in a voice of well simulated sadness and regret.

The friend of Percival Wayne gazed steadily upon the strange, dark-browed man before him:

"I should be very sorry to bring such accusations against anyone without sufficient proof," he continued, "for much I admire your people, Mr. Phillips. There is much in their forms of observance that is consistent and praiseworthy—but, pardon me, I am an outspoken man; I mean no offence—but do not some of your people deem it no sin to wrong a Christian? I ask only to obtain information."

"Some of our unfortunate brothers may be ignorant enough to harbor such sentiments. I ask you, sir, with equal candor, are there no Christians who deem it no sin to cheat and betray a Jew?" There was no touch of anger in his voice; it was deeply sad; it appealed to the best feelings of the good man that was questioning him.

"Too true, too true, sir!" he replied. "I have no prejudices of creed or belief. I think we are all brothers in the eyes of one Universal Father—that is *my* creed, sir! But the letters my friend Percival received? They were threatening, cruel, bitter letters! telling him his child lived, and would be brought up an enemy to her father's faith. Those letters, sir, nearly deprived my friend of reason! They brought him to the verge of the grave. Was it not a bitter foe who wrote them?"

Manasseh succeeded admirably in concealing his demonine joy. He replied in the same subdued and deprecating manner:

"Must it have been a *Jewish* foe? Could not some Christian enemy have conceived the plan?"

"True, true; I believe Percival never thought of that. But I cannot see that he could have an enemy at all; so good, so noble and generous as he is!

"And that little girl we have seen a bride today is your only child?" he questioned.

"My only one," was the answer of Manasseh, and his voice sounded tremblingly, as with strong affection: "The hopes of myself and my beloved wife are bound up in that child; her future happiness is our constant prayer."

"It seems a strange thing to me, as a Christian and an Englishman, to see so young a child become a bride. May I inquire when you intend the marriage to take place?"

"When she herself shall desire it. We use no compulsion in the matter; we fix no time. I, too, am an Englishman, although an Israelite, and I yield to the customs of the ancient law. My Leila will be happy; we have well chosen for her."

"Your child's name is Leila?"

"It is, sir. May I inquire your name? Our host gave it, but it has escaped my memory."

"My name is Withers, at your service. May I inquire what place in England was your home?"

Manasseh mentioned a distant country town, far removed from B—. At the close of the festivities, Mr. Withers warmly pressed the proffered hand of the man he had doubted. Manasseh spoke so feelingly of duty, and all human obligations; he spoke with such deep, religious fervor, that the single-minded Englishman accused himself of injustice, in no sparing terms. Shina returned not to the company; but the little bride resumed her place with European freedom. Her father had whispered to her that she must retain her Hindostanee name of Leila, and henceforth give no other. Therefore when Mr. Withers questioned her, she told him she was Leila Phillips; that she loved her kind, gentle mamma ever so much; that papa was very good to her. Had she only mentioned her mother's name, the one familiar word, Shina, would have uplifted the curtain of mystery. The Englishman returned home, muttering to himself: "What a fool I came nigh making myself! Because this Mr. Phillips looks like Percival's vague description of a servant man! All the Jews look alike, more or less. This is a gentleman, the other a menial; he is called Phillips, the rascal's name is Moshem—a little difference there! The child don't look a bit like Percival; and if she was stolen, it is not likely they would idolize her so. The mother looked as if she would worship her; the father talks of her with tears in his eyes. But, at first, the idea struck me so forcibly—I imagined he colored at the name of Lea. No wonder, poor gentleman, when he told me he had an only sister who died at the age of sixteen named Lea. That explained his changing countenance; what a fool I came nigh making of myself!"

True hearted man! He knew not of the chameleon forms of deceit and wrong.

Lydia's voluble tongue found ample employment on disrobing her little mistress that night.

"It's a beautiful angelical, unsurpassed beauty you are, Miss Leila, as master bids me call you. I'm no advocator of changeabilities of surnames and titles in generalities, or I should have been married a hundred times over if I hadn't put a higher valuation on my moral propensities and advantages of religious life in early training. But I'm a conscientious woman, and love the laws of our blessed Legislator more than the temptations of glittering pearls and ore and flesh pots of Egypt and jewelry. And when you're married, Miss El—, Leila, I mean, I'll stay with you forever, if I drop down dead the very next minute after I see you in the holy bondage of matrimony. Miss El—, Leila, dear, it's customary to give a present to the officious attendant as is a ministering to mind and body all the time, with scrupulosity of affection and tenderness of waiting like a patient lamb! What are you going to give me, dear?"

Cosella gave her a gold piece. The woman's small eyes glittered with joy; she kissed the coin and the hand that gave it, and was breaking forth afresh, when the child interrupted her:

"Please, don't talk now, Lydia; I want to think!" she said.

Lydia clasped her hands in wonderment, retreated a few paces, and was silent. Cosella, resting her brow upon both hands, thought long and deeply. Her thoughts were strange, wild, mingling, and confused; there blended with them prophetic glimpses of the future that thrilled and oppressed her heart.

Manasseh proceeding to his wife's chamber, he found her sitting in her festal robes with eyes that bore the marks of long-continued weeping; with hands folded upon her lap. She started at his entrance. He locked the door, went up to her, and said:

"We have had a narrow escape, Shina! That man is one of my enemy's spies. But you nearly betrayed me. Woman! You are my evil genius! When will you learn to control your silly nerves? By heavens! If we had been discovered by your folly, you should have rued it. We must leave this city, but not suddenly—not so as to arouse suspicion; and we must deceive them all. Listen, Shina! You must pretend to receive a letter from England—from your mother, or some near relation; that letter recalls you on account of some property. Mind you act well your part, as you fear my lasting displeasure! We will take passage in a homeward bound vessel, but we will not actually return. I will determine soon whither we shall bend our steps; but we must mislead the emissaries of Percival Wayne, curses on his name! He must not search for us out of Europe. Now, remember, you receive that letter tomorrow."

"Nothing but wandering, endless, endless wandering!" passionately exclaimed Shina. "Oh, Manasseh! cannot you excuse me from this task? I cannot dissimulate—indeed I cannot! My mother rests in her grave—shall I invoke her memory to a falsehood? I cannot. Manasseh, you ask too much of me!" The poor woman wept.

His brow contracted with the gloomy frown she feared so much.

"What a conscientious fool!" he said, mockingly. "Remember, madam, *I* command you, and I am your lord and master; you have no will, no responsibility of your own. Be grateful for the privilege; if you feel scrupulous about using your mother's name, take that of any other relative. I leave this matter in your hands; I will not have all the trouble of that child to myself. You *love* her so much, take your share of the securing of that love."

"I cannot lie—I cannot act and deceive; I am incompetent; my soul recoils from it!" cried Shina, wringing her hands.

"I will teach you; you will be an apt pupil. I know the motive that will bend you to my will," he replied with concentrated fury, pushing her forcibly into a chair.

"My life is one of deception and false appearances throughout! I cannot —I *will* not lie in the pure presence of that innocent child!" she said with sudden energy.

"*You will not?*" He looked into her face. Shina veiled her eyes with her hand.

"Listen, Mrs. Phillips, Shina Moshem, listen! The law in this land, our Rabbinical law, grants divorces. There are plenty of Eastern women, young and fair, who would be willing to be mothers to *my* child. Tempt me not— try me not too far! Do my bidding, and the child shall know no other mother. Disobey me and—"

"No, no! God in Heaven, no!" cried Shina, wildly flinging herself upon her knees before her tyrant. "Manasseh! I will do all—all! Never again say those words! Leave me that child, that soul, that heart, that life, of mine! Beat me—kill me—let me die for her—but separate us not! Oh, promise, Manasseh, promise! You will not cast me from you; you will not give my place—the place of Cosella's mother—to a strange woman? Promise, Manasseh, as you hope for heaven, promise!"

He smiled a quiet smile of victory as the tortured woman, looking upon him with pallid face and wildly imploring eyes, poured forth her anguished entreaty. He took the little silver tablet from his bosom, and kissed the sacred name thereon engraved:

"By the holy commandments herein contained, I swear!" he said; "as long as you obey, you shall retain your place. You know now what is before you."

The solitary woman kissed the despot's hand. Her all of hope and love was centered in that one living thing—the child of her adoption. Through her affections that stern fanatic bound her to his will—plunged her pure soul in the darkness of deception.

Alas, for will! Alas, for seeming destiny!

6

Awakening

Over the world, with weary footsteps straying,
With fainting heart that vainly longs for rest,
Elysian glimpses of home's sunlight straying,
In luring mockery, o'er the soul's unrest.

—C. W.

As time sped on, the novelty of change and travel lost its charm, even for the young Cosella who vainly yearned for home quiet and repose. Although so much of the beautiful, rare and sublime in art and nature was presented to her view, to impress everlastingly upon her soul their images of poetic beauty, their powers of inspiration, yet true to the first great dictate of a woman's heart, Cosella, while yet a child, longed, wept and prayed for *home*. She turned with listless mien from the lavish magnificence of Eastern life, from its dazzling display of wealth, its architectural wonders, that, though in ruins, bore the impress of sublimity, fraught with olden legends and the antique records of that storied land. Even from the art galleries of Italy, from its marble palaces and sites renowned in song, the child turned with sighing heart to gaze upon the hamlets embosomed in the flowery vales, the cottages nestling amid the forest's depth. Amid Nature's scenes of grandeur and of still repose she longed for the artist's power, that she might retain those glowing sunset tints, that she might imitate those swaying branches rustling to the evening gale; catch the last sunlighted reflection upon the roseate floating clouds above the sea; that she might immortalize the human face, when truly divine it gleamed with the seraphic illumination of pity, goodness and love.

From the great deep with its mysterious voices telling that forming soul of God and life, the child turned her fervent gaze up to the burning stars, and in one lustrous, far off, shining, silver orb fashioned for herself a life of love hereafter, a home amid the beautiful. From the busy mart, the artificial life of cities, she turned, in contemplation, to the humble wayside homes, and sighed regretfully that such a resting place was denied to her.

Again and again the deep was traversed, the great cities of the earth passed by, the mountain's windings followed, and the placid rivers gazed upon, and still no home repose awaited the longing weary hearts of Shina and Cosella; still the demon of ambition, the raging thirst for gold, the shadow and the unrest, dwelt in the darkened soul of Manasseh, and urged him on to endless wandering.

There are those who say that there exists no standard of right; that conscience is educational, a conventional thing, that lives not of itself. Cosella's awakening soul, her thoughts, her aims, her motives, were a living example to the contrary. Her sense of honor, truth and justice was innate—strengthened, it must have been, from above—while all around, from earliest childhood, threatened with subversion every aspiring thought. Intuitively she recoiled from the maxims and sophistries of Manasseh, delivered with so much holy unction. Her quick understanding pondered over the vacillations, the superstitious teachings of Shina; and earnestly, promptly, lovingly, the truth was accepted, revealed and understood by that angel-guarded child. Ever the voice within repelled the theories of vengeance of a dread and fearful God; ever the child-soul turned lovingly to the God of love, enshrined in beauteous forms, in all surrounding Nature's vastness and loveliness; ever that still, small, untaught voice applauded loudly whatever reached its inner shrine that was all true and pure; ever faithfully it turned from the man-made laws that fettered to the God mandate that gave righteous liberty.

At twelve years of age, Manasseh's character stood partially revealed before her, and she felt increasing the vague fear, the shrinking mistrust, that ever bound her in his presence. She knew him as dishonest, untruthful, compromising with the world. From the narrow, fettering creed he taught, from the wearying ceremonials, with their gaping, soul void, Cosella turned with ill-disguised repugnance, and from her own soul sought the light and guidance; and there truth spoke unalterable: "Thou shalt not deceive either God or man!"

Thus slowly developed in that neglected soil the germs of thought, of artistic beauty and poetic expression. There truth came bringing glorious trophies early won, and religion, pure, untrammeled, unfurled her snowy banner, and love inscribed his mighty name. The influences of earth could not contend against the angel mother's guardianship, nor win the victory from angel hosts.

Too early, alas, the cloud weight of premature thought rested on Cosella's brow, and that momentous inquiry of the future pressed on her child-heart with foreboding gloom.

Ever from her soul arose a cry, voiceless but mighty, freighted with earth's heaviest burden of woe and longing—a cry intense and prayerful that in its response would be gifted with deific power to save—the human heart cry for love!

For she found it not in Shina's arms, close nestling to her heart; something was wanting in that most-devoted affection. Cosella often turned her tear-filled, asking eyes up to the starlit heavens and mutely questioned them.

Thus, early was the soul-tie linked betwixt her spirit and heaven; the attractions of the upper world enfolded, unconsciously, her being; the music of the spheres rolled over the listening, unfearing heart; the altar flame was lit, unknown, within the secret, deep recess; the spontaneous, eloquent, oft wordless prayer was the tribute of an inspiration freely given; the dreams of night and waking were revelations from an inner source; the star worlds glistened with magnetic, soothing power; the ideal realm, the true, the beautiful, unfolded to the dreamer's sight. Against its charmed walls the serpent forms of worldly wrong sought vainly for admittance. False religion, mammon-worship, and the host of unruly thoughts and images could not approach the golden door, could not breathe in the fragrant atmosphere of the poet's, the dreamer's guarded realm.

Thus, world-traveled, yet unworldly-wise, the soul light deepened in the child's dark eyes, and the thought-cloud rested on her brow; strange thoughts dwelt in her mind, unspoken, uncommunicated, save to the ear of night, the breast of ocean, the keeping of the clouds. The faint bloom on her cheek deepened with the vague, delicious, growing hopes; it paled beneath the foreboding shadows that drew ever near. And thus Cosella emerged from childhood, and stood upon the threshold of a new life, a novice to the world, with even then a shadow of distrust lingering on the sun-lighted path; even then, with a presentiment of mighty trial, turning from the great, open, beckoning, changing world, to the ever radiant dream-land, the music world of song, the whispering of spirit life.

⌒

The stars of heaven look down upon the placid river; the cocoa waves its crested head, the giant palm bends whisperingly to the murmuring waters. There, strange and dazzling with its gilded spire, the tall pagoda stands amid environing foliage, and clustering fruit trees. The boat glides indolently with the current and Cosella sits with folded hands and upraised brow, her soul communing with the unseen world. Thus run her thoughts amid the silence of the night, the strangeness of that Indian scene.

"They say that thou art afar off, great God! Enthroned in majesty, with kingly pomp and power. I cannot hope for, believe in Thee, thus. To *me*, thou art *everywhere*; love, beauty, poetry, warmth, and song! Thy voice is in the wind, in the thunder's roar, in the cataract's fall; thy might and glory manifest in all! And *here*, oh Father-spirit," the girl touched her heaving breast, "here in this heart I feel *thee*, life, power, aspiration, strength, and love! The spirit worlds, for I feel they are innumerable, they are all ladders of ascension, worlds of changing, unfolding beauty; life cannot be stationary, nor heaven monotonous. Action, knowledge, wisdom, love, and power, all is in the soul; can it be quenched by death, extinguished by the hand of God himself? No; age after age I shall progress, unfold, aspire. I shall become angel, seraph, spirit of love and knowledge! I shall tread the mazy pathway of the stars, I shall learn of the mysteries of life, I shall know love, and behold my God in higher forms of thought and being. Spirit-life! Worlds of mysterious beauty! Tremblingly, fervently, I aspire to your opening portals! Open, oh, golden gates for me!"

Then over the rapt enthusiast's face there passed a gleam of roseate light, and low, exquisite melody floated downward from the starry orbs, and faith dwelt sun-crowned in Cosella's awakening heart.

Apart, with gloomy brow and fixed eye, sits Manasseh, and his heart is troubled with the mercenary cares of life. He fears no longer the living vengeance of Percival Wayne; but luring and mocking voices urge him on his restless course; gold the guerdon—wealth the purchase of tranquility. The stifled moans of conscience break through the iron armor of his soul. Successful in spoiling the trusting; traveling in ease and luxury, still ill at rest! For he dares not seek a home; but drags over the wide earth the unwilling wife; the dreaming and unfolding girl.

"Soon," he mutters, gazing fixedly at the young Cosella, "soon she will be a woman; she is strictly attentive to her prayers, to every ordinance of our holy faith, but she is not zealous as I would have her. She is abstracted, dreamy, fanciful; she inherits much of *his* nature—curses yet upon his name! She braves me too! She will not lie for me. When I bade her affirm an assertion I made yesterday before the European we met at the village, she refused to do so, whispering that she would not tell a falsehood for the world. Had Shina dared to do this, I would have felled her to the earth! But *she*, this pale, fragile girl, her eye gleams with her mother's fiery spirit. I dare not touch her in anger, but I will yet curb her soul."

Never, never, so wrong, Manasseh; for angels guide and guard her from thy power!

Shina sits gazing sadly upon the young girl, who beholds her not, enwrapt as she is in dreams. "She loves me," murmur the melancholy lips, "but her thoughts, her strange, peculiar feelings are her own; she guards them watchfully, she tells me not her girlish dreams. Oh, Ella, darling! once, when I am laid to rest, thou wilt love me better!" The soft eyes are filled with tears, but Ella sees not, her gaze is on the distant worlds.

The boat sways to the current, the night wind sighs, and spicy odors from the forest's depths are borne to the river's banks. The silence of night enfolds the scene; the wanderers drift on.

～

The sun shines on the golden bosom of the Egyptian Nile, blazes over the sacred plains of Palestine, and lights the wanderer's pathway through the sandy desert. On the Red Sea's track the ancient song of Israel is sung by girlish lips, and like the Miriam of old, Cosella stands upon the headland's top and renders praises to the Lord of hosts. By the pearl islands, the palmy groves of Persia, lingers the awakening heart; not all enthralled by superstition she dares to worship in silence the visible glories of the Great pervading Spirit; she cannot confine to given form or shape. Past the rocky coast of Araby, and past the Green Sea's beauty; images of poetic reverie, sweet food for song in years to come. All swiftly passing, merging once more into the broad expanse of ocean, the grandeur and solitude of the overarching skies.

Again for months the wanderers lived upon the sea; the soothing calm, the sublimity of the storm, alike welcome to the fearless girl, who reveled in the tempest's power, and called in glee unto the threatening waves. Then, as an island paradise beckoned the shores of flowery Java, and beneath its burning skies, amid its gorgeous growth of fruit, and flower, and foliage, loitered harmlessly the fearless Northern girl with rose decked cheeks and elastic step of health and youth.

But Shina bent to the fatal breath of its perfumed airs. For months she lingered in the grasp of fever; then pale, emaciated, sadly smiling as usual, she was restored to health. Wildly, madly, had she prayed for life; wildly, despairingly, had Cosella entreated for her to God, and for a while the boon was granted. They were nearer to each other than before, for the girl had watched by the sufferer with all a daughter's devotion and untiring love. What Manasseh's thoughts were none could tell. Strong and unbending in his will-power, he yielded not to disease; he overcame fatigue and braved the changing and unhealthy climes. With his usual superstition, he attributed his exemption from disease to the favor of Providence, bestowed in reward for his punctilious observance of the laws of Moses. It was to his temperate habits, his abhorrence of swine's flesh, that he owed his manifold escapes from malignant illness. But, although favored with health and strength, his soul was darkened with remorse and fear—with threatening superstition—at times with torturing skepticism. Fearful of the hereafter, Manasseh often hoped that the immortality he feared would prove a dream; he impiously prayed for annihilation when the earth life should close, for the words "reward," and "punishment" rang in his guilty soul like knells of doom.

Not long did the wanderers rest; again the fiat went forth; again the white sails fluttered in the spicy breeze, again the ocean spray dashed in the face of the light-hearted Cosella; again the prayer arose from Shina's tortured heart for home and rest. The grouping islands passed, the long days over, the shores of summer-garbed Australia met the delighted eyes of the weary voyagers, and again poor Shina sighed, "Would that we could here find a home!" But it was not to be.

For a little while only they rested among their people, of whom there was a number in the principal cities. Once more, mother and daughter listened delightedly to the chanting of the ancient songs of Israel. Upon many of her race, Cosella looked with the supreme disdain of the untried heart that has not yet learned its first great lesson of charity; many of them had been sent from the land of their birth for theft and plunder, for various derelictions against law and order; to the honor of Israel be it said not once in a hundred years is one of her children found guilty of taking life. Oppression, cruelty and inflicted wrong have brought forth harsh, repelling traits of character; but the Israelite, be he ever so fallen, so degraded, shrinks from blood guiltiness!

Upon the mixed community of that strange far land, the innately true and just Cosella looked with repugnance. She withdrew from society as much as possible; she sat much alone, listening abstractedly to Lydia Elster's strange discourses, for amid the many changes of her wandering life that voluble personage followed her young mistress; submitting, as she said, with "the courage and invincible fidelity of a Jewish martyr to all the horrifications of traveling in heathen lands among idolatrous worships, and eating things against her blessed conscience of right, the holy law and the prophets of Moses;" but it was self-interest, not love, that linked her to this family; for Manasseh gave handsome presents, and she bore all insults meekly, and followed their fortunes with a view to making her own.

Cosella was not surprised, though Shina was, when one day she presented herself before them, with a demure countenance, but determined air, saying:

"Mistress and Miss Ella, you know I've been serving you faithful and unchangeable for a number of countless years of time, as was spent journeying in heathen lands among savage beasts and birds of prey, and all sorts of dangers to soul and body. Miss and Madam! Now, as I am safely landed among the chosen people, and meet nothing umbrageous to my immediate designs of settling in life and plenty, I feel it a Scripture duty to look out for the old age that is coming, though there's no signs of it in me, in my personal presentation; but I can enter the mercantile community on my own responsibility of comprehension, and keep the Sabbath and the feast and the fast days holy, and rest my weary body, without being tossed about on fishes' backs on the great ocean, and sleep without fears of Christian robbers and Indian snakes, and earthquakes, and fevers, and mosquitoes, ma'am. If you please, I wish to applicate for my discharge from the honorable duties of my situation, as it is becoming too burdensome and disadvantageous to my years and standard of health. Will you speak to the master, madam, for I do dread and despise to be brought in circumference with his fumigated mind."

Cosella laughed outright. Shina, smiling sadly, said:

"I thought you would always remain with us, Lydia."

"So I thought, madam; but fate ordinates the changes of mortality," replied the waiting woman. "I must obey the dictatious rules of over scrupulentious conscience as bids me forsake my sins and break no more commandments. I've been thinking a great deal lately, and I see the enormities of my misdemeanors of forgetfulness toward our holy religion, and I believe in repeting while we're young, and turning our thoughts to religion, and laying up a little money for the rainy day. Besides—" here Lydia fidgeted a little while with her handkerchief and apron-strings—"there is a young, honorable, well-to-do gentleman, has been paying me complimentary expressions on the faxinations of my modest appearance and style of twilette (toilet); and—and, madam and Miss Ella, I heard this morning that his attentions were to matrimony, and I confabulated with my own discrimination of intellectual knowledge, and made up my mind—"

"To marry the young man?" interrupted Cosella, with a mischievous smile.

"Yes, miss, yes, madam, I shall be a honored and respected lady. Mr. Isaac Moses Poodlestock—"

"*What?*" burst in again the young girl with hearty laughter that could no longer be restrained. "Mr. What?"

"Isaac Moses Poodlestock, Esq.," gravely replied Lydia. "I think it's highly indecorous, and unmanageably ungenteel in a young lady to laugh at a gentleman's name and title in that way. He's a gentleman every inch, and would be a prince if justice was done in the world. But I'm engaged, anyhow, and I think it's only common civility and manners to congratulate and give presents to a young bride."

"But this is very sudden, Lydia," said Shina. "We have been here only three months; how long have you known the gentleman?"

"What's the odds, ma'am?" sharply responded the woman. "I can't afford time to waste in investigatories and spendthrifts of persons; he is an

English Pole, and a gentleman, and a finished tiptop Hebrew scholar. Has learned to kill poultry, and writes as fine as a microscope; he's got a new and old clothes' shop, and sings in the kire (choir) of the synagogue. Why shouldn't I marry such a man? And he loves me and vows I'm beautiful to the sight. Oh, Miss Ella! He writes such poetry; you'd go into convulsions of admiration, you love rhyme so. What he says jingles just like snow bells."

"You ought to love Jaspe very much, Lydia," said the mischievous girl, taking up her mother's pet dog.

"Why, Miss?" queried the puzzled Lydia.

"Because he is a part of your intended's name—poodle-stock," laughed the merry Cosella. But Lydia fired up at this innocent sally.

"Young ladies that are only chits of girls, without school knowledge or accomplishments of music and fine arts, etcetera, ought to hold their tongues, and not speak before older and wiser personages endowed with perspicuity of sight and strongholds of understanding; children ought to play with skipping ropes and dolls, and leave the reflections of matured time and wisdom to the regulations of those that know and to the Lord. I'm my own mistress, Miss Ella; I'm no black Hindoo salaam bowing Hottentot; neither am I a salamander or a rattlesnake, or a constricting boa! I'm a rationalized individual, considerably elevated above the humbleness of my menial capacity by the finer construction of my optical delusions! I'm a free thinker, Miss, and I ain't afraid of the great can of Persia, nor of all the evil spirits in the immiserable universe. I'm a daughter of the covenant of Jacob and Esau; I'm a true religionist, and no new fangled demigog or neckbreaker; I'm going to find the master, as I can't reason with that young gigglepate!"

Angry and excited, Lydia flounced out of the room.

The gentle Shina held up her hand deprecatingly; but Cosella's mirth could not be restrained. She laughed over the dog, until thoughts of the shaggy terrier, her first canine friend, sent a melancholy shadow to her face; poor Selmo rested on the Indian river's banks—her tears had watered the spot. With Selmo's remembrance arose many images of the past—the vivid panorama of her first remembered wanderings. Cosella grew pensive and fell silent.

Lydia was married to Mr. Isaac Moses Poodlestock and received from "the master" a handsome bridal gift.

In a few months the wanderers sped forth again; now, that for years no tidings had been heard of Percival Wayne, Manasseh feared not to call his young and growing daughter Cosella.

It wanted a few days of her sixteenth birthday when they landed at the beautifully situated, rural town of Santa Lucia, in South America. The tropical shores were luxuriantly robed with their gorgeous flowery vestments; the graceful cocoa skirted the sea-washed banks, the crimson coffee berries glistened ruby ripe in the sun; the delicious odors of the mango and the guava were drifted out to sea. Blue and dazzling shone the unclouded sky of beauty, but as she stepped upon the green, inviting shores, Cosella's heart was filled with foreboding, with sadness deep and unutterable.

7

The Dawn of the New Life

Enthusiast! Dreamer! Such the names
Thine age bestows on thee,
For that great nature, going forth
In world-wide sympathy;
For the vision clear, the spirit brave,
The honest heart and warm,
And the voice which swells the battle-cry
   Of Freedom and Reform.

                —Grace Greenwood

In the town of B——, in England, in a plainly furnished room overlooking a modest garden and the distant winding river, sat two friends interchanging thought and planning hopefully for the future. They were both men in middle life; the dark hair of the one was intersected with many silvery threads, and lines of care and thought had deeply furrowed his brow; but his eye beamed brightly, with a quiet, holy, serene joy, a sweet smile of satisfaction ever played around the firm well-shaped mouth. Years of toil and study had bent his frame; it was growing erect once more under the influence of a new born hope and faith.

His companion was younger, more erect, of more majestic presence. A great grief, borne hopelessly for years, had paled his cheek and settled its impress on his brow and lip; but the large, blue eye beamed hope, encouragement, undying faith. There was about this man an irresistible attraction; it called little children to his knee with one asking glance; it won tenderness, confidence and respect from young and old. It was the attraction of goodness, nobleness, purity and strength, calling to its own heart the good and true, to share with them the treasures of a mightily dowered soul; calling to its side the helpless and the erring, to impart the strength, the hope and faith they lacked. Young girls looked up to those soul-reading, tender eyes, and trusted him with all their sorrows; oppressed and degraded women clung to that life- and hope-bestowing hand and learned great lessons, and turned thenceforth to the light of peace and virtue. Men hardened in crime, in the fashionable vices of the day, looked on him with reverence. There was something in the tones of his voice, never to be forgotten, if once listened to; it never borrowed one accent of anger; low and sorrowfully, as if laden with tears, it dwelt upon the follies, the vices of man, the wrongs, the deprivations of women. Eloquently clear and thrillingly melodious, it spoke of an era of light, joy, love and harmony, soon to dawn for earth. Whenever he had traveled, loud blessings followed him; and, though many smiled in derision at his enthusiasm and prophetic hopes, a few tried hearts fully understood him. Among their numbers first and nearest ranked Almon Fairlie, his friend and correspondent for many years. Now, after a three years absence, they met again—these thought-brothers, these kindred souls—and with a woman's tenderness and solicitude beaming from every feature, Percival Wayne addressed his friend:

"I see you looking more hopeful; joy and faith dwell in your eye, my brother! And my heart is gladdened that the new life's dawn is around you too. I have been across the ocean, to far India, to China—I have met with responsive souls in every place. Wherever I go—among the heathen, the poor idolators, the varied beliefs—everywhere the same sure-founded hope of immortality, the evidences of spirit communion, at which our learned societies laugh in scorn; everywhere the idea of a God—all spirit, all pervading; everywhere glimpses of beautiful truths, amid the superstitions and vagaries of mind. And you, my brother, how have you fared in your experiments? By day and night, have I listened to the welcome sounds that at first arrested our attention, and many loving messages from the immortal dwellers have I received. But that I dare not give this joy, this knowledge, this wealth of love to man—that troubles me; for oh, how blest were earth, if the truth, beauty and holiness of spirit-communion, the certainty of life unending, were accepted by all!"

Over the fine face swept a shadow of regret; tears trembled in the large blue eyes, tears of tenderness and sympathy for the benighted man! The glow of enthusiasm faded from each hope-lit feature; and sadly quivered the tender mouth; great thoughts surged in the longing heart, thoughts freighted with the Christ love, for the redemption and happiness of humanity.

"I have fared well," responded Almon Fairlie, "for I seldom go beyond the limits of my garden wall. I cannot speak of these things to the people around me; they look at me in silent wonder and think me crazed. And this not from the unlearned and stupid, but from the intellectual and the thinking few. Oh, Percival! Man is so steeped in gross materialism, while the churches promise heaven and rest and forgiveness for all sins by late repentance and another's atonement, what need is there to develop the spiritual faculties, to work for salvation ourselves, to bring the spirit realms to our homes and hearts? A hopeless task, my brother! A thankless office to endeavor to enlighten the understandings of men, who live in ignoble ease, bound by their fettering creeds, content to eat and drink and *pray* as they have been told to do—prayers of the lips only, the soul hath no part in them! Percival, I sometimes despair of the race."

"Not so!" said his friend, and anew the glow of love and confidence irradiated the pale, spiritual face. "There is hope for all. What say our spirit-friends? There is in every soul the germs of angelhood; we, blinded brothers, behold it not. See, Almon, I have dealt with bandits, and found honor and fidelity among them. I have held intercourse with men convicted of deep, heinous crimes; there was darkness blight upon their souls, but God was still there, one ray of His divinity, one sun-flash of His consciousness was revealed. I bowed before it, even as it was enshrined in an erring, fallen brother's soul. I have met degraded women, lost to virtue, shame, reflection; the obdurate heart could not be melted by prayer or entreaty; they defied the world! But one of these I saw bend over the early violets, and from her hard eyes fell tears, the human tributes of affection. I heard her story afterwards. The early violets had been her mother's favorite flowers, they had been placed in that mother's icy hand, and had decked her bosom for the grave. The ever whispering, ever watchful angels entered that poor girl's soul, with the fragrance of those early violets, and by the open door entered the victorious hosts of heaven! She is now one of the redeemed ones of earth. Another I saw fondly caressed by a little child, and beneath that angel spell, the long pent-up waters were set free. She wept, and her tears were healing balsam. That child handed the erring one to peace. Oh, Almon! There is much—all to hope for in humanity, for it is a part of God!"

Almon replied not, but looked appealingly to Heaven. At last he said:

"Come, our meetings for the last three years have been of the spirit only. Let us renew our sittings; perhaps our spirit-friends will favor us. Do you remember, Percival, our first experiment with the sounds, when first we tested the intelligence?"

"Do I remember? Shall I never forget it—that twilight hour that brought peace and certainty to my soul? Since then, alone as I stand on earth, have I not been blest with spirit visitants, with music from the spirit-home, enriched with treasures of knowledge, with the wisdom transcendent; all of earth and Heaven, the glorious assurances of love?"

Oh, at that moment the face of the long-suffering one was illumined by the light within! It was enwrapt and beautiful. The glow of inspiration rested full upon it; the low, deep, fervent tones were soul-fraught with melody; foreshadowings of the heaven the spirit yearns for, settled upon the longing heart.

"Come, friend!" he held out his hand, which was cordially taken and held by Almon, who drew up a small table before them both. Soon, the tiny raps were heard, and a smile, sweet and peaceful, stole anew to the toil worn face of Percival's friend.

"We come in love!" was spelled out, for they had learned the first lessons, and had studied how to hold communion with the invisible intelligences.

"We would teach you of charity, forbearance, gentleness. Love is the watchword to the stoniest heart.

"Soon, a few years more, and our mission to earth will be acknowledged," was rapped out in reply to Almon's interrogatories.

"This method of communicating is tedious. Your friend will speak for us." Almon, settling back in his chair, looked tenderly upon his friend, folding his hands and intently listening.

The eyes of Percival Wayne closed slowly; a peaceful smile stole over his face; again the heart-glow illumined it. Inexpressibly sweet and loving came the words:

"Cast all thy sorrows in the Father's bosom, thy fears unto the winds; for strong and mighty and predominant is the power of good, and it shall rule forever. Weep not for the counsel unheeded, the loving words repelled, the truth unanswered; they live and breathe the word, the thought, the motive, from age to age eternally! See, the pure sunlight falls over desert places, over flowery beds, over good and bad alike in its impartial love. But on the flowret's heart it rests a glowing blessing, calling forth its choicest perfume; ripening the golden fruit it comes; calling forth the pure heart's songs of welcome. Over the arid waste it falls a brightening power; on the cold rock it plays; perchance, amid its jagged fissures, calling forth some timid blossom, a tuft of grass. From human souls, hard, cold and callous, the sunshine of human love may call forth some hidden power, some angel-blossom crushed and faded by the storms of life, the iron hand of man's oppression. Oh, seek not for the evil, but for the good that is of God; and in the cherishing and upholding of one virtue, one spark of Deity, you overcome a multitude of sins.

Even now, the dwellers of the spirit-worlds are marshaling; for the loud, glad proclamation has gone forth that we can return to earth, and impress with noble loving thoughts the souls of those we love. A few years more, as you count time, and from the mountains and valleys, cities and villages of the New World, will the Truth go forth, proclaimed by the lips of noble, fearless men, of inspired and high souled women. There will be antagonism, opposition, suffering; but Truth will prevail. The new light will dawn for countless hearts; the belief of a progressive life, of a heaven of affection and action will be accepted by the true and good; and the ignorant, the bigoted and the opponent will follow in due time.

There is work for thee in this cause, Almon Fairlie! When thy aged mother shall have passed away, the last tie that binds thee to thy native shores shall be broken, and thou wilt be wholly ours! In the ranks of reform, the champion of bold, fearless speech, the revelator of things beautiful and high and holy, thou shalt be found, thou weary toiler! Strengthened for the good cause, endowed with new life and youth and vigor. In the New World lies thy future field of labor; there thou, too, Percival, shalt meet with the crowning joy of thy life. Farewell, my brother!"

The eyes of the speaker unclosed; he returned to outward consciousness. The friends silently embraced; then they spoke much of the future, and of the Truths about to be given to mankind.

That night, with the starlit heavens above, the husband stood beside his Lea's grave; but he wept no more. No disappointment paled his cheek, no hopeless sorrow rained in tear floods on the sod, but joy and full fruition of all earthly hope dwelt in his breast. He leaned upon the marble tombstone; with outstretched arms and voice that trembled, not with fear but tenderness, he called in tones sweet, trustful as love's earliest invocation: "Come, Lea, come!" He saw her with the spirit's eye, white-robed and star crowned, with the lustrous Oriental eyes that won his heart; with the swaying grace of her girlish figure, the majesty of step that became her so well; with the raven tresses decked with gemmed and glistening flowers; with the light of purity above and around her, the impress of a divine humility upon her perfect face.

The pride of earth was gone; the majesty and innate power of spirit possessed its place; but exalted, and intensified, love beamed from every lineament, spoke to the soul of him, her chosen one, long ere her lips unclosed.

Life warm, breathing, musical, the language of another world spoke to the listening soul:

"I am with thee day by day, my Percival! I shelter thee from danger; I watch thy every step in life. Never on earth could I have been to thee as I am now. I would have kept thee by my side forever; now thousands shall bask in the glory of thy spirit, and gather strength and will from thee! Thy love shall bless the human race. In the New World, Percival, blooms the garden of thy life; I shall be with thee in thy labors; I will welcome thee there. There, hands as loved as mine, an eye as loving shall greet thee; fond, youthful lips shall press thy weary brow; one worthy of affection be folded to thy strong, brave heart, my Percival!"

"Oh, Lea! Never, never! I never shall love but thee!"

The dark, gloriously lustrous eyes of the spirit looked love into his soul; a sweet and reassuring smile wreathed the fine rosy lips:

"You do not comprehend, and I may not tell thee yet. Thou wilt not give my place to another, for spirit law forbids. The record of our marriage is preserved by angel hands; it is eternal. While God's kingdoms last, I am thine and thou canst choose no other bride. Ours was on earth a union of the spirit; rejoice, rejoice! For in the ever-unfolding worlds beyond, we two shall wander hand in hand, soul joined to soul eternally!"

He knelt before the spirit, often veiling his dazzled sight from the resplendent light of love and joy that broke from the dear, familiar face; for still its glorified features were familiar, the purple gleam upon her raven hair, the peculiar smile, the wide forehead, the easy, gliding, swan-like motion, all so like Lea, the earth-won bride, the wife of one short year!

Kneeling upon the summer carpet of dewy grass and fragrant blossoms, with the hand of his spirit wife laid on his head in blessing, the soul of Percival Wayne drank deeply of the spirit's love; and the new life gathered strength and beauty, and nestled in his bosom with a host of newly admitted thoughts and angels that in the coming era were commissioned to bless and elevate mankind.

"Tell me of our child. Is she on earth, or does she dwell with thee, beloved?" entreated the father, with a saddening heart.

Again the eyes of Lea looked reassuring love and faith into his soul.

"Question not yet. I may not tell thee. Follow thy impressions. Thou art pure and just; thou canst trust thy inner promptings. The New World calls thee. Go!"

A fragrant breath, warm as a summer's zephyr, fanned his cheek, filled his heart with reverential love. Slowly the vision faded, the starry gleam was gone. Percival stood alone by Lea's grave.

A few months he tarried with his friend; then, urged by spirit voices, he left again his country's shores, and sailed for the New World. Almon Fairlie, watching by his mother's bed, with the sorrow of the past locked in his breast, dreamed hopefully of the promised future, and of the spirit's mandates unto him.

↬

By the vine covered porch of her sweet rural home sits Solita Mendez, and the uneventful years have passed by and touched her lightly. Still willowy in grace, her girlish figure sways as if to music heard by her dreaming heart alone. Still gloriously beautiful, her eyes beam love and kindness on the world around. Her voice is tender and musical as of yore. Somewhat paler is the face, but it is with thought, not sorrow. The rare golden hair still falls in its own luxuriant wealth of curls, but they are put back from the lovely face in a less girlish fashion. Her dress is simple and elegant—an exquisitely embroidered muslin robe, the sleeves looped back with ornaments of pearl and coral. She loves this vestal garb, and seldom wears aught but white. Her aunt lives with her still. The bluff old uncle is in the land of souls.

As Solita sits by the casement of her home, the green valley beyond that is skirted by the towering hills, the waving forests of fruit, the coffee plantation, the spacious garden—all hail her mistress. But not upon the variegated earth, so lavishly adorned, rest her thoughtful glances. They linger on the mountain's cedar-crowned summits, and thence her thoughts roam to the past, so dear and life-fraught; to the quiet churchyard in B——; to him, the good, and true, and noble whose image she looks upon daily, whose soul-features are graven on her heart, for whom her love grows day by day more angel like. Strange human web of life! A few ocean-miles, a stretch of land lies between Solita's heart and that of the young Cosella, who daily, hourly implores for love.

The new life, dawning, glowing, whispering, advancing, is nigh to Solita too, although she knows it not. The strange, unbidden thoughts, the vivid dreams, the flashes of a higher consciousness that thrill her being, give evidence of this.

Upon the ready and disciplined souls the spiritual agencies are at work; and for the labor of redemption, bands of earnest thinkers and willing hearts are organizing. The watchword has gone forth; the fate of oppression and wrong is sealed; the angels of earth join with the host of heaven. Of earth's chosen ones, Solita, the true and good, is one.

↬

In the upper land, the realms of soul, a mother's heart is striving for the happiness of a beloved child on earth. Lea, beholding, with a spirit's prophetic gaze, the gathering sorrow clouds around her child, seeks to avert the trial hour, to throw the sunlight of love and joy upon the darkness. But the discipline of life is good for the expanding soul; even a mother's sympathy, a loving spirit's prayer, may not avert the sorrow so necessary to the soul's growth of strength and light. From the yet untraversed worlds, the upper realms of higher life, a vision passes before the mother's soul. She recognizes her daughter's angel-marked pathway, and bends her will unto the love and power of God!

She saw the young girl, daring, free, courageous, the possessor of wealth and power. The poetic tendencies of her soul, her hitherto slumbering artistic tastes, found expression in lavish display. The house she dwelt in was adorned with the choicest offerings of art, the rarest pencilings of genius. Wealth and munificence reigned around her, beauty and ease enwrapped her being with repose. Then Lea read her daughter's soul and found there the highest, noblest aims of life buried beneath the weight of flowers, all aspiration stifled by their languid perfume; tropical indolence, luxuriant heedlessness, in the place of the once uprising energy, the lofty, up-soaring thought.

The young heart was closed to the cry of suffering, for it knew not of the world's woe without. In that charmed atmosphere, in that fairy-land of repose and inaction, the high-souled capacities lay dormant, the spirit progressed not.

The gazing mother sighed for the useful life thus rendered valueless by the power of worldly circumstances; then from the golden music-freighted heavens above came, sweet and tenderly, the voice that bade her look again.

She saw the child she loved yield to the potent magic of a first and happy love. She saw her follow the chosen one of her young dreams from the altar's side to the loving home he had prepared for her. She loved him for his external gifts—the music of a love-laden voice, the manly beauty, strength, and grace of form and feature. She was too young, too inexperienced, to read the soul. Sorrow had not yet unfolded her intuitions; she had gained no strength on the battle-field of life; she knew naught of soul-love; she had not learned to look beneath the surface. Youth, beauty, music, seeming, had won her guileless heart. To the first strong spell of life she yielded without thought.

The mother saw the wild and daring spirit of her child imprisoned by the mandate of her own lips; and as years sped on, feeling, thought and judgment ripened in Cosella's breast. She saw the stifled aspirations newly uprising with a mighty power; she beheld the passionate love departing, slowly, wearily and sadly—dying of neglect and disenchantment. With the light of early womanhood upon her brow, the light and splendor faded from the heart of the unloved wife; and wild and rushing, dark and menacing, swept thoughts of freedom over her soul that were shudderingly banished as suggestions of a tempting power.

The spirit mother beheld with trembling sympathy the daughter of her love drooping and fading beneath the waning glory of life; pride, joy and love departing, leaving the darkened spirit sunless, plunged in the densest night of heart despair and unbelief. One by one the energies died out, the aspirations folded their silver-bright and rainbow wings in heavy sleep; the young heart closed upon the sweetest charities, the holiest trust of life; and as in a desert, bleak and waste, the changed, wronged spirit wandered on, accusing heaven, cursing the fairest boon of God, turning from the name of Love with a shudder and a sigh of pain.

"Look again, and murmur not!" the sweet voice whispered from above, and again the vision changed; and by the rugged path of teaching adversity, Lea beheld her child, toiling, struggling, weeping, suffering, aided by the angel hosts. Alone by the couch of death; alone in her first bereavement's hour, alone amid the environments of toil and privation; no hand to guide, no voice to cheer, no mortal lips to utter welcome, no hearts of earth to up- lift to the sunlight glory of affection that early-tried young spirit. But as her eyes penetrated the densest storm cloud's gloom, she saw that ever near her child hovered shapes and beings from the upper worlds. The music angels came with breath of harmony and whispered to her mighty stillness; the spirit of song nestled closely to the weary heart and called thence plaintive strains of poesy. The angel of charity set free the ice bound streams of feel- ing, the purest love warmed there the suffering; the mightiest inspirations whispered there; glowing prophecies, heavenly hopes, immortal blessings, thronged around her; amid the utmost loneliness, she often sang aloud in joyous recognition, she offered unto heaven the tribute of a grateful heart.

Lea beheld the child of her affections passing through the shadow vales of life, drinking deeply of its Marah waters, fainting often by the wayside; often resting 'mid the gloom of graves. But the heart was strengthened, hal- lowed, purified, and exalted by the ordeal. For every trial, the soul of that young spirit bore fresh blossoms destined for immortal perpetuity. The tears of grief watered the once arid ground, and it brought forth fragrance, color, beauty, gems of truth and holiness that would adorn her life eternally.

At the close of the necessary, love-fraught ordeal, even the spirit's eyes were dazzled by the opening glory of the portal leading to the new life, thenceforth awaiting Cosella. She came there crowned victoriously by the angel band; the jewels she had won by soul effort, by adherence to the true, clung to her flowing hair, and shone forth resplendently from breast and brow. The garments of her virgin purity flowed white and radiant; the lily wand was hers, the halo of love encircled the martyr head. This was her spirit's portraiture; the mother smiled in joy and triumph. Then again she saw the earth life spread before her child's wandering feet and seek- ing heart. Years had passed on, and trial and storm had fulfilled their mis- sion; the salutary influences, the heaven-sent uses of sorrow, had been ac- knowledged; the cross had been meekly, lovingly pressed to the quivering lips; freedom, truth, and peace were found within the soul as in the world around her and above. With sweet, submissive looks, the heart said humbly, thankfully, "Thy will be done!" The mission of adversity was fulfilled.

Then life spread, broad and beautiful, earnest, grand, and fraught with blessings before Cosella's gaze. Then all good thoughts and holiest resolves nestled to her soul; then all the angel graces and white-robed charities abode with her; then God and angels spoke, and were recognized; then heaven was nigh and felt. Then in soul, and to the mortal sight, they met, father and child, long severed! Then upon the noble face of a long-tried champion of truth, the loving eyes of the daughter rested; then for the life of solitude and pain was made amends; then the designs of the all-overruling One were fulfilled—the angels sang aloud for joy!

"Thou wilt be, as ever, her guardian spirit!" said the voice, whispering to the mother's heart. And in view of the coming joy, the dawn of light and peace, the spirit bowed her head in humble, grateful compliance, and looking upward said, "Thy will be done!"

The music of acceptance rolled through the sunlit heavens in a fervent strain of loud thanksgiving joy; flowers fell around the spirit kneeling there, gemmed blossoms from the upper spheres. The sunrays of musical light quivered on her upturned brow; the glory of the unseen heavens was reflected in the lustre of her adoring glance. "And now to return to earth awhile," she murmurs; and as she leaves her blest abode, a line of rainbow light streams from the sunset heavens and bends to earth, announcing the coming of a bright and willing messenger.

Meanwhile, Cosella, restless of the future, questions her own soul, and asks of dreams the response; and thus was the impression given, the prophecy of the future made.

8

The Dream's Reply

I called on dreams and visions to disclose
That which is veil'd from waking thought, conjured
Eternity, as men constrain a ghost
To appear and answer.

—Wordsworth

She found herself before an ancient and spacious building that stood apart from the city's crowded thoroughfares, grey, solitary, yet inviting. Wide steps led to its massive oaken portal, which yielded to the girl's slight touch without a sound. The warm sunshine illumined every nook and recess; bright and cheerful was the aspect of that home of wealth and elegance.

Into a spacious apartment Cosella entered by the wide-open door that was half concealed by the silken curtain folds. She paused in admiration as the novel decorations there met her eye. From the ceiling to the very floor, arranged by some artistic hand, draped most harmoniously, fell the rich folds of the finest, most gorgeously-tinted Cashmerian cloth, veiling, as with a shower of stars and flowers, the quaintly-carved frames of the huge mirrors gleaming there, reflecting all the varied splendor so lavishly displayed.

The wreaths and leaves upon the carpet seemed imbued with life-like brilliancy and truth to Nature; the footfall of the wandering intruder fell unheard amid the mimic moss and blossoms. The swaying crystal pendants of the chandeliers dispensed their sportive rays of rainbow-tinted light; the sunlight, streaming through the rosy curtains, flickered on the rare old pictures, and their massive frames revealed the costliness of marble, ivory, gold and porcelain there lavished with a generous hand.

The love of the beautiful, the poetry of art, swelled high and rapturously in Cosella's breast as she paused before the breathing canvas, the inspired work of the sculptor, the delicate textures, the rich warm colorings that adorned that beautiful and silent home. It was silent, notwithstanding its luxuriant appointments; no sound of life came through its hospitably open doors; no voices of grief or merriment; no sounds of childish glee; no familiar watchdog's bark; no chirrup of a bird! But the silence was not oppressive; it was calm and holy, as if the spirit of contemplation brooded there, by the home altar, even 'mid ease and elegance, in poetic reverie uplifted to a higher world of beauty, heeding not the outside tumult of the busy mart.

Cosella thought not of intrusion, but she wandered from hall to chamber along the silent galleries and passages meeting no living thing. Through elegantly-furnished apartments, where stood solitary couches draped with snowy lace and linen, and surrounded by light-blue silken hangings; where the same gorgeous luxury reigned; through chambers glittering with silver and crystal ornaments, with the wealth of painting and the triumphs of art; the treasures of the sea she passed; ever guided by the warm, cheering sunshine; pausing, wondering, yet not afraid; meeting no impending stairway, no obstacle in form or menace; on, through the chambers, the downy galleries of wealth and ease, until the limits of that deserted house were reached, and narrow, hemming and unexpected grey walls arose, excluding the fervid sunshine, rendering drear the uncarpeted space that marked that home's wide boundary.

Cosella looked up; a winding stairway, tortuous and wide, wound up afar into the very clouds—its steps of clean, white wood, its banisters of burnished oak. For a moment the young girl paused and thought—reflected deeply, clearly, vividly. How easy to retrace her way through the same beautiful halls and chambers, and, passing through the opening portal, return to the busy world, the customary life. The ascent before her might be long and toilsome—wherefore attempt it? Two voices whispered; but that of the encouraging angel was sweetest, though lowest; it whispered, pleadingly: "Child, the stairway leads to higher regions, to a purer life; wilt thou, for ease and wealth, resign the noble victory born of toil? Would'st thou not behold the future, robed in emblematic garb? Ascend, then, spirit! Come with thy heart unspotted, thy hands yet pure; come, it is time!"

She yielded to the sweet, persuasive voice, unknowing what its language meant, yet filled with the resolve to know more of the life beyond, above. Not without effort was the determination made, not without a sigh of regretful longing for the life of ease below; and yet the angel conquered.

The timid girl, endowed with renewed strength, with hasty feet and calm prayerful heart, ascended the first steps, then paused and took a long, long breath. Then she sped on, resting whenever her panting breath demanded a respite from the motion of her willing feet. The stern, grey, cold walls encompassed her, shutting out the merry world with its varied sights and sounds. Departing sunrays flickered o'er her path; but all was still, solemnly calm; no sound of life stirred there.

Suddenly the wanderer paused, and smiled with surprise and wonder; for the grey, cold walls that on each side rose up, whichever way the tortuous stairway wound, were covered with the leaves, the abundant blossoms of tall and stately trees that decked in the fairy green of earliest summer's glory entwined around and sprang from the dark cold stone. The drooping clusters of the star-like fragrant flowers were of the purest white; no colors mingled with the vivid emerald tint; life stirred amid the dancing leaves, and whispered prayerfully from the blossom's heart of incense. Thus accompanied, the child of earth sped on, until the twilight neared apace, and she paused to rest awhile upon the broad white platform just above.

She reached it and gazed down; beneath her lay the vast and populous city, its church spires pointing heavenward, its tall monuments gilded by the last beams of day. She saw the thronging crowds, the jostling seekers of pleasure and business hastening from place to place with ant-like speed in most diminutive stature. Like playthings glistened the emblazoned equipages, the prancing steeds, the costly robes of fashion. The frivolity of a life of pleasure, the insignificance of earthly pomp and power, spoke to the gazer's heart, as viewed from that flowery height; and she turned from the surging city, with its host of idlers, to the roseate clouds floating far above—to the waving, singing music of the wind amid the trees—to inhale the fragrance of the pure white flowers that lined the pathway within reach of her outstretched hand.

On, on she sped; and the twilight shadows deepened, and the sun departed, leaving the floating clouds to retain awhile their golden fringe. From the faithful toiler's sight the city was withdrawn—she was alone with gathering shadows, solitude and clouds!

For the first time, the calm of faith departed from Cosella's panting breast, for amid the stillness was heard the tramp of heavy footsteps—a pursuer—and her troubled heart presaged it was an evil thing on her track! Wearily, heavily, yet up lifting her soul in prayer, the maiden passed swiftly on; pausing in sheer exhaustion to recover her failing strength a moment, then rushing blindly, madly on; feeling in every strained nerve and sinew of her trembling frame that life, *soul life* and happiness depended on her speed! For, far above, in the misty rolling clouds, she beheld her journey's end; she saw a little cottage, environed all by clustering roses, jasmine, and honeysuckle, overgrown with ivy, a sweet though humble sanctuary that beckoned amid a surrounding landscape of inconceivable beauty; its hospitable door, wide open, dispensed a roseate light that illumined the steep pathway, and bathed the last step of the guiding ladder. The light came from a roseate orb suspended, lamp-like, in the open door—suspended there mysteriously amid a gauzy veil that softened its intense warm radiance.

With arms outstretched, with a loud cry of joy and recognition, Cosella reached the portal, fainting, weary, breathless; and amid the solemn silence the pursuer's footsteps were unheard. With foot upon the magic threshold, with trembling hand veiling her dazzled sight, Cosella was about to pass on, when a voice said soft and tenderly, "Not yet, return!"

⌒

With a start and a moan, Cosella raised herself in bed to find the moon-light streaming on the floor, to feel the sea breeze laden with the forest's spicy odor, to find the beautiful ladder of ascension gone, her journey 'mid the clouds—a dream!

Shina listened to her child's recital with reverence and much attention. She was a firm believer in dreams.

"But perhaps you have read of such a house, my Ella," she remarked. "Your memory is retentive, you are poetical; perhaps you have mixed your daily thoughts with something you have read and so produced the dream."

Cosella smiled, and replied that she had not thought of anything like it.

The same week the dream repeated itself—vividly clear and distinct in its every detail; swerving not in the least from its first portrayal; ending with the accomplished journey and the cottage home, with its mysterious beacon. Shina looked grave when Cosella told her of the strange dream's repetition, and she racked her brain for its interpretation. Thenceforth, for many months, that vision was presented to the young girl's sleeping eye; and light-hearted and careless as she was, she would say in a bantering tone:—

"Good night, mother; I am going to my dream."

Manasseh was not told of it; it might have shaken his superstitious soul with terror.

Cosella had invoked the future's revelation. With maidenhood and thought came questionings of the soul, to which the strange, uncalled for dream responded.

⌒

One evening Shina complained of headache and restlessness; the next morning she arose pale and haggard, and though she went about her usual avocations there was a listlessness in her step and manner that betokened physical pain. To Cosella's anxious inquiries, she replied, "That she felt languid and weary, but hoped soon to regain strength." But as day after day passed on, her face grew more sunken, her eyes more supernaturally brilliant, crimson spots burned on her cheeks, and the little wasted hands felt hot and feverish. For many days Cosella prepared for her the simple soothing beverages in use among the natives, but they failed in reaching the disease; then, without Shina's sanction, she called in the physician, who gave her much hope, recommended diet and repose.

Oppressed with a vague terror, Cosella slept in her mother's room, and watched the perturbed slumbers, and administered the cooling draught.

She had known no other mother; despite of the veil between their souls, she loved her; now she mused painfully and thought of what the future would be without her. Alone with Manasseh—her strange, incomprehensible father! She shuddered involuntarily.

He had been away three weeks visiting the capital. One starlight morning he returned; and Cosella, glad of the presence her mother longed for, threw herself into his arms with tears.

He followed her to his wife's apartment; he started back in surprise at her altered appearance. A shadow of doubt and fear overspread Shina's face; she looked eagerly up to him.

"Must I die, Manasseh? *Is it written*, so soon? Am I so changed that there is no hope? Must I leave Co——, my child, leave you?"

"Pooh, pooh! Nonsense!" said Manasseh, assuming a bantering tone. "You are a little sick and nervous, that's all."

"Manasseh!" she continued; "I feel that I must speak, come of it what it may. Ella, my child, leave me alone with your father."

With tear-filled eyes Cosella left the room, carrying with her Jaspe, her mother's pet dog. She knew not why, she fell down on her knees to pray; but as she wept and supplicated for the dear one's life, as if conscious of the negation, the futility of that prayer, poor Jaspe whined pitifully at mention of his mistress's name!

Meanwhile the husband and wife sat side by side, and Shina's eyes were lustrous with the resolve of principle that was formed, alas, too late. Never had those eyes looked so into the stern, world-hardened face of the relentless man. What was there in that penetrating glance so to unnerve his soul? To cause a nameless dread to overcome him, who long since had buried peace, and tried to stifle memory? They burned into his very soul, those glances of appeal and determination. Unconsciously his voice softened as he addressed her:—

"What is it you would tell me, Shina?"

She passed her hand across her brow as if to collect her thoughts. The voice with which she spoke was firm and even, unlike her usually low and trembling tones. There was solemnity and fervor, the fire of awakened soul, in the address of the stricken, wasting woman.

"Manasseh!" she said, "I know not whether my last hour approaches, whether this disease is fatal, but I know that the time has come for me, for you, to *repent*. Start not, I mean it; I fear no more your anger. I know not whence this sudden change; but I feel as if an angel had spoken to my soul that the time has come for expiation, for atonement. Cosella is a woman. I say not that you shall humble yourself before her by an avowal of the past; but, Manasseh, as you value peace and happiness, listen to me this hour! Advance not in the fatal path of dishonesty, in the crooked ways you have entered upon—by all that is sacred in our holy teachings, I implore you!—for it will lead to ruin. Are you leading aright the soul of that innocent child, that victim of the snare *we* laid for her? I have steadfastly endeavored to imbue her mind with the love of truth and virtue; you would teach her only the love of gold, the falsehoods of the world. Oh, Manasseh! I forgive you all *I* have suffered—my sleepless nights of remorse, my days of anguish, the misery of endless wanderings—*all, all*, if you will but henceforth be an honest man, a true father to that poor child, so unconscious of the webs around her.

"Perhaps," and she regarded her wasted hands and cast a look into the mirror by her side, "I may soon leave this world. Oh, God! Dread God of Justice! I cannot leave my child!"

The energy and moral strength that sustained her bent beneath the recurring sway of tenderness. She burst into tears; wildly glancing upward, she cried, in piercing tones, "Have mercy, God! Oh, do not let me die!"

Swift and varying were the emotions that swept across the sun-burnt face of her husband; anger, surprise, menace, and mockery dwelt there by turns. He said in a cold unresponsive manner—

"You are ill and excited, and your language is that of fever. You had better go to bed and obtain the needful rest."

"It has been ever so!" cried Shina; "the curse of my life has been my guilty submission to your will. I am ill, but I am sane; Manasseh, listen to me, I implore you; if for naught else, *for Lea's sake!*"

Alas! The angel spell of that sainted name had long since departed; perverted by his craven soul, it invoked the demon of discord, and swelled the heart it should have calmed with bitterness and rage.

"Speak not *her* name again!" he almost shouted, "or see, frail woman, I crush you thus!" and he seized her with a vice like grasp, until a low moan of pain escaped her. "Idiot! Maniac! To rave *to me* of duty; to speak *to me* of that Christian girl within my power! I have not stolen from our people; I have not violated Sabbath or festival when I could help it. I do not deny my religion here, even amid the Catholic unbelievers. Dare *you* prate to me of right and wrong, to me, who am your head and lord? Obey your destiny, woman, without repining, and dictate to me no more. Hark, too! Never again, pronounce the name of Lea. I will not hear it from your lips!"

Shina paced the floor awhile, then with a sudden impulse she cast herself at Manasseh's feet, and with tenderest entreaties besought him to return to the paths of honesty and truth; to find some humble home where they might live safe and respected.

"Think of the innocent girl I was—think of the degraded thing I am, Manasseh! Falsehood and deception have steeped my soul in shame. I dare not meet untremblingly a stranger's eye. I cannot gaze upon that child's face, save with a pang that she would spurn me if she knew I wrested her from her father's arms. Shall she live to become false and sinful as I am, or will *you* drag her soul into guilt through the gateway of religion? *Religion*, Manasseh? I feel that it is fanaticism, revenge that you call by the sacred name. Shall she live—this wronged girl—to scorn you for your treachery? Come, we believe her father surely dead; she is ours indeed; let us do by her as we would by a daughter heaven had sent us!"

"The Christian's child—*my* daughter!" he fiercely replied. "Woman, you know not the sweetness, the triumph, the glory of revenge! I have no love for that girl; beneath her apparent gentleness and submission she hates me! Her father's spirit lives in her."

"Have you sought to win her love? Have you ever spoken to her as a father, a teacher should? Hear I not daily the sophistries you strive to twine around her soul? To confuse her moral sense, to blunt her pure perceptions, to bend her noble nature, her disinterestedness, her unswerving principles to your mean thirst, your vile pursuit of gold! Manasseh, if I am called by the death-angel, and you succeed in counteracting my influence, in plunging that pure soul in sin, I tell you that all the fiends of Gehenim will pursue you to your latest day! Remorse, endless, fiery as the burning lake lost souls are rolling in forever, will be your portion! Take from that white tablet the signature of God, so fairly written that it sparkles from her eye and brow, impress upon it the blackened characters of your worldly soul, the records of guilt—and God will punish you; punish you, Manasseh, until in sackcloth and in ashes you bewail, and cry, and shriek aloud in vain!"

"What has come to the woman, is she mad?" cried her husband, and astonishment for the moment overcame even superstitious terror, and the rage that trembled in every limb.

But the craven fear had departed from Shina's soul; in that hour, like one inspired she spoke, dreading no consequences. Her true self—just to womanhood, purity, and nature, vindicated its right, crushed so long by slavish submission and superstitious dread.

She heeded not her husband's angry glances, she retreated not before his menacing approach. She folded her arms, gazed unflinchingly upon his erect and stalwart frame, and still the lightning flashes of vindication broke from her eyes; the crimson hue of determination burned brightly upon either cheek, the usually low and faltering voice, borrowed tones of impressive strength and solemn prophecy!

"*Beware! Beware!*" that changed voice rang loud and clear through the apartment. "Spare Percival Wayne's pure child, or dread the vengeance of offended God! You are leading her from her mother's soul, but you will not prevail, for angels guide her. You and your legions cannot harm, cannot approach to taint her!"

Still the bright burning eyes were fixed on his; fear blanched not the countenance, no palsy of terror shook the strong brave heart; although white and convulsed with passion, his face bent close to hers, his strong grasp on her wrist, he cried to her to cease her raving, to return to the submissive mood so well befitting her. Calm and unmoved she stood, and smiled in pity, not in mockery.

"For years," she said, "I have been the silent tool of your will; the submissive slave. I deemed it a wife's duty to obey. I fulfilled the letter—obeyed you even unto wrong. I know not why I speak to you thus, Manasseh, but the words will come, bitter, accusing, cruel as they are! I am urged to speak thus to you, before whom for many years I have trembled, by a power beyond my own; words and thoughts come thronging, crowding, I cannot restrain the whelming tide! I speak unto your conscience, husband! Shall I appeal in vain?"

"Until the last day you might expend your breath, and never move *me* from my fixed purpose," he replied; "and now, woman, as you value your health, *your life*, be still! I once more bid you cease your tirade. Utter another word of reproach or menace, and—" his cruel grasp tightened around her wrist, the other hand was upraised with a threatening gesture.

Again Shina smiled. "I feel no pain," she murmured.

"Shall I recall you to reason—to sensation?" he cried savagely, and he shook the feeble frame; but no moan of pain escaped her, not a vestige of fear swept over the illumined face.

"Will you not give us a home in our native land, where we can worship God in truth, and live in honor? Will you not take me and the child to some safe retreat, and so expiate for the past, your wrongs to me and her?" demanded the clear, silvery, unfaltering tones.

"No! By the sacred tablets of the law! By the oath I have sworn! By my life! No, *I will not!* You shall wander through the world *forever!* You shall have no fixed habitation, you shall form no friendships! You and she shall be obedient to my will, my projects; *she* shall know no love, no affection for one earthly thing, save where *I* dictate, where I bid her bow at the world's shrine of gold! She shall—"

"Hold, Manasseh! I have done my duty, have revealed to you the soul you deemed all bent beneath your will. Now, listen! In a lonely isle, deserted and forgotten, you shall breathe your last, without a friend to moisten your lips, to wipe the death dews from your brow. *Alone, alone*, with grinning and accusing fiends, vainly suing for the mercy of Heaven, a cold, grey, barren stone, sinking deep, deep, deep, into utter darkness. Manasseh, this is your fate!"

For a moment a breathless silence reigned; for the superstitious soul of the plotter was shaken with a dread presentiment; ashy paleness overspread anew his face, his knees trembled beneath him; he caught at a chair for support. Then with a loud cry, all the evil of his nature aroused, he rushed towards the inspired speaker, who still endowed with a strength indwelling not in that frail and stricken form, stood there with eyes uplifted, with outstretched hand, and crimsoned cheek—the trembling, yielding woman, transformed into the gifted seer!

His heavy hand fell on the bare white shoulders; he tore the covering from her head, and rent her still abundant jetty hair; she uttered no cry, offered no resistance, but said in a lower voice:

"I will warn Cosella—she shall know all—even though you kill me!"

With impious appeal to Heaven, with imprecations too terrible to record even on this gloomy page, the infuriate madman rent her robes, and plied his desecrating hand upon the feebly shrinking form.

"At God's judgment-seat you will be called—to answer—murderer!—deceiver of the good!—*I* shall accuse you!" feebly murmured Shina.

He would have killed her in his fury; for his face was that of a demon, and demons lent him strength; but his harsh, discordant voice, his dreadful imprecations reached Cosella's ear, as with swollen eyes and slow steps she passed by the chamber.

The young girl entered, and drew back with an exclamation of terror, for Shina, with disheveled hair and torn garments, lay, to all seeming, insensible upon Manasseh's arm; and he with livid face and horrid curses was bending over her.

"What have you been doing to my mother, sir?" impulsively cried Cosella, and she grasped his uplifted arm.

"I—I—nothing—she was excited—nervous—I—" he stammered confusedly.

"You have been maltreating her, sir! Mother! *Dear* mother!" she cried, bending over the now pallid face and kissing the brow, "what has *he* done to you? Oh, mother, dearest, speak to me!"

The music of affection in that voice, never so intense before, aroused her from the torpor that had succeeded the previous excitement, the faintness consequent upon her tyrant's usage.

"Release her! Give her into my arms; this is not the first time she has suffered at your hands," Cosella cried loudly. "Dare to touch her while I am by, and by the Heaven I believe in I will forget that you are my father, and defend *her* to the death!"

Cosella stood close by him with arms folded defiantly, with eyes flashing indignation, with anger and command in her tones. One blow from his strong arm would have felled her to the earth; but he dared not touch her! A gleam of Lea's spirit was in her eye; he quailed before it. The sweetness and imperativeness of her mother's voice spoke through her lips. Manasseh laid the form of his wife upon the bed, and like a coward fled from the room.

With tears and kisses Cosella bent over the woman, who for her sake had suffered so much. The spirit's energy was gone, the physical anguish usurped its place; only the girl's light touch and tender words had power to soothe. Throughout that day and night, Cosella moved not from the sufferer's side, and Manasseh, guilty and abashed, walked to and fro outside, listening to every sound from within, fearing, trembling, that Shina would reveal the secret of the young girl's birth; praying that death might claim her ere the revelation could be made.

One by one, slowly the stars of affection, that never had beamed with intense filial luster for him, were extinguished in Cosella's breast; fear, distrust, indignation; haunting shadows, vain outreaching for a better, holier love, invaded the lone sanctuary of her thoughts. She knew not why, sleeping and waking, she dreamed of a pair of calm and sorrowful blue eyes beaming from a pale intellectual face, that, looking into her soul, awakened there the filial love the stern, dark-browed, cold Manasseh never could call forth.

9

Bereavement

Thine eye's last light was mine—the soul that shone
Intensely, mournfully, through gathering haze;
Did'st thou bear with thee, to the shore unknown,
Naught of what lived in that long, earnest gaze?
　Hear, hear, and answer me!
Thy voice—its low, soft, fervent, farewell tone,
Thrill'd through the tempest of the parting strife,
Like a faint breeze: oh! from that music flown
Send back *one* sound, if love's be quenchless life!
　But once, oh answer me!

　　　　　　　　　　　　　　　—Hemans

For fourteen days and as many weary nights, Cosella watched by Shina's bed, and hoped and prayed, and stole away to weep unseen. Manasseh hovered like an evil shadow in the sick chamber, scarcely daring to meet the searching eye of Cosella. What secret conferences he held with the sufferer seemed to exhaust the remnant of her strength; they left her with traces of strong agitation, with pallid face and trembling limbs. The courageous girl, determined to brave all for the sake of her she called mother, boldly told Manasseh that she would not leave the room while he remained; and she was rewarded by the grateful pressure of poor Shina's hand; by the stern man's murmured acquiescence; he dared not openly manifest all the deformity of his character to the child of Lea.

Shina faded slowly away; and two natures appeared warring within her soul; at times trembling when her husband's step was heard, shrinking from his eye, answering him in the subdued and faltering tones of yore; then gazing upon him with a blazing eye and burning cheek; speaking strangely of wrongs committed and sins unrepented of; a language that appeared incoherent to Cosella, and which Manasseh, in her hearing, attributed to the effect of fever. Sometimes, gazing upon the child of her affections with all a mother's tenderness, speaking to her of God and Heaven in so appealing and solemn a strain, that Cosella's tears poured forth in answering tribute; then again, silent for hours, as if communing with her inward self, she would lie gazing upwards with folded hands. Sometimes bodily resigned and patient, then piteously imploring for life and health; her varying moods racked the young watcher's soul with agony; an agony suppressed by the dominant will, the prayerful energy of that untried heart.

At last the physician gave no hope; and Manasseh, with real or affected sorrow, clasped his knees and implored him again to try his skill. Perhaps even his callous heart was touched, perhaps when truly aware that the suffering, patient victim would soon be removed from his sight, he felt a pang of pity and remorse. Who shall say that for the time the better angel touched not the perverted soul?

Cosella heard the fiat, and deathly paleness overspread her face; she bowed her head, until the long, flowing curls concealed her eyes, and cried aloud to God for mercy.

The good physician fondly stroked her head; he was a father himself, and reverently said, "God *will* be merciful, my child!"

The young girl hastened from the room, and in the silence of her own chamber, she threw herself upon the matted floor and wrung her hands; all, all the wealth of love and indulgence lavished so bountifully upon her rushed upon her heart with overwhelming force.

"She alone of all on earth has been so true, so tender!" she sobbed. "I cannot love my father. I fear him; what will be my fate when she is gone? The perverted doctrines *he* strives to inculcate—I know—I feel them false! Yet I shall have to bend, to yield to him, as she, the loving martyr has done through life! Oh, *mother! mother!* how can I live without thee! They say that prayer can move Thee Judge of life and death! Grant to my soul this boon, my mother's life! Oh, he will drag me from place to place, the tool of his pride and ambition! He will sacrifice my young affections, my holiest aspirations to his unholy thirst for gold! I detest the robes, the glittering trinkets he decks me with. I have never seen a love gleam in his eye; a meaning is there, so vaguely dark and terrible, it makes me shudder! Mother! Oh, mother! Do not leave me! Or take me to rest with thee! I will not—I dare not stay with him!" she cried with increasing agitation. "If she dies I will fly—away from here, far hence! Alas, where? But woe to him fate compels me to call father! Woe to him if his sacrilegious hand dare touch her or me again in anger. I would beg my bread from door to door before I would submit to such an indignity. Oh, forgive me, Heavenly Father! I think of self while she is dying!"

Subduing the uprising of her fiery temper, curbing by affection and prayer the rebellious surgings of her soul, Cosella passed into her mother's chamber; her pale face composed, a smile upon her lips, giving no sign of the anguish that rent her heart.

The superstitious Manasseh dared not tell his wife that the shadow of the death-angel's wing was on her brow. Cosella could not unclose her lips to frame the fatal words, and the pale sufferer knew not of the impending change; but tortured the dear child she kissed and blest so fervently with playful allusions to the summer skies, the meadow flowers, the winter's glory of her native land, which soon as her health was restored she would revisit.

Alas! Cosella knew that soon she would behold the immortal plains, the angel bowers, the unfading summer glory of the heaven impressed upon her own poetic soul! The heaven she dreamed of, not the promised land of theology.

The young girl had not slept for many nights; she trusted not to nurse or attendant, but with her own hand ministered to the loved one's wants. That night she watched the startled slumber, the restless, wakeful eyes, with all a daughter's tenderest solicitude; and upon her wounded, silently bleeding heart fell sweet and soothingly the murmured thanks from those dear, fading lips: "God bless my good, dear child!"

Midnight's starry hosts looked down in solemn calm upon the sleeping earth, the waking, tortured hearts. They beamed in at the open window to witness the vigil of love, the completion of sacrifice. Cosella, bending tearfully above her mother's couch, saw the change that once seen can never be forgotten, the seal of death upon the lovely face. Yet there was nothing ghastly or appalling in the changed aspect of that loved countenance, though the hues of earth had left it, and the unseen mystery was fashioning every lineament; burning, rapt and unearthly from the tender lustre of those dying eyes, so filled with all of love's intensest depth; heralding the high and mighty conquest of spirit over matter; speaking serenely and solemnly conscious from brow and lip and cheek! Cosella saw and understood, though never before had she been in presence of the departing; and even there, amid the strong first agony, an angel whispered, and her soul believed: "This is not forever!" The cold hand feebly sought the young, life-warm one; it was wet with the tears that hour could not control, and the lips of the dying sealed on it the tender kisses of acceptance. Cosella started as she heard the changed voice; it sounded afar off—yet musical; it already borrowed tones no more of earth!

"My child!"—she bowed her head to listen; her dark curls swept the faintly pulsating breast—"I shall soon behold the scenes I long for—but it will be from above. *I know*—weep not, my darling! my faithful angel, weep not! God will guard you; his blessed angels will shield you! Read to me the prayer of night. I die far away from home, fulfilling the curse pronounced upon our fated race—scattered to the four parts of the earth—wanderers and accursed! My child! Cherish in your heart no hatred—love all; the Father loves all his children. Ella, promise—"

She faltered; her breath grew short; still her appealing tender gaze sought the veiled face. A shower of passionate kisses, a flood of tears fell on her brow and mingled with the death-damps there. Cosella could not speak; emotion stifled every word.

"Promise, Ella, promise!" said Shina, low and sweetly.

"What, dear mother, what shall I promise? All, all, everything; but never again to be happy when you are gone!"

And a wild defiance arose in her bosom; she pillowed the loved head upon her arm, cast the other around her, and in silent and reckless daring braved death to tear her away! In after years, when the mystery of death was divested of its terror, when a better faith had taken the place of gloomy teachings, Cosella wept in penitence of her impious sorrow that would have retarded a soul's ascension, and from her own lips have removed the bitter, most salutary draught of trial.

"Rebel not against God, my child! Daughter of my love—my heart!" feebly implored the maternal lips. "Promise, that through life—in joy or in sorrow—through trial or triumph—exalted or low—whatever fortune betides—or circumstances bring—you will—child of my soul—be ever true to your own sense of right—ever obedient to what I—weak, sinful, erring as I am—have taught you. Ella, be ever true and pure!"

As if in presence of the Infinite Jehovah and his assembled angel hosts; with all the solemnity and fervor that marked the ancient offerings unto the Most High; with thrilled heart, all nerved for every earthly sacrifice, Cosella kissed the cold hand she held, and said aloud:

"I promise, mother, so help me God!"

A smile of ineffable peace and triumph stole over the wasted face, and the weary eyelids drooped; the sweet lips murmured gently:

"Now read the prayers."

"Shall I call father in? He bade me call him when you awoke."

"No, dearest, let him rest. Tell him—in the morning—that I forgive him —for all—that I bid him remember his promise. There is a package of papers—I wrote them; they are yours; you will find all there—that I have not strength—cannot—dare not tell you. You will always love me, my Ella?" she questioned suddenly and anxiously.

"Ever, ever, dear mother! Who on earth has been to me like you? Who on earth shall I find like you? Mother! I cannot pray! I cannot take my eyes from off your face. I shall be desolate, forsaken, *lost* without you! *Mother!* You cannot—you *shall* not leave me!"

And cries and sobs broke from her tortured breast; but in that hour the weaker one was strongest, and Shina's voice pleaded low and soft without one shadow of reproach.

"This is sin—rebellion—my child! God is good, and orders all things wisely. My loved and cherished daughter, read to me the prayers for the night."

Cosella laid her softly down, and kissed her lips and brow without a word, but deep sobs swelled from the stricken heart, and in low, faltering tones, blistering the page with her burning tears, she read.

The prayer was long; in many portions sublime and elevating; unconsciously she gathered comfort from the sacred promises, and upraised her soul in the resignation born of faith. Shina followed the prayer with her lips and heart. When Cosella closed the book, she said:

"Repeat the *Shemang*, my beloved child!"

Fervently, reverentially, with upraised eyes, and hands meekly folded, she repeated the sacred asseveration of God's unity:

"*Hear, oh Israel! the Lord thy God, the Lord is One.*"

With pious fervor, Shina repeated it. She made a feeble sign for Cosella to draw near.

"Remember your sacred promise!" This was said in a thrilling whisper. "Ever obedient to God's will—mid change—of joy or sorrow. Love me ever—receive my blessing—" the cold hand lay on the bowed head with its clustering curls—"when tempted, called away from duty—remember! Be ever true and pure!" The lids closed softly over the hazy veil drawn quickly over the intense and lingering gaze that rested on Cosella's upraised face; the love light of the tender eyes was withdrawn; one last, long, lingering pressure, and the stiffened fingers relaxed their hold; a low sigh—a faint, melodiously whispered "good night!" and with a smile upon the calm and wasted countenance, without a struggle, the spirit passed away!

How long Cosella stood there, enrapt in prayer or contemplation, she knew not; when she looked around the nurse was gazing upon her in speechless terror. She had awakened to find the lady dead and cold, the daughter with fixed eyes, immovable as a statue, gazing with prayerful attitude upon her mother's face!

The voluble mulatto woman commenced her lengthy prayers and condolences, but the bereaved heart replied not; and the woman, hastening from the room, awakened the servants and officiously aroused the master from his slumbers to inform him of the sad event.

Manasseh started from his bed with an exclamation of horror and surprise. Hastily throwing on some garments, he rushed to his wife's room to find his tortured victim cold and still, and smiling in the repose of death; Cosella standing by with cheeks as pale as those of the departed, the tears of a first mighty bereavement stealing down her face, inundating hands and bosom with their briny flood!

"Dead—dead! my Shina gone!" he cried with an outburst of sorrow that seemed real, for it startled the girl from her deep trance of grief.

"Oh, forgive, forgive, my wife!" he sobbed, as he pressed kisses on the unresponding hand.

Cosella placed her hand upon his shoulder; its light touch thrilled him mightily, and he bowed his head upon the coverlet. "She bade me tell you that she forgave you *all*. I would have called you, but she deemed you weary, and desired you to rest. She died calmly, happy as an angel! I have delivered my mother's message. I leave you here—for I must to my chamber. I am overpowered with fatigue."

Why was her voice so calm and stern? She gave no sign of grief, save by the tears that unrestrained rolled down her cheeks and by the mortal pallor of her face. Manasseh looked upon her with reproachful eyes; so calmly, coldly she delivered his dead wife's message! She met his eye with unquailing glance.

"What said she besides? Peace be to her soul!" inquired Manasseh, rising not from his kneeling posture by the dead.

"*She bade me be ever true and pure!*" replied Cosella, firmly. "And I have sworn to do her bidding." There was so much emphasis in the words; such haughty defiance of all wrong in the solemn promise that, even in that hour, the guilty plotter felt he could not cope successfully with that brave, true girl. He made no reply, and Cosella, kissing silently the brow of the dead, passed from the room.

"Cold, haughty, unfeeling girl!" he muttered, for he could not read the refinement of sorrow that scorned external revelation in his presence.

Alone in her chamber, the angel hosts beheld the tributary offering of bereavement. The flushing dawn and the rising sun beheld the yet unfinished conflict, the wrestling of a heart untried.

The same day, Cosella demanded of her father the papers entrusted to his care. He answered her with indignation for the unseemly haste she manifested; he accused her of heartlessness and self-interest, so soon to break in upon his sorrow. She turned away with a mocking smile—with a haughty, contemptuous gesture, she left the room. Manasseh's glittering eyes followed her with deep menace in their depths.

He was compelled to dispense with the ceremonies of mourning, the prayers for the dead repeated by the assembled ten, for he was not among his people. He would not permit his wife to be interred in the Protestant burial ground of the town, set apart for the use of its foreign residents. He bought the ground for Shina's grave; a lovely, sequestered nook, some miles above the port, situated between rising hills, in full view of the ocean, dense with tropical foliage, with wild flowers and willow shades.

A simple monument was erected there—it recorded her name and age; it told not of her martyr life. When the funeral pageant moved down the street—when the last kiss had been impressed on the marble brow, the last look given—Cosella turned to follow with the throng. She had been told by Manasseh, that it was not the custom of the country for women to attend funerals; but what cared the loving heart for custom?

There was no long line of carriages, no hearse, with its appalling gloom. The coffin was carried by the friends of the departed—the dark cloth that covered it was strewn with flowers.

Wrapping a black silk scarf around her, putting on her white straw hat, Cosella was about to step into the sunshine, when her father's hand was laid upon her arm.

"I command you to remain," he whispered low and threateningly, for some persons yet lingered near the house.

"You have compelled me to return from my place by the departed. Am I not troubled enough that sacrilegious hands must touch her, profane eyes have seen her in her shroud? Will you, too, submit me to annoyance? Back into the house immediately!"

"I will see my mother to the last!" Cosella firmly replied.

"You shall not!" he cried, tightening his hold upon her.

"I appeal to these gentlemen," he said aloud. "My daughter persists in accompanying the funeral, though I tell her it is contrary to the customs of the land. The heat is excessive, the willful girl will make herself ill!"

"Your father is in the right, young lady." "Do not add to his great calamity by opposition." "Young girls must be obedient," said those around; and with a cry of mingled rage and sorrow, at one bound, freeing herself from her father's hold, she ran, tear-blinded, crushed and wounded, to the chamber that had been hallowed by the presence of her gentle guardian.

She heard the retreating sound of footsteps; then all grew still, and anew the sorrow fell; the utter-darkness environed, the desolation, vivid and palpable, enfolded her! With tears and sobs, she called on Jaspe, the faithful dog, who since his mistress' death had refused to taste food. He was not in the house. "Her dog is permitted to follow," cried Cosella. "I, her child, am forbidden to pray upon her grave!"

Long before Manasseh returned, the good old physician sought the mourner's presence; he carried something wrapped up in a dark cloth; it was the lifeless body of poor Jaspe, who had breathed his last upon the new-made grave! Fidelity and devotion strong unto death, beautifully manifest throughout Thy world's creations, endowing with the attributes of angels the lowliest things!

Cosella clasped the faithful creature in her arms, and kissed him reverently. With tears of earnest longing the full heart cried aloud, unconscious of another's presence.

"Oh, that I were in thy place, dear Jaspe!—that I could die upon her grave and be at rest! I envy thee, so good, so true! Thou could'st not live without her! Even her dog has left me! Oh, Jaspe, Jaspe, last, faithful friend! I am alone, alone!"

The good man could not behold, unmoved, so deep a sorrow. He stooped down to the suffering girl, who was crouching on the floor, with the dead body of the little favorite in her arms, and with paternal tenderness he lifted to his own the pallid, tear-stained face, and kissed the young, saddened brow. "Have faith in God, my daughter; in his mighty hand he holds healing for every wound of earth!" he said.

"I am alone, alone!" was the wild, anguished reply; and the kind comforter knew that words were vain in that dark hour.

In after years, Cosella, thou didst kneel to bless God for trial, to sing thy loud thanksgiving songs for every suffering past, for every pang of earthly sacrifice that led thee to the altar's side! From the graves once enshrouding all of love and memory arose the angel forms that led the way to heavenly gates—arose the invocations bringing ministering seraphs, power and conquest, might and glory, joy and triumph, to thy soul! But the initiation was terrible, the conflict dire; the first draught of suffering was bitter as gall, and the quivering lip shrank from the proffered cup.

10

The Web of Destiny

Oh, I envy those
Whose hearts on hearts as faithful can repose;
Who never feel the void, the wandering thought,
That sighs o'er visions—such as mine hath wrought.

Love covered all with rose-like flowers,
A fragrant, but an *early* thing;
The spirit's almond tree that buds
And blossoms in its spring.

Not many days after the funeral, as Cosella was sitting immersed in thought and grief, she was called upon by a lady, who with the usual friendliness of that hospitable clime had frequently sent a fragrant and choice *bouquet*, a dainty dish of fruit to the departed. This was her first visit to the house, and as if in keeping with the occasion she was attired in black, and wore a black veil thrown lightly over her head. The face that met Cosella's inquiring look was one usually brilliant with animation—now overcast with the semblance of tenderest sympathy; the large, dark, restless eyes were suffused with tears. She was of slender frame, and her every movement possessed the swaying grace of the Creole. Her hair, dark and lustrous as that of Shina, was disposed in massive braids around her face; when unloosened it fell to her very feet. On her matronly brow no impress of care or sorrow lingered; the hand of time had touched her lightly indeed, stealing not one rose shade from the finely-cut lip, leaving the cheek fresh and rounded as in earliest youth. Her brown but clear complexion wore no roseate tint; the full and sparkling eye flashed and melted alternately; but the tide of emotion swept not its ruby flood athwart the pale yet brilliant countenance.

With a sudden movement, quick, graceful and impulsive, she rose as Cosella entered the room and taking her hand said, in a voice replete with music, "*Mi querida hija!*" (my beloved daughter).

Without a word of reply, the young girl cast herself upon the stranger's bosom and wept aloud, wept long and silently. The tender eyes that looked upon her rained plenteous tears upon her early woe; the soft arms enfolded her most lovingly. For a brief space Cosella deemed she lay upon her mother's bosom, and amid the great, choking sobs of her bitter grief she murmured, dreamily, unconsciously, in the soft southern tongue, "*Madre mía!*" (my mother).

"God is good, he does all for the best—be comforted, my child!" said the sweet, soothing voice. Cosella, understanding as yet but little of the language, yet knew the meaning of those soft, low, sympathizing tones.

"She was all of earth to me!" was all the quivering lips could utter. The stranger held her closely in her arms, murmuring sweet words of encouragement, of motherly affection, of religious trust. The attentive ear of the mourner heard her speak of the consoling Saviour, the blessed Virgin, and the ministering saints. Her heart felt deeply. How far off, how unsympathizing with her sorrow was the dread Jehovah she had been taught to worship and fear. For the first time the Jewish maiden thought of the agonies of that mother, revered by thousands—of the sorrow and sufferings of Jesus of Nazareth.

"Come home with me, my daughter; my heart, my house, all shall be thine; my husband and my sons will love thee," said the lady's caressing lips. A shower of kisses fell on Cosella's upturned brow. She understood—her heart interpreted the language. "Good, kind friend!" she whispered, "what is your name?"

"Teresa Hernandez de Almiva," she replied.

Cosella started. "You sent the beautiful flowers *she* loved so much, the fruits she loved to gaze upon and feel their freshness when she could no longer eat? You are the friend who so kindly sympathized with the stranger, alone upon her sick bed? Oh, señora, I thank you, thank you from my soul, for her dear sake!"

The impulsive, loving untried heart poured forth its gratitude in tears and fervent kisses, showered on the lady's hand and brow. Teresa replied with a solemn benediction invoked for her coming life. They conversed awhile by signs, and Teresa understood that the young girl's father was a jealous guardian—that she dared not give a promise of visiting her until his permission had been obtained; and Cosella listened with a thrill of joy to the fervent protestations of affection, the loving assurances of this newfound friend. When the lady left the house, Cosella threw herself upon her knees beside her mother's vacant bed, and cried, as if unto her spirit hovering there, "Mother, dear, lost mother, God has sent a friend, a guardian angel, to thy lonely child!"

She obtained Manasseh's permission to visit the Señora Teresa, and he led her to the house. With much politeness and show of gratitude for the interest manifested by the wealthy lady for his motherless child, he allowed her to remain for the day.

The fine artistic tastes of Cosella met with much that pleased and aroused her from her brooding sorrow in that home of elegance and ease. The snowy matting on the floor, the curiously tinted swinging hammocks, all wove by the Indians' swift and graceful fingers; the rare old mirrors; the valuable pictures; the costly yet airy-looking furniture; the waving curtains of palest green that excluded the fervid sunshine; the porcelain and alabaster vases, filled with choicest flowers; the pure white marble, and the glistening shells—all brought their refining, breathing influences wherewith to soothe a heart's first grief.

It was not to the mere external that Cosella clung; the inner power of the beautiful, its poetic charm, its unspoken witchery it was that attracted through the eye her soul. The separate influence, the peculiar charm of each beautiful thing, called forth a feeling pure and elevating, thoughts akin to prayer. From the visible surroundings her spirit soared aloft and reveled in fantastic imaginings not all unreal; dreaming of the beautiful beyond above.

But it was the hand of affection that unlocked the portals; the music voice of Teresa de Almiva led her to the ideal land once more. Her hand it was that first uplifted the heavy pall of despair from off her soul; her loving summons bade her return to life and hope; ever docile at affection's call, the untried child responded gratefully.

She was sitting alone one day in the house that ever seemed pervaded by a mysterious presence, the shadow-form of the departed; thinking sadly, regretfully of the past, and turning from the future's looming shadows, when Carmela, the mulatto woman who had watched by her mother, and who was yet retained in the service of the daughter, entered. She held in her hand a *bouquet* of choicely assorted flowers; silently she busied herself in looking around the room for a vase to put them in.

"Give me the flowers, Carmela, I will take care of them," said Cosella, and as she received them and inhaled their delicious perfume, the small eyes of the woman glittered with joy—a triumphant smile played over her face. She said, half-audibly, as if talking to herself—

"If the person who gave me those flowers could see how well they are received— "

"Who sent this bouquet?" asked her young mistress suddenly.

"The same hand that sent them while the Señora lived; it sends them every day to the young lady."

"It is not the Señora Teresa de Almiva," said Cosella, thoughtfully, "for she denies having sent any since—"

"Oh, no, it is not the Señora Teresa—"

"Who is it, then?" she demanded eagerly.

"I dare not tell you," replied Carmela mysteriously.

"Why not? Ought I not to be grateful to the kind friend who sends me such beautiful tokens?"

"If you knew *who* sent them, you would be grateful, for that person loves you better than anyone on earth."

"Who *can* it be? But no one loves me better than the Señora Teresa, she is my second mother, Carmela."

The woman smiled a strange, peculiar smile.

"There is a better love than even a mother's, Señorita."

"A better love?" replied the innocent girl, "what on earth or in heaven can be better, higher, holier, than a mother's sacred love? Oh, no, you are mistaken, Carmela."

"You are young, Señorita Cosella," said Carmela, in that soft southern language, they pronounced her peculiar name as if it were written *Coseya*; rendering it far more musical and soft.

"Someday you will learn of another love to which that of daughterly affection is as nothing. I speak from experience. But you understand the language of flowers; come, read the messages contained in your bouquet."

Her soft, dark, questioning eyes bent on the fragrant treasures; she touched them lightly with her finger as she translated their unspoken tongue.

"The white rose, 'thou art my divinity'; this rich rose pink, 'love pure and devoted'; this sprig of mignionette, 'Thy virtues exceed thy loveliness'; this leaf from the lemon tree, 'secret hope'; this beautiful rose, with leaves and thorny stem, 'I hope and fear'; this blue flower, I forget its name, I know signifies 'acknowledgement.' Oh, there are so many here I cannot go on."

"What means the pomegranate flower, Señorita?"

"That? It is a declaration of love."

"And that is the significance of the offering. Do you now understand the giver?"

"I—I don't know whether I do," replied Cosella, confused and puzzled she scarce knew wherefore.

"Will you promise secrecy if I tell you? Mind, not a word to anyone."

"Yes, yes, I promise!" cried the young girl, eagerly; "Carmela, do me the favor to tell me!"

"It is from a young gentleman; he loves you better than his life. He does not approach you, because he respects your grief. When you become quite calm and consoled, he will speak to you—not before."

The face of the attentive eager listener was suffused with blushes. A strange uprising of a sudden joy, then a vague disquiet stole through her strangely thrilled heart, the flowers fell from her hand and lay for a moment unheeded upon the floor. Then she stooped for them, and once again inhaled their fragrance; her drooping eyes dwelt on their loving significance; the

first vague, girlish dream of love enthralled her being, the first ideal longing seeking its embodiment.

She dared not ask his name; but the wily Carmela, reading her expressive face, said in a whisper:

"The cavalier who loves you is handsome and accomplished. His father
once held a high position at the Court of France. You know him, you have
seen him; your father has had business transactions with him. It is the Señor Salvador del Monte.

Cosella remembered; at her thought invoked, his image stood before
her—young, handsome, and breathing of love—bowing in homage before
her—the ideal of her youth's first promise, her awakened heart's first hope.

"And he loves me?" she questioned low and dreamily.

"Better than aught on earth. You are to him like the far off shining stars
of heaven, the light upon Our Lady's face!" replied the waiting woman,
who, like most of her nation, was endowed with superior facilities of expression, with a poetic range of thought.

But at her comparison with the Virgin mother, the dreaming girl aroused
from her strange reverie; a sudden fear and pang, a gloomy cloud of superstition rolled athwart her soul and bade the music-beatings of her heart
be still.

"*He is a Christian,*" she murmured, and her cheek grew pale. "I dare not
love one of another race." And, covering her face with her hands, she desired Carmela to withdraw. The woman cast a sidelong, triumphant glance
upon her as she left the room.

Thenceforth conflict abode in that girlish soul; the eager, prayerful longing for love, now partially revealed and understood, was to be repressed and
overcome as something sinful; the spontaneous worship of her heart and
mind was ever to be withheld; it dared not go free and blithesome forth
into the universe of God, and seek among the beautiful and true its resting place. Love, the white winged messenger of heaven, doomed to wear
the galling fetters of a narrow creed, the worldly aspect that was to ensure
acceptance from her bigoted father—it dared not approach in its own unveiled glory its angel nature. And Cosella's soul rebelled. She seemed suddenly to have taken an all-embracing view of the future, and she shuddered as she beheld. Her fate would be lasting bondage to the belief which
she shrank from even then; fetters of creed and custom would bind tightly
down those upsoaring pinions that so often fluttered in the musical airs
of spirit-land. Her father would sell her for gold; the world's approved and
church-applauded bondage would bind that free, wild, daring, seeking spirit
to some mercenary clod of earth, and call that mockery of marriage a holy
union!

Cosella knew and felt that among the maidens of her race marriage was looked upon as woman's highest attainment; but of the spiritual tie, that passionless and holy was when matter first existed, will remain while He, the Source of Love, exists; of this—of all the subtler links and pure attractions that form the harmony of soul with soul, they of the world, the sensual, mercenary, and creed-bound, know not; and in *her* soul, an overwhelming joy and a mighty sorrow, it was foreshadowed all!

Then and there her soul uttered a vow unto the ear of heaven; and amid the trials and temptations of desolation and orphanhood, angels of strength and goodness upheld her fainting spirit whene'er it wavered in its holy purpose. She vowed that never, through force or artifice, for wealth or home, for self or others, would she become an unloving wife—would she take upon herself false marriage vows. Holy and unbroken has that faith been kept, 'mid tears and trials, amid the scorn and desertion of the world!

Untutored child! Poor dreamer! All enrapt in the ideal life whose portals close upon antagonism, falsehood, and deception—what couldst thou know of the borrowed guise of angels, of the simulation of love, of the plots of earthly daring?

She met the giver of those taken flowers, and her heart-speaking face revealed the inner consciousness and acceptance. She met his admiring glance; she heard the tender modulations of his voice in timid adoration to the loveliness she had never cared for, thought of, until then. She bowed unto the magnetism of a strong and earnest will that seemed so loveful and tender even of her every glance. Unarmed, untaught, unwarned by experience, she loved before she was aware; loved an ideal living in her own pure soul, her own poetic fancy.

He spoke to her of God loving all his children with an equal love; of the beautiful laws of attraction that heed no difference in creed or station. He told her he was free from superstition, from the church's thrall; she, that was all of life and joy to him, would she not turn from cold and chaining doctrines to the heart-warmth of love, the sunlight of home and peace?

And Cosella listened as one entranced, and half bowed her heart in acquiescence, half smiled upon the eloquent pleader; then stole to her quiet chamber to weep and grow rebellious at the conflict in her soul.

She made no confidant, not even of Teresa de Almiva. She guarded the secret of her growing love, until, with a seeming giant's strength, affection coped successfully with bigotry, and out of the discipline of the heart, long, long continued, cruel and bitter as it was, grew freedom, bright and glorious soul freedom!

His words of love, his tender solicitous looks, his presence every day, would have sufficed for her heart-happiness for years. But the trial-cords were to be tightened, the choice was to be made, another darkened page of life unrolled, another Marah fountain tasted, whose bitter waters clave to the soul for years.

From the adjoining island of Canida that was inhabited by many of their people, tradesmen and visitors often came to Santa Lucia. Among their number was Jeshurun Lopez, a Portuguese Jew, wealthy and avaricious, a widower in middle life. Manasseh and he grew intimate friends, and between them it was settled that the young Cosella should become the wife of one so totally unsuited to her elevated mind and refined spirit. Unconscious of the doom pending over her, she was called to her father's presence some seven months after her mother's death.

"I am glad to see you recovering health and spirits, my child," he began. "I see that reflection, my counsels, and the aid of our holy religion have strengthened you to overcome your grief for the loss of *her*—whom yet I cannot—" He covered his face with his handkerchief. Was it real grief that convulsed his frame, or was it mere hypocrisy?

Cosella remained unmoved; but her heart accused her that for a stranger's untried love she had accepted joy so soon, while the willow branches deepened over the mother's broken heart. She sighed, and Manasseh hearing that sigh continued:

"Sorrow no longer, my beloved child; she is with God, where the Cherubim and Seraphim veil their faces before the splendor of God's majesty. His people will yet be restored; we shall return to our ancient dominion, and Israel shall rule above all the nations of the earth. Our feet shall be upon the hated necks of our Christian foes. The faith, the blasphemy of Nazareth shall be blotted out of the universe. They shall implore mercy of us, even as we have entreated at their hands so many centuries. The cursed abominations of their idol worship shall—"

"Father," interrupted Cosella, "can it be right to curse, to invoke evils on our fellow beings, our brothers?"

"*Our brothers*, girl! None are but those of the covenant, the scattered tribes of persecuted Israel. Is the Christian *thy* brother? Does he not hate, scorn and avoid thee? Are we not as dust beneath their feet, we, 'the unbelieving Jews,' for whose conversion so many missionaries are sent abroad? Ha, ha, ha! They may spare their trouble; no man in his senses will fall from the worship of the one true God to the adoration of that incomprehensible mystification, the Christian Trinity."

She had always listened silently and with perfect unconcern to his tirades against others' belief, even to his denunciations of his fellow-men. Now her bosom swelled with indignation. She was about to reply, but he continued:

"Listen, my daughter. For years you and I, and she who is with God, have been wanderers upon the face of the earth. We fled from despotism, bigotry, from the Christian pursuer. It beseems me now to think of you. You are no longer a child. You must take upon yourself the dignity and the cares of womanhood. You must think of marriage, Cosella."

She started, paled, then crimsoned to her very brows. Manasseh gazed upon her with earnest scrutiny. She drooped her eyes beneath his gaze; a strange fear fluttered at her heart.

"It is a father's place and duty to speak to you of this," he continued, "since *she* is gone to rest. You know, Cosella, that with us, children of the ancient covenant, it is incumbent to marry. We wait with longing pious hope for the Prince of David to be born among us. Our women may not remain unmarried; and she who is childless is divested of God's blessing. I have chosen a husband for you, Cosella."

She grew deadly pale, looked piteously imploring into his face, and stammered forth:

"I—I do not wish to marry—I will not—*never*, NEVER!"

"Wouldst thou rebel against the highest law, the wise decrees of the Almighty, given through his inspired servant, the lawgiver, Moses, blessed be his name? Would you rebel against a father's authority, that power that is next to God's? Would you render yourself liable to the olden penalty of stoning to death for disobedience? You will not—*never*? Speak not so again to me, Cosella!"

Manasseh was becoming wildly excited.

She was upon the verge of bursting into tears, of loudly exclaiming against his tyranny; but she forced back the swelling tide, controlled the indignant rush of feeling.

"I am too young yet, father; let me live as I have always done; I desire no change."

"But, foolish girl, it is woman's destiny to be married; for this has the Creator placed her here, and he has made the husband responsible for the deeds and vows of the wife. She has it much easier than we, for while all the precepts and ordinances are binding upon us, she is absolved from all accountability by her husband's word and will; even as I now am responsible for your every act, my child."

"Am I not then a moral and accountable being? Am I a mere nothing in my Creator's world that I may not think, act, feel, do right or wrong in my own soul?" burst forth Cosella.

"You may not sin, either willfully or ignorantly, without suffering; but I, your guardian, am responsible for your deeds; for the woman's soul is not like the soul of man; it is given to our guardianship and custody."

"I feel that I am free, that God will judge *me* for *my* works; that my soul is equal to that of man, my spirit on a level with his. I feel—"

With crimsoned cheek and flashing eye she was continuing, but with an imperious gesture, Manasseh silenced her.

"You must not speak of these things; you are too young, too unlearned—it is presumptuous! Obey your parents, fulfill the requirements of the law; this is all that God asks of *you*, as a woman!"

She saw that his anger was rising; she knew that it was useless to argue with him. The pictures of her mother's martyr-life rose vividly before her; those soft, brown eyes looked meek and lovingly into hers. She bowed her head before that cherished memory; unmindful of her tyrant's presence, she cried with freshly-wrung heart and streaming tears:

"My mother! oh, my mother!"

He uttered an exclamation of impatience, but she heard him not; she wept until the storm of feeling subsided, until the words of the dying had sounded with solemn, clear distinctness athwart the gathering shadows of her soul. She wiped away the tears that glistened on her cheeks and trembled on her lashes. She looked in Manasseh's face and said, in a sweet, imploring voice, all childlike and submissive:

"I wish to be good, my father. I will obey you in all else, but you will not urge this on me; I cannot marry yet—"

"There is no hurry, child," he replied, considerably softened by her manner; "but I tell you today that you may think and prepare yourself. The husband I have chosen for you will be here in a fortnight."

She made no reply; but her beseeching eyes, her folded hands demanded, "Who is the man?"

"You would ask me who it is? Well, child, you need not be so bashful with your father. It is my friend, a wealthy, honored, influential man, a thorough Israelite, a business man, my brother, Jeshurun Lopez."

"No—oh, my God—no!" cried Cosella, springing from her chair; "that sullen, old, avaricious man? I marry *him*? Never, never, never!—by the grave of my mother, never!"

"Girl, how dare you swear by her grave? By aught on earth? You are mine to dispose of, to give you up to whom I see fit. Dare you oppose your puny self to my strong will and power? Did *she*, your mother, ever frustrate one plan of mine? Can you think you will? Cosella, tempt me not to anger; the law of the land, the law of our people gives me power over you. Obey as becomes your youth."

"Obey!" she cried, indignantly; "seal my own life-long misery by wedding a man I despise; a mercenary, avaricious wretch! Bind my young, hopeful life in such a tie? Live, without love, for worldly pomp and glitter? *I will not*—I cannot—I *dare* not!"

The impulsive girl stood revealed before him! There was strength, and daring, and energy, in her attitude, and form, and bearing; he felt that he coped with a mighty and courageous spirit, enshrined in that frail, willowy, girlish figure; he measured the cost and the danger, and then passed heedlessly, blindly on.

"What is this you prate about?" he said, with that chilling irony, that stinging sarcasm, that so often and so long had sent hopelessness to Shina's withering soul. "What know you of misery or blessedness, of motives, or of character? Say, girl, what know you of *love?*"

He seized her arm, and looked upon her blanching face with a searching, deeply-scrutinizing look. That soul of honor could not feign or equivocate; he felt her tremble as a reed, rudely shaken by the blast; he saw her crimson with the maiden consciousness of her pure secret revealed. A groan of bitter agony and disappointment burst from the fanatic's breast. His voice trembled with rage and terror as he pursued the inquiry:

"Have you dared—has your soul become alienated from the worship of your fathers? Has some Christian miscreant dared—God of Abraham! I would sacrifice thee, as did the Hebrew chief of old! Tell me—you say you dare not lie, you would not lie for me, your father—*tell me*, or dread the punishment of offended God, what know you of love—whence come these thoughts, this reasoning? *Quick, quick*, Cosella! As you value peace and life! Answer me!"

Her voice trembled with emotion, not with fear, as she responded: "These thoughts come to my soul in solitude; I think good angels send them; they strengthen me and exalt my heart. I feel that it is sinful, wicked, to live with those we love not. I despise Jeshurun Lopez because he lacks the noblest attributes of manhood—justice, truth, and honor. I must revere and love the man I marry. Rather the grave than life with the man you call a brother!"

"Father of Israel! This is some evil spell, some work of Satan! You have been too much alone with these Christian vipers. You shall no longer go to Teresa Almiva's. You are tainted with the horrors of their belief. Gracious Heaven! Can it be possible that repugnant fop, her son Carlos, has won your heart from God?"

"No, oh no! Indeed, you judge not rightly," Cosella cried, with such an accent and fervor of truth, he dropped that hasty surmise.

She trembled with apprehension, but she wavered not; her truth sworn soul was firm amid the impending danger.

"*Tell me!*" he cried, and again held her firmly and bound her beneath his steady gaze; "have you been false to the teachings of the departed? Have you in thought or deed forsaken the path marked by our holy faith? Have you dared to think of—dream of—a Christian lover?"

"I have not been false to *her* teachings; I have not sinned against her dying words in thought or deed; I have done naught I blush for in the sight of God or man," she answered proudly, and her head was erect with conscious right; "but," she faltered, the quick tears veiling the flashing eyes, the pale cheek crimsoning, "though you condemn and cast me forth, though you *kill me*, I will avow the truth—I love a Christian!"

A loud cry, more like a howl of an infuriate beast, burst from Manasseh. He sprang toward her; he could have crushed her then. She neither moved nor spake, but stood with folded arms and pallid cheek, defiant, fearless and erect!

"Thou shalt not escape my vengeance! Thou shalt be thwarted, apostate! —sinful, guilty wretch! While thou livest thou shalt repent, in sackcloth and in ashes, for this day's confession of thy grievous sin! Without delay, my plans shall be achieved."

He rushed from the house. A stunning sense of some great woe to come fell on the maiden's breast. "But I have told the truth!" she murmured, lifting her brimming eyes to heaven; and from within, the still small voice cried musically clear and triumphant, "Well done! Well done!"

As she passed on to her chamber, she heard a knock for admittance on the outer door. Before she could retreat, Carmela had opened it, and Salvador advanced toward her. The trial she had passed, the danger that overhung, the dread, uncertainty and sorrow overcame her. With a sudden impulse, childlike, tender, innocent, she threw herself upon his breast, and wept for the love so heralded by gloom and woe.

With his arm cast fondly around her, he soothed her into peace and calm, she murmuring all the while, so fondly and confidingly, "Oh, Salvador, be thou my saviour. I trust in thee, I love but thee so well!"

11

The Second Sorrow

Scratch the green rind of a sapling, or wantonly twist it in
the soil,
The scarred and crooked oak will tell of thee for centuries to
come.

—Tupper

Oh! Fair as the sea-flower close to thee growing,
How light was thy heart till Love's witchery came,
Like the wind of the south o'er a summer lute blowing,
And hush'd all its music, and wither'd its frame!

—Moore

From the day of Cosella's confession of her love for one not of her race,
Manasseh watched her closely, and by prayers, promises and threats endeavored to obtain his name; but the young girl's lips were sealed. She said
her secret was her own, and she proudly guarded it. No longer permitted
to go out alone, weary days and weeks passed by, and she saw not Salvador;
but every day the fragrant flower gift was sent, her tearful eyes and longing
heart read from it the unalterable love, the unfailing hope, the renewed vow.
This was her only solace, for her young life had become drear indeed. She
was to be kept under this close surveillance until she would promise to accept the hand of Jeshurun Lopez. Cosella looked with impatient hope and
firm resolve to the time that would render her actions free—one little year
and she would be mistress of herself. Unworldly child! She had no idea of
the distribution of property, of the value of gold, of the homage rendered to
it by the world. Love beautified life; and she believed all promised friendship true and lasting—all hearts as guileless as her own.

Sadly and cruelly was the young hopeful spirit tried by him who called
himself her father; bitter denunciations, loud revilings such as poor Shina
had for life endured fell on Cosella's sensitive ear, arousing her to wild retort, crushing her soul with its weight of despotism; and calling forth bold,
startling thoughts of freedom, not from the legal bondage only, that gave
her to his care so long, but from the soul fetters of the narrow belief that
sanctioned force in place of soothing love.

Ever careful of the world's opinion, his manner toward her while in the presence of strangers was affectionate as usual. He still permitted her to visit the Señora Teresa; but he went with her and remained waiting in an outer apartment while the friends conversed. Cosella possessed a wonderful aptitude for the acquirement of languages; she could soon converse freely with that dear and gentle friend. Manasseh, without the remotest suspicion, and for reasons of his own, permitted this intercourse, little dreaming that the first lessons of the Christian faith were being instilled into his daughter's moulding soul. They came accompanied by superstition, it is true; but still the history of the gentle, long-suffering, all enduring Saviour, the poetic idea of his Virgin mother's life and agony, the beautiful doctrines of the interceding saints and holy attendant angels could not fail of impressing the susceptible mind of a young girl brought up in solitude of spirit—of binding chains of poetry and beauty around a heart that yearned for love and worship, finding it not in the stern belief of her father. Unknown to him, she had accompanied her friend to the Catholic church; the sweet, heart-breathing hymns, the triumphant and supplicatory music, the fragrance of the swinging censers, the flower-decked altars, the fair, sweet, pensive face of the Sorrowing Mother, the lights and priestly forms, the adoring multitude inspired the wondering and enthusiastic girl with feelings of intensest worship; for she was young, imaginative, solitary; and music and beauty, light and fragrance, called forth the irresistible prayer, the grateful tears, the tribute of involuntary homage unto God.

And Teresa de Almiva kissed her brow and invoked the Holy Mother's blessing upon her, saying soft and fervently: "If you were but a Christian, my blessed child!"

The motherless girl dreamed of the sweet consolations of the Virgin Mother's love and care; until the poetic fancy became to her longing heart a near reality, and she, too, knelt before our Lady's image, with the filial veneration that was in truth addressed to her who hovered near and unseen, the spirit mother, Lea!

She had heard the history of Jesus, not from the enlightened and just Israelite, who speaks of him with respect and pity, but from the fanatical Manasseh, from the unlearned of her nation. She had deemed him an impostor, striving for kingly honors, performing miracles by magic art; one who taught pernicious doctrines, and was justly put to death for his manifold transgressions against the law. Now from the lips of her maternal friend she heard the Christian's story; the very opposite of what she had been taught. That embodiment of celestial womanhood in Mary, that idea of all forgiving love in Jesus, the faith in guardian angels, all was irresistibly attractive; it was life, warm, promising, poetically beautiful! And then, it was the faith of Salvador, and though he seldom spoke of religion, would she not be happy to belong to the belief that was his?

Yet was there conflict in Cosella's soul; the old prejudices, the strong habits of years, battling with new views, new thoughts and emotions. Betwixt the outward and the inner conflict her cheeks paled and the rose-tint fled her face, and hours of bitter weeping, silent wrestling waited on her solitude. The world saw not, heard not, thought not, of what she endured; they who saw her richly attired, surrounded with comfort and elegance as became the only daughter of a wealthy man, knew not that the father, so ostentatious of affection in public, showered the direst invectives, the most startling denunciations, upon that tender head; that his hand heavy with anger had fallen on her bare white shoulders, that he had dragged her by the long dark hair; and often at the dead of night had threatened her with death unless she vowed obedience to his will. And the young girl, strengthening with suffering, yet often growing wild with her misery, fearlessly confronted him with accusations that thrilled his guilty soul with terror. She often said to him—

"Your conduct takes from my heart all filial love; I have long since ceased to respect you; for my mother's sake I guarded some remnant of affection for you; it is departing swiftly; when the last star sets I will be free; I will leave you, despite of the world, your threats, your faith. You will die alone, alone, calling in vain upon the child you tortured into fear and hatred!"

Manasseh, remembering Shina's words, shuddered and turned pale.

He could not wring from her the name of him she loved; he could not bow her soul to compliance with his mercenary plans. When Jeshurun Lopez called, Cosella would not see him; threats and violence were expended in vain. The suitor felt his case was hopeless.

It was then that Manasseh formed a plan; he would return to Europe, and leading Cosella to the customary forms of worship, seeking for themselves a home amid their people, she would forget her sinful love; he saw that, with such a character, force was not to be employed. He turned to gentleness and argument.

The weight of a great sorrow fell upon her when his announcement was made. Leave Santa Lucia, leave Salvador, perhaps forever! Those who have felt the foreshadowed pangs of parting with what to them was all of life and hope can feel for the despairing heart, the boding, wailing soul that cried aloud for help. She obtained permission to visit once more her mother's grave alone, and through Carmela it was arranged that Salvador should meet her there. The mulatto woman accompanied her thither. Manasseh deemed he had bribed her to fidelity, he little knew the reasons for her broken faith.

It was a delicious autumn afternoon; but in that land of unfading beauty the earth was robed in all its summer gorgeousness. Over the sea the sunbeams flashed, and answering diamonds seemed to dance upon the rippling waves; clouds, roseate and golden, lay upon the mountain heights; afar, on the horizon's verge, fantastic landscapes shone in fairy hues of purple, green and gold, crimson and azure, the cloud-land of the poet's realm. The early vesper song of birds issued from the thickly clustering groves; the incense of the flowers was poured upon the cooling air; the music of the ocean waves mingled with the Eolian whisperings of the breeze, so richly freighted with the forest's spicy greetings. The crystal waters dashing from the hill-side, speeding gleefully amid the cedars' ranks, fell into the awaiting pass beneath, and mingled with the river's sunlit flow, that meandering, rippling softly, sped on its quiet way beyond the quaint rude bridge that traversed the town; faithful to their destiny, the waters rushed into the salt embrace of ocean, ever singing, ever peaceful, ever clear.

Cosella passed along the beach, her long black veil drawn over her pale face—the tear-filled eyes she would conceal from all the passers-by; her mourning dress trailed in the sands; her scarf gathering up the fallen blossoms, the fragrant leaves, that strewed the ground. She looked upon the sea, the hills, the sky; life's burden was so toilsome, its pressure so heavy on the untried heart, she wept for rest, and even prayed for death's deliverance.

But when she reached the grave, the hallowed stillness surrounding it that was occasionally broken by the chant of birds, the murmur of the sea, she felt rebuked and silenced. Even from the cold marble, a tone of love, sweet, calm, and reassuring, spoke to her soul of life and hope. Carmela walked upon the beach; while weeping, praying, and expectant, the orphan stood beside the lonely grave.

The willow drooped its branches lovingly above that sheltered spot; the trailing vines clasped round the cold, white stone, their blue and crimson flowers mingling with the jessamine stars, the fragrant roses, the falling clusters of sweet mignonette. It was as a flower garden, that weary wanderer's last resting place. It was the home so longed for, close by the sea, beneath the willow's shade, amid the forest's silence, and the flower's sweet breath!

She was kneeling by the tomb, her tear-filled eyes upraised to the illumined glory of the heavens, her small hands crossed upon the aching breast; her dark curls, lifted by the caressing winds, left free the pale young face so prematurely stamped with sorrow, the brow so full of thought.

She heard a slight rustling amid the branches; she did not move, but a soft blush dyed her cheek, a sweet hope filled her being. Salvador, having exchanged a few words with Carmela, stood before her.

He looked upon her with a questioning, pitying glance; a shadow of tender compassion stole athwart his fine proud face; a sigh escaped his heart. The voice in which he said "Cosella" was melodious with the breathings of pity only. Alas, for her! The inexperienced, blinded, trusting girl—she deemed it the melody of love!

He raised her gently from her kneeling posture, and sat down on the flower-studded ground beside her. She looked into his face with all the truthfulness, the undisguised affection of her nature; and with tear drops freshly gathering in her saddened and beseeching eyes, said mournfully:—

"I must leave you, Salvador!"

"Leave me?" he looked searchingly into the appealing face. There was surprise in his tone; was there the sorrow of love?

"Yes," she continued; and the gathered heart-dew rolled slowly down her cheeks, and studded, like diamond drops, the folds of her mourning garb.

"My father intends to sail for Europe in the first vessel that offers, and I must accompany him. Oh, Salvador! You know not that he is cruel, unjust, unkind. Never, never can I tell you all I have suffered and still endure! Oh, I fear, I dread, this journey! Salvador, I shall never behold thee again!"

The floodgates were removed for that hour; the regnant self-control gave way. With sobs and incoherent speech, maddened with long suffering, wild with grief, she implored deliverance of him she loved so fondly, purely.

"Oh, save me from my father's cruelty, from this cold and bitter separation! Salvador, friend, brother, all to me! Take me to thy home, thy heart, thy protection! I cannot go with him across the sea!"

For a moment, wild and fleeting, a strong temptation crept into the soul of Salvador del Monte; his arms were outstretched involuntarily to the lovely suppliant, longing to rest upon his sheltering bosom. But there was good within that soul, at least then, in that sunset hour of holiness and calm. The watching angels had averted the danger of which she dreamed not, knew not; sorrow was in the young Cosella's path, but sin was put aside.

"Listen to me, my loved, my *good* Cosella," he replied, and his voice trembled with emotion. "I cannot take thee to my home, for I have none; my parents are in their grave. I can offer thee no safe asylum; and I cannot— wed thee—yet. I cannot explain, dearest, not now! There is one way for thee—flee from thy cruel father to the protecting arms of the Church. Thou wilt find friends. But if thou wouldst follow the advice of him who loves thee, Cosella—he, who would not behold thee wretched—submit for one short year more. At its expiration, if thou dost not return, I will follow, seek thee, do all things for thy happiness!"

"You will? My father vows never to return to this land. Will you, indeed, seek me? Salvador, I trust thy word, thy faith, for thou art all of earth to me!"

"I am unworthy of such love, such pure devotion! Mother of God forgive me!" murmured the young man.

"*You* unworthy! Who then on earth is true and honorable? Oh, speak not so humbly of thyself, thou sole friend of the orphan!"

Those pure and loving eyes! They burned deep into his soul; that voice so eloquently pleading! It aroused all the dormant good within. He could have folded her to his heart and knelt before her as to some saving angel; but he resisted the impulse—he kept his new-formed vow.

If then, following the dictates of truth and justice, he had told her all, how much of suffering he would have saved that guileless heart; what longing hopes and glooming fears, and vain, vain, dreams of the future, a few words would have dispelled! But his soul lacked strength and moral purpose. He dared not tell her! So when with that sweet, unguarded smile of hers, the unconventional manner, the spontaneous heart warmth so innocent and unrepressed, she said:

"Promise me, on my mother's grave, Salvador, that you will not forget me—that you will sacredly fulfill your promise, and I will brave and suffer all!"

He replied with seeming fervor and tenderness:

"I promise, Cosella! Within a year I will rejoin you; only write and tell me where you are. If in the uttermost end of the world, I will find you!"

"My mother's spirit hears you, Salvador! And here, the most sacred spot of earth to me, will I give to you my plighted vow. In one year's time I will become a daughter of your church. Were *she* living, I feel she would not blame me. Here, take this ring—it was my mother's; take it as a token and a memory of the faithful Cosella. Oh, think of me—pray for me often! Forget me not!"

She leaned against the monument for a moment, lost in the pain of parting. Deep sighs heaved the breast of Salvador. She deemed them the tribute of a grief shared with her own. He knew his sorrow was wrung from feeling's depths by the retributive, ever watchful hand of remorse!

"God is here!" said Cosella, low and fervently; "he hears our words, and reads our secret hearts. In his Divine presence, before the angels that unseen surround us, for my peace and faint heart's sake! Repeat once more thy promise!"

Slow, as with a painful effort, and his face was pale the while, he answered:

"In the presence of God, upon this hallowed spot I swear to thee! No other woman shall ever become my wife!"

A solemn stillness followed, amid which the young girl's heart beat rapturously; with head inclined and folded hands, she had listened as to a benediction given from above. The twilight, sudden and star lighted as it comes in that tropical clime, had overspread the heavens. The vesper song of birds was hushed; upon the still air chimed the evening bells.

"Farewell, Cosella—beloved and true—farewell!" said Salvador. "I dare not enter thy doors. I do not visit Doña Teresa, and even there I could not see thee. But I will behold thee once more ere you leave our shores. Carmela will arrange it. See, the stars have come; 'tis time for thee to retrace thy way. Farewell, Cosella; God and good angels guide thee ever!"

"*Farewell, farewell!* dear Salvador. My blessing and my love go with thee!" she replied, amid her tears.

He took her hand, he held it long and tenderly, and pressed on it a reverential, parting kiss. "Good, pure and true," he murmured, "once more farewell!"

She held his hand a moment; one more fond look into his face; her girlish lips were impressed on her mother's ring, her token gift to him. It was the first and last caress that passed between them. Cosella stood alone beside her mother's grave, his farewell nestling to her heart with glowing promise.

Salvador hastened from the spot with sorrow in his soul; he said no word to the awaiting Carmela; he rushed past the calm ocean-skirted scene with flying steps, averted eye, and troubled heart. Perhaps in that parting hour he truly loved the guileless, unsuspecting, and devoted girl.

Cosella returned home with peace and hope admitted to her soul. She announced to her father that she was willing to obey his commands, and leave Santa Lucia whenever he desired.

"So, so; no more rebellion!" he muttered to himself. "She is becoming sensible. I really feared she would throw herself upon the protection of some of these cursed idolaters! I see the thought has never entered her head. Once away from here, she will forget all her youthful nonsense. She will make a good Jewess yet. I will guard her from all outside influences. I will be good and kind to her, and give her presents, so she shall forget all harsh treatment. Give a woman a pair of new gloves, or a costly trinket, and you wean her from all sorrow. I thank my Creator, who has not made me a woman."

Manasseh took his daughter to the shops next day, and bought her several dresses and a costly veil of black lace. She smiled in acknowledgement, wondering in her heart how man could be so blind as to seek to heal heart wounds with external gifts.

When apprised of her departure, Teresa de Almiva loudly expressed her sorrow, and urged Cosella to remain and join the church, which would prove her support and refuge; but she had promised, and would not retract;

in a confidential hour she told her friend of her betrothal to Salvador del Monte.

The speaking face of Teresa was overspread with an expression of sadness and alarm; she was about to make some impulsive reply, to enter a protest or give advice; but Cosella, who had not noticed the change in her friend's countenance, said in those determined, fervent tones so usual with her:

"Much as I love you, my mother's friend, I would not be willing to return but for *his* sake, for I have suffered here so much, *so much!*"

"But if he—if circumstances prevent the fulfillment of his promise, Cosella?"

"I will return, if in the given time he comes not, though I return as a beggar! I will join your belief—I will be unto you as a daughter."

"The Holy Virgin and all the Saints strengthen your resolve, my child!" said the lady; and she knew that through human love she was linked to the new faith. Teresa de Almiva was a zealous enthusiast in religion—she calculated well.

In three weeks from the day she had received Salvador's promise at her mother's grave, Cosella, with her father, embarked for England. The Señora Teresa and her husband accompanied the voyagers on board. Of Salvador, the young girl had caught a passing glimpse from her balcony. He waved his hand, and smiled adieu. On the morning of her departure he sent, by Carmela, a choice bouquet, and amid its glistening leaves lay hidden a tenderly written farewell—first and last missive of his love—long was it guarded by the faithful heart that trusted so fully—long were the faded, scentless flowers treasured, above all gold and gems!

With many tears, Teresa folded Cosella in a parting embrace, and whispered in her ear: "Return to us, whatever befall you, my daughter! Come to the Virgin's bosom, to your second mother's loving heart!"

And Cosella gave her sacred promise.

Once more upon the sea; Manasseh plotting busily, dreaming of wealth and worldly honor, exulting in the success of a part of his plans; for he had borrowed a sum of money from the Señora Teresa, unknown to his child, who would have warned the lady. He never intended its return; but Teresa, for Cosella's sake, was willing to oblige him—to lose the gold, if necessary—for the pious hope predominated in her soul that she would be won, a willing, zealous convert to the Mother church.

Dreaming of things more beautiful than gold or earthly treasure, Cosella, too, plans for the future, and exults in the blessed consciousness of the loved and loving.

12
Light on the Pathway

I could have loved thee—could have yielded all
My heart's beat, warmest feelings up to thee,
Freely and willingly, without recall,
With real, transport, purest ecstacy;
Did I not with instinctive feeling learn
This love of mine thy heart could ne'er return.

—Max

But thy deep peace doth on me fall,
The frenzy of my love is gone—
The holy love remains alone.
There comes a solemn calm o'er all,
The storm is hushed within my breast,
Beneath the quiet stars I rest!

The spacious synagogue was crowded with its Sabbath worshipers; the ancient, unchanged prayers ascended to the God of Israel; the chant of youth and maidens was the same that echoed through the mountain passes of old Palestine, and sang victoriously from the Red Sea's banks, the desert's solitude. A stranger and a Christian, clad in deep black, the insignia of mourning around his hat, sat amid the zealous worshipers; and as his eye turned to the gallery above, where the richly clad and jeweled daughters of Judah sat, his glance rested again and again, with a pleased, strange and new emotion, upon the face and figure of a young, pale girl, wearing also the mourning garb.

There was something inexpressibly sad and tender in the expression of her face, in the sweet firmness of the finely cut lips, in the drooping lashes veiling the dark, soft, brilliant eyes, that, upraised once, had sent a thrill of strange remembrance to the gazer's heart. Sorrow, premature and heavy, was impressed on the speaking face, but hope and faith and trust were there also. Almon Fairlie, a deep reader of human character, a man with intuitions largely unfolded, read much of that undisguised aspiring nature; she was so like one he had known and loved in early youth—the memory, the resemblance, was thrilling, startling! Alas! No angel whispered more; he knew not that the face he gazed upon would be led to Percival Wayne's seeking, longing sight, the richest boon that earth or heaven could give. He knew not that he gazed upon Cosella Wayne!

The maiden's thoughts were far away with him who vowed his love beside her mother's grave—with him she deemed so true and loving. From the customary worship, the familiar scene, the remembered orison, her spirit wandered to the tropic land beside the fair Madonna's shrine; her heart was not with the prayer upon her lips; and in her soul anew the conflict raged; her spirit cried aloud for help and light.

The psalm was chanted, with thanksgiving joy; the young, fresh voices rendered praise unto the mighty Lord of Hosts.

Oh, give thanks unto the Lord, for he is good; for his mercy endureth forever.

Oh, give thanks unto the God of gods; for his mercy endureth forever.

To him who with understanding made the heavens; for his mercy endureth forever.

To him who stretched out the earth above the waters; for his mercy endureth forever.

Who formed the sun to rule by day.

The moon and stars to rule by night.

To him who smote the Egyptians in their first born,

With a mighty hand and outstretched arm; for his mercy endureth forever.

To him who led his people through the wilderness.

To him who smote great Kings.

Who remembered us in our low estate; for his mercy endureth forever.

Oh, give thanks unto the God of heaven; for his mercy endureth forever.

Then, lower and more solemnly, the reader sang the hymn of Sabbath praise, and the congregation joined in with fervor.

The soul of all living bless thy name, oh Lord, our God! And the spirit of all flesh shall continually glorify and extol thy memorial, oh our King! For from everlasting to everlasting thou art God, and besides thee we have no King, Redeemer, or Saviour! Thou art God of the first, and God of the last, the God of all creatures, the Lord of all generations; who is adored with all manner of praises; who governeth the world with tenderness, and his creatures with mercy. And the Lord slumbereth not and sleepeth not; he rouseth those who sleep, and awakeneth those who slumber; he causeth the dumb to speak; he looseneth those that are bound; he supporteth the fallen; and he raiseth up those who are bowed down. Although our mouths were filled with songs, as the fullness of the sea, and our tongues with hymns, as the multitude of its billows; and our lips with praise, like the wide extent of the firmament; and our eyes with brightness, like the sun and moon; and our hands extended, like the eagles of heaven; and our feet swift as the hinds; we should nevertheless be incapable of rendering sufficient thanks unto thee, oh Lord, our God, and the God of our fathers, or to bless thy name for one of the innumerable benefits which thou hast conferred on us and our ancestors. For thou, oh Lord, our God, didst redeem us from Egypt, and release us from the house of bondage; in time of famine thou didst feed us; and in plenty thou didst provide for us; from the sword thou didst deliver us; from the pestilence thou didst save us; and from sore and heavy diseases thou didst relieve us. Therefore the members of which thou hast formed us, the spirit and soul which thou hast breathed into our nostrils, and the tongue which thou hast placed in our mouth—behold, they shall thank, bless, praise, glorify, extol, reverence, sanctify, and ascribe sovereign power unto thy name, oh our King! For every mouth shall adore thee, and every tongue shall swear fealty unto thee; every knee shall bend unto thee; and every stature shall bow down before thee. Who is like unto thee? who is equal unto thee? who deliverest the poor from him that is too strong for him, the poor and needy from their oppressor? Oh, thou, the great, mighty, and tremendous God—the most high God—possessor of heaven and earth! We will praise thee, we will adore thee, we will glorify thee, and we will bless thy name; as it is said by David: "Bless the Lord, oh my soul! And all that is within me bless his holy name!"

Also in the congregation of the tens of thousands of thy people, the house of Israel, shall thy name, oh our King, be glorified throughout all generations; for such is the duty of every created being in thy presence, oh Lord, our God, and God of our fathers, to thank, praise, extol, glorify, exalt, ascribe glory, bless, magnify, and adore thee, even beyond all the songs and praises of thy servant David, the son of Jesse, thy anointed.

These praises read and chanted in the ancient Hebrew tongue, they contrasted strangely with the modern garbs, the shaven faces, the changed worship of Israel. And Almon Fairlie, dreaming of the past ages, stood in spirit in the consecrated temple, so lavishly decorated with gold and precious stones. Now, past were all the offerings, the sacrifices of that ancient people; the high priests divested of their dignity, the march of progress forbade the soulless offerings of beasts and birds, and conservative Israel still bound by formal rules and olden precept, amid their wandering lot, maintained the given law—upheld that most beautiful of all doctrines, that star of love and lustre burning brilliantly even amid the night of Judah's banishment—the unity of God!

Then from the worshipers around, from ark, and desk, and hymn of Sabbath joy, the stranger turned to the pale, pensive face above that so singularly attracted him. His upward glance met the young girl's wandering eye. She smiled faintly, for his look was not that of insolent admiration or rude curiosity; then her flowing curls concealed her face; she was bending again over her prayer book.

He sought Manasseh, that benevolent featured stranger, and when the services were closed, and Cosella descended from the gallery, she was met by both.

"My daughter, Rachel Cohen," said the father. Again another name, assumed she knew not why it was, because with necessary prudence Manasseh foresaw that it would not be well for him to call his child by her peculiar name in her native land; and then the English metropolis was not far from B—.

"My Christian friend, here, who will honor us with a call—Mr. Fairlie," he continued. Cosella bowed; the stranger looked long and earnestly into her face, sighed deeply, bent reverently before her, and she passed out of the house of worship leaning on her father's arm.

From that hour Almon Fairlie loved the Jewish girl; with his matured and world tried heart, with all the hoarded tenderness of his nature, with all the strength of his advanced manhood; it was to him the crowning effort of experience, the last sharp sorrow overcome; his spiritual self unfolded rapidly and he became a world's fit teacher. In after years, Cosella knew he loved her, and in her soul dwelt a sweet, tender, and sisterly love for him; but she never knew how he had loved her first; she never knew what agony the conflict cost him, nor how grand and victorious his soul became through her.

He called upon them often; he read much of Cosella's soul, and somewhat of her sufferings. He spoke to her of his new-found belief, of the proofs of spirit evidence, the beautiful demonstrations of the life to come. These conversations, lofty, mystical, and deeply religious, charmed the young girl. Oh, that she had confided to him all, that she had had time to make of him a still closer friend!

He told her of the maiden he had loved in early youth; the beautiful in soul and feature, the intellectual and the gifted Emma Ashton. How silently and uncomplainingly she yielded to the fatal disease that bore her to an early tomb. Cosella's tears fell fast as he told her of the maiden's dying words and peaceful transit to the other life.

"And you are so like her; so *very* like!" he said; "her voice, her gliding motions, the expression of the varying face, the same bright, yet tender eyes, of the same shade of color, but her hair was lighter, here were ripples of gold upon the chestnut curls. Let me call you friend for her dear sake." And Rachel, as he called her, acquiesced.

One morning, when her father was absent on business, and Almon Fairlie called, she came into the room holding a sealed package in her hand; her face was suffused with blushes, the voice with which she addressed her friend trembled with agitation, but the fine lips were curved with resolve; she was about to ask a favor of her friend.

"He would be happy to oblige her."

It was not the usual manner with which that conventional phrase is accompanied. She felt the tone's sincerity; tears started to her eyes. "I know that I can trust you," she faltered. "I need a friend and my heart tells me you will be one."

"For life and eternity," he replied, taking her hand; "confide in me, that package?"

"It is my journal; a diary of my uneventful life, interesting to one person only; here is a letter to go with it. Will you forward these—without the knowledge of my father?"

She saw his surprised look, she was grieved and silent.

"Will you not be candid, *sisterly*, with me, Rachel? May I not know your heart?"

"Yes!" she replied with a sudden impulse. "I would not do a clandestine thing, but you know not my father. You think me happy, beloved, and cared for by him; you know him not. It pains me to speak thus of him— my father—but it is truth. Do you doubt me, Almon Fairlie?" She addressed him thus familiarly, after a three months' intercourse, and he called her sister Rachel.

"Doubt *you*?" he said in a tone so strangely fervent it caused her to start. "No, no, I believe all you tell me, but it is new, surprising. Your father?—"

"When you come again, and he is absent, I will tell you all, and you will pity me. I cannot live this life much longer, and he who waits for that letter is—"

"Your affianced lover?" said low and tremulously Almon.

She bent her head in acknowledgment. She saw not the sharp spasm of pain that passed over his features, she beheld not his sudden paleness, she dreamed not of the conflict and the victory within the breast of the strong noble man before her.

"My sister," his voice had regained its calm; "give me the package; the heart of him who loves you shall be rejoiced with its tidings. I go at once to fulfill your wish; remember your promise, confide in me, your brother!" and so saying, he hastily left the room. Cosella turned her grateful glance to Heaven.

Several weeks passed, and Manasseh was ever present; the young girl could not find the opportunity she sought. But one day he was absent on urgent business, he might not return that night, he said. She dispatched a messenger to Almon Fairlie, and he promptly obeyed the summons.

"You may think me bold and undutiful," she said, with a slightly faltering voice, "but you will not blame when I tell you all, even of my father. Oh, friend! He is kind to me only in the presence of strangers. Because I revealed my heart to him in obedience to the dictates of truth, he curses and reviles me! See, brother Almon, the marks of his anger;" she held out her rounded arm, and pointed to a scar upon her neck. His face blanched with grief and terror.

"*Your father!*" he exclaimed. "Impossible! This man can have no feeling of parental love! But forgive this outbreak; go on, dear Rachel."

"He to whom I am plighted," she continued with modestly veiled eyes, and cheeks suffused, "he is not of our faith, and for this my father denounces me and swears to keep us parted. He knows not his name; he could not wring it from me by menace, cruelty, or violence; but Salvador has promised, and I know he will fulfill his sacredly given word—he will come for me, no matter where I am, when my eighteenth birthday is completed. And in this hope I live; else life were valueless, for it is embittered by discord, by contest and cruelty. I shall forsake my father's faith, but I shall gain a home, a true heart's love, and is not God the father of all?"

"Assuredly he is," replied Almon Fairlie. "But this young man—have you known him long, my sister?"

"Not many months." she said softly.

"And you feel that he is worthy of your love, your trust?"

She answered not in words; she raised her earnest, truthful gaze to his face; it was eloquent with love and faith. Almon stifled a rising sigh, and gave not utterance to the doubt and fear within.

"Let me tell you all while I have time, for I know not how soon my father may prepare for our departure; I feel impelled to tell you all, for I have never met with such a friend! Oh, Almon, brother! It grieves my heart, it pains my soul!—not even Salvador knows all I have endured—still suffer! The father I should love and revere, he is dishonest, mercenary; revenge and fanaticism occupy his soul! For gold he would sell me, his only child; he would have me seal my bondage and misery for this life to ensure him a luxuriant old age. Oh, brother Almon! The falsehoods and deceptions I have witnessed have embittered life and darkened my faith! My poor mother! The weight of wrong rested gloomily upon her gentle heart. For his sake she submitted to treachery, deception, falsehood. Oh! In what an atmosphere have I lived! And yet my soul worships truth and honor, and feels the glory of obedience to the right."

Truly a votary of the beautiful and the true! She stood with clasped hands and eyes enkindled before him; the strength of her spirit beaming gloriously from her illumined face.

"God bless, and shield, and save thee!" he uttered fervently, and his hand rested upon the young girl's head in benediction.

"I must hasten to tell you all before he returns," she continued, seating herself by his side and looking confidingly into his face. "I will tell you of my mother's sufferings, and my own, and you shall judge betwixt my father and me. You do not blame me for my apostasy to the faith of my fathers?" she questioned suddenly, an anxious shadow stealing over her animated countenance.

He took her hand and said:

"I would have rejoiced to have beheld you free from *all* creed shackles, but I see that it may not be; perhaps it is well. There are great ideas, lofty thoughts, slumbering energies in your soul that will, *must* awaken into life, expression, action. You do not at present comprehend my belief; your heart is filled with the external beauty of a new, false religion. Forgive me, Rachel," he said, as he saw her grieved look. "You know I would not offend you; forgive me if I utter an unpleasant truth. Some day you will awaken from this dream, which is of the imagination only, dear child! You will find sorrow, disenchantment in life; only in the soul can peace and heaven be found! You will find it; my spirit foretells that you will one day accept a faith that makes life beautiful, that banishes the fear of death, brings angels to our homes and hearts! But I listen; tell me all of your past life and sorrow. Where were you born, dear wanderer?"

"I have been told in England, not far from the Metropolis; my dear mother left a package of papers that I know not why she attached much importance to. I feel that a mystery concerning myself was connected with those papers; I believe they were in the dear departed one's handwriting. Before my eyes, in triumph and in mockery, my father cast them into the sea! Brother Almon, dear, true friend! I have had strange thoughts come upon me of late—listen;" she lowered her voice to a whisper; drawing close to him, she said: "I have dared to think, to dream, imagine, hope, *that he is not my father!*"

Almon Fairlie started with surprise! He seized her hand, looked long and intently into her face. She was trembling with the disclosure that had escaped her. In his brain, strange, wild, and thronging ideas chased each other rapidly; a vague indefinite hope and fear rose in his heart and took away the strong man's breath!

"There is no resemblance!" he murmured.

"I have heard strange words fall from my mother's lips," she continued; "but whether it was the truth she uttered, or the mere ravings of fever attending her last illness, I cannot say. She incoherently accused my father of a great wrong toward a Christian foe; of that Christian's injured spirit she piteously demanded forgiveness. Oh, Almon! Mine is a strange, wayward destiny. I say *my mother*—I fear that even she had not that claim upon me. She whispered of such strange and fearful things in her unquiet sleep! Yet, oh! I loved her dearly! And yet, and yet—there always seemed a gulf between our hearts. Of these things I have written to Salvador, and now I speak to you; but the papers are lost, and *he* will never tell me! Oh, that my dreams were true, that at least I were not *his* child!"

"Father of humanity! Father of spirits!" prayed Almon Fairlie, "give me light—oh, give me hope!"

Cosella was startled by the paleness of his face, the agitation of his manner.

"Tell me, sister, dearest—have you ever heard the name—but no, not yet!—have you ever borne another name? Is Cohen, your father's, *his* real surname?"

She was about to reply, to confess to him that her name was Cosella; that her mother's name had been Shina; that Manasseh Moshem was her father's name (for this she had heard in conversation between him and the departed).

"I will tell you all; trust you as I would my mother," she said. "My name is not Rachel, my father's name is not Cohen. Mine is—"

He held her hand, looked eagerly into her face, and trembled for the coming words, trembled with uncertainty, the overhanging glory of a near and priceless joy! There was a rolling of carriage wheels, a loud knocking at the portal. Cosella paled and the tears rushed to her eyes. Dread and coldness, the anguish of disappointment, fell on the spirit of Almon Fairlie!

"It is my father returned!" she whispered. "Another time I will tell you all."

Already his footsteps were heard upon the staircase. Cosella turned to the flowers by the window, and bent over them to conceal her emotion. Manasseh entered gleefully.

"Ah, friend Fairlie here? I am happy to see you, sir! Rachel, my love, I have returned much sooner than I expected. Come, kiss your tired old father."

The young girl advanced reluctantly and received the false embrace. Almon Fairlie's breast was heaving with indignation; he bowed, but did not take Manasseh's proffered hand.

The quick eye of the plotter saw that there was something wrong; the unusual coldness of his Christian friend, the restraint of his daughter, and anger rose within his heart.

When Almon had departed, he cast aside the conventional smile and the smooth manner, and addressed Cosella in the loud, harsh, imperious tones that had become familiar to her ear:

"What have you been telling the cursed infidel? Have you been wailing and repining before him, say? His manner is changed and distant; instantly tell me the reason, or—" the maledictions he evoked, the curses that fell from his lips shall not be recorded upon this page. Cosella remained silent, pale, seemingly unmoved.

"Will you speak?" he thundered. "Perhaps," and a gleam of malice shot athwart his face, "perhaps he is in love with you, and I interrupted his confession. Perhaps my exemplary daughter, having forgotten her Catholic lover, is willing to accept this free-thinker, this fanatic, this enthusiast! But before you shall wed a Christian—see, girl! I will destroy you, thus!" he broke into fragments her ivory fan, Teresa de Almiva's parting gift, and threw the broken pieces toward her.

Cosella smiled with bitterness and defiance:

"Almon Fairlie is my *friend and brother*," she at last said, and her cheeks glowed, her voice faltered with indignation. "You may spare him and me your jealous surmises. I was speaking of my mother, of my past life—"

"You dare to reveal the past to a stranger? Without my permission to speak of your travels, of *her*, God rest her soul! Have I not expressly forbidden you to mention the countries you have lived in? What have you told the Christian? I insist on knowing all."

"I cannot, and *I will not* repeat every word I said," replied the defiant and indignant girl.

With a savage cry he rushed toward her; his arm was uplifted to strike, but Cosella evaded the blow. With ashen face and flashing eyes, she cried to him:

"But once again touch me in anger, and by the Lord you impiously invoke, by the Father I believe in, I quit your roof forever! Though it be to beg my bread from house to house! Strike me if you dare! One blow, and I am no more *your* daughter!"

She gained the door, and fled weeping and despairing to her chamber.

The next day, when Almon Fairlie called, Manasseh was as studiously polite, as cordial as ever; but Cosella entered not the room. Her father said she was indisposed, and desired her friend to excuse her.

They conversed long and earnestly. When Mr. Fairlie left the house,

Manasseh, casting aside the mask of friendliness, self-control and indifference, rushed into Cosella's chamber with almost frantic mien, and storming, raving and cursing direfully, accused his child of treachery, deceit and faithlessness to him, her father and sole guardian.

In vain the poor girl wept and defended her motives, and sought from the infuriate man an explanation of his incoherent words. In vain she protested that she had not given any of their former names to Almon Fairlie—no clue to their past lives. He spoke wildly of imminent and pressing danger, of escape and vengeance. He threatened the innocent girl with death, if the pursuer overtook them.

Alarmed beyond measure, breathless with fear, deeming her strange father crazed, she listened, comprehending not, guessing not, alas, of the cause of his guilty terror, dreaming not of the possible nearness of relief and joy.

He left the house, locking the bewildered girl in her chamber. He was absent until late at night. Then, with savage triumph, he announced their departure on the morrow.

"Where, oh Heavenly Father, where are you going to drag me?" cried Cosella.

"I," he mockingly replied. "The ship will do the dragging; and you ought to be sincerely grateful to me for taking you out of London fogs, and snow covered streets, back to your beautiful tropic shores. Ah, I see you are pleased, Miss Rachel."

"Return to the tropics!" she cried, in joyful surprise. "Are you in earnest? Where—to what port?"

Hope, fear, trembling joy, impeded her further utterance.

"Back to Santa Lucia. There is a vessel ready to start early in the morning. It is not my choice to return there; but it is the first opportunity, and I have not a moment to lose. But I shall not remain there a week. I shall go to the island of C——, among our people."

"And I will remain," said Cosella, mentally. And she hastened to commence preparations for the hasty departure.

Next day at noon, when Almon Fairlie called, he was told that Mr. Cohen and his daughter had left for the country. Stunned and bewildered, that true friend cried in agony:

"Too late, too late! I shall never behold her again! Oh, Percival, the hope, the joy is past! Uncertainty and dread return. Oh, gentle, loving girl! Perhaps *his* child! Shall I ever look upon thy face again?" And he returned to his lodgings, weary and worn with grief.

13

The Teachings of the Fathers

Say not the law divine
Is hidden far from thee;
That heavenly law within may shine,
And there its brightness be.

—Psalms of Life

The stormy voyage over, the familiar shores of Santa Lucia have met Cosella's longing gaze, and the balmy zephyrs of that land of bloom and fragrance have caressed her brow as with a greeting sign. With loudly throbbing heart she stepped on shore, and overcome by the thronging memories of her first landing there, she wept afresh for the beloved one gone, the martyred one at rest from strife. As she turned to look upon the familiar scene, to be recognized by some lounging negroes upon the wharf, she saw, amid the figures strolling upon the beach, enjoying the sunset's calm and coolness, one form that sent the tide of joyful recognition to her face, suffusing it with a grateful blush. It was Salvador del Monte; but he was not alone. A lady, seemingly young and beautiful, leaned on his arm. Cosella could not distinctly see her face, but the white-robed form was pliant and graceful, the long black curls waved sportively around her face, and the lace veil, that becoming head covering of the women of that clime, fluttered upon the wind, caressed her cheek, and fell to her waist like a softening cloud. His head was bent toward her; their attitude was loving, confidential. A strange pang, a sudden terror, swept across Cosella's heart, a blinding mist of tears obscured her vision. For the first time, the demon of jealousy invaded that pure soul's sanctuary; the ever attendant phantoms of doubt and distrust flapped their black wings exultingly, as they passed the open portal, hitherto so guarded by love and hope. A burning blush overspread her face, and still the sharp fierce pain contracted her breast, as her father's voice harshly called her from the spot. She looked again. He was still fondly looking in the lady's face. Even from the distance, she felt that it was with looks of love he regarded her. How carefully and tenderly he readjusted the veil, so rudely dealt with by the evening winds! A deep, dry sob burst from Cosella's heart as she followed her chiding, impatient father.

They took rooms at a hotel for a few days, and then removed to a small and neatly furnished house that overlooked the sea; for Manasseh, forgetful of his vow not to remain over one week at Santa Lucia, became immersed in business cares and plottings. Associating much with his fellow Hebrews from the neighboring islands, he forgot to strictly watch Cosella, whose silent sufferings and paling cheeks he scarcely deigned to notice. He led her to her mother's grave; and when she threw herself, bitterly weeping, on the ground, and cried to God for help, he deemed it but a renewal of her grief caused by the memory of the departed. He knew not that she wept for blighted hopes, in all the anguish of a loving heart's disappointment.

Carmela, the shrewd and crafty woman, had again been taken into their service; but she too was changed. She evaded the young girl's inquiries concerning Salvador del Monte; and when, at her desire, she took to him a few hasty lines that were blotted with tears she returned, bringing no message, no token of acceptance or remembrance; nor could she assign a cause for this sudden change, this cruel and inexplicable silence.

Days, weeks, passed on. Cosella knew that Salvador was in the same town, and yet he came not, though her father was often absent, even for days. He sent no message; he had forgotten her!

The hitherto light-hearted girl, whose sunny temperament upheld her amid all the trials and changes of her wandering life, now bent beneath this last and heavy blow of destiny. She cared not to go abroad, and Manasseh, beholding her quiet and obedient, deemed her past dreams forgotten, and laid his plans accordingly. He was harsh and stern as usual, but he was abstracted also—often plunged in deep reverie. The girl was becoming a heavy burden upon his hands. He could not bend her to his will in all things—that he clearly foresaw. He could not make of her an accomplice in his dishonest, mercenary plans, as he had done of Shina. Ever in opposition, in bold defiance, she had arrayed herself against him, strong in her feebleness, triumphant in the knowledge of justice and truth. He feared her secretly, and formed wild, vague projects of deserting her—for she was not his child, and her soul had wandered from the faith he had hoped to bind her with forever. Her persistent opposition to his plans, her steady defence of honesty and just dealing, her denial of the sophistries he strove in religion's name to twine around her life—all this had rendered her hateful in his sight. He thought no more of the rebuking gleam of Lea's eye, so truly mirrored from Cosella's dark and flashing orbs. He thought no more of the noble spirit he once had loved; of the voice repeating its music from the daughter's tongue. Revenge had usurped the place of every fine emotion. He only saw the demon of defiant strength, as he termed it, bursting from her eyes, speaking in every gesture. Henceforth he dreamed of vengeance upon Cosella, the daughter of his Christian foe.

But he forgot that she was amid familiar scenes; that her mother's grave sanctified those tropic shores, and gave to them the home-charm elsewhere wanting. He knew not that the subtle spells of a new religion were wound around the girl's imaginative soul; that the music and splendor, the pageantry and the consolations of a poetic faith, had charmed and won the longing, loving, yearning heart; that Teresa de Almiva, permitted to visit her, was the wily temptress, leading her from the olden worship to the modern shrines, where—oh, terror to his bigot-soul!—Jesus of Nazareth was adorned with praises, his virgin mother received her suppliant's offerings of love and tears.

Ever gentle, loving as a mother, Teresa sought to lead that young and pliant spirit to what she deemed the haven of salvation. Her father enforced the precepts of the Mosaic law with threats and harshness; her friend spoke eloquently, sweetly soothing of the grace of Jesus, of the maternal love of Mary. Was it a wonder that the untried, seeking, crushed and wounded heart yielded to the potent spell?

And Manasseh dreamed not of the danger.

He sat one afternoon, reading from the Hebrew volume before him, the "Proverbs of the Fathers," then turning to the English translation and reading therefrom for the edification of Cosella, whose thoughts wandered far away from these ancient sages, with their utterances so strangely compounded of sublime truths and absurd superstitions.

"Can the teachings of these idolators, or the doctrines of Christianity anywhere, compete with the wisdom of our sages? Who is like unto Moses, the inspired law-giver, who performed miracles in the name of the God of Israel; who smote his enemies into the dust before him? Who, among their false prophets, is like unto Joshua, and the leaders of our tribes? Truly, *we* are God's chosen people, and shall yet be gathered together from the four quarters of the earth, to return to Zion, the holy city of our King! We shall yet hold dominion over the nations of the earth; our feet shall be upon their necks, and they shall yield us tribute. Father of Israel! God of Abraham, Isaac and Jacob!" continued the fanatic, with earnest appeal to heaven, wildly raising his clenched hands: "Speed, oh speed the day, when thy holy city shall be rebuilt, thy scattered children return to their rightful land, the dwelling place of her Kings and Princes! Listen, Cosella—how I hate that name! I would much rather call thee Rachel—listen, and gather wisdom from the sayings of the fathers; I will continue to read, so you may understand and learn."

Cosella replied not, but bowed her head in acquiescence, and Manasseh read with emphasis:

"All Israel are entitled to a portion of future happiness, as is said, And thy people shall be all righteous; forever shall they possess the land; the scion of my planting, the work of my hands, that I may be glorified.

"Moses received the law on Mount Sinai, and delivered it to Joshua, and Joshua to the elders; and the elders to the prophets, and the prophets to the men of the great synod. These said three things: Be careful in giving judgment; train up many disciples; and make a fence for the law.

"Simeon the Just was one of the last of the men of the great synod. He used to say: The world is sustained by virtue of three things, namely, the law, divine worship, and active benevolence.

"Antigonus of Socho received the tradition from Simeon the Just. He used to say: Be not like servants who serve their masters for the sake of receiving reward; but be like servants who serve their master without a view of receiving reward, and let the fear of heaven be upon you.

"Jose, the son of Joezer, of Zeredah, and Jose, the son of Joehanan, of Jerusalem, received the tradition from them.

"Jose, the son of Joezer, said: Let thy house be a house of assembly for the wise men; and cover thyself with the dust of their feet, and drink in their words with thirsty avidity."

"This," continued Manasseh, in explanation, "alludes to the custom of scholars sitting on lower benches than the teachers, who thus scattered, as it were, the dust which their sandal-shod feet had gathered in their walk to school, on the scholars.

"Jose, the son of Jochanan, said: Let thy house be wide open as a refuge; and let the poor be familiarly received in thy house; and do not hold too much converse with womankind; the wise men say, whoever converseth much with women, bringeth evil on himself, and thus neglects the study of the law, and at last will inherit hell.

"Joshua, the son of Perachiah, said: Procure thyself a master; and acquire thee an associate; and judge all mankind favorably.

"Shemaiah said: Love labor and hate dominion, and seek not to make thyself known to those in power.

"Abtalyon said: Ye sages, be cautious of your words; perhaps it might be that ye be doomed to captivity and be carried captive to a place of infected waters (a place where learning is rare and crime prevails); and the disciples who follow you might drink of them, and thus the name of God would be profaned.

"Hillel said: be of the disciples of Aaron, loving peace, and pursuing peace; loving mankind, and bringing them to the study of the law."

"There!" exclaimed Manasseh, exultingly; "this is wisdom, such as their Christian Scriptures cannot boast of. I will not read the entire chapters, but give you sentences here and there, from the blessed traditions, the sayings of our wise Rabbis of Israel."

"Reflect well on three things, and thou wilt not lapse into the power of sin: Know what is above thee; a seeing Eye, and a hearing Ear; and that all thy actions are written in a book.

"Hillel said: Separate not thyself from the congregation; nor have confidence in thyself until the day of thy death. Judge not thy neighbor until thou hast reached his situation; neither utter anything which is incomprehensible, in the hope that it afterwards may be comprehended. He also said: The rude man feareth not sin; the ignorant cannot be pious; the bashful cannot become learned, nor the impatient be a teacher.

"The same Rabbi also once saw a skull floating on the face of the water, and said to it: Because thou didst drown others, thou wast drowned! and at the end will those who drowned thee, also be drowned.

"He also used to say: He who increaseth his flesh, multiplieth food for worms; he who multiplieth riches, augmenteth care; he who multiplieth wines, increaseth superstition; but he who augmenteth his knowledge of the law, augmenteth life; he who attendeth much at schools, increaseth wisdom; he who increaseth in reflection, augmenteth prudence; he who exerciseth much charity, multiplieth peace; if one hath acquired a good name, he hath acquired it for himself; if one hath acquired a knowledge of the law, he hath obtained for himself immortal life in the future state.

"Rabbi Jochanan, the son of Zaccai, had five disciples; he used thus to designate their respective merits: Eleazer, the son of Hyrcanus, is like a well plastered cistern, which loseth not a drop; Joshua, the son of Chananya—happy is the mother who bore him; Jose, the priest is very pious; Simeon, the son of Nathaniel, feareth sin; and Elazar, the son of Arach, is an increasing spring.

"He once said to them, Go and consider which is the good path in which man is to maintain himself. Rabbi Eleazer answered, A good eye (contentment); Rabbi Joshua said, A worthy companion; Rabbi Jose said, A good neighbor; Rabbi Simeon said, One should foresee the probable consequences of an undertaking; Rabbi Elazar said, A good heart. He then said unto them, I prefer the sentiment of Elazar, the son of Arach, to yours, for in the scope of his words are yours included.

"They said three things; Rabbi Eleazer said, Let the honor of thy companion be as dear to thee as thy own; and be not easily moved to anger; and repent one day before thy death. When asked by his disciples how this could be strictly followed, as no one knows the day of his death, he answered, Then be ready every day, with penitence and good deeds, as though it were your last. Warm thyself by the fire of the wise; but be careful of their heat, that thou be not burnt; for their bite is as the bite of a fox, and their sting as the sting of a scorpion, and their hissing as the hissing of a poisonous serpent; and all their words are as coals of fire.

"Rabbi Joshua said: Discontent, unbridled passions and hatred of mankind, remove a man from the world.

"Rabbi Jose said: Let the property of thy companion be as dear to thee as thine own, and prepare thyself to study the law, for it cometh not to thee by inheritance; and let all thy actions spring from a reverence of God.

"Rabbi Simeon said: Be careful of reading the Shemang, and the ordained prayer; and when thou dost pray, look not on thy praying as a task, but let it be a sincere supplicating of mercy in the presence of the Supreme; as it is said, For he is gracious and merciful, long suffering, and of abundant kindness, and repenteth of the evil. And never regard thyself as an ungodly person in thy own mind.

"Rabbi Elazar said: Be diligent in the study of the law; and know how to reply to the unbeliever.

"Rabbi Jacob said: He who journeyeth on the road, meditating on the law, and interrupteth his study, and saith: how beautiful is this tree! Or, how handsome is this field! is considered by the Scriptures so guilty, as having by his sin forfeited his life.

"Rabbi Dossa, the son of Harkinas, said: Morning sleep, wine-drinking at noon, conversation with children, and spending one's time in the place of assembly of the ignorant, remove a man out of the world.

"Rabbi Elazar, the Mudai, said: He who profaneth holy things, despiseth the half festivals, putteth his neighbor to shame in public, breaketh the covenant of our father Abraham, and expoundeth the law contrary to its true sense, although he be well learned in the law, and possessed of good deeds, will yet have no share in the eternal life.

"Rabbi Akiba said: Tradition is a fence to the law; tithes are a fence to riches; vows are a fence to abstinence, and the fence to wisdom is silence. He used to say, man is beloved of God, because he was created in the image of God, but it is an additional love that he was informed that he was created in the image of God. Every thing that is done, is seen by Providence; though freedom of choice is given to man; the world is judged with goodness, though every thing is judged according to the multitude of deeds. Whatever man does is done on a strict accountability—he is at *liberty* to sin, but is always within the *meshes* of retribution.

"Rabbi Eleazar said: He who performeth but one precept even, obtaineth for himself an advocate: and he who committeth a single sin, procureth himself an accuser: repentance and good deeds are a shield against punishment. It is not caprice in God to reward or punish, but each act claims and obtains its recompense, and only amendment and repentance can avert the evil which we have merited.

"Rabbi Yanai said: We cannot account for the prosperity of the wicked, nor the sufferings of the righteous.

"Rabbi Jacob said: This world may be likened to an ante-chamber, in comparison with the future world—prepare thyself in the ante-chamber, that thou mayest enter the drawing room. One hour employed in repentance and good deeds in this world is better than the whole life in the future one; but one hour's tranquility of the spirit in the future world, is preferable to the entire life of this.

"Rabbi Simeon, the son of Elazar, said: Attempt not to pacify thy neighbor in the moment of his anger, and do not console him while his dead lieth before him; ask nothing of him in the moment when he maketh a vow, nor be desirous of seeing him in the time when he is humbled. Samuel, the younger, used to repeat the following verse: Rejoice not when thy enemy falleth, and let not thy heart be glad when he stumbleth, lest the Lord should see it, and it be evil in his sight, and he turned his wrath from him.

"Elisha, the son of Abuya, said: He who teacheth a child, is like the one who writeth on clean paper; but he who teacheth old persons, is like one who writeth on blotted paper.

"Rabbi Elazar Hakkappar said: Those who are born are destined to die, the dead to live, and they who are risen from the dead, to be judged—that we may learn, teach and understand that he is God, also the Former and Creator; that he also understandeth, is the judge, witness and suing party; and he will also judge us hereafter, blessed be he! for in his presence there is no unrighteousness, no forgetfulness, no respect of persons, and no acceptance of bribes. Know, also, that everything is done according to accountability; and let not thy evil passions persuade thee that the grave is a place of refuge for thee, for against thy will wast thou formed; and against thy will dost thou live; and against thy will must thou die; and against thy will must thou hereafter render an account, and receive judgment, in the presence of the supreme king of kings, the Holy One, blessed is he! With ten divine expressions of will was the world created; meaning that in the history of the creation we find ten times the expression, 'And God said,' which is the creative energy—no other power is required to effect the will of God. But could not God have created it with one expression? But this was done to punish the wicked, who destroy the world that was created with ten expressions, and to give a good reward to the righteous, who preserve the world which was created with ten expressions.

"There were ten generations from Adam to Noah, there were ten generations from Noah to Abraham, to make known unto us how greatly God is long suffering, as all those generations constantly provoked him, until Abraham appeared and received the reward of all. Our father Abraham was proved with ten trials; ten miracles were wrought for our ancestors in Egypt, and ten at the Red Sea. Ten plagues did the blessed God inflict on the Egyptians in Egypt, and ten at the Red Sea. Ten times did our ancestors tempt the blessed God in the wilderness. Ten miracles were wrought for our ancestors in the holy temple. Ten things were created on the eve of the Sabbath, in the twilight, and these are they: The mouth of the earth, the mouth of the well which accompanied the Israelites in the desert, the mouth of Bileam's she ass, the rainbow, the manna, the rod of Moses, the Shameer, the letters, the writing (on the tables), and the tables. And some say, also, the demons, and the grave of our legislator Moses, and the ram of our father Abraham.

"Seven sorts of punishment are inflicted on the world for seven important sins: When some people give tithes, and the others do not, a dearth from want of rain ensueth; but when the whole do not give tithes, a famine caused by tumult of war and want of rain ensueth. For not giving the priest's portion from the dough, a famine of destruction ensueth. Pestilence is inflicted on the world for the commission of sins declared punishable with death in the law. The sword is brought into the world on account of the denial of justice and the perversion thereof. Wild beasts come into the world on account of false swearing and the profanation of God's name. Migration is inflicted on the world on account of idolatry, bloodshed, and not allowing the land to rest in the Sabbatical year.

"There are four qualities perceivable in those who bestow charity. He who is willing to give, but doth not wish that others should give, is stingy with others' means; he who liketh to see others give, but will not give, is avaricious with his own means; he who is willing to give, and that others should also give, is pious; he who will not give, and liketh not that others should give, is wicked.

"He who possesseth the following three virtues is of the disciples of our father Abraham, and he who is possessed of the three opposite vices is of the disciples of Bilaam the wicked. A good eye (contentment), an humble spirit, and a modest soul, characterize the disciples of our father Abraham.

"At five years of age a child should be put to study the Bible; at ten to that of the Mishna; at thirteen he is to observe the precepts; at fifteen to study the Gemara; at eighteen he is fit to enter into wedlock; at twenty to pursue his avocations; at thirty he is arrived at full strength; at forty, at understanding; at fifty, to give counsel; at sixty he is accounted aged; at seventy he is called grey; at eighty he may be accounted to have attained a rare age; at ninety he is bending over the grave; at a hundred, as if he were already dead, and past from and useless to the world.

"And it is said: 'And the tables were the work of God, and the writing was the writing of God, graven (*Charuth*) upon the tables.' Read not (*Charuth*) graven, but (*Chayruth*) freedom; for none can be accounted as free but those who are engaged in the study of the law. Five possessions hath the holy, blessed One appropriated to himself in this world, and these are they: The Torah (law) is the first possession; heaven and earth are the second; Abraham is the third; Israel the fourth; and the holy temple is the fifth.

"Rabbi Chananya, the son of Akashya, saith that the holy, blessed One, being pleased to make Israel worthy of enjoying happiness, had enlarged the law with many precepts, as it is said: 'The Lord was pleased, for his own righteousness' sake, to magnify the law and make it honorable.'"

"The Señora Teresa de Almiva," announced Carmela at the open door; and, closing the sacred volume, Manasseh politely advanced to meet the lady. Cosella's eyes brightened with joy.

14

Temptation and Trial

Yet was there light around her brow,
A holiness in those dark eyes,
Which show'd, though wand'ring earthward now,
Her spirit's home was in the skies.

—Moore

Come to me, thoughts of heaven!
My fainting spirit bear
On your bright wings, by morning given,
Up to celestial air.
Come in my tempted hour,
Sweet thoughts! And yet again
O'er sinful wish and memory shower
Your soft, effacing rain.

—Mrs. Hemans

After a few polite inquiries concerning the Señora's health, Manasseh left the room; and Cosella, throwing aside all restraint, fell weeping on her friend's bosom. "*Querida, mi hija!*" (my beloved daughter) she fondly murmured, "tell me all! Some new grief weighs upon you; I see it in your altered countenance, your laggard step, your utter indifference to life, Cosella. Will you not confide in me, your second mother, your best, your truest friend?"

"I will, I will!" cried Cosella; "you shall know all, and advise me as a mother would a child. Oh, Señora Teresa! Oh, mother! Salvador del Monte—" She covered her face with both hands, and turned aside, sobbing convulsively.

A shadow of surprise and anxiety passed over the Señora's face. It was the first time since her return that Cosella had mentioned that name. She said, with somewhat of impatience in her tone, "Well, my child, tell me of him."

"You know, my friend," she sobbed, "that I have loved him, that still, for his sake, I would forsake my father's faith. On my mother's grave he vowed eternal love to me; yet, since my return, not a message, not one token of remembrance, not a flower, even, has he sent to me! How have I forfeited his affection? What have I done? Why is he thus alienated, and I left so desolate?"

"No, no—not desolate, not forsaken!" said Teresa de Almiva, folding the weeping girl to her bosom; "here beats a maternal heart for thee, willing to protect and cherish, to accept thee as a daughter for evermore! My husband, proud and stately as he seems, loves and esteems my Cosella; he will be a true father; my sons shall be thy brothers, our home thy resting place, dear, weary wanderer! The blessed Virgin's arms are opened to receive thee, the smiling Jesus beckons! Come to the church, my daughter! Forget this first, fleeting, romantic dream—forget Salvador del Monte!"

"*Forget him!*" cried Cosella. "Oh, Señora Teresa, have you never loved that you so coldly, so cruelly bid me forget?"

The still beautiful and graceful matron smiled a quiet and significant smile, and fondly stroked the young girl's brow.

"*You* have been fortunate from your birth," she continued wildly; "*you* have never felt the utter loneliness that has always been *my* portion. You have been blest with affection; how can *you* feel aught of want in a world so beautiful as yours? You can bid me forget the fondest hopes of my existence, bid me cast life and glory from me. Oh, my mother, if she were living, would not bid me forget!" And she turned aside and wrung her hands in the bitterness of her reproachful mood.

"You are unjust, dear girl—you wrong your truest friend! You comprehend me not, beloved! I, who with the holy Virgin's sanction am in the place of your mother now, I would not inflict the smallest grief upon your heart, my child! I have not spoken before, because I feared to grieve, to offend you. I know your pride and spirit; I know you have sorrow enough to bear, my patient one; but now I tell thee, speaking to thee as a mother does, he is unworthy of thy pure young love."

"Unworthy?" A faint color tinged Cosella's cheek—a great fear fluttered at her heart.

"Shall I speak, Cosella?" demanded the Señora in a low, faltering voice.

"Yes, speak, and tell me all, for I cannot live in this suspense; tell me what black waves rise between us, what wall of separation has been placed betwixt our hearts!" cried the tortured girl, with wildly appealing glance.

With pity and tenderness Teresa gazed upon her and sighed heavily; tears trembled in her eye as she replied: "My child, come, give me your hands; rest your poor, throbbing head upon my bosom! Cosella dearest, sorrow and disenchantment come to all with time. Salvador del Monte loves a young woman! Start not, Cosella—let me finish my painful task. I had hoped you would have heard this from other lips. Whether she is his wife or his mistress none can tell. No one knows her family. She is young, and still beautiful, and is the mother of two children. We cannot believe him wedded; for he has sought several of our wealthiest and loveliest maidens, and after the consent of their parents and guardians was obtained, he broke from his promises and returned to his first allegiance—to Inez Montardo—who, I have heard, is with him now in town. He usually keeps her secluded in a country house some twenty miles from here, so that few have seen her face. She receives few visitors, walks out only with him. It is a mystery, and its weight seems to prey even on Salvador himself. This I long knew, but dared not tell thee; it is a grievous task to me to tell this to my loving child!"

"It is the woman I beheld! She is Inez Montardo; and he vowed love to me! Oh, it is not true—there is some terrible mistake—it was not Salvador!" cried the pale and agitated girl.

"By the blessed Virgin of Mount Carmel, by my patron saint, it *is* true, my daughter—poor, crushed heart, it is the truth!"

"And you all allowed me to go, to return, to believe him! You left me to dream and hope so long! You told me not of this, that I might brand him a deceiver to his face! Oh, is this punishment for my forsaken faith? Am I indeed guilty, and justly decreed by God? I know not—I have none to advise and lead me! Is it a trial to crush my soul for some great wrong? Or is it but a passing dream that darkens life? For this have I crossed the sea, have I wept and hoped and prayed for—for this, this awakening?"

With eyes upraised to heaven, clasped hands, and hurried utterance, she paced the floor, the first great shadow of a wrong inflicted by the hand she trusted, falling densely on the future she had pictured so vividly bright and beautiful.

Teresa vainly sought to calm her, to reason her into quiet, to speak to her of hope and a better love to come. It was in vain. In tears and sobs, in wild appeals to heaven, in outcries and reproaches, her grief found vent; and the friendly voices of consolation were unheard amid the tempest of her soul. When Teresa at length left her, it was in an exhaustion of grief; and the zealous believer trusted that now that Salvador del Monte proved recreant to his love, the ministrations of sorrow would lead the wrung heart within the church's saving fold. She kissed her brow at parting, and fervently commended her to the Saviour's holy guardianship, to the blessed and sorrowing mother's care.

There was somewhat of calculation in Doña Teresa's heart while planning for Cosella's future. Her son Carlos loved the young girl, and had confided his hopes to his mother, who approved of his affection and smiled encouragement upon him. Once recovered from the stunning blow of Salvador's faithlessness, a convert to the church, her daughter by the church's sanction, she would in time learn to love the handsome and agreeable Carlos, and by a union with him rejoice his parents' hearts.

But Cosella would never learn to look upon Carlos de Almiva other than with a sister's eyes.

The young man called sometimes at the quiet house, with flowers that his mother sent, with inquiries concerning the health of father and daughter. Strange to say, Manasseh never expressed himself bitterly concerning these visits; he seemed to have laid aside his suspicions of the young man once so loudly maintained. Cosella, entirely unaware of the secret hopes entertained by her friend's son, whom she always called *hermano* (brother), gladly welcomed his coming, and when her father was at home acted as interpreter between them.

Teresa de Almiva called every day, and sought by every loving artifice to revive the drooping spirits, to cheer the fainting heart of the sorrowing girl. Eagerly, tenderly, she besought her to seek her home's protection, the sanction of holy church for removal from her harsh father's guardianship. Still Cosella wavered, and lingered, until the thronging, urging necessity impelled her on, and the timid, shrinking spirit acted for itself, took the first great step toward freedom and a better life.

One day young Carlos had delivered his mother's flower-message, and silent and embarrassed he sat opposite the pale abstracted Cosella, regarding her with respectful tenderness. His heart was troubled for the sorrow so legible upon her face; he longed yet dared not to seek her confidence.

He saw her start suddenly, color deeply, and tremble with sudden agitation; she waved her hand from the window; Carlos, rising hastily, beheld Salvador del Monte passing on the opposite side of the street. Her secret was revealed, and the shadow of a great disappointment fell on his young, proud, ambitious spirit. He heard her murmur, "He comes not!" and with a sudden impulse he seized her hand, kissed it sadly, and withdrew without a word.

Cosella still sat by the window, alternate hope and fear within her breast, for Salvador had bowed to her in passing. When Manasseh returned home, "Who has been here this afternoon?" he inquired.

"Carlos de Almiva," she replied.

"Cosella, I want to talk to you," continued her father. "I disapprove entirely of your reserved and distant manner to some persons. I esteem the Señora Teresa as much as my conscience permits me to esteem an unbeliever, and you, I have remarked, are shy and distant from her son, who I am inclined to believe looks on you with a favorable eye. Take my advice and follow my bidding, and it will be well for you; do not cavil, and seek argument with me, it is not your place; leave all responsibility to me, and act my will. Do you hear, Cosella?"

"I do, but cannot comprehend what you demand of me," she replied.

"Teresa de Almiva is wealthy; she loves you, you can exercise much influence upon her. Exercise it in behalf of your struggling, weary father. Be pleasant, and smile upon her son, and so reach the mother's heart that she may acquiesce in our plans."

The twilight shadows veiled Cosella's proud and scornful face; only her white dress fluttered in the cooling breeze, her hands moved nervously about.

"What is your plan?" she asked in a calm, cold determined voice.

"Cosella!" he replied eagerly, "I am engaged in a speculation that may make my fortune, but I need capital, I have not sufficient means. It is no sin to take from these unbelievers, we shall not impoverish them, for they have riches. Listen to this Carlos who I think loves you, smile upon him, fondle his mother, and obtain from her the sum I need; I will never, never, ask this favor of you again, Cosella, but a fortune is to be won, girl! A few unmeaning words can obtain it."

She rose and stood before him. "Would you sanction my love for a Christian?"

"Holy father Abraham! No, girl. Why ask me such a question? I mean that you shall only feign an affection—I would curse you forever if you dared to make it real!"

"So for mercenary purposes, you would have me lie, and simulate the holiest feelings in our nature? You would make of me a vile and base deceiver, a lure, a thing of seeming, a false, degraded being, daring all things evil for the love of gold!" her voice was loud and shrill with the intensity of its indignation.

"By our blessed law-giver, girl! Not so loud! Dare you think yourself possessed of more honor than your father, your guardian, who is responsible for every act? As yet, you are in my power; do my bidding, or, as I live, I will so embitter your life that you will be glad to obtain peace and rest by means which I dictate! Did *she*, the departed, ever oppose my will?"

"You plunged one of the purest souls into error and degradation; you steeped her pure heart in all the blackness of remorse! Do not—dare not invoke the memory of my mother! If ever angels surrounded you, it was because she invoked them by her patient smiles!"

"Girl, this is enough! You tongue's free license must be limited. Silence!" he thundered; "never speak of *her* as a martyr and a saint! She was my tool, my slave, as you shall be, by heaven!"

"No! By the God of truth and justice—*never!* You broke her heart, mine you shall not wither by the blight of sin. I will not pander to your greed of gain! I will not feign affection or friendship, to forward one mercenary design of yours! I will not steep my soul in falsehood! Never, hear you, for your sake, will I step out of the path of right."

He rushed upon her in the gathering darkness; his heavy hand descended on her shoulders thrice; she was about to scream for help when a loud knock at the door was heard. With an oath, Manasseh released her; with clenched hands and loudly throbbing heart, from which at that moment every gentle vestige, every better feeling was swept away, Cosella rushed to her chamber, crying wildly as she sped past him—

"You are no longer my father! I scorn and despise you, and you touch me again at your peril!"

He stood for a moment overwhelmed with astonishment; then seizing his hat he left the house, in his blinded fury seeing not, caring not, who was the visitor admitted to his daughter's presence.

It was Salvador del Monte! Tremblingly, Cosella returned to meet him; she had arranged her hair, bathed her tearful eyes, and readjusted her disordered dress. There was a tempest within her soul, daring resolves, and half-formed, vague and recurring wishes; wishes that bordered upon the unknown confines of sin were nestling to her heart! She raised her eyes; the face of Salvador was sad, yet tenderness was beaming from it, and the smile of joyous welcome sat on his lips. Carmela had placed the lamp of cocoanut oil with its encircling wreath of evergreens upon the table; the Hebrew volume lay closed beside it.

"Welcome to Santa Lucia, Cosella!" were the first words Salvador addressed to her; they swept away the mountain load of doubt and fear, the wild despair so long an inmate of her heart.

"Am I welcome, welcome to you, Salvador?" she falteringly demanded, and her hand was extended in greeting.

"Ever welcome! Ever dear and welcome!" he replied, as he took the extended hand within his own, and held it long.

"Why have you not called before?" she ventured to inquire. She saw a shadow sweep athwart his face.

"Listen to me, Cosella," he replied; "I come to your presence in fulfillment of a duty. I owe you an explanation for my seeming neglect; it was for love, for tenderness, for respect for you, Cosella, that I came not, that I answered not your letter from Europe, your messages to me since your arrival. I must speak to you tonight, even if your father returns. I must claim and obtain this interview. Cosella, I dreamed, I hoped, you would forget me!"

She looked him in the face, without a word. He saw that it had paled, that its outlines were sharpened by grief and blight; he sighed for pity, with conflicting feelings.

"I know that you suffer much; that you deserve a happier lot," he continued. "From the pages of your journal I have read your heart and sufferings; willingly, gladly would I lead you forth into a life of love and peace—but Cosella, *I may not!*"

He saw her blanch with terror, turn faint with suddenly departing hope. In his strangely vacillating nature, the slumbering tenderness awoke again; his voice was soft and melodious, as he entreated her to forgive!

"Yet you promised to love me, upon my mother's grave; you vowed that I alone should be the one near and dearest to you! Do you remember, Salvador?" How mournful sounded the reproachful accents!

"I did," he falteringly replied: "and I do love thee, Cosella; but I can never wed thee or any other woman!"

She started from beside him; no sound escaped her quivering lips; only her mute, reproachful, and beseeching gaze, riveted upon his countenance, told of the deep agony within. He had been less than human had he not pitied her.

"I would not have led thee on to love me, Cosella," he said, in faltering tones; "but I knew your lone heart pined for sympathy. I thought you loved me first."

"*I!*" surprise, indignation, unconscious maiden pride spoke in that quickly uttered little word.

"Carmela told me so," he continued: "and for the love of one so good, I would not prove ungrateful. Cosella, a vow that oft has galled my spirit chains me to another; I cannot, dare not forsake her. It is not love that binds me now, and yet I cannot give thee, I honor, thy fitting place. We must not meet again; or if, indeed, thy love for me be strong, we need not part. Choose for thyself. I will lead thee hence, and thou shalt be all to me—my life be dedicated to thy happiness."

She had aroused from the first shock of bewilderment, and though her lips were bloodless, and a shudder thrilled her frame, she said, in a firm voice that faltered not at all: "Are you wedded to this—is Inez Montardo your wife?"

"Who told you her name?" he cried; "no, Cosella, I am not married; and yet a vow I dare not break binds me to her forever. I cannot tell you how all this came about; it was my youth and inexperience, her grace and beauty that enslaved me. I know, now, that she is not my soul's ideal. I know one who would respond to all my highest, noblest aims, my loftiest ambition; one whose mind is a repository for the beautiful, whose heart is the throne of poetry and music, an embodiment of the spiritual and the pure! I would love this child of nature; worship this poetess; breathe with her the airs of dreamland; bend in homage, not alone to outward loveliness, but lowly bend to mind and spirit-beauty. Pity and condemn me not—for, Cosella, *I dare not!*"

She understood him well. Anew the blissful security of yore stole to her fluttering heart, and stilled awhile its pain. Again the music breath of words, profaned, alas! too often by worldly usage, stole to her listening ear. With the sighing of regret, the humbled tone of sorrow, she heard the blessed words, "I love thee!"

A vision spread before her of the secluded, flower-environed home of love; the skies above it were radiant with golden light, and roseate with the reflections of soul; the air was full of melody, the flowers there glistened in the diamond dews, the gemmed leaves danced exulting to the music-freighted wind's request; the ocean sang its hymn of perpetual joy. The voices of the clamoring world reached not that peaceful spot; the blissful solitude was untrodden save by the presence of the one beloved, the lingering foot-steps of the angels. From tree, and fount, and ocean, leaf and flower, sky and sun-gleam, the sweetly tempting voices called: "Come from the world, the strife, the unending conflict! Come to the home of peace and love!"

She stood like one entranced; and he read well the passing emotions of her soul. Athwart the melodious waves, wafting her spirit to forgetfulness, came the voice, the words so dear: "I love thee, Cosella; wilt thou not abide with love and me? What is the world, its forms and usages, to thee?"

The world! What had it done for her? Solitude had enriched her mind and heart; abroad the perversions, the intolerance, the grossness of her fellows, repelled the loving, generous, aspiring spirit. The world's condemnation —though young and untaught, she knew that it rested on the purest motive and the most exalted action; that often its crown of bays decked mercenary brows; its judicial ermine, and its robes of honor, were bestowed on plotting, worldly tricksters; that the gorgeously woven veil of fashion and conventionalism concealed the monstrous vices, the hideously repellant sins and mockeries of society. Intuitionally, the innocent girl knew this; and love, to her, was sacred, lasting—it dreamed not of earthly desecration, or of sin against its innate holiness.

And yet he who would have tempted that pure young soul to error was not wholly evil in his vacillating nature; but his spirit had not grown to the heights of sacrifice, to the glory of renunciation. Long had he struggled with the purely material bond that fettered him to Inez Montardo; his spirit had gone forth in search of a purer, higher affection—had sought the embodiment of what his loftier faculties, his spiritual nature, craved for in woman; and ever the yet clinging earthly attraction, the mistaken sense of honor, had led him back into the bondage that dragged his spirit down—twined around its upsoaring wishes, the chains of sense that left that spirit powerless for good.

He told her that he loved her, now that he knew and appreciated her mind and heart; he drew a glowing picture of the future, all imbued with the diviner light of heaven; no grosser flattery, no word that could have aroused her pure soul's indignation did he utter. With fervid eloquence, with respectful tenderness, he besought her to become his saving guiding angel. And she?

Oh, blame her not, if hope awhile
Dawned in her soul, and threw her smile
O'er hours to come!

And that, beholding only hope, and love, and freedom, she forgot awhile the fearful cost at which these precious boons alone could be purchased.

She was alone, unaided by outward strength, walled in by no home sanctities, guarded by no warning tones of love. Already the words of assent trembled on her lips; beneath the wondrous spell her yielding heart sent the rich love tide to her face, illumining its paleness with a fervid joy. She advanced to Salvador, she was about to place her hand in his, when a low, vague sound—a note of memory, struck by the passing angel of the hour—vibrated to Cosella's soul. The spirit aroused from the unholy enchantment; the fearful wrong stood fully revealed before her—no more a rose-crowned angel, but a looming horror and a fearful doom!

A sound, as if a spirit's wing
Had struck a chord from out the string,
Passed dimly through the hushed saloon,
And died away beneath the moon.

Clear, silvery, thrilling, with intense solemnity the words of the dying Shina re-echoed through the silent room, heard only by the startled soul: "*Be ever pure and true!*" There was no dread of the world's conventional scorn; no fear of human interdiction came to overcast the soul's desire for freedom with a clogging pall; it was the spirit's injunction, the mandate of the divine, the warning utterance of the inner consciousness that aroused her from that dangerous dream; it was the spirit-mother's hand that broke the fascinating web; it was the aiding angel-band that strengthened the young girl's fainting heart in this her tempted hour!

She knew not that guardian angels hovered near; that the air was musical with the songs of their encouragement. She felt them not stroking her throbbing brow, inspiring her heart with the love of the right. But the extended hand was quickly withdrawn; the crimson flush died out from her face; the pain and the suffering returned to her breast; but with it mingled firm resolve, unshaken determination. Salvador saw and felt the sudden change. Her voice startled him, it was so unnaturally firm, so strangely it vibrated to his soul!

"Go!" she said, and there was sorrow but not anger in the tones; "come not again into my presence; return to Inez Montardo; I will not become as she is. If you cannot break unholy bounds, you cannot keep the holiest vow. I forgive you, Salvador; but come not here again. Never will I look on your face again. Yet one word more: I never sought your love; you sent me daily gifts of flowers; Carmela said they were the offerings of your love. Deem me not so devoid of pride and feeling as to seek affection unbestowed. Henceforth there is one sanctuary only for my affections—it is in Heaven!"

He would have detained her, he would have poured forth his soul in penitence for the pain inflicted, he would have told her of Carmela's treachery, but she glided from the room; he heard her swiftly retreating footsteps along the passage. With sorrow, shame, remorse in his bosom, he fled from the house, nearly overturning Carmela at the door. To his muttered malediction upon her for her falsehood, she replied with a mocking and exultant laugh that rang in his ears like fiendish glee.

When Manasseh returned home he found Cosella in her chamber, lying on a lounge, her dark curls veiling her face, immovable and apparently sleeping. He called her several times, and receiving no answer muttered that "The girl slept like a stone," and left her, as he deemed, to repose and silence.

The morning sun shone on the colorless face, the pain stamped brow; the wrung heart cowered from the light of day, and longed for the darkness even of eternal night! Undisciplined human affections, undeveloped faculties, unappreciated powers—strengthened, subdued, and spiritualized by suffering, ye were preparing for the future's might and glory!

15

The Virgin's Shrine

In the deep hour of dreams,
Through the dark woods, and past the moaning sea,
And by the starlight gleams,
Mother of sorrows, lo, I come to thee!
The troubled joy of life,
Love's lightening happiness, my soul hath known,
And, worn with feverish strife,
Would fold its wings—take back, take back thine own.
                                            —Hemans

On the brow of a sloping hill, amid a dense grove of cedars, beneath a rude canopy of stone, stands the weather beaten, yet romantic shrine of the "Virgin of Solitude"; and her image, attired in sable robes, a crown of sun-rays on her head, is decked with the daily flower-offerings of her votaries. The face is sweetly pensive; a mighty inspiration of love and grief gave to the artist's soul the power to form that image of sorrowful beauty. The fierce tropical storms often rend her robes, and tear the diadem from the placid brow; the tear drops of the storm cling to her trailing vestments, and glisten with a living semblance on the marble cheek. Her maiden votaries renew the faded robes, and replace with love and reverence the fallen crown. The fondly superstitious believe that she performs many miracles, and the loving and sorrowing repair to her shrine to implore her motherly intercession for the object of their affections. The flower-wealth of the surrounding gardens appears to be lavished on the place; the air is redolent of fragrance; the streamlet, leaping over its pebbly bed, bears flowery trophies to awaiting ocean; garlands and chains of choicest blossoms hang from the stony archway; the Virgin's robe sweeps showers of lilies to the ground; the feet press on a carpeting of roses. The sunlight falls, quivering and subdued, athwart a mass of foliage, tropical and luxuriant; the stars of heaven gleam magically brilliant on the wavelet's course; the moon illumines with resistless charm the upturned pensive face, the small and delicately sculptured hands of Mary that, imbued with life-like fervency, seem raised to heaven in mute appeal. Some cunning device of art has colored and illumined the upturned eye that ever seems swimming in a mist of tears.

And there Cosella, the Jewish maiden, often kneels in prayer, at morn and eve; escaping her father's vigilance, and the gloom of unshared thoughts. Thither, with Teresa de Almiva, she wends her way and weeps her tears upon the flowery sod. Thither, when the curtain of night enfolds the slumbering shore, she sits and dreams, and thinks the mysterious voices of the grove and sea give answer to her wordless prayer.

One early morn—stars yet twinkled faintly in the roseate mist of dawn—Cosella came to the sweet shrine alone, a fragrant offering of pure white lilies in her hand. She started with surprise, with wonderment and admiration as she neared the spot; for kneeling there, she saw the Virgin's living counterpart, a lady clad in mourning robes, whose pale and beautiful countenance was uplifted in enwrapt devotion, whose dark eyes swam in tears, while the sweet lips moved in supplication.

The young girl gazed upon her as if she were some vision of spiritual beauty thus suddenly embodied before her in that silent and poetic spot. The golden hair that lay in massive braids upon her cheek, the delicately molded hands, the wondrous eyes, the girlish figure, the thought-matured and intellectual brow, the indescribable charm of her face and attitude—all bound Cosella with a power as of enchantment, speechless, admiring, thrilled and wondering to the spot. Where had she seen that face, so strangely beautiful? Never to her waking sight had those Madonna eyes been turned; yet somewhere surely, mayhap in the land of dreams, their soulful glances had rested upon her, even as now they rested on the Virgin Mother's face.

The lady turned and saw Cosella standing there with folded hands; a flush of vague recollection stole to her cheek, far back into the linked past her star-gaze wandered; that dark haired, pale and pensive girl—where had they met before? She could not solve the problem—unknown, yet strangely near to her; unseen until that hour, and yet so familiar in every lineament—surely they had met in dreams if not in actual life.

"This is a sweet spot for prayer and contemplation, señora."

The stranger started, and the rose-flush dyed her very brow. What was there in the plaintive melody of young Cosella's voice that so strangely, wildly stirred her heart?

"A fitting place of prayer, indeed," she replied, but her sweet voice faltered with its strange emotions, and to Cosella's troubled soul came soothingly the love tones of that voice.

She looked into the lady's face; so much of holiness and peace was there, of strength and purity, of faith and resignation, the sorrowing one bent her heart in homage to its spiritual power. She said low and eagerly:

"You are a stranger here, señora; I never met with you before."

But to Solita's listening soul there came the unuttered thought, "You are a friend, long, long foreshadowed in my heart's best dreams."

"I lived in Santa Marea," replied the lady.

"I know thee and I love thee," fervently responded spirit unto spirit.

"Will you sit down beside me?" said Solita, motioning to the flowery seat at the foot of the rude shrine.

She smiled assent, and placed in her hand the lily offering destined to the Virgin. Her hand lingered long in Solita's clasp; a sweet, soothing influence was upon her, as if near and living, the face of Shina beamed upon her, and the peace of by-gone days returned. As if pitying angels had led her to the sanctuary of one true human heart, forgetting present woe and future dread, she sat like one entranced in paradisean vision, blessed and favored by that one glimpse of Heaven athwart the darkness of her lot. Alas! That ruthless hands should tear her thence, that the inexorable fiat yet went forth: "On—on through life and trial; thou art not ransomed yet!"

And yet, oh blinded human foresight! Oh doubting human heart! The ruthless hands obeyed the angel's mandates, to themselves unknown; the decree of trial was the trumpet tone of Divinest love, revealed in suffering.

"You are in mourning, lady?" said Cosella softly, gazing tenderly into the face so sweet and calm.

"I have worn this garb for several years; not that I mourn my friends or relatives, but because I like it. My parents dwelt with God long since. I am alone on earth."

The mournful melody, the lofty resignation of those words!

"And I wear mourning for my mother," faltered Cosella, and the quick tears started to her eyes and fell upon Solita's hand.

She said no word of consolation, and made no protestations of relief or friendship, but silently, lovingly she kissed the mourner's brow, and folded to her beating heart the sorrow-bowed young head.

The long repressed emotion of Cosella gave way beneath these silent demonstrations of truth and love. The crushed spirit revived beneath the salutary showers of awakened feeling; she sobbed upon the stranger's breast, and with tears and kisses she asked her name.

"Solita Mendez," replied the embodied Purity and Grace. "You are not a native of our land," she continued, twining around her slender fingers the dark brown curls of her weeping companion. "Your accent is English, though in complexion and manner you are like the children of the sun. I speak English, too, my friend."

She said "my friend," in the grateful mother tongue, and Cosella, now able to converse more freely, joyfully clasped her arms around the new-found friend, and cried:

"You speak my native language?"

"I do; and you speak ours well—only your accent betrays you somewhat.

Now I will tell you my history, then demand in just return the narration of yours." A sweet smile accompanied her words.

The glorious sun had risen, and the sea was aglow with crimson light. Scattered diamonds, life imbued, seemed dancing on its scarcely rippled surface. Full, grand, and free, varied and harmoniously blended, arose from thicket, grove and forest, the matin song of birds. The sky's blue canopy was spread, and fleecy, golden edged clouds peered from its depths, like sunny-locked cherub heads, heaven's infant world of beauty, keeping watch over awakened earth. The fishing boats sped swiftly across the tranquil waters, and the flagging sails of ships drooped indolently. The leaves and flowers whispered low unto each other, and the tall grass swayed in greeting fragrance to the morn. The Virgin's shrine had not yet been decorated, but at her feet lay scattered the flowery tokens of the arch above; and a garland of white roses, blushing pomegranate blossoms and dark green myrtle leaves was also there. It was the votive offering of Solita to her patron Lady.

They sat together, hand in hand, telling each other of their lives and aspirations, of their hopes and dreams. Solita's story was soon told; and Cosella related, with many tears that hemmed her utterance, of her joyless and solitary life, of her mother's death, of her utter loneliness and desolation in a foreign land.

"You have a father still left to you; rejoice in the possession of that one sweet earthy tie," said Solita, with upraised glance to heaven.

She saw not the added pallor that overspread the young girl's face; she saw not that her lips were about to unclose in a harrowing revelation; but, rising from her seat, she said:

"Come, if you can, tomorrow, at the same hour. This is a holy meeting place for friends. But today, if you have leisure, and desire to see me, call at the first house on the hill in the *Calle del Monte*; you will find me at home. Or, my friend, I will call upon you."

Embarrassment and confusion held Cosella speechless. The *Calle del Monte*! It had been named so by the father of Salvador, the proud hidalgo, who once held it as his own. How the name recalled the poignant memories that would not slumber! She dared not invite Solita to her home, for the irritability, ill humor, and suspicions of Manasseh had increased tenfold of late.

"My friend," she said at last, after a painful and protracted silence during which Solita had anxiously and tenderly scanned her blushing, troubled face, "I must be frank with you. I dare not invite a stranger—not even you whom I love—without my father's previous consent. He is strange, moody, irritable. I dare not thwart him, señora."

"You are not happy at home, dear child," impulsively exclaimed the sympathizing friend. "But call me Solita—call me so forever. I am many years older, but I would be your sister."

Again Cosella folded her arms around her, pressed grateful kisses on the placid brow, the golden hair, the lily-hued delicate hands.

"You have not yet told me your name," whispered Solita.

A sudden resolve, an impulse swift and prompting, to tell this angel all, uprose in her heart. She would not betray Manasseh; and her strange English name, so metamorphosed by its Spanish substitute, would be safe in that honorable breast.

"I have a story to tell you," she began, with faltering voice and downcast eyes. "You will not think it strange? You will not misjudge me?"

Solita's calm and steady gaze assured her of her earnest sympathy.

"I have a friend in this town," she continued, "one who has been as a second mother to me. But what I am about to tell you, I have not confided even to her. My name—"

"Ella! Ella! Are you up there? Call out, if you are, immediately. Who ever heard of such a freak as getting up before daylight to run into the woods? Ella—I say, Ella, are you there?"

It was Manasseh's loud and angry voice. Cosella trembled and turned pale. She gasped for breath, then called out, hastily:

"I am coming, father—coming directly."

"It is my father," she continued, breathlessly. "I will be here to-morrow, though he seek to prevent me. I promise. I *must* see you again. I have much to tell you. Love me, pray for me. Farewell, dear sister!"

A parting, hurried embrace, a lingering pressure of the hand, and Cosella darted down the sloping hill, and, flushed, excited, defiant, she scarce knew wherefore, she reached her father's side. Solita, taking another path, regained her awaiting attendant. Had she met Manasseh then, she would have read all of Cosella's hidden suffering; she would, with her soul's clear intuition, have read the treacherous designs, the false soul and assumed position of her friend's reputed father. Passing slowly down the mountain slope, gazing with admiring eye and prayerful spirit upon the vast and gorgeous scene, she said, in low and fervent tones, as if it were in invocation of a blessing: "Shall we ever meet again? Oh, grant, Most Merciful, that I may meet once more with Percival." And to the sea, the wind, the whispering flowers, she told the name, still guarded, loved and cherished, of Percival Wayne.

"What on earth or in heaven were you doing up there?" rudely demanded Manasseh, as Cosella approached.

"I met a lady, and we enjoyed some pleasant conversation, or I should have been home before this," replied the young girl.

"Met a lady? Who is she—any one you know? How dare you leave home without my permission? Wandering away so far, too. I forbid you ever doing so again."

The angry retort rose to Cosella's lips; the remembrance of Solita restrained its utterance. She replied to her father's questions that the lady was a stranger, very beautiful, refined, and engaging in her manners.

"Was she richly dressed? Had she any diamonds on? What is her name?" he eagerly inquired.

The daughter's lip curled with scorn as she replied to his questions, that it was not likely the lady would display her wealth at early dawn; but her dress and manner betokened ease and elegance; she was a lady in the highest, noblest sense of the term.

"What took her up there?" he demanded.

"Probably the desire to pray to the Virgin of Solitude," said Cosella.

"The Virgin of—*what*?" cried Manasseh fiercely. "Is one of their accursed images up there? And you, a Jewish maiden, dare to go near that unholy place? that gathering of abominations! *You* go to look upon the stone and wooden images forbidden by our laws! *You* gaze upon the face of Mary, the mother of the impostor Jesus! *You*, a descendant of the house of David! From this day forth you shall be watched, apostate girl! Think you that your holy ancestors can rest even in their consecrated graves beholding your wickedness?"

He would have beaten her in his fury had they been at home; as it was, he feared some loiterer upon the road might see him; but he tightly grasped her arm and bade her move quickly. Outwardly composed and stoical, she made no reply, but defiance and resolve surged mightily within.

"To-morrow, to-morrow," she thought; "and if Solita be true, as I would stake my life she is, all this shall change."

Manasseh led her hurriedly along the streets, smoothing his brow and composing his angry voice as they neared their habitation.

"Go in now, my child; you must be fatigued with your long walk," he said, as a group of neighbors passed.

But when he confronted his child in the silence of her own chamber, when no earthly witnesses were by, he poured upon her such a torrent of invective and abuse, the tortured girl closed her ears against his voice's sound; but when infuriate and blinded with his bigoted seeming of holy horror, he approached to strike, Cosella looking him full in the face, with one of those glances that often made him quail, said loud and fearlessly, with folded arms and unblanching cheek:

"Strike if you will, but rue it! The moment you touch me in anger, I seek for refuge in a neighbor's house, and I accuse you before the tribunals of the land!"

Then the moral coward shrank before the resolute girl, and muttering direst imprecations upon her, he fled from the room to still the tempest of his wrath by a timely perusal of the "wise sayings of the Fathers."

Cosella murmured hopefully and longingly: "To-morrow! Oh, to-morrow!"

Next day, long before sunrise, Solita Mendez, anxious and expectant, awaited the young girl, whose face had beamed upon her so appealingly lovely, so pensively familiar. The sun dispersed the lingering stars, the bird choir sang their matin hymn of rejoicing, the forests waved their salutation to the sea, and yet she came not. Higher and higher rose the brilliant orb of life, until its fervid beams played 'mid the thicket freshness of the Virgin's cool retreat; and on the path beneath, the sands grew burning, and the pebbles shot forth vivid, jeweled flashes of light and heat. With a sigh of disappointment, with a heavy heart, Solita retraced her steps.

For three mornings she waited, with anxiously expectant hope, beside the Virgin's shrine, for the young girl's returning footsteps. In vain; she came not. In tears Solita watched and longed for her. In vain she made inquiries; she could not be found by her description, and Solita knew not her name. There were many foreign residents in the place, several young motherless girls living with their fathers.

But she determined to seek for herself; the quiet and retired family she was visiting could give no clue; she would go out and inquire, and she felt the effort would not be made in vain. By her heart's strong affection she would find her friend. But when the fourth day came, a letter from the trusty attendant left in charge of her house in Santa Marea was handed to her by the host. It told of the arrival of a stranger, who ill with fever and delirious, at his urgent and repeated entreaties had been removed from his quarters at the Hotel to Villa Paz, Solita's rural home.

"I had your orders, my lady," wrote the faithful Francisca, "that I was to do all the good I could in your absence; I know your tender-heartedness toward the poor and strangers, and when repeated messages were sent that this poor foreigner called out incessantly your name and desired your presence, I deemed it my duty to you and my own conscience to fulfill his desire. Last night he was brought hither, pale, feeble and delirious; but our good doctor says he will recover with careful nursing; he is a handsome man, and his linen and his wild sayings even betray the gentleman. The doctor says the fever was brought on by over-exertion of mind, and that your presence may do him much good. He calls two other names, one a strange outlandish one I cannot remember; the other is Lea; that was his wife. The doctor says he is a gentleman of talent and fortune, and his name is Percival Wayne."

"Merciful Providence! my prayer is heard!" cried Solita, and, with a wild outburst of mingled joy and sorrow she fell upon her knees and kissed the letter.

"He will not die! I know, I feel it! He will be restored to life, to usefulness, and I—I shall behold his face again, hear once more that voice so dear!"

All thoughts of finding the young girl were abandoned. Alas! If she had known how near and dear to his heart was that lost one, she would have lingered even then.

At sundown, a sloop for Santa Marea bore the hopeful, sorrowing, expectant and grateful Solita to her native town.

Meanwhile Manasseh, soured by disappointment in his business speculations, vented the fullness of his wrath upon the defenseless Cosella. With bitter sarcasm he assailed her; with threatenings and dire denunciations he embittered her days, and he shouted his schemes of vengeance to her wakeful ear at dead of night. Tried beyond the bounds of human endurance, her spirit goaded on to desperation, she, invoking heaven's high aid, and taking counsel of her own soul's prompting, took the first great step into the world.

16

The Step into the World

Grows dark thy path before thee?
Press on still undismayed;
Heaven shines resplendent o'er thee,
Though earth be wrapped in shade.
And God, thy trust, hath given,
With word from swerving free,
The angels of high heaven
  A charge concerning thee.

                        —Psalms of Life

"I will bear no more! I will go out into the world—beg, starve, die, if I must! But, tyrant and torturer! I will submit no more! My wasted childhood, my fleeting youth, passing in sorrow and in darkness—my imprisoned soul, my torn, raced heart—my spirit, that you strive to darken and demoralize—all call for deliverance, and I can bear no more! You would make me cold and calculating, selfish and false—you would sell my soul for gold! My very being shrinks from you, my love is extinguished;—it cannot be, if there is truth in nature's voices, that there is one tie of blood, one link of spirit between us. I can stay no longer; I must go forth—away—into the world!"

With cheeks crimsoned with her strange excitement, with eyes aglow with daring resolve, with determination impressed upon her face and figure, Cosella stood defiantly before her reputed father; and as the wild words fell loud and piercing from her lips, his face grew fiendish in its expression of hatred and malignity; the bitter mockery, the ringing sarcasm of his first inquiry, startled her, she knew not why, as with an electric shock.

"*Into the world?*" he said slowly, scanning the fragile form before him, curving his lips into a sardonic smile. "What can *you* do there?"

"I can work, I can toil for a livelihood. I can ply my needle, or do the veriest drudgery, if there be need. Anything, everything, for peace and home and rest!"

"Work?" he repeated, in the same sneering tone. "*You work?* You indolent, helpless, wild, untaught thing! *You* ply the needle? Six months of sedentary life would kill you, you stormy petrel! You unworldly simpleton! *You* work in the kitchen—with those dainty hands, that never brushed away a cobweb! See, I will unfold to you the picture of your future life, such as you can make it by due obedience and submission to my will; such as it will be, with the curses of offended God upon it if you disobey. See, I have reared you tenderly; the mistaken indulgence of—your mother, has kept you aloof from household knowledge, from the kitchen drudgery you think yourself so fitting for. Your wandering life has deprived you of the advantages of steady attention to study. You know nothing of life, of the world, of science, of human nature, and I—have kept you thus ignorant, *for a purpose.* You might have become a painter, a finished scholar, a wit, or a poetess, had you followed your bent, had your native talents been cultivated. But such is not your destiny. You have dared to step outside of the boundaries marked by our holy laws, by the commandments that restrain your weaker sex; you have dared to think, to speculate, to reason, where you should yield only implicit faith. Would you, weak girl, be wiser than your forefathers? Go back into your place, become the loving and submissive wife of one of our own faith, and pray that God may pardon your rebellious strivings for unreal things and forbidden themes. You are fitted by nature and your mode of life, only for the luxurious ease of a tropical life; for the ease of wealth, the comforts of fortune. These can be yours if you act wisely."

"If I perjure my soul and immolate my conscience on the altar of *your* God, I can be rich and happy?" cried Cosella, with blazing eyes.

"Not so loud, girl! Or by Heavens, I crush you to the earth!" exclaimed Manasseh. "Blasphemer! Fallen, wicked soul! How dare you take His holy name in vain?"

"I meant not the holy, ever-worshiped name of Him, my Heavenly Father!" cried Cosella, with reverentially folded hands and fervent upturned gaze: "I meant the demon that you sanctify in words and elevate above Him; your idol, law, and Deity! Your worshiped Master—*Gold!*"

He ground his teeth in fury, his fingers twitched convulsively, as if longing to silence with their murderous clutch the truthful utterances of the unfearing girl thus braving him. With a violent effort, he folded his arms, composed the quivering lip, and said, again in the slow, measured accents that distilled their venom of sarcasm and blight upon her listening heart:

"Now for the other side of the picture; in place of home and ease and honor, wealth and plenty, you throw yourself upon the tender mercies of the world. Fool! Idiot! Romancer! The friends now smiling upon you bow to you as *my* daughter, the representative of my wealth and position; take away your silken gowns, your diamonds, and your adornments, and who will claim you as their equal? You may take some menial occupation; oh Israel! who will then acknowledge you? And when toil and misery and privation press upon you, you will turn to what the world provides in such cases; from starvation labor and humiliation, from servitude and necessity, you will turn unavoidably—and mind it is a prophecy I speak—to some glittering temptation, and the pure, proud, chaste Ella—well, never mind your surname—will become that scorned and loathed thing, the branded outcast of earth, the accursed of heaven—a fallen woman!"

A piercing cry of indignation rang through the room; with wildly uplifted arms, with eyes that burned and flashed with conscious power, cheeks crimsoned anew by the wrung heart's denial, with spirit quivering from the inflicted cruel outrage of these words, she came so near to him, that her dark curls almost swept his face. Manasseh started back in affright; at that moment he actually feared the dauntless, inspired girl. For they were prophetic tones in which she made reply; that on her brow was the signet of angel promise; the strength and excelling power of resistance upholding that girlish frame was from a foreign and a higher source; the vow then registered was prompted by unseen and wise and pure intelligences, who when they left their charge left in her keeping the memory and the influence of truth and right:

"I scorn your prophecy of evil! I trample under foot your invocations for my soul! I may toil and battle, starve and die, but I shall never sin for bread, for life, for aught that earth can give. You are not the exponent of God's will; my own soul is the best translator of His will and power. *You* cannot mold my destiny; it is in His hand. My fate is to do right, act justly, and doing right I shall be happy. Never, while my conscience lives, my reason is retained, will I willfully forfeit my Father's favor, or relinquish my inheritance to the blessedness of immortal life! Never shall I become what you so wickedly portray. I will be true and pure and good, so help me God, forever!"

Even he, the cold, unscrupulous dissembler, was for a moment awed by the solemnity of her voice and manner; but he had taken too many steps in wrong to retrace his way. That bold, courageous, dangerous girl! So unapproachable by artifice and menace, how should he bow that proud unconquerable spirit? A dark and fiendish plan formed suddenly in his whirling brain; he hailed it with a sudden joy.

"You persist in refusing to accompany me to the island of Canida—do you still continue in that determination?"

"I do," she firmly responded, "and no promises or threats can move me. Leave me here with friends, or abandon me as you will. I will no longer travel with you. I love you not as a daughter should. I shrink from your religious teachings—your dangerous maxims; I will be free! I am, as you often say, a burden and a tax upon you. Relieve yourself, let me go free into the world!"

"Into the world!" he repeated, scornfully. "You would soon go out of it. I care not for your love; your submission is all I need, and that I will compel you to give! Next week we go to Canida."

"I go not with you!" said Cosella resolutely.

He scanned her again from head to foot.

"You persist in this mad resolve?" he questioned.

"So help me God!" she replied, and quailed not beneath the searching lightning of his eyes.

"So help me, the sainted shades of my holy ancestors!" he burst forth, "if you persist in this, you shall be rendered houseless, friendless, and penniless through your own words. Listen, girl! Hitherto I have shielded you from the world. Leave me, and I abandon you to its scorn, its malice, its detractions! I brand you with a father's curse, I proclaim your disobedience to the world. You care not? You defy me even there? I will blast your prospects, cause the pure and good to turn from you in holy horror. I will tell tales of you that shall cause you to blush to meet a fellow-being! Ha! You tremble, dare you brave this?"

"*All, all*, that *you*, and such as you dare tell! My actions are open to the day; I fear you not."

"Not yet cowed down," he murmured; then, in a loud voice he continued; "I will brand you with the taint of infamy! I will proclaim you as a *bastard to the world!*"

For a moment she stood aghast and breathless, gazing upon him with dilated eyes, a wondering horror impressed upon her face. Drawing a long, deep breath, she cried—

"It would be but another falsehood added to the list. I defy you! I believe you not; your story will not meet with one moment's, one soul's belief."

"But I tell you, girl, *it is true*! You have forced me to this revelation, which would have gone to the grave with me were it not for your provocations. I swear to you upon this holy volume," the hypocrite placed the Jewish scriptures to his lips, "that this is so!"

She felt as if consciousness was about to forsake her; strange, wild suggestions, flitted athwart her throbbing brain; her heart beat violently; the erst warm, indignant blood seemed to congeal in her veins and freeze the bonding life currents. At length, her pale and quivering lips said faintly—

"And you—are you—my father?"

"Of course, you silly fool! But Shina was not your mother."

Such a cry of anguish as escaped those pallid lips; with clasped hands, reproachful gaze, and faltering utterance, she called upon God for mercy, for she felt as if bereft of all! Now that certainty had come, she felt anew the loss of Shina, and wept afresh the burning tears of bereavement. Shame, humiliation, dread, filled her soul; bound, shackled yet in the world's conventional forms, she deemed herself a scorned and lowered being; and over her crushed soul's future she cried in poignant, hopeless sorrow, in unavailing self-accusation. False and unscrupulous as she knew Manasseh to be, she also knew his superstitious veneration for the symbols and forms of his religion, and she thought not that revenge and cruelty could lead him so far to outrage truth as to perjure himself by oath upon the sacred book.

"Will you now go with me and become submissive and dutiful?" he inquired. Her face grew stern and scornful as his own.

"I will not!" she replied. "I will abide my destiny, not as you would make it, but as God disposes of me. Take your revenge! Proclaim me to the world as you will, my conscience is guiltless of all wrong. Though all scorn and despise me, He will accept me for his own. But my mother, tell me of my mother! If there be one spark of human feeling, one glimmering of pity in your soul, tell me of my mother!" she cast herself at his feet.

He looked upon her in silent triumph, with a fiend's malignant joy.

"She was a poor, rough, uncultivated girl—a servant in my father's family," he replied.

Cosella shivered as if a cold northern blast had reached her.

"Is she living?" she asked imploringly.

"Long since gone—long since sleeping in her grave," he said.

The young girl sighed; mingled feelings of pity and regret, of relief and thankfulness, swayed the troubled heart.

"Will you consent to remain with your father *now?*" he again inquired.

"*Never!* Now, more resolutely than before, I say again, *never, never!*"

"Swear it upon this volume, the holy record of our people."

"If an oath be necessary, I will take it. By this, and by what is holier far to me, by my own consciousness of right, I swear! I go not from this place with you."

She kissed the book, and placed it on the table. Manasseh saw that he was foiled in every effort; he could not cope successfully with that indomitable spirit. His face grew livid with rage, for his prey was about to elude him; he saw the danger of the present, the looming terror of the future, and his self-control was gone!

Seizing her slight frame in his strong arms, placing one heavy hand upon her mouth, he plied the other with infuriated force, and left the crimson impressed on her slender neck and bared white shoulders! She struggled violently to release herself, but he held her close; showering between his fearful curses those relentless blows upon her shrinking frame. He unwound the long dark hair that lay in a massive coil around her head, and by it dragged her through the room! Her small white hands vainly struggling in self-defense; the glossy floating ringlets that concealed the death-pale face, the bending form, all that could remind him of the sainted Lea, touched not one chord of feeling, awoke not one stray gleam of pity in his soul!

At last he removed his murderous grasp and cast her from him, and her loud and piercing cries for help rang through the house.

"Silence, or I shall kill you!" he cried, with a rapid glance around. "The servants are away, and if you call in strangers you pay for it with your life!"

She found her scarf, and wrapped it around her; she fled to the inner chamber and brought thence her veil; she threw it over her disheveled head and tear stained face:

"God will protect me!" she said with a faltering voice. "I go, forever!"

She saw him point a pistol at her breast. With a bound, and a shriek that startled the passers-by, she gained the threshold; she sped along the passage with frantic haste, and gained the street. Unconscious of the observation she attracted by her hurried gait and disordered dress, she passed on, hearing not the voices that addressed her; seeing not the curious, amazed, and compassionate glances cast upon her. Faint, breathless, almost bereft of sense and feeling, spurred on by the one dominant thought of flight, she reached Teresa de Almiva's dwelling; she passed its hospital portal; she entered the familiar sitting room.

Alone, and beautiful as ever, the lady was seated at her embroidery. A slight rustling at the door caused her to turn her head in that direction. She looked at the closely veiled figure that advanced toward her with surprise not unmingled with alarm. With a kindly impulse she arose to proffer her assistance; a trembling hand put back the veil; pallid, tear stained, so changed by grief and terror that Teresa de Almiva uttered a loud cry as she recognized her, Cosella knelt before her friend and called wildly and imploringly upon her to save her, to shield and hide her from her father's rage!

Overwhelmed with sorrow and indignation, the lady removed the young girl's veil and scarf, put back the unloosened hair, the veiling ringlets from the disfigured face.

"Merciful Trinity! Thrice blessed Virgin Mother!" she exclaimed, as her eye rested on the crimson marks on neck and shoulders, "what brutal hand did this?"

"*My father!*" hoarsely whispered Cosella; "I fled, or he would have killed me! I will never return. Save me, *mother, save me!*"

The Señora Teresa burst into tears.

"Here thou art safe, safe and sheltered, my beloved child!" she cried, showering fond kisses on the upturned brow. "Fear not, *he* shall never again molest thee; but tell me, Cosella, wilt thou be indeed my daughter, wilt thou accept the Virgin Mother's love, the church's saving grace?"

"*I will, I will!*" fervently replied the wretched girl; "henceforth I obey you—I rend all former ties. I will be yours, the blessed Virgin's child!"

"Praised be the Lord for evermore! Thanks blessed Trinity! Thanks holy guardian angel!" cried triumphantly with zealous joy the faithful Catholic; and Cosella, still kneeling at her feet, bathed the kind hands with tears, and told the story of her father's cruelty, the humiliations he had cast upon her by the revelation of her birth.

"It is not true, my daughter; believe him not! He said it only to distress you, to keep you in the snares of his false religion. Believe me, it is not true, my darling!"

Cosella looked up with a wan smile and vowed obedience to the new faith. And thus it was she took the first great step into the world.

17

Spirit Teachings

How pure in heart and sound in head,
With what divine affections bold,
Should be the man whose thought would hold
An hour's communion with the dead.
In vain shalt thou, or any, call
The spirits from their golden day,
Except like them, thou, too, canst say
My spirit is at peace with all.

—Tennyson

The winged shafts of calumny had flown hither and thither, and many gazed on young Cosella with suspicious eyes, or curled their lip in derision, or turned coldly from her proffered salutation. For true to his word, Manasseh, with great show of grief and wounded feeling, bewailed his daughter's disobedience, her love for the world's gayeties, her boundless extravagance, and desire for change and travel, that caused his paternal heart so many pangs! Of what he had revealed to her concerning her birth, he said naught, for good reasons of his own; but with well simulated sorrow he insinuated much that, in the world's hasty judgment, branded forever with ineffable stigma her maiden fame. This wound, deepest of all inflicted by that cruel hand, rankled deep and sore for years. A haunting specter on her path of life, a terror and a looming woe, it was the nightmare of her pure, proud soul.

Fearing that proceedings might be legally commenced against him for personal violence against his daughter, when the first tempest of his fury was allayed, Manasseh Moshem (for that was his real name) packed up his remaining valuables and departed for the Island of Canida, without seeking to behold again Cosella. At the demand of the Señora Teresa, whom he feared (for he yet owed her a sum of money), he sent the young girl's wardrobe and her jewels, retaining, however, the most valuable portion of her diamonds.

Every day Cosella studied the catechism and the prayers of the church preparatory to her admission to its sheltering fold. Let us awhile to another scene of earth; and beyond earth, to glean of experience, spiritual truth, and better knowledge. Come!

⌒

The ever beautiful and unselfish Solita sits watching the slumbers of the now rapidly recovering Percival Wayne. His face is yet pale and haggard with ravage of illness, but the clear and powerful intellect rules in its accustomed place. A sweet placidity rests on his brow; in his sleep he dreams and murmurs: "Lea!" and the mention of that name causes no more a pang to the hushed and happy heart of the patient watcher. As a child, reverentially listening to a father's teaching words; as the neophytes of old bent to their sage's admonitions, so she, of the aspiring heart and cultivated spirit, drank in of the angelic wisdom flowing from his unconscious lips. As health and strength returned, the benign influences that taught and counselled, ever leading him upward, resumed their control; and wise, and pure, and loving intelligences, spirits of the redeemed and advanced, angels of the music and the poetic realms, gave, through the favored and fitting organism of that true, pure man, their sagest counsel and their loftiest themes.

At first, Solita, startled and alarmed by these strange revelations, by the seemingly unnatural condition of her friend, dreaded the hours of his entrancement; but as time sped on, and her heart awakened to those angel teachings, and her soul expanded to the magnificence of celestial love and heavenly wisdom; as her intellect unfolded to the comprehension of mighty truths and spirit laws, she linked these grandly beautiful revealments with the dreams and vague prophecies, the foreshadowings of her childhood, the visions of her earliest youth. And with tears of gratefulness, with quiet ecstasy and holy fervor, she welcomed what the world denounced; what material minds derided as the impossible and the visionary. By her own heart's responsive beatings, by her own soul's acknowledgment, she knew these things were truth.

Thus, when the ever unfolding spirits of the love and wisdom spheres of knowledge, the advanced minds, from realms of beauty, light and wonder, spoke through the mortal organism of her dearest friend, Solita, often clasping her hands with tearful joy, cried in her fervent gratitude:

"Of this have I dreamed and thought and pondered; such hopes have come to me at morn and at twilight! So have I imagined the spirit world; such the emblematic colors of the celestial raiment; this have I asked of life."

One day the controlling intelligences said:

"This new philosophy, this faith upreared upon the granite foundations of reason and nature; those laws upheld by the inherent power of God within them, shall be proclaimed to earth; and studied, revealed and acknowledged by numbers now resting in religious indifference, or rocked upon the sea of educational prejudice and blind belief. The bigot and the atheist, the scholar and the unlearned; maidens and youths; matured minds and gray-haired loiterers by the wayside; all shall become participants of the knowledge of immortality; many shall become its teachers unto their fellow men.

Listen to our prophecy of the coming time, ye, its first exponents—ye moral pioneers of a cause unheralded by trumpet tones, or waving, kingly flags! Many aspiring and poetic minds shall give through heavenly aids to earth the inspirations of the Lyric heavens. The music of far distant spheres, translated as it may be into mortal tongue, shall delight the listening, wondering thousands assembled in the free vast temples of God's nether world. Ye shall be told of love, and heaven, and home, of the soul's glorious transfigurations, of the power of spirit and the wondrous force of law. Eloquence and might, and genius shall unfold their shining, varying garb, and earth acknowledge the superior wisdom of the heavenly spheres. And, as time rolls on, to the selected, trial chosen souls of the purified and victorious ones, the highest revelations of the purest spirit-life shall come; fraught with such overwhelming glory, it shall kindle into songs unheard of since the world was born—into such music as the seraphs of the upper realm delight in. From the inspired lip the gemmed discourse shall fall, and through their influence, erring souls be ransomed, and aspiring hearts be led through the valley-shadows of life and trial unto the land of realization, the music-world of delight! But they who stand upon this moral height of angel power have climbed there step by step, through densest glooms of sorrow; their feet have bled, passing over the cruel rocks; their brows have been lacerated by the trial-crown; their souls have called in anguish unto him who ever hears! For them, earth's every joy has receded, that heaven might come near; for them, the joy and hope of life has faded, that immortal hope and joy might bloom; for them, the desolation of orphanhood, the stings of poverty, the desertion of friends, the removal of love, the destruction of home and peace; for them, the bitter waters of a thousand Marah founts, the scorching wastes of utter hopelessness, the wintry plains of desolation; for them, the tempest and the deserted ship, the desert isle and solitary cave, the daily crucifixion and the burial of earth's choicest hopes. But, oh, triumphant victory theirs too will be, the ascension of the spirit from the material clogs of life, the removal of the soul from selfishness, the upraising of the heart unto the nearness of Omnipotence! The victor over temptation and wrong, the moral conquerer, the truth-sworn, charitable and forgiving, the brother of the lowliest, the humbly great, the childlike and the pure—these, and these only, shall be the guiding, battling, truly winning spirit of the age.

In vain the inspirations of the higher life, the revelations of its power, shall come to men, if their influence be confined to mere externals. If the angel mandates of purity and truth be not fulfilled in daily life; if from the public rostrum only the presence of the countless host is heralded, and the inner consciousness respond not to the thrilling thought of spirit-witnesses; if in language only is religion taught, and love proclaimed, vain is the advent of the new era, vain the labors of the myriad worlds! But, if the soul entranced by the descriptions of beauty, love and power, will respond in sympathy, in effort, self-denial—then truly will the spirit-hosts draw nigh, and earth shall sing her matin song of redemption soon.

Self-denial, even of all the heart demands, the soul has yearned for, when the angels of discipline command. Down with thy battling will that would confront defiantly the immutable laws of Deity. Undisciplined affections, worldly attractions, selfish aims, all, all must yield beneath the fiery ordeal that purifies and leads to God! From the human soul divine all that would darken and degrade must die, as withered leaves drop from the healthy branch. Where there is suffering there is sin and wrong, perversion and misdirection of the Godlike faculties. Tears and pain and woe, disappointment and gloom and care, are of the earth—the progressive spirit, the regenerated soul, knows them no more. While the least particle of earth's grossness clings to the robe of love, while wavers yet its heaven ascending flame with one breath of low desire—while yet one taint of selfishness rests, glimmering, in friendship's breast—there will be suffering; for not all of heaven is there. While slander, envy and detraction live, ye cannot breathe the airs of paradise, if but their faintest reflections linger on your souls. Untiring effort, therefore, for the good and true, and all the aided resistance of the God-like will to wrong, and man shall ascend into a higher life, and taste of heaven's beatitudes. Know you not the right by its pervading holy thrill of divine consciousness? Feel you not the degradation and the conscious sense of wrong, that is not educational, not the effect of prejudice, but the whispering of soul and Deity? Oh, ever, thou moral combatant, distrust the argument repulsive to thy soul's highest intuitions; discard the doctrines that would enthrone *self* above thy brother, that would miscall thy lower nature's promptings, the voices of thy God!

Through innumerable changes of matter has the inherent life-principle worked out its glorious mission, and now the spirit man stands lord of all upon the tributary earth. And it is for the full development of spirit, for the subjugation, complete and entire of the animal, that thou must labor and strive unceasingly, ever guarding the portals of thought and sense, ever exercising, expanding and elevating affection, until it beam a star wreath from thy brow, a glory from thine eye, a promise of celestial compensation in thy heart. Ever must thou conquer passion, until, a willing slave to spirit, it crouch obedient at thy feet, oh, angel-man—oh, seraph woman!

Ye, the first laborers in this field of action! Ye, the first receivers of the light and truth of other worlds—oh, guard well your hearts! Treasure well your soul's best impressions. A power and a magnetic force is breathed o'er earth that may attract unto high heaven itself, or enchain relentlessly unto the dust. Beware of all that recognizes self as pre-eminent; trust not the voices that tell beguilingly of *rights* that are not *soul laws*. Believe not in mere attractions of the external; trust not the allurements of sense; they are false and deadly, all! Give to the angel-world thy heart for keeping; build in those upper realms thy fanes of soul worship, thy shrines of consecration, thy permanent abodes. Cast from thee all that would retard thy spirit's advancement; all that would upraise a barrier betwixt thyself and angel visitants.

The problems of life may trouble and perplex thee often; they are thy needed discipline; thou mayst walk solitary through the earth life, and the coming of love be as a sorrowing angel to thy breast. But faint not, waver not! Have faith and hope; such is thy needed discipline, and solitude for thee is good. The tears and sufferings, the doubts and fears, the earth love's usual accompaniment, are its angel purifiers. Through their ministrations, affection is spiritualized until it glows with light and power divine; until, submissive as a babe, it rests at the good Father's feet; willing that trial should come, that sorrow should enfold, that it may grow more intensely beautiful, more angelically wise. When thus the human heart is sanctified, it is ready for translation to the higher spheres, and it lives its spirit life even on the earth, and meets its Ideal in the communion of the soul. Then is the brow of earnest and unfolded manhood, the pure and truthful brow of woman, fitted for the bridal chaplet of the skies, and the star of love, burns lustrously, the guiding beacon of their souls.

Yes, gentle sister, thy earliest thoughts, the suddenly-occurring poetic fancies that winged their way to thee in sunbeam, shower and blossom, wind and wavelet's tone, and rainbow's message, they all were impressions from the upper worlds. Thou hast heard the dying cadences of celestial song, the whispered watch words of the spirit hosts. The fragrance of our lilied bowers has been wafted to thy sense; immortal roses, unseen by thee, have decked thy innocent breast. Yes, dear intuitive one! Thy dreams are true, the foreshadowing of thy earnest soul will all be realized. The flowers in celestial land are gemmed and musical. Our tall trees bend to sweetest melody; the grass in instinct with sound. The emerald's deepest lustre tints the unfading leaves; the rubies' blended rays flash from the rose's heart; and pearl-like gleams the lily's stately cup. The harebell glistens with the sapphire's glow; the diamond's splendor breaks from the environing crown of foliage in rainbow shafts of light; and the topaz beckons from the tufted mounds. And each one has its own God given song, its own thanksgiving hymn uprises, musically fragrant, an offering of love unto the beautiful.

At morn and eve, this floral concert, uniting with the songs of birds unknown to earth, charms ear and heart with unrivalled harmony. It were too much for mortal ear and heart, these triumph songs of soul, those glad refrains, these heavenly welcomings; once, thou and all shall hear them.

Here beauty reigns, crowned Empress, before whom adoring nature bends in reverential homage; before whose sceptred might she brings the tributes of her wealth; the offerings of genius, fame and love. But it is the *inner* beauty that is thus worshiped here; it is unselfish love, undying faith, hope, truth, and charity that wear the angel garbs. In emblematic colors, gemmed and radiant, gleam the won trophies of the soul; the lowly virtues, the lofty aspirations, the meek self-denials, the sweet amenities of spirit. There are destinations here for those who have lived the purest, noblest lives—those who, in humble walks amid the daily toil and weariness, yet fed their souls on heavenly manna, and lived for sacred duties, well fulfilled; these are the highest, because the happiest, here.

Awaiting and thirsting spirit, eager for the draught of life, the gift of vision, and the dawning of inspiration, be a patient laborer yet awhile; slowly thou art working for thy soul's advancement, for the future's culminating joy. Wait patiently, in hope and faith; for love and knowledge, heart-rest and home-peace, shall be thine—thine when thou hast earned their possession, when thou shalt be fitted in the angel's sight, for thy peculiar mission."

Three months passed on, and with hospitable joy she watched beside and tenderly waited upon the best loved friend. In that short time, aided by the unseen influences, she was led to the inner light that was so beautifully cheering, so life warm, new, and inspiring; and sweet Solita, understanding as it were, intuitively, the glorious spirit theory, and rapturously thankful for the boon accorded, ceased to fear the angel visitant that, in the guise of impression, brought great and often startling thoughts to her musing hours, inspiring her with poetic fervor, with musical delight, that improvised sweet songs of Heaven to the accompaniment of her plaintive voice.

Soon, and she had charmed all weariness and pain from the brow of Percival. He called her often Cosella; and she, without one tremor of embarrassment, bade him look upon his cherished image, guarded so long and faithfully upon the household shrine. And he told her of Almon Fairlie, his friend and brother, the pupil of the spirits and the expounder of the truths of immortality.

Strange it was that Solita should not think of the young girl that had so strongly touched her heart in Santa Lucia; strange that she never mentioned their meeting to Percival. It seemed to be obliterated from her memory.

"You look so little changed, dear sister," said he one day; "only I miss your flowing curls. This braided hair gives you a majestic, a queenly grace. Your picture smiles more than is now your wont; but you are unchanged in heart; you are stronger, lovelier and wiser, though, now than before."

He took and held her hand, looked tenderly and earnestly into her face, and with a consciousness of perfect trust, she calmly returned his gaze; those pure and intuitive souls read each other fully. He knew that she had loved him in sorrow and in tears; that his image had been her guiding star through life; that she had entertained the glowing hopes of earth, and feared with a maiden sense and dread of wrong. He knew that she had prayed and supplicated heaven as do the loving and impassioned souls for whom no earthly fruition blooms; that sometime, in the discipline of the past, a flitting of jealousy and despair had passed over that love-warm and vestalic heart; that she had appealed to heavenly justice against the law that bound him to the spirit of Lea; that often, with outstretched arms and longing soul, she had called him, far across the sea, to come and brighten all of life and love for her. He knew it all; and she felt that he read the inner tablet of her soul life; yet, although the rose hue of acknowledgment dyed her pearly cheek, she averted not her calm and steady gaze. In those clear wells of deepest feelings and holiest thought, he saw it written:

"The struggle and the pain is past. I love thee still, but not with earthly longing. I know that all of *fraternal* love and confidence thou givest to me, and to me alone on earth. Gratefully I acknowledge the gift, and accept thy right; thy highest love is for that one beatified, my spirit sister, Lea."

"Am I now truly thy brother?" he asked her tenderly.

"For life and eternity," she fervently replied, and smiled. "And she, your wife, your progressing and awaiting angel, she is my sister, is she not?"

"Forever!" he responded. And a kiss of pure, fraternal love sealed the compact, holy and divine, between those kindred souls.

There are those of this world ever smiling in derision of what they have not learned to comprehend. These, from the lower standpoint of conventional adherence and customary denial of the, to them, "far, bright and unattainable," will mock this portrayal of a soul's experience, this picture from reality. But she who, commissioned by her spirit guides, ventures to portray in earthly and imperfect utterance the disciplining process whereby human hearts are made the vestal fanes of spiritual and divinest love, she *knows* these things are true, and feeling their beauty and their holiness, presents them to the world, unheeding that world's cry and mockery; and believing that love all passionless, and good untainted may be within the reach of all, she goes to Memory's stronghold, to the deep caverns of Experience, to the star-lit summits of the promising future, and tells you what treasures she has found!

Remember that the woman's soul I write of had grown to heights sublime by constant effort and heart-watchfulness; that beneath the spiritualizing process of guiding angels, she was beyond the reach of earthly taint, of aught that could pervert so angel-like a nature. And he, yet in his manhood's prime, beautiful in soul, and schooled in long-suffering, he was wedded to that higher world wherein his heart-angel dwelt. The love that he bestowed upon Solita Mendez, the sister of his adoption, was worthy of the consecration of the purest seraph hosts. To both it was a precious gift, a compensating joy.

We leave them to the perfect communion of their understanding souls, and return to the poor child groping in darkness for the light that glimmered and disappeared, until heart and spirit sickened, and the gloom of utter skepticism shut out the beauties of earth and heaven. It was the work of seeming Destiny; so she, the sufferer, cried aloud unto the mocking glory of day, the oppressive silence of the night. Be still, oh soul undisciplined! It was the will of God, the sanctified work of his chosen and ministering spirits!

18

Changes

The spiritual ministry of Night
Is all unknown. Day rules the sensuous mind;
But Night the fettered spirit doth unbind,
And through the silver palace-gates of light,
In dream and trance, she bears the soul away
To the wide landscapes of the inner day.

—T. L. Harris

One outward change, combined with many sad and solitary soul awakenings, has passed over the young Cosella. One sunny morning, amid conflicting feelings that rent her spirit while they decked her face with a mortal pallor, she became a convert to the church. Attired in the white robes of innocence, with flowing veil and myrtle wreath around her brow, she knelt at the altar's foot, and was accepted as the daughter of the Virgin mother. Amid the solemn tones of the rejoicing hymns sung in commemoration of her adoption of the new faith, there lingered, vague and troublingly, a whispered discord that caused her heart to flutter with a conscientious fear. The lady Teresa and the stately Don, her husband, called her daughter; and the stricken heart for a while reposed, as it fondly deemed, beneath the projecting care of parental love, new found and blessed. She even adopted the name of her godfather and mother—for in that relation they stood to the young convert—and for some months a dreamy quiet, a salutary stillness, visited the soul long tempest-tossed and weary.

Then followed strange and troubling dreams that, like haunting phantoms, pursued her even by day. Now and then the heavy dream curtain was uplifted by a small white hand and the spiritual glories of far-off, teaching worlds revealed. There, amid lilied bowers, beckoned smilingly the beatified face of Shina, and, sweetly encouraging, her lips repeated her dying mandate, "Be ever pure and true, my child!" Standing erect in queenly majesty, or kneeling at some woodland face, she beheld a mysterious beauty, a woman's form, veiled in a robe of light, from which gleamed magnificently a hundred stars! A mystic diadem of rainbow hues encircled the lofty brow; a wand of power was in the tender hand. As a gush of celestial melody, thrilled her voice to the heart depths of the enraptured dreamer; as a heavenly benediction, her sweet smile fell upon her. Strange and mighty revelations pertaining to the realms of soul life, whispered watch words of the seraphic host, teachings from the inner shrines of being, sagest counsel, and saintly encouragement, were vouchsafed to the dweller of earth. And when timidly veiling her sight from the resplendent glory of that vision, Cosella ventured to inquire, "Who art thou, oh most beautiful?" the music voice replied—

"I am thy guardian angel!"

And she awoke, strengthened and encouraged, and on her spirit fell the love charm of celestial guardianship, and the balm of resignation settled on the sorrowing breast awhile; for her trials were not yet ended.

One memorable night, Don Almiva was absent, and the young girl shared the spacious sleeping apartment of the Señora. They had retired early, and suddenly Cosella awoke to find the friendly "light of stars" withdrawn, the room shrouded in darkness, and the sea-breeze sighing faintly amid the curtains of the bed. In the corridor without, a lamp of cocoanut oil was burning dimly. For a while she lay there, pondering on the past, and dreaming of the future, while a heavy weight seemed to fall upon her heart, and a hushed suspense, a fearful expectation, took possession of her faculties. In vain she strove to banish the superstitious dread creeping so coldly over her frame, chilling the warm life currents, causing her heart to throb so wildly. At length, unable longer to endure the oppressive stillness, she spoke in a trembling whisper to her friend.

"What is it, Cosella?" replied Doña Teresa.

"I cannot sleep—I am afraid—I feel strangely!" and her teeth chattered with cold; she raised her hand to her brow, as if to dispel the crowding, fearful thoughts demanding access.

"Have you been awake long? I, too, feel strangely; I have not slept for some time, but feared to disturb you, so I did not speak."

Cosella noticed that the voice of her friend faltered. "Shall I bring the light in here?" she timidly demanded.

"Not yet, child; wait awhile; perhaps this oppressive feeling will pass away. What time in the night is it, I wonder."

"Do you, too, feel as I do? As if we were encircled by unseen things, as if invisible forces were directed against us, as if some impalpable evil surrounded, as if haunting spirits came to—" She stopped and wiped the perspiration from her brow.

"*Santa María del Carmen!*" cried the now thoroughly alarmed Señora. "Don't talk so, Cosella! Holy San Antonio shield us! Holy Father Saint Francis, Saint Barbara and Saint Paul, guard and save us from the demons that waylay and ensnare souls! Pray, Cosella, pray! Holy Virgin of sorrows, I am oppressed and alarmed this night! To thy maternal protection I confide myself—save us, mother of God!" And now thoroughly excited, the lady counted her beads, and implored her goddaughter to pray for relief.

For a while Cosella strove to obey; her lips unclosed in the customary forms of prayer, but her heart went not with the formula. It was as if some spell held every faculty in awaiting and breathless suspense for some greater terror yet to come. Powerless, she crossed her arms upon her bosom; silently she turned her eyes to Heaven; deep, within her soul, unuttered by the quivering lip arose the cry for help! And to the calm and beautiful regions of Faith and Love uprose the invocation that called her guardian angel to her side.

A soft breath, balmy and healing as the Southern violet freighted breeze, played over her brow and cheek; and she drew a long, long sigh of relief. Then, in the corridor without were heard strange hollow sounds, signal knocks of the invisible messengers, or summonings from the unseen shores; who then could tell? Upon the walls they rapped again and again, over the floor they rolled—these strange, weird, midnight sounds! For which humanity had no interpreters then.

And Cosella listened with a beating heart, but with a courage not her own; her eyes sought for flickering shades and passing forms, but naught met their strained and eager gaze. Trembling, upon the very verge of fainting, Doña Teresa grasped the curtains of her couch and cowered from the darkness, the stillness broken at intervals by the mysterious sounds.

The silver-tongued clock in the bed chamber rang out twelve! There was silence for a while, broken only by the labored breathing of the lady, and the deep drawn sighs of her companion. Then the knockings were renewed, as if with exultant glee or fiendish satisfaction. Over the walls, across the floor, into the chamber, they passed, unheeding the mortal terror they occasioned. But when loud and continued rappings were heard beneath the very bed on which Teresa de Almiva lay, the last remnant of her self-control took flight, and she broke out into wild, almost maniacal ravings; she accused herself of sin and dissimulation; she uttered startling confessions to the ear of heaven, and frantically implored the intercession of the Virgin to shield her from Satanic power.

Cosella heard but half of what she said, for her senses seemed bound in a trance of wonder, almost devoid of fear. A deep significance that time would solve she felt lay hidden in that midnight manifestation. But the strange sentences, the self-accusing words that broken and dreamily confused and mingled with her own busy thoughts, fell on Cosella's ear; they startled and alarmed her, she knew not why.

Gradually the sounds departed; growing faint and few, until the former stillness reigned, and the friendly stars beamed in at the casement.

Assured that the strange visitation was over, Cosella left her bed and approached that of her friend. She was breathing heavily, and her hands were ice cold. For some moments she spoke not; and when her goddaughter held the lamp toward her, she was startled by the strange expression, the disturbed features that met her view. Surely some great wrong, or some grievous sin, preyed heavily upon the lady's soul. Quick as the lightning's flash, the thought and suspicion darkened the young girl's trusting faith, and with a repelling gesture was as quickly dispelled, for it is so sweet to love and trust; the cruelest awakening is that of the confiding heart from its dream of worth and affection. Yet such is the inevitable destiny of those whom the angels love—whom celestial guardianship ordains for the wearing of the trial crown, that they may gain the final palm branch of immortal victory. Such was Cosella's destiny.

"Virgin mother!" exclaimed Doña Teresa, when her calmness was somewhat restored. "Are all the devils gone? Oh, have we dreamed all this, Cosella? What have I said? I was beside myself. I know not what I say or do when I am alarmed. You will not notice anything I have uttered, my daughter, my love, my dearest one?" and the loving arms were thrown around the neck of the innocent girl, and tender, maternal caresses soon dispelled the sudden and fearful illumination that had threatened to break upon her. She kissed her friend and soothed her fondly; and when it was required of her to keep secret the strange occurrences of that night, she unwaveringly complied, and felt not a doubt intrude itself upon her mind.

Time passed; no changes in that sunny land disrobed fair nature of her summer vestments; no cold winds tore the rejoicing flowers from their forest homes; no ice breath froze the limpid streams; no snowy robes enfolded in a death-like sleep the wealth of earth; no blighting frost-touch withered; and no season's desecrating hand despoiled the gorgeous coloring, the emerald verdure of the woods. Summer, full and joyous, garlanded with bloom and warmth, rested in benignant blessing o'er that paradisean clime. But o'er the human heart, the autumnal and the wintry changes passed. God had made the soul-realm beautiful, but man invaded it with desecrating wrongs, and stripped its Eden bowers, and froze its crystal waters, and tore rudely down its loftiest fanes of worship.

Slowly over the young Cosella's life that should have been an offering of devoted peace and joy there gathered the gloom clouds and the tempest heraldings of suspicion, doubt, and disenchantment. Over the heart aspiring to love had been cast the earth-woven veil of fear; the gathered flowers of purest friendship changed to cypress and mourning weeds; the unread soul drank deeply of the bitter draught of disillusion, and questioned of high heaven if love and purity, trust and truth, were indeed things of this life? And for a while there was no response to the anguished invocation.

Bereft of love, the pride of maidenhood and honor had come to her soul's rescue; she was strong and brave in that grandest and holiest element, conscious purity; and before the all-seeing eye of God, before the all searching gaze of angels, she would have shrank and blushed for shame to harbor the weakness of loving where affection was unworthily bestowed. Therefore, though she suffered keenly, it was not long; for she felt that she had falsely embodied a divine and lasting Ideal; she cast no love aside; but hallowed, exalted, sanctified, enshrined its holy image on a still loftier mind throne—gaining by the suffering and the experience the sorrowful mistake of its first unwise earthly enshrinement.

But in holiest friendship she deemed the ark of refuge gained. Every aspiration and thought were confided to the maternal guardian she deemed so true and good. On many subjects they agreed; on some they differed. Doña Teresa continued to urge upon her charge at every available opportunity the necessity of love and marriage as the great and only ultimates of a woman's destiny. And when Cosella offered fraternal and universal love, in place of exclusive dedication, her matronly friend smiled derisively and called that a dreamer's plan.

Soon it was manifest that she strongly desired a union between her son Carlos and the new convert to the faith.

Cosella frankly told her that she cherished only a sisterly affection for her son; and when the mother spoke of the love that would grow out of companionship and time, it was Cosella's turn to smile derisively. She knew too much of its divine nature, of its spiritual demands, to believe its heart-tokens could blossom from the soil of fixed indifference; and, as time passed on, a shadow brooded betwixt her friend's heart and her own, and home was darkened by it.

There came a frequent visitor to the house, a Spaniard of lofty presence, courtly manners, and reputed wealth. Instinctively Cosella shrank from him, she knew not why. In after years she learned that it was the unfolded lily bloom of purity within her soul, shrinking from the serpent's gleam. A refined sensualist, strangely mingling philosophy with grossness, this man approached the ear and heart of woman. His stern materialism was veiled by adroit sophistries, as was his theory of life and pleasure. Not many compliments did he waste upon the angel-guarded girl; for they elicited neither smile nor blush; he learnt to guard his speech, his eyes, in her presence, and often when she left the room he would murmur with a sigh of relief, "Thank fortune she is gone!"

At first Doña Teresa seemed to share Cosella's fixed aversion; she expressed herself with indignant warmth against his frequent calls, and concluded, with the public voice, that he had caused the death of his wife by cruel treatment and unfaithfulness. But soon this changed; gradually she grew to tolerate his presence, then to declare herself his friend, and to admit that public opinion had vilely slandered a good and noble man. Looking up to her, as to a model of goodness and virtue, Cosella strove to share her views; but ever that insurmountable shrinking, that unaccountable repulsion, checked the intended speech or the friendly smile. Ever some intuitive whisper, some sudden uprising of soul said to her audibly: "Beware!"

And Doña Teresa rebuked her; at first gently and lovingly, at last sternly and strongly, for her marked avoidance and willful rudeness to Don Hyronomo Lanuz; and finding that her explanations only drew forth ridicule, the poor girl took refuge in tears; and the shadow brooding by the hearthstone swelled and darkened into gigantic proportions, and a new and mighty grief raged in the bosom of Cosella Wayne.

By degrees, the maternal fondness once displayed was altogether withdrawn; and coldness, irony, and petty humiliations substituted therefor. She was taught to feel as a dependent in the home once so freely offered. From Doña Teresa's husband she ever received kind words and gentle greetings; but he was often absent, and when at home often retired to his room and remained there for weeks, having his meals brought to him there. Carlos, despairing of ever winning Cosella's affection, sailed for Europe with his brother; and she was thenceforth taunted with having driven them from home and country.

A heavy curtain of mystery, that seemed to guard from the world some great and grievous wrong, enfolded that once happy household. And beneath repeated strokes of petty tyranny, the heart of Cosella seemed dying out. Cold, and doubt, and apprehension, settled on her spirit; she grew pale and worn again with weeping; and but for the encouraging voices of the night, the dreams allotted, the glimpses of the hereafter, her reason as well as her strength would have yielded beneath the intolerable pressure of unmerited suffering.

The crisis came at last. The weary heart received the stunning blow of certainty. She became assured of the worthlessness of her she had trusted with such fond and filial love. Doña Teresa de Almiva, the honored lady, the devout worshiper at the Pure Mother's shrine, the respected wife and mother, was false to woman's truth, to her marriage vows, to God and purity!

Oh, the bitter, bitter disenchantment! How cruel the rending of the heart fibers that clung around that woman's soul with such devoted, pure and daughterly love! She had borne coldness, scorn, ingratitude; but oh, this revelation of a soul despoiled of beauty, light and truth! Alas! Unconsciously was Cosella led to the discovery; her pure ears listened horror-stricken to the pleadings of unhallowed passion, and startled, they drank in the yielding woman's sinful avowal of return. She saw the tempter draw the mother she had reverenced to his breast. She heard the words of endearment that should be uttered only by the pure in heart, that were a blasphemy of love's divinity, on the lips that desecrated their hallowed utterance. With a reeling brain, a stricken heart, she uttered a piercing scream that must have startled the guilty plotters and fled from her unsought hiding place—fled with wild and headlong speed, until at the end of the far garden she was caught in the arms of the black slave Panchita, and lulled to rest upon that faithful and God-serving heart.

"What is it, darling—my little child, my pretty one, what is it?" said the old woman; and through her blinding tears, Cosella saw the glory of sympathy illumining that homely face, and felt the force of truth and tenderness in her endearing, childlike words. Her arms thrown around the bondwoman's neck, her young head nestling on that true mother's heart, she wept her sorrow, but would not tell its cause.

"Who is with the señora, my pet?" whispered the old woman.

"Alas! Alas!" cried Cosella, with a fresh burst of grief.

"Is it Don Hyronomo Lanuz?"

Cosella looked upon the woman. Intelligence, honesty, truth, beamed from her ebon face; her large eyes were filled with pitying tears. Soul read soul in the exchanged glances of mutual sympathy, sorrow and indignation.

"Panchita knew it long ago, *queridita*" (little dear), she said, softly. "And Panchita knows what honor and duty is, though her skin is black; and she has never learnt from books. Oh, my child! You are the Virgin's child; *she* alone can be a mother and protector to your innocence. Panchita is old, and black, and ugly; but she can look the Virgin Mother in the face, and feel that she is worthy of her sacred intercession. Do not remain here, my pet darling; for some day there will be a terrible outbreak, and the unholy deeds will be brought to light. You, young and innocent as you are, will be called to an account, maybe. Flee this house, my child, for evil spirits hold possession of two souls in it. Take old Mamma Panchita's advice; flee as you would from sin!"

"Where, oh where, my God, shall I find refuge? Oh, that I were in my mother's grave!" cried the stricken girl, with a wild, appealing glance to heaven.

Panchita gently rocked her in her arms and continued: "You have many friends, dear lamb; any of them will receive you gladly, and give you the shelter of a home."

"I loved her as a mother! She was all of earth to me! And, *now*, to be so cruelly deceived! Oh, is there any truth on earth?"

"There is, darling, much truth, and love, and good; and there is more in heaven. *There* old Panchita will meet *her* children, and there she will be blest with the sight of the Saviour of the world, and with the glorified face of his holy Mother!

Even amid her crushing sorrow, Cosella could not refrain from deep admiration of the humbly religious soul before her. With an impulse of tenderness at once true and graceful, she kissed both cheeks of the aged negress; and the warm tears that rained upon her face, their grateful acceptance, the fervent embrace, the inspired "God bless you, good and loving child!" was ample compensation for that spontaneous little deed of love.

"I shall sorrow for your departure, señora; but it is for your good. Your old black mama advises you to go. I will go to seek you sometimes, *quer-dita*; but, oh, leave soon, for I feel a great black thunder-cloud! I see it in my dreams, and I feel the hot sulphur air streaming from it! It is settled above this house, and if *you* stay the storm will burst upon you, too. Oh, promise me, Señorita Cosella, my pet child, promise me that you will go!"

"I will; most assuredly, I will," she sobbingly replied. "I could not eat another meal in this house; I could not sleep; the guilt and horror would chase all slumber from my eyes. I will go, my good Panchita; I will go tomorrow. Heaven bless you for the words of comfort you have spoken. Oh, Shina! Oh, mother! Would I were sleeping by thy side! But, whatever betide me, believe that ever I will fulfill thy dying words. I will be true to God and the right!"

There is a sublime majesty in sorrow that invariably wins the homage of the good and disciplined. The faithful negress gazed in almost adoration upon the inspired beauty of the young girl's face, and then, resting her bony hand upon the bowed head, she blessed her solemnly; and by the responding thrill of deep emotion, Cosella felt that the bond woman's untutored and beautiful prayer was accepted of the Father and registered by his angel hosts.

Slowly, calmly, and determinedly she returned to the house. She entered the drawing room to find it occupied by Don Hyronomo Lanuz alone. He arose to greet her, but she turned upon him a flashing glare; indignation choked her utterance, for a torrent of rebuke, of overwhelming accusation, sought for speech. He read the storm and its cause, and his dark cheek paled, his fierce eye quailed, beneath the steady accusing gaze of the brave pure girl. In confusion, he seized his hat and muttered some incoherent apologies. One word alone escaped the tightly compressed lips of Cosella—"*Tempter!*" He trembled beneath that one uttered word and hastily fled from her presence.

It needed some strong incentive, some powerful mental stimulant, to urge Cosella in braving the anger and the censure of her godmother. For many months her spirit had been bruised and almost broken by daily trials and a thousand variations of treatment. But where principle or duty was involved, the timid girl grew strong and resolute, and the opposition of the world could not turn her from her purpose.

It was with perfect self-possession, with calm and dignity, that she presented herself before the señora, and told her of her intention of leaving her home and care. Doña Teresa gazed upon her in astonishment, as yet with no suspicion of her real motive.

"What new freak is this?" she said, knitting her brows. "Have I insulted your highness' dignity by some oversight? Or, have I failed to respond to some of your sentimentalities as you deem I should? Have I put a check upon your extravagances, or denied you some foolery? What occasions this new freak? Where do you desire to go?"

"I will not reply to your ironical words, nor enter upon any self-defense, Doña Teresa. Where I shall go I know not just now; perhaps to Clara Maldonado's. She has often invited me to her home. I wish you to understand, also, that I leave your house forever!"

"Leave my house *forever?*" repeated the señora. "Call me *Doña Teresa?* Are you insane—or what is it ails you, girl? Why do you not call me godmother, as is your duty? Do you not know that I have spiritual authority over you?—That you dare not leave my guardianship without my consent?"

"You cannot withhold it, madam!" replied Cosella. "And I no longer call you godmother because I deem you unworthy of the name. Your coldness, your neglect, your cruel treatment of me, I could all forgive; but this last terrible revelation—"

"*Of what, girl? Of what?* Speak, speak! Must I compel you?"

The lady's face was livid; with a trembling, eager clasp, she seized Cosella's arm. Looking her steadily in the face, Cosella said: "You are no longer as a mother to me. I know you!—*you are false to God, to womanhood!*"

There was silence between them for a while—breathless, uninterrupted reading of soul with soul. Teresa's eyes wildly sought those of her once-loved daughter. Cosella's gaze fell not before the searching scrutiny. She felt the hold upon her arm relax; her godmother fell back in the chair she had risen from, and two bright crimson spots dwelt amid the pallor of her cheeks.

"Go!" she said, in a stifled voice; "go when you will and where you will;

but if ever—" she paused awhile, and then said, in a low and menacing voice: "Beware, Jewess! Beware! If you breathe one word—not all that your father has said shall form the smallest atom of the terrible accusations that *I* will pour upon you! Breathe but my name, or couple it with—no matter— you understand me—and I will drag you from that pedestal of purity on which you so loftily enthrone yourself. You have driven my son from his home. You shall not stand between me and my happiness! Go, and may the demons attend thee! Thou spy and curse upon the household!"

"Madam!" replied Cosella rising, and her manner was replete with dignity and self-respect; "I will not stop to talk to you of the sorrow I have endured on your account, for I believe you incapable of a pure affection. I see now that your love for me was all a scheme, a pretext. *I know you*— consequently I no more respect you. If you have not the love of right and the fear of wrong within your soul, no foreign interference can prevent you from sinning. I am a young and inexperienced girl; but I feel that you are preparing a woeful return for the sins you commit. Señora Teresa, as a wife and mother, God and his angels hold you guilty! Your rest is broken; you are haunted by fearful visions; your contentment and peace is gone; your temper, once beautiful and gentle, is turned to one of gall and bitterness. I fear not your menaces, señora; and if your conscience, your own soul, be not a sufficient accuser to lead you back to innocence, fear not that Cosella will lead you there by force. But in the name of the mother who bore you, I entreat you go no further in the path of sin."

She would have said more; but the thoroughly stung and vindictive woman arose, and with a malediction such as Cosella never dreamed could pass those lovely lips she violently thrust her from the room.

The doubly orphaned girl spent the night in prayer and in tears. The next day, collecting her wardrobe and the few trinkets left to her, she left the house wherein she had suffered so much, without another parting look or word to the unworthy woman she had clung to so lovingly. The husband and father was away from home, and Cosella was spared the pain of parting with him who had been ever good and kind to her. She departed with the blessing of the old Panchita on her heart.

19

Retribution

Silently, strangely the darkness
Has fallen upon thy way,
And the hands of no earthly morning
For thee shall open the day.

In a large and richly furnished chamber that overlooked the sea, upon a bed of suffering and remorse, lay Manasseh Moshem; and to his darkened sight the heavy and oppressive air was peopled with accusing phantoms; with the embodied sorrow his iron hand had inflicted upon the defenseless. Wailing and loud lamentation, entreaty and menace, prayer and denial, were wafted to his ear; and white hands, worn and attenuated, beckoned through the environing gloom. It was his dark soul's revelation unto itself that thus obscured the mid-day brightness; that, casting out the warmth and fragrance of the surrounding summer-world, brought demons to his pillow and the gaping grave before his sight!

The room was deliciously cool and inviting; soft folds of lace fell before the lofty windows, and swept the carpet of palest azure, on which white lilies and life-like glowing roses were scattered with profusive hand. From vases of Parian marble and most delicately tinted porcelain, the sweetest flowers of that abundant clime exhaled their choicest perfume. Rare pictures, in massively carved and gilded frames, adorned the rose hued walls; and on tables and shelves of curiously wrought workmanship of ivory, pearl, and tortoise shell, glistened many costly specimens of mineral beauty, treasures from the mine and the sea, caskets inlaid with precious stones, and ancient volumes bound in softest velvet and in gleaming gold.

The green, low, drooping awning outside sheltered the open windows from the admittance of the too fervid sun rays; the sea breeze swept unobstructed through that spacious chamber; laden with a briny fragrance, it rustled amid the rosy curtains that overhung the bed; toying with the flowers, waving mid the silken folds of couch and screen, it lingered, that blessed ocean breeze of healing! But it brought upon its cooling wings no freshness for the burning brow of the sufferer, who, with wildly distended eyes, and arms tossed aloft, saw not the glorious sunshine; heard not the soothing murmur of the sea; heard only the accusing thunder tones of conscience—

saw darkness and dread phantoms there—and felt the glowing breath of a furnace upon his tortured heart and brain.

He lay thus for hours, tossing helplessly from side to side, in utter agony of frame and soul; muttering incoherently, crying out loudly, praying with eyes averted from the mocking fiends that surrounded him! And as he lay there, the pale azure satin of the nearest couch changed to a floating bed of clouds on which reposed in magnificent, terrible and accusing beauty, the spirit form of Lea! She came to sit in judgment on his soul for the wrongs committed against her child. The waving lace of the sweeping curtain folds, they changed to spectral messengers, unpitying and stern, that came to call his doomed and lingering soul from earth. From the soft carpeting of flowers; huge serpent shapes arose that twined around the downy ottomans and hissed from amid the roseate folds of the pearl-studded Oriental seats that decked the room; their fierce eyes glared upon the transgressor, and endowed with mortal utterance, their forked tongues whispered, "Retribution!"

From the pictured, smiling landscapes on the wall, descended winged and horrible demons, wild birds of prey with outstretched sable wings; they perched upon his laboring breast, croaked hoarsely in his ear, and snatched his trembling fingers from his eyes! At the open door, passing noiselessly between its folds of azure silk, entered the arisen spirit of the much-wronged Shina, her dark hair put smoothly back, her pale face, sharpened by sorrow, gleaming stern and reproachful through the misty veil that pitying angels had woven from her earth-shed tears. From the open book in her hand, he read in blood-red letters there inscribed the record of her wrongs; the manifold and pardonless sins committed against her life; and, at the close of each page was written the ever recurring fearful word, "Retribution!"

There, in the corner, stood, accusing and defiant, the mother of Lea Montepesoa. There, Shina's gray haired father pointed to him with a threatening mien, both asking and demanding that justice for their meed, of which they had been deprived so long. The imperious dame of Israel, the neglected father, both cried for "Retribution!"

In from the casement stepped, also pale and stern and unforgiving, the living father of Cosella; from the golden, massive goblet in his hand, he poured upon the shrinking, wasted wretch before him the crystal draught therein contained. It rolled upon him in a fiery stream, scathing, burning and withering with the lightning's power! In vain he shrieked for respite, pity, forgiveness; the blue eyes of Percival Wayne, robbed of all human tenderness, glared fiercely upon him, his lips with the disfiguring impress of utter scorn upon their placid curves repeated the one judgment word, "Retribution!"

Then, as if imbued with life power, large gold coins rattled on the carpet, and huge sacks of gleaming silver were emptied over seats and bed. Now from the ceiling fell a golden rain; and precious stones, for which affection, truth and honesty were bartered, were thrown in at the open windows. White doves, bearing in their beaks rich bracelets flashing with the diamond's rays, chains of untold value and scintillating gems, flew hither and thither, as if in search of a resting place.

The golden shower fell heavily upon the sick man's breast, and beneath its accursed weight he lay as one crushed and breathless, yet intensely alive to pain and sound. Around him flashed, danced and quivered, with blinding rainbow hues of splendor, the covetously sought for treasures of the earth, the objects of his unholy search; they burned him where they touched his shrinking flesh, or dissolved in air beneath his frenzied grasp; while the demon host applauded, and the night birds waved their dusky wings and hoarsely croaked for joy!

The white birds dropped their glittering trophies, and they changed to wildest reptiles 'neath his gaze. The burnished gold and emerald beauty of the serpent's form clung to the curtain folds of his bed of torture; their steel like tongues darted shafts of agony to his soul, and whispered, "Retribution!" to his sharpened sense.

The sapphire and the ruby glistened from the lizard's scaly form; amethyst and amber in the mocking clutch of shrieking vultures! And pearls worth a prince's ransom were twined around the sable wings of huge and motionless bats suspended in the lurid atmosphere. Stray gleams of palest light, or dazzling glare and heat of most intolerable fire, revealed these distorted phantom shapes; then all again was darkness, and through it broke the sounds of weeping, menace and accusation that appalled his guilty soul. One panorama after another filled with looming horrors and fantastic terrors spread before his inner sight, for he was alone with conscience then; and no voices of sophistry drowned the clear, ringing, thundering tones that spoke incessantly the one recurring fearful word, "Retribution!"

Then, as a picture of the future, invoked and wrought by his most impious soul, he saw the life of Cosella unrolled, and stretching far, far away from hope and love and gladness, into the dim shadows of misguided purpose; into the valleys of moral perversion; down, down, into untold depths of sin and sorrow, incurred through him who was her banc through life! He saw her paling, day by day, beneath her inflicted wrongs; and, as her youthful figure lost its all of freshness and elasticity, as her eye grew dim with the midnight toil and the unquenched tears; as the last lingering ray of beauty and of hope died out, he saw deep in her heart the struggle, and the curse with which she named him! And to her darkened spirit's groan of helplessness, to her farewell sigh to duty, God, and virtue, his tortured soul, comprehending all, re-echoed the anguish and the misery with a loud and fearful cry for mercy!

It was unheard; no soft touch soothed his brow, no human hand raised to his parched lip the cooling draught, no softly modulated love tones whispered peace; he was alone, forsaken, left to die of fever and neglect! Once in a while a stealthy step sounded outside the waving folds of azure silk that screened the door; a swarthy and malignant face appeared, and listening intently to the cries and groans that racked the sufferer, he, the intruder, smiled a fiendish smile of satisfaction and muttered gleefully, "Soon, soon, he will be still!"

The day passed on, the last sunbeams that ever would greet the earthly sight of Manasseh Moshem fell aslant upon his pillow. Perhaps it was commissioned by angelic power to arouse that guilty soul to the first effort of restitution. He opened wide his eyes, looked searchingly around, and the gleam of returning consciousness illumined his haggard face.

"Water—oh, water!" he vainly supplicated.

He heard the cooling, mocking flow of waves beneath his window, the droppings of the fountain in the court below. A deep groan burst from his heart; then came the conviction that he was left to perish there of thirst and pain; and then followed resolution, brave and atoning, even for that dying man!

The God so long and practically denied, the truth and justice desecrated so vilely; the outraged and accusing laws divine and human, all were meekly invoked and reinstated in the soul-realm in that supreme and self-investigating hour!

"I will make restitution as best I can and leave the result with God!" he murmured. And he arose from his sick bed, all worn, emaciated and feeble unto death as he was; he threw around his shrunken form his dressing gown of cool, white linen, and deliberately fastened it around his waist by its silken cord of blue; then with faltering steps, but strong, unwavering will, he reached his writing table, and dropped into the cushioned chair that stood beside it. His trembling fingers lit the silver lamp, and drew forth the materials necessary for writing. For two hours his pen flew rapidly over the paper, and his plentiful tears rained on the pages of his last confession. At length he paused:

"Oh, they will not send it! I am in the power of murderers!" he cried, with an appealing look to Heaven. "My labor is in vain; yet something tells me she will receive this letter. I must hasten; I have only to tell her her father's name."

A mist overspread his eyes; he seemed overpowered by some sudden shock or influence that seemed anew to paralyze his senses; his hand could only trace the first letters of the Christian father's name; the pen fell from his powerless grasp; the letter, with its unfinished revelation, lay upon the desk; and Manasseh Moshem, reverentially covering his head and rising slowly from his seat, repeated aloud in clear and thrilling tones the sacred asseveration of God's Unity, the accepted prayer of Judah's scattered host:

"Hear, oh Israel, the Lord thy God, the Lord is One!"

And stretching forth his arms, and bowing low unto the ground, as before the judgment seat of the eternal, his spirit passed away, even before his lifeless body fell prone and heavily to the floor!

He lay there until dawn, and then the swarthy and malignant face bent over him, and looked around the room with covetous and guilty glances. He espied the letter upon the desk; he sat down to peruse it, taking no further heed of the human clay before him.

"Well," he muttered in the Spanish tongue, "he does not accuse any one of his death, he gives no account of his sickness; and as this will prove to her what a rascal he has been, she will not enter into any minute investigations. He died of fever. *That* is evident; it is a malady peculiar to our climate. No one will dare to suspect *me*, and I will write a most brotherly and feeling letter of condolence to the señorita. I wonder who her father is? And why the devil, who has always assisted this blasphemous Jew, did not assist him to write out the name of the Christian gentleman? By San Antonio! The young lady will be grateful for the news; but as she is adopted and cared for, I have still less compunction in helping myself to what I need."

And the reputed pious, seemingly wealthy, and ostentatiously charitable Don Jorge de Mas, opened casket and draws, and peered into all the secret nooks of the curiously constructed writing desk. His swarthy countenance lighted up with fiendish exultation, for he found much that was valuable in ancient coins of massive gold, in precious stones and rare trinkets. But in a secret drawer of the writing desk he found a roll of bank notes, and a purse heavy with modern gold pieces. There was a fortune there that would have saved the world-untried Cosella from toil and hardship, from the harsh experience of the thorn-covered pathways of necessity. It was not to be. The wronged girl's patrimony went to stranger and unlawful hands.

When the sun rose high and gladdening above the hill-tops, the robber ceased his search and laid the lifeless form upon the bed. He folded and superscribed the letter, and arranging a few trinkets in an ivory casket, he placed Manasseh's confession therein, and inditing a long, hypocritical missive of condolence, he directed all to the Señorita Cosella Maria de Almiva, in Santa Lucia; and, taking the casket in his hands, he left the room to seek for a fitting opportunity to send it. Soon it was known that the stranger, so *kindly and hospitably* entertained at the retired mansion of the Señor Don Jorge de Mas, had departed this life; and as he could not be interred on the consecrated Catholic soil, the señor, in his kindness, permitted the poor heretic to rest within the limits of his plantation, and when the plain grey stone was placed above him, no one caviled, questioned, or marveled; still less did they entertain a doubt of the devout and Christian gentleman who had sent the wretched man into another life.

The prophecy of Shina was fulfilled. In a solitary island, where here and there the scanty residences deck the earth's enameled beauty; alone, forsaken, conscience-struck, abandoned of all save God, he breathed his last on earth!

20

Manasseh's Letter

Wherefore so sad and faint, my heart?
The stranger's land is fair;
Yet weary, weary still thou art—
What find'st thou wanting there?"
What wanting? All, oh! All I love!
Am I not lonely here?

—Hemans

Several weeks have elapsed since Cosella left the luxurious home of Doña Teresa de Almiva, and sought refuge in the humbler but happier one of Clara Maldonado. The ever kind and jocose husband of her friend received her as cordially as did Clara herself, and their two lovely children were glad to have the señorita come. It was indeed a fitting resting place for Cosella's wounded spirit; and whatever their humble means afforded was placed at her disposal with frankness and good will. The good old Panchita called often to see her; she heard from her that her godfather had returned, that the Señora had held a long and private conversation with him, and that the Señor had never mentioned Cosella's name. "*She* has told him something," said the faithful negress indignantly, "or he would not so neglect his God-child." The young girl sighed wearily and accepted her fate.

Her manner, paleness and abstraction proved to Clara that some great grief weighed upon her mind; but with true and intuitive delicacy she forbore from questioning her. And Cosella was silent, not from fear, but for shame of the unworthy woman once deemed her maternal guide. It was with her a season of unrest that preceded the coming storm; strange dreams haunted her pillow, and a wild desire to wander far from the scenes of her discipline took possession of her every wish. Only while in the presence of Clara, or while pressing the children to her aching heart, and replying to their innocent prattle, did she feel the soothing calm of that happy home; and for the hour she forgot the sorrow and the foreboding that haunted her.

One afternoon, Clara's husband returned from the post office with a letter and a package directed to the Señorita Cosella Maria de Almiva. "There, young lady," said he smilingly, "is news for you, and I doubt not a handsome present; come, please gratify our expectant curiosity; see, the children are staring at you, open-mouthed, hoping for a good supply of candies. Clara, by her looks, thinks a fortune has fallen to your share, and we are all ready to wish you joy of your good luck, Señorita."

"Cosella Maria!" (she was thus called often since her admission to the church). "What is the matter, my friend?" and the sympathizing Clara hastened to take the package from her hand.

"Open it, pray it open," said Cosella faintly; and her trembling fingers proceeded to unseal the letter she held in her hand. She was so long about it that Clara had untied the parcels and cast aside the wrappings ere she had perused the first lines. She recognized an ivory casket that had belonged to Manasseh, a few trinkets lay therein and an open letter which she saw was in his handwriting. Her heart gave a loud throb of pain; then by a sudden and powerful exertion of the will, she gave her attention to the missive she held in her hand. Her friends looked on in silent wonder.

"This letter is from the island of Tulic—I have no correspondent there," she murmured. "And this casket, with a message from my father, what can it mean? Lord! Give me strength!" she fervently implored. And hastily she read the letter.

She read it through, with a blanching cheek and with eyes dilating. Not a sound escaped her lips; when she had perused it all, and read the signature, she snatched up the casket and hurriedly left the room.

"Some great calamity has occurred to our poor friend!" said Clara, and she burst into pitying tears, in which her tender hearted children joined.

Cosella entered her chamber, bolted fast the door, and sat down, pale and stern and tearless, to the perusal of Manasseh's last confession.

She read it once, and the crimson of a sudden joy, the pallor of a soul-deep grief alternated on her changing face. Low exclamations burst from her lips. "I thank thee, oh my God!—oh mother, Shina! Father! Where, oh where!"—and then with another effort to be calm and still, she read the letter again; and drank in its overwhelming revelations of life and blessedness; its testimony of penitence and wrong.

She perused it for the third time, and not until then did she realize that Manasseh, her cruel guardian, her calumniator, her ruthless foe was dead!—With a prompting of exultant joy she clasped her hands, thankful that she was liberated from his grasp; free and glad and proud that she was not his child. Then came the human pity; the mild-eyed womanly angel of compassion knocked at her heart, and the wronged girl's tears fell on the letter indited by a dying hand. "God forgive thee as I forgive!" she murmured, and then she thought of him in his sunny moods, and in view of his tardy but soul-wrung penitence, of the appeals to her woman's heart for charity, she wept the heart floods of divinest pity o'er his death.

Then came the thought that indeed he had spoken truly, that the loving Shina bore to her no tie of motherhood; that in a far land she rested who had given her birth. And then amid the isolation, and the sorrow and thankfulness, there broke a gleam of divinest light and hope. Her father, her loving, true, much wronged and seeking father, he lived perhaps; and she would meet him on the earth. For Manasseh had written thus: "often have I been deceived with tidings of his death; as if it were a punishment for my sin, his haunting and *living* image ever pursued me. Only two years ago I heard from him, he was then in England. Oh, forgive, forgive Cosella! I will make restitution as our law demands. May you meet and be happy, for in this my dying hour will I confess that he who has the right to call you daughter is one of earth's noblest men. The veil of prejudice is withdrawn. I stand upon the portals of another life. I feel—I know my immortality *now*; and I tell thee, thy father is a brave and most heroic soul. His name, oh wronged and persecuted child!—his name is Per—" thus far the failing hand had written when the summoning angel called. A bitter cloud of disappointment lowered over her expectant hopes; and she wept for the unfinished revelation; she cried aloud that Heaven was unjust thus to defraud her of a daughter's rights. But even amid the storm of frustrated hope, there arose to her mind's vision the welcoming form of him it was her will to seek throughout the universe! Tall and majestic with the power of innate nobleness; lofty-browed and eloquent of speech; with face untouched by the desecrating hand of time; unmarked save by the beauty-lines of thought; with eyes of heaven's serenest, holiest blue, her father stood before her, opening wide his arms, smiling with deep tenderness; calling by name to come and cheer his life! And as before some beckoning reality, she bent her knee and reverently bowed her head, invoking that most sacred boon, a father's holy benediction.

She had learnt her mother's name; she knew the history of her proud grandmother, the sorrows of her father's lot; and from that hour a wild but fixed resolve dwelt in her breast; she would seek her father; she would travel from place to place, guided solely by the intuitions of a daughter's heart, and if he dwelt on earth she yet would find him. Poor Cosella! She thought not of her dependent condition; she forgot that she was bereft of fortune; she knew not that the grandest aspirations of the human soul, the loftiest impulses of truth and goodness, are often fettered in their expression by the iron hand of stern necessity; by the galling bands of penury. The dreamer knew not this; the denizen of fairy land deemed not the earthly pilgrimage so paved with difficulties; she who worshiped heart-wealth could not deem the world's obeisance was most deeply rendered unto gold!

Therefore she dreamed amid her sorrow of home and blest re-union, of happiness and joy; and yet there was a gleam of prophecy, spiritual and true, in all the varied imagining of her love-yearning soul.

Cosella bathed her face and arranged her hair; then calmly walked into the sitting room and told her friends of the announcement of her father's death. But when alone with Clara she told her all, and received that true friend's condolence and sympathy. "I shall have to unlearn to call *him* father," she said, with a tearful smile; and from all the world beside she guarded her secret.

For some months afterwards new and strange feelings struggled in Cosella's breast. Gradually awakening to the bitter sense of dependence, she began for the first time to think of the daily effort necessary for material sustenance. She had ever been surrounded with plenty, often with luxury; she had never accustomed her hands to toil, nor her brain to labor. Her humble friends lavished upon her every kind attention, and in return she compelled them to the acceptance of various gifts; such as dresses for Clara, pictures for the adornment of the sitting room, play things for the children. Cosella thought not, cared not for the diminution of her resources; she knew naught of the value of money; none but Manasseh had ever vaunted to her its mighty influence upon the world. She dispensed gifts with a generous hand. Until she had no more to give; and with folded arms and eyes that sought help from above, she queried of herself: "*What next? What shall I do?*"

She heard of Salvador del Monte occasionally; she caught a glimpse of him sitting by a woman's side upon the balcony of a house. But resolutely she turned away her head, and when once he sent her a message she declined receiving it. There was no wavering in her soul when conscience pronounced her fiat. Hoping, waiting, praying of destiny for a change to come, the months passed on; and many changes passed over the interior life of the awaiting one. Religious scruples arose; conflicts of reason with traditionary teachings. Which was the path to heaven? Was it the faith professed by her mother's people, to the last upheld even by the scattered, persecuted tribes of Israel? Was it the Christian faith, with all its panoply of church and form? Was it right for man to make unto himself embodiments of things unseen, and worship them in lieu of the divine realities? Was Jesus of Nazareth indeed the very God? And was that God a spirit, infinite and all-pervading; or was he some grand, incomprehensible personality, dwelling afar in space where time is not? *And heaven?*—was it a place of never-ending day, where Jehovah sat enthroned in kingly pomp, where a blaze of glory veiled the Father's countenance, and the occupation of the angels was to sing and glorify him alone? And that mystery of the Godhead—

the Christian, the Catholic Trinity—could the human intellect accept it and the human heart approve? The never-varying monotony of heaven, the earthly glitter of its golden streets, the imperial pomp presiding there as in the court of some worldly despot—was it a sufficient compensation for the trials and discipline of life? What was to become of the holy ambition, the ever upward tending aspiration, the love that demands fruition and continuance of eternity? What is life devoid of action, incentive, progression? What is the hereafter, if divested of the noble affections that embellish earth? What of the untold capacities, here but half unfolded; the yearnings half untold; the spirit-links of soul that would stretch from world to world up to the infinite conception? What of the slumbering emotions no wand of earth could reach; the vague foreshadowings of angelic prowess, spiritual dominion, holy conquests? The thousand guarantees of immortality, how should they be realized? In selfish rest within a glittering, sensuous heaven; in prayer before Jehovah's majesty; in withdrawal from all human and angelic sympathy? "No, oh, my soul!" responded, silver, clear, the promising voices of intuition within that seeker's breast. "Believe not creeds and rituals, they are the work of man. From a low standpoint of moral fear and grossness he has hitherto beheld his God; he went *outside* of his own soul to grasp the infinite, and found only shadows—looming horrors, myths of man's formation. He has cast aside the ever-renewed and holy volume of nature to grope amid musty books made sacred by the impress of antiquity. The *soul* ever gives a truthful response; divest it of fear; fill it with human and divine love; cast aside the trammels of creed and the teachings of priest-craft; question not thy educational prejudices, thy passions—they are of the earth; but inquire of thy freed soul, and the truth will respond.

God is no malignant tyrant, sending wars and pestilence upon his much-loved earth. He is not jealous of thy human tributes rendered unto the beautiful in art or nature. *He is a spirit*, present in each form of life, speaking in a thousand voices, all of love. When creeds and churchly dogmas cease to satisfy the hungering soul, from nature's fountains flow forever the myriad streams of living truths. The bloom upon her sacerdotal vestment is as pure and fair, today, as ever; there is within her wide arcana all that earth life can bestow upon the student's soul. Her crystals teach the fashionings of divinity; her piled rocks tell of the successive ages of unfoldment; her vegetable realm teems with the life-spirit, her floral treasures with the Godlike attribute of beauty, her mines' wealth with the correspondences of soul. Not a flower blooms, nor a brooklet murmurs, nor a tall tree waves in the passing wind, but finds a link within the human soul. "From the atom up to God," the interminable chain ascends. And there are chords within the human breast responding to the wild bird's note, to the eaglet's cry; to the Eolian breathings of the summer breeze, as well as to the rending of the thunder-cloud and the passing of the storm. There are souls on earth to whom the voices of the sea are the teachers of a mystic lore. Beside the wave-washed beach they learn what life shall be; how death can be overcome, and heaven be gained. In that hallowed spot of voiceless prayer they compose sublimest poems, never to be recited until the material veil shall be withdrawn, until the loved and parted shall meet in the Elysian star-worlds. Vows of sublimest self-abnegation, promises of soul-enfranchisement, efforts for a world's redemption, have been outspoken and outwrought in presence of his recording witness—the guarding, faithful sea! Some vestal hearts have sung their hymnings of devotion beneath the silver stars of night, and to the lily's ear have breathed what man can never know. The wild-wood solitudes have trained strong souls for the battle of this life; and the mountain's mist-encircled grandeur has inspired the epic poems, the heroic actions of the age. Calm, peace, and sweet endeavor have been borrowed from the river's onward flow; and the songs of joy that have blessed the laborer have arisen from the wafted inspirations of the sunlight and the dancing leaves. Thus everything that bears the semblance of the beautiful appeals to human knowledge—instructs, and charms, and soothes—for it is ever God that speaks therein.

But *heaven*? Where I shall meet my mother. Shall we there wander listless, hand in hand, surrounded by a blaze of glory, feeling naught save self-satisfaction? No employment, no incentive to effort, no good to be achieved? And that other place—too terrible to think of! There those I have loved may dwell in perpetual torment, and I may not lend the helping hand!

I am a human creature, full of faults, inharmonies, and conflicts; my eyes are darkened to the heavenly light; suffering and disenchantment have made me bitter, oft rebellious. I repine when I should submit; I know not yet the wherefore of life and trial—the necessity of being, of endurance and of sorrow. But this I know, all faulty as I am—within my soul there gushes forth a fountain of forgiveness that by its sweetness I know is divine. I have been cruelly wronged, deprived of my rights, despoiled of love, and disenchanted with the promises of friendship. My soul is full of skepticism, bitterness, and suspicion of humanity. Forgive me, God, that I have dared to arraign *Thee*! It is not thou who inflictest suffering, but thy human children upon each other. Earth and sky are as beautiful, as true, as in my childhood's days. *Thine* aspect changes never! Yet I, striving to imitate Thee, learn to forgive. And from my soul I do forgive Manasseh, cruelly as he has sinned against me. Yet the priest tells me that he is in hell; that the gentle, loving, timid Shina, she whom I shall ever love, burns in perpetual torment, not for the sins of life, but for the difference in belief! Oh, *can* this be, and art thou just? Answer me, oh voice of God! Oh sacred intuition! Tell me, is there an eternal hell?"

The soft breeze that invariably preceded an impression fanned her brow; calm descended on the anxious heart; a sweet atmosphere of peace through which the commissioned angels communicated enfolded her thought. Framed into words, thus was the response:

"There is no arbitrary decree nor place of punishment; but natural, beautiful, and inevitable consequence that is the spirit's compensation for its every act. The heroic, self-denying soul, yielding obedience to the moral and physical laws that are immutable, is a spiritual conqueror; and in the hereafter, the soul-victories achieved, the illumination of truth and knowledge obtained, shall form for itself external surroundings of the utmost beauty. The purely loving shall dwell in Eden bowers, such as their young imaginations pictured; all that the mother's heart desired and dreamed of for her noble boy or lovely girl, shall there be realized. Not an aspiration shall be lost, nor one hope remain unsatisfied; the material barriers removed, the soul is free to act, to live, and to achieve. Therefore the poet's eye shall be gladdened by the beauty-forms of the celestial worlds; the artist's soul drink in the varying panorama of the fadeless realms; the minstrel there shall hear the music-voices of the stars, the floral concerts of the blessed earth. And there will be *labor* for all; labor of love, and aid, and sympathy; works of truth and goodness; communication of Heaven with the worlds beneath.

The faint reflections of celestial heavens of beauty and of peace may dwell within the human spirit while it swells amid the discords of the earth-life. Angelic discipline, self-effort, will and truth, may bring these bright reflections; and you may dwell in joy, though surrounded by external inharmony. And thus with the opposite picture; violation of natural and divine law, inevitably entails remorse and untold suffering. Hell, with its demon shapes and lurid fires, dwells in the guilty breast; and it burns on, when the shores of eternity are gained, *but not forever.* Thou, fallible and human creature, canst forgive; and thinkest thou the infinite possesses not that holy attribute in an infinite degree? Human hatred would not consign its bitterest foe to a life-long torture, and yet it tells thee of a God implacable and unrelenting; the chimera of tyrant's brains; the offspring of ecclesiastical fear and love of power, is this avenging and unforgiving Deity! The true God is a loving father and a bountiful mother unto all souls.

All sins must be self-expiated; no church, no priest, is invested with the power of forgiveness. The soul must, from its gained summit of spiritual insight, *learn to forgive itself,* ere happiness can be obtained. And this can alone be done by substituting deeds of love for deeds of hatred; by living purely in place of living vilely. On *self* depends the gaining of salvation, or the soul's immunity from evil. Pure and lofty aspirations will attract kindred influences that will strengthen the first feeble effort in the right. But the first effort must be made by the human will; it is the voice of God asserting its supremacy; it is the God within dictating through the reason, the affection and the intellect; and all that conflicts with it is of the grosser nature, and must be overcome in order that the Divine may reign supreme. That voice hearkened unto obeyed, the angels of inspiration hasten to the soul to assist with their encouragement; to strengthen with their power; to elevate, refine and purify; therefore no vicarious atonement can suffice; no priestly absolution benefit; no churchly ceremony sanctify. On *thyself* depends thy present and thy future destiny; knowing the beautiful compensations of good, the direful and inevitable consequences of evil, what soul would choose the latter?

There is a conscious self-respect, intuitive to the soul that makes it shrink from the arraignments of conscience; it would not blush for shame before its own august tribunal; it would stand erect on the mountain heights of spiritual freedom, and proclaim itself a worthy child of God! But in the homage paid to externalities, in form and creed and ceremony, this consciousness has been lost sight of; and many a soul harboring deep the hellpangs of remorse has been proclaimed forgiven by the judgment of man. Many a human heart tortured and devoured by self-accusation has received the church's symbol of admission, the outward sign of the remission of its sins.

Follow the voice of truth and honor; the mandates of purity, the laws thou feelest are divine; and break from off thy soul the fetters of superstition that render thee fearful as a slave! Leave all thy troubled questions, those thy intuitions cannot solve, to the guardian care of Time. Revelation, insight, spiritual discernment, come to all that truly seek; but the earth discipline is needed, and thine is not ended yet."

"Strange that I should have such thoughts!" said Cosella to herself. "They come sometimes unbidden, at other times invoked. What strange, new fancies crowd upon my brain! Perhaps it is wicked in me to indulge them. Heaven help me, I know not! I seem lost in a labyrinth of doubts; what human hand shall draw me hence? Oh, that I might know of the Future, that a spirit might appear to me and tell me of the other world!"

Not yet, not yet, Cosella! For a while the shadow and the doubt, then wilt thou emerge into the free and glorious sunshine.

The external beauty of the faith that had captivated her poetic fancy was fast losing its every charm; for Cosella had learnt the hollow mockeries it concealed. Her active mind could not refrain from reasoning, her heart from questioning; she ceased to pay her usual devotions to the Virgin Mary; she neglected the confessional; weary, dispirited, skeptical, she fluctuated betwixt olden opinions and the thronging thoughts that overcame her. A feeling of longing, of home-sickness, a restless desire for change, for a return to the cold regions of the North, possessed her. She often prayed to God to send her deliverance, to reveal to her in what place her father sojourned. Then for days a strange exaltation seemed to enfold her spirit; she seemed to feel her father nearing. This was succeeded by a sad revulsion of feeling, in which she wept and wildly accused her wayward fate. The strong and unyielding grasp of an iron necessity approached; the tenderly nurtured, dreamy Cosella was troubled by the invading phantoms of compulsory toil and privation; but as yet they only loomed mistily in the distance.

She retired as much as possible even from the little world surrounding her; when she walked out, it was to Shina's grave or to the pebbled beach. A settled melancholy brooded upon her face; Clara was tender and sympathizing; but Cosella for a while turned away from all human sympathy.

"If I can only find my father," she would think, "I would believe that God is good and that life is beautiful; while that joy is denied me I can only mourn. Soon I shall be penniless, a burden to my friends; before that time arrives I must away—away from here!"

21

Above the Clouds of Earth

Eye hath not seen it—
Ear hath not heard its deep songs of joy;
Dreams cannot picture a world so fair,
Sorrow and death may not enter there.

—Hemans

Thou toiler for the multitude! Stay awhile the earthly record, and come in spirit to the heavenly land. Though thine eyes be veiled and thine ear yet closed, a gleam of beauty and a low, faint strain of joy is vouchsafed unto thee; a revelation from the worlds of soul. Calm all the anxious throbbings of thy heart; be silent, all ye voices of the outer world! Uprise, winged aspirations! Nor stay your flight until the Morning gates are reached!

Oh, world of life and youth external! Thine atmosphere of blessedness encircles me! thy pearly gates unclose; thy fragrant summer wreath is at my feet, thy crystal streams flow on toward the ocean of Infinitude! The grandeur of thy wisdom-temples and thy mountain-shrines—the beacon fires, the love-plains of the soul's divine repose; the marriage bowers, and the trysting fanes; oh, blessed land! They break upon my spirit's vision, all mistily overhung by my earthly imperfection's veil!

And wandering 'mid the avenues of light, resting by the sunlit fountains, praying by the wildwood shrines, mine eyes behold the faces of the glorified and blest. I hear them joining in the harmony of worship unto the true and living God:

Father! With uplifted vision,
Freed the spirit, purified the soul—
Gaze we upward to the worlds Elysian,
Where the planet isles in music roll.
Where thy sun-winged messengers outvieing
Thoughts intensest speed, are borne along
To the nether worlds, in pity hieing
With the heaven-born gifts of love and song.
Starry isles, the sacred fane of angels,
Gleam upon our loving, prayerful sight;

And love divine, the soul's evangels
Graves the tablets of eternal right!
Father-spirit! From thy inner glory
And abounding Mother-love, we crave
Pitying response to Earth's saddened story,
Light to guide her souls beyond the grave!
By the tombstone broken hearts are kneeling,
Doubt and fear with moral storm are rife,
O'er the senseless clay in vain appealing,
For the tokens of another life.
Priests are held the guardians in whose keeping,
Rest the treasures of celestial lore;
On the Present's knowledge falsely heaping,
Musty records of the myths of yore.
Thundering curses o'er the affrighted masses,
See, they hold dominion o'er the world;
Forged devices of the heavenly passes,
Fierce decrees of endless wrath are hurled.
By lips fallible, and weak, and sinning,
That presumptuous dare of thee to tell!
And with fabled glories seek the winning,
Of immortal souls from priestly hell!
Father! We, thy spirit-children, gifted
With enfranchised souls and hearts at peace—
Would, inspired by Thee, by Love uplifted,
Labor for a darkened world's release.
From the spirit-orbs in distance gleaming,
From th' encircling ocean of Thy Will,
From heights of power, and depths of loveful dreaming,
Benignant wisdom speaketh to us still.
Of the sunrays of that Inspiration,
Of the waters of eternal Truth,
Of the blessed soul's transfiguration,
And the amaranthine blooms of youth—
Of the love fanes, and the marriage bowers,
Of the soul-laws of the upper realm;
Of the life-bark, freighted with God-powers,
Angel-guarded at the prow and helm,
Would we tell Thy children; creed-bound, weeping,
As the orphaned, outcast ones of God;

Tell them, Life is endless—death no sleeping—
 That no heart-pulse rests beneath the sod?
They should know Thee, Father! From the pages
 Of thy Life-book, Nature, true and fair;
And the teachings of the bygone ages,
 Steep no more their souls in doubt's despair.
Earth is calling! Myriad souls are pining,
 God and Father! List the anguished cry!
In thy Love and Wisdom boons designing,
 Bid saving angels to the rescue hie!

A kingly form, majestic in his bearing, with the innate nobleness and worth of soul, steps from amid the spirit-ranks. Light undulated in rainbow waves around his form; its condensed rays illume as with a diadem's transcendent lustre, the lofty brow; the scepter of moral conquest is held in his uplifted hand. That is no servile homage that is rendered unto him; the bowing of love-crowned and lily encircled brows; the folding of strong and tender hands is no mark of deference such as earth renders to her princes and her rulers; it is the tributary meed of the soul's obeisance, law-giver unto Honor, Truth and Wisdom. That kingly soul has gained the victory in a hundred spiritual conflicts; that noble heart has won the mountain summits of Submissive Will; that regal hand has unlocked the treasures of celestial life. And public acclamation and the inner dictate have enthroned him intellectually; have given into his care the teaching of souls—to his keeping the watchwords of Progression. In musical utterance his eloquent speech flows forth, and is recorded upon the tablets of Eternity:

Oh; earth benighted! earth enslaved! thy sorrows
 Have touched my soul with shafts divine of Love;
For thee uprolls the curtain now—the morrow
 The dawn of Truth is breaking from above.
Thou wert my birthplace, mother! and I love thee,
 With all the grateful memory of young years,
And with responsive blessings I will seek thee,
And with sweet heaven-songs chase thy hoarded fears.
Father of souls! Before thy Omnipresence,
 I bow the head and meekly bend the knee;
Awaiting from the Love-realms of thy Being,
 The consecration of my ministry—
To bear to earth Immortal truths, and win
The faltering, creed-bound souls of men from sin;

Commissioned of my heart and Thee, I go
To teach redemption to the world below!

From the azure and rosy clouds, vibrating to a strain of heavenly encouragement, there fell upon the bowed imperial head a diamond-tinted shaft of light. It was the signal of divine approval; and by its inspirational power he felt commissioned from the source of Truth.

"Blessed, thrice blessed, art thou, co-laborer for the earth's redemption!" sweetly sang the spirit hosts. And he was led to the roseate and pearly gate by the hands of the true and pure.

Radiant with the beauty born of heroic deeds and lofty soul achievements, a woman-angel, clad in the azure vestments of the beatified, leading by the hand a child immortal, thus addressed the silent ranks:

Is it not woman's province earth to bless,
With the heart offerings of Love's sacredness?
A spirit's holiest task is to reclaim
Its children from their heritage of shame.
To break off fetters from the souls that pine
In churchly prisons, for the light divine;
To priests to whisper of a higher fame,
Than controversial fury in God's name!
On childhood's heart to pour the love of truth,
And beauty's secret to the ear of youth.
And to the mother and the maiden speak,
Of soul laws binding on the strong and weak.
To stand a guardian-angel by the side
Of tempted virtue; to the sorrowing bride,
And weeping mourner, teach the law of love,
God's mandate of reunion from above.
Be this my mission; bending heart and knee,
I seek Thy blessing, Spirit of the free!
Life of all souls! Maternal source! Whose grace
In love-lit splendor decks the human race!

Around the kneeling form there fell bright golden and violet-tinted rays; a sapphire star, unseen before, glistened on her brow, and a wand of magic power was in her hand; with a gentle gesture of farewell she turned to her companions, who showered flowers upon her pathway. Close beside the music-opening portal she paused, and gazed upon the little child that in its snowy vestments, with its wreath of jeweled roses, rested by the fountain's murmur. To her inquiring gaze the little angel's lips responded in a gush of melody:

> I will go with thee, beloved, to the dark and stormy
> earth,
> And my soul shall whisper comfort to the mourner by
> the hearth;
> Where they weep for angel children, past the golden
> flowing tide,
> Where the seal of sorrow lingers, there wilt thou and
> I abide.
> I will press the rosy blossoms of my star wreath to the
> lips,
> Of the captive and the mourner, waiting for their life's
> eclipse;
> I will speak of home and heaven, to the toilers of the
> land,
> And the pure and the forgiven, shall behold me as I
> stand.
> I will sing sweet songs of comfort to the erring and
> the wild.
> And will tell the sorrow-stricken that he is the Angel's
> child;
> I will go with thee, beloved! by my ministry to aid,
> The beautiful to blossom, in yon world which He has
> made.
> To the Father of the Living! To the Mother of all
> souls!
> The tide-flow of devotion through the boundless ether
> rolls!
> And his spirit child invoking, all of Inspiration's
> might,
> Lowly bows the heart and spirit in His omnipresent
> sight.

Oh, the delicious tidal flow of melody that descended from the unseen realms! Beneath its solemn and thrilling visitation every knee was bowed; beneath the glory-flood of crimson splendor that enveloped that radiant child-form, every eye was veiled. Meekly triumphant, inspired and joyous, it approached the maternal guardian, and the twain descended to the awaiting earth.

From the angelic band of responsive hearts and united souls stepped forth a youth; the embodied and exalted counterpart of the fabled god of music. A garment of the golden hues of morning, embroidered with the pearls of poesy, threw around him its ample folds, and at the waist was girdled by a zone of precious gems his soul had gathered from the mine of thought, the seas of revealment. A coronet of sky-blue flowers that glistened gemlike and transparent, encircled his youthful forehead, and stray gleams of jeweled luster broke from amid the sun gleams of his golden hair. The thought fires of celestial wisdom mingled with the angelic tenderness that shone from those cerulean eyes; in his hand he held the lyre of heavenly teachings; and as he stepped forth, all bowed their heads and spread their hands toward him, while he sang:

I would leave the starry bowers, and the fanes
Of my soul's divine abode,
To bear to yon darkened world of sin,
The love-light of our God!
To bear to its weary, storm-tossed souls
The palm branch from above,
With the magic of Truth to unbar the gates
Of the poet-realm of love.
With a mission of grace and of saving power,
I would bid the mourner arise;
And in worship of soul seek the Infinite One,
In the inner life's paradise.
With a word to the erring that shall bid them unfold
In the rays of forgiveness divine;
With a song for the toiler, a hymn for the lone,
Deck with beauty the desolate shrine.
To the mourner's ear I would whisper the lore
Deep guarded in ocean's wild caves;
Of the spirits that glide, and the music that floats
O'er the sapphire and crystalline waves.
To the lovers of earth I would tell of the homes,
Of the blessed twin-angels of life;
From my silver-voiced lyre I would bid them beware
Of the clamoring phantoms of strife.
On the heart-wedded souls in yon wearisome earth
I would pour the full tide of my song;
On their sanctified brows, on the love-guarded hearth,
There should linger no shadow of wrong.

On the soul that aspires, on the worshipful heart,
I would cast the sweet spell that is mine;
Till it broke forth exultant in triumph's refrain
And the earth wore its semblance divine!
I await thy behests, gracious Author of Mind!
I wait for the token of joy—
That shall animate soul, and shall sanction the toil
Of the chosen of Heaven's employ!

It came, the sunlit token of acceptance; breaking through the amethys-
tine splendor that encircled it; and the poet's spirit seemed to float exultant
in the music-broken air.

"Blessed, blessed is thy mission to the world!" sang the admiring host,
and with bowed head and eyes that glistened with sympathetic heart-dew,
he passed beyond the pearly gates.

A vestal Grace, wrially gliding over the enameled plain, advanced. The
nameless beauty of the soul's serenest expression dwelt upon her perfect
face; its lines revealed in all the rhythmic symmetry that ruled her form;
the holy eyes were upraised to the glorious skies, and inspiration's glory was
enwraptly mirrored in their azure depths. As a veil of living sunbeams, her
unbound tresses fell around her, and the mystic splendor of the silver Star
of Even was reflected on her flowing robe. A wreath of lilies, fragrant with
the outbreathed purity of soul, was twined around the queenly head; from
the flowerets' heart-depths sparkled light, and murmured music. All heads
were bowed, all hands outstretched in welcome, as she approached. The
cloud-messengers lingered to hear; the birds suspended for a while their
liquid strains of rejoicing; the floral harmony of spirit-land was hushed,
while she, the angel, sang:

I know that life divested of love's power,
Is barren of fruition; that the flower
Of Truth unfolds beneath its sunlight dower.
I am beloved of God and angels; man
Alone refuses me the right to scan
Creation's glory, and the Future's plan.
I am immortal! Yet they call me dead,
And say my kindred loves from earth have fled;
That Eden's love-light from the world has sped.
They call me "Dreamer by the vestal fane";
Earth's voices tell me it is all in vain,

The wish and will, its holiest souls to gain.
And yet, methinks, within earth's homes there dwell
Souls that but need my spirit's kindling spell
To bid the grossness of the world farewell!
I hear sweet prayers arising from that world;
And music, that the planets must have hurled
Through space and time, till peace her wing unfurled
Upon some sacred tablet of the heart;
Bidding the phantoms of its ill depart;
And seraph's calling, love-lore to impart.
I see within the darkened homes of earth,
Amid life's disillusions, spirit dearth,
Winged aspirations couching by the hearth.
I will unto the untaught souls declare
How angels live in soul-bands, free and fair;
How vestal brows love's lilied chaplet wear.
I will teach man the serpent form to shun;
Tell him accusing chimes in ether hung,
Ring out the horror of a soul undone!
I will tell mothers that their children bear
The impress she has chosen they shall wear,
Of demon foul, or sylphlide of the air.
And I will whisper to the maiden's sense,
Of purity's divine Omnipotence;
The mystic glory that she draws from thence.
Thou! Who art e'er enthroned in love's own light
By Thy soul's quickening power and conscious might!
I pray Thee arm me for the coming fight!
I would release Thy children from the gloom
Of earthly grossness; and the spirit doom
That evil works beyond the shielding tomb.
I would behold the earthly serpent crushed,
Beneath the conquering woman's foot; and hushed
All groveling aims from life-founts that have gushed.
I would make love supreme, my God! for Thee;
For the lone hearts invoking death's decree—
And for man's great and godlike destiny!
And not a breath of lower earth's desires
Should mingle with the incense, that aspires
Unto the soul's eternal heaven-fires!

Loud plaudits rent the azure and cloud-jeweled dome; then solemn silence fell upon the multitude, and a prolonged re-echoed hymn of sovereign gladness swept from the empyrean above, enfolding all the prayerful hearts assembled there in a hush of most ecstatic joy. Around the invoking spirit fell a silver shower; and unseen hands cast o'er her kneeling form the emblematic lilies of immortal growth. While yet that cloud of glory lingered, she had reached the gate, and with one more look of love and longing, she sped to the calling world below.

There came next, a matronly form, whose brow was decorated by the love crown of motherhood. Beautiful with eternal youth, the wisdom of ages dwelt within her soul. Eager to redress the wrongs, the skepticism, the sorrows of the earth, she stepped forth, leading by each hand an angel-child; and all who gazed upon her blest her as a ministering spirit. She cast her eyes, so full and tender, toward the overarching sky, and from her true heart burst the melody:

> I dwell in the land of my heart's desire,
> I pray by the true God's shrine;
> I am robed in the amethystine glow
> Of a motherhood divine.
> I wear on my brow the diadem
> Of its consecrated aim;
> And the music-waves of my soul respond
> To the love-call of my name.
> I would leave the home-lit glories
> Of my heart fane, shrined above;
> Hastening to the angel rescue,
> And the seraph's work of love.
> I would bear to earth the tablets
> Of the life-laws framed by thee!
> And would tell the fettered millions
> Of the freed soul's destiny.
> I would bid the mourning mother,
> From the great bereavement turn
> To the star-world's magnet glory,
> Where the constellations burn.
> I would lead the aspiration,
> Winged and fearless to the goal
> Of love's infinite revealment,
> To the sunlit heights of soul.
> I would to that world of sorrow

Bear the messages of truth,
Angel watchwords of reunion,
And the blessed spell of youth.
I would cast the prayerful incense
Of the heart's divinest need
O'er the darkened household altar;
From the crushing soul-bonds freed.
Man, erect in godlike beauty, shall upraise the
triumphant song
Of the blessed earth's redemption, love-taught by the
angel throng.

A flood of amber light shed around the suppliant spirit proved the divine acceptance of her offering, and again the solemn music of celestial hosts was heard. With sweet smiles of gratitude and farewell—the spirit-mother leading by the hand the graceful angels sped upon her commissioned way. Many sought the same boon for earth. Sages, child-like hearts, maternal guardians, moral heroes, loving youths, and most celestial maidens prayed for the earth's redemption, and for the divine approval of their laboring souls.

And thus, to some portions of the world, from upper hands of love and knowledge, were the glad tidings borne; and thus the new era was inaugurated; the earth blessed anew with the spiritual intercourse of old.

The beautiful scene fades slowly; the glorified faces grow dim; the music dies away in a soft lingering strain of regret. The pearly portal closes; once more the diamond spray of fountains blends with the shifting splendor of the skies above. A misty veil o'erhangs the beautiful revealment.

"Return to earth and record earthly scenes, thou toiler for the multitude!"

22

The Realities of Life

And ye, who sit aloft in earth's high places,
Perchance amid your wealth ye scarcely know
That Want and Woe are leaving fearful traces
Upon the toiling multitude below;
From your abundance can ye not bestow
A mite to smooth the thorny paths they tread?
Have ye no sympathy with human woe?
No ray of blessed hope and joy to shed
Upon the weary hearts that toil and pine for bread?
                                        —Sarah T. Bolton

The scene is changed. From the unveiled realms of soul land, we lead thee to the darkened earth; from the luxuriant Tropic landscape to the wintry gloom of the far-famed City of Brotherly Love. And there, amid life's stern and sad realities, we meet again with the changed Cosella. She has drank deeply of the trial draughts of orphanhood and dependence since last she prayed beside the willow shaded grave of Shina. Unable longer to endure the indolent monotony of her life, she has left her humble friends, and the shelter of their cosy home, resolved to defy her destiny and perhaps realize the wild hope living at her heart. With a morbid eagerness, she seeks in the newspaper for tidings of the father she knows not how to name; she walks the streets peering anxiously into the faces that bear resemblance to the one her fancy pictures. She has put aside her costly robes and sold all her valuable trinkets. She wears the livery of toil, and on her face is the badge of untold suffering. From the poetic life of ease and leisure, she has descended to a dependent's scale; and in the houses of the proud and fashionable she is received on most unequal terms. The proud, brave spirit, that deemed itself companionable to the highest, is superciliously shown the place the world allots to toilers. Women devoid of soul-culture address her condescendingly; men divested of the heart rules of politeness call her in a commanding tone. And while the indignant flush mantles her cheek, and defiant glances break from her eye, her lips are silent and the high heart is wrung with all the bitterness the unappreciated know of. Cosella, the dreamer of the beautiful, the free, wild, soaring spirit, is imprisoned by the requirements of the daily needs. She, who gazed upon the glories of the sunset from the Ganges' sacred banks, she who stood beside the sphynx in solitary meditations, who drank in soul draughts of life lasting inspiration on the Alpine mounts—she is now that saddest, most unheeded things of earth, a seamstress for her daily bread!

No more the soothing lullaby of ocean charms her to sweet dreams of poesy; no more the garden's fragrant wealth invites her wandering steps; the heavens, so blue and sunlit, gleam strange and far above the thronged house-tops, and the message of the golden stars is intercepted. The even monotony of one of the finest cities presses heavily upon her; the snow-white marble of the door steps, the long interminable rows of brick houses, the denuded trees that primly line the street, the falling snow, the ice, the cold, the chilling rain—all, all external changes correspond to the gloom of soul in which the stranger is so deeply plunged.

Brave girl! Alone, unaided, save of spirit hosts, she crossed the ocean and reached the land renowned for liberty. She sought for aid and friendship from those of her mother's race; she had read much of the tie of sympathy existing between those of the same faith, and she dreamt of protection, maternal guidance, fraternal help, and sustaining friendship. Not one of her dreams was realized.

She was rudely questioned as to her worldly means, her parentage, her past life. "What can you do for a living?" was demanded. And when she replied that she had been unaccustomed to labor, she was told that she "must learn to make herself useful."

Thus repulsed, she resolved to keep her own secret and trust to God for the fulfillment of her most cherished hope. She therefore gave her inquirers such portions of her history as she deemed necessary, and locked the rest within her breast. For a few weeks she lived in one of those economical boarding-houses abounding in large cities, where low prices are in vogue, and the fare is correspondingly execrable. Then, finding her scanty means rapidly diminishing, she again made application to those whose law enjoins pity and protection for the orphan and the stranger.

I will briefly sketch *from life* some of the young girl's experiences in the wealthy, piously-reputed and benevolent city of fraternal love.

"Can you do housework?" asked Mrs. S——, a pious, ignorant and fortune-elevated lady, of the shrinking and embarrassed applicant.

"No, madam," replied Cosella; "I have never had occasion to perform it."

"Vere do you come from?" queried the Americanized German.

"From Santa Lucia in South America."

"*Tear me!* Dat is fery far off, is it?—near Ingland?"

Cosella explained.

"De Spanish Main!" exclaimed the lady; and going to the head of the kitchen stairs, she called out: "Modder, modder, come here right avay! Here is a gurl all de vay from Spain; she vants something to do; come and see her."

She was submitted to the scrutiny of the old lady, who, taking the young girl's soft hand, said, in German:

"Little, good-for-nothing hands! Never did any useful work."

Cosella blushed painfully. "I understand German," she said to the younger lady.

"You do? My! How fery queer; vere did you learn? And can you talk French, and Spanish, and Portekeese?"

"I learnt from—my father," replied Cosella. "I speak Spanish and understand French."

"Can you sew?"

"I can."

"Can you make dresses? Make sherts and poys' pantaloons?"

"I cannot make dresses, nor boys' clothing; but I have helped to make my father's shirts. I can sew very neatly."

The coarse wondering souls before her little knew of the heart-pangs of wounded feeling, the depth of humiliation, she was enduring.

"Vell, de neatness is all fery vell; but I vant some one to sew fast as blazes for me. How many days vill it take you to make a shert?"

"I cannot tell, madam."

There was a whispered consultation, during which she was scrutinized from head to foot. Then Mrs. S—— rejoined, "You may come next Monday, and I vill have de sewing ready, and if you suit me, I vill make some arrangement to keep you. You vant a home and your board, and dat I vill give you, and you needn't sew on Saturday—ve alvays keeps de Sabbat holy."

The old lady murmured as she retired, "*She* can't do much!"

This was her first introduction into the world of actual toil. At the appointed time she came, was reprimanded for her tardiness, and the pile of work was placed before her. Never had she sat at one continued task for a whole day. But she bore up bravely, never uttering one complaining word, though her temples throbbed with pain, and her fingers, unused to such continued labor, ached wearily. Her handiwork was admired, but she was told she must learn to sew faster. She was shown into a cheerless, fireless room, and she slept, after the day's toil, and her dreams were sweet.

From early morn until eleven o'clock at night she was compelled to wield the needle; making garments for the children, which Mrs. S—— cut out, mending and braiding and stitching until her eye-balls ached and her head was tortured with a weary pain. For all this she received her board, and now and then a paltry present. She sat all day in the close cellar kitchen, and was the constant butt of the cross old lady and the rude, untrained children; the only drop of balm mingling in the bitter cup was the kindness and urbanity of Mr. S——, who treated our poor girl as became a gentleman; but he was away from home the greater portion of the day, and knew not to what tasks she was subjected. He would often say to her, seeing her ply her needle in the evening, "I fear you will injure your eyes, Miss Phillips" (to that name Cosella had returned). But she, knowing too well what was required of her, smiled gratefully and continued her work.

At dusk on the Sabbath eve she was allowed to lay aside her tasks; and if the weather permitted, she would steal forth into the open air. The Sabbaths she spent reading, and in taking exercise. Sometimes she accompanied the family to the synagogue, but her feelings of devotion had departed; she saw only the outward form; she read the many shams, the seeming, the mockery of true worship; and she sought for light within, telling no mortal soul of her internal struggles.

The heart that is repulsed by the world, its wealth of love unacknowledged, its soul-needs unresponded to—that heart of necessity turns to its inner resources, and forms to itself responsive and beautiful ideals. On some imaginary shrine (imaginary because impossible of realization in this life) it places its votive offerings of genius and faith, of truth and affection. It endows with life and color, warmth and music, this beautiful ideal: adding to its conceptions of undying glory day by day until it stands face to face with its invoker, and its creator becomes a longing votary. Then in the actual life, mayhap, someone bearing a faint or strong resemblance to this image in the heavens appears; and the seeking heart, enwrapped in its own fair and pure illusions, casts the mantle of its dreams upon the earthly embodiment, who thenceforth becomes a God to be worshiped for his attributes; a hero form to be enshrined with loftiest deeds; a ministering spirit, an earthly friend. With all things high, great and good, this one idea mingles, and the heart rendered plastic by sorrow receives the fair and false impression it deems indelible. Thus are wayward loves admitted—thus the mistakes of life are made.

Solitude, uncongeniality, morbid fancies that gained strength by nurture, past trial, and present uncertainty; the dreams she brooded over and the uncommunicated thoughts had weakened the strong resisting heart of Cosella. As time passed on, and the hope of meeting her unknown father grew faint and wavering, the hoarded filial tenderness, the woman's love sought for a resting place amid the turmoils of life and destiny. She found none she could compare to her noble father. But she gave anew the treasure of her love, unsought and unasked for; she showered its heart-wealth on an unconscious head; she endowed with superhuman glory one who returned not the blessed gift. She waited for his footstep, listened to his voice, and wove sweet heart-dreams from his smile.

He was the music teacher, who came thrice a week to instruct the eldest Miss S—— in the rudimentary elements. The strange, fantastic and bewildering harmonies that he drew from the ivory keys were accompanied by Cosella's unspoken improvisations of prayer and love. Sometimes, Mrs. S—— repaired to the parlor, and, as a favor, the seamstress was allowed to follow her, to listen to the music while she sewed. Thus it was that she gazed upon the intellectual face of the teacher, that sometimes she met his beaming eye and encouraging smile. One day he entered into conversation with her. His home was upon the banks of the Rhine; there yet dwelt his aged parents. Cosella told him of her travels; and warming with a touch of the olden enthusiasm, her cheek glowed with its recovered roses, and the light of a new-born hope illumined her eye. Mrs. S—— had left the room for some moments:

"You are out of your sphere, young lady, in this capacity," he said, as he took up a portion of her sewing.

Cosella thanked him with a grateful smile and a tear. "One noble heart appreciates me," she thought, and her dreams that night were golden with the future's promises.

By degrees, she learnt that he was engaged to a young lady of the city—a lady fair, and young, and wealthy. For a time, Cosella struggled with the sorrow and the revelation, urging upon herself that she had no right to blame—no permission to love unsought; then veiling still more carefully every vestige of partiality, she sought to meet him as a sister and a friend. But the heaviest blow her heart had yet received was when he came one day, with a flushed cheek and glittering eye, and in faltering tones and unsteady gait gave every token of intoxication. Mrs. S—— had graciously permitted her to sit with herself in the parlor that afternoon; and when he entered in that miserable condition, Cosella felt a deathly faintness creeping over her, and her work fell from her trembling hands.

"Vat is de matter?" said Mrs. S——. Then in a loud whisper: "Are you not used to see dipsy mens? *He* is often so."

Cosella picked up her work, but could scarcely control her agitation. He, the supposed embodiment of her every thought of nobleness—*he*, thus abased, degraded before her!

"Vell, Mr. E——, I s'pse you vont give any lesson dis afternoon?" said the lady of the house.

He replied incoherently; he attempted to relate some news, to joke with Cosella. She merely lifted her rebuking and tear-filled eyes to his face and shuddered as she gazed upon it. The beauty of its intellectuality was gone; a gross expression rested on its every lineament; there was a revolting gleam in his eye. Gathering up her sewing, and saying: "Please excuse me, Mrs. S——," she descended to the cellar kitchen.

She could not go to her room to indulge in the luxury of tears; that was denied to her. She had no maternal friend to whom she could confide her sorrow and her disenchantment. The coarse, materialistic souls around her, what knew they of those finer feelings that are at once the blessing and the bane of the thus endowed? In her heart's depths Cosella murmured: "God pity me! There is no truth, no love, no real good on earth!" Then with an impulse of womanly sympathy, all devoid of envy, she thought of his fair and fortune-favored bride and said: "God help her, too!"

"What are you so still and sorrowful for?" queried the old lady who had been silently regarding her. "Are you thinking again of your father and mother? It's of no use to fret for them; they are in heaven; and you ought to be thankful that you enjoy health and such a comfortable home. If you indulge in crying, you will spoil your eyes, and then you can't do Sophy's fine stitching; and no one will marry you if you fret and grow ugly."

Cosella's tears were falling fast; and to the old lady's tirade in German, she replied in the same language that she was not thinking of her father and mother, and could not help the intrusion of sorrowful thoughts.

Mrs. S—— laughed at her heartily for her affectation, as she styled it, in not being able to bear the sight of "dipsy mens."

Mr. E—— gave no lesson that day; and it was long before he returned to the house. Cosella sought in vain for an opportunity of conversation; and failing to find it, she wrote him a long and sisterly letter warning him of the depths to which his infatuation would lead him; calling upon him for his parents' sake and in the name of his young betrothed to cast aside the tempting cup. It was such a letter as could only emanate from the heart of a true and loving woman, who laying all of self aside strives only for another's good. Whatever impression that missive made upon him, she never heard of it; for soon after its delivery the S—— family removed to another part of the city. The music lessons were discontinued, and she saw Mr. E—— no more.

She heard, long afterwards, that he had been ignominiously expelled from the house of his intended by her incensed father for presuming to present himself in a state of total inebriation. Cosella mourned for the lost dream and the broken idol. It was one of those experiences buried deep in the breast that brook no revelation. But it added to the darkness of skepticism that enfolded her being as with a moral pall.

Wearily, wearily the weeks and months rolled on and the cheek of Cosella paled, and her once buoyant step grew laggard. The close confinement told upon her health and spirits, and the hated employment was a constant source of rebellion to her every feeling. Once in a while an impatient word escaped her; a reminiscence of the past was alluded to; the desire for a home of her own was expressed.

"Vell, den," was Mrs. S——'s unfailing reply, "vy don't you git a home? Vy don't you marry Mr. Helmerskop and git a servant of your own? You can git him any day you vants to; he tells me he likes you ever so much—vy don't you have him?"

"Mr. Helmerskop is old enough to be my father," replied Cosella, with an angry flush upon her face "Besides, he is vulgar and conceited, a braggart and an ignoramus!"

"*My! My!* Vat big vords all for noting; never *you* mind if he is old enough to be your fadder; he's got money; vat you call vulgar, and conceity, and all de rest? Poor gurls must not be so partickler."

"Poor girls can retain their self-respect, Mrs. S——," replied Cosella, and she applied herself vigorously to her sewing, disdaining any further discussion upon the subject.

Mr. Solomon Helmerskop was an ancient Hollander, a queer old bachelor, full of strange conceits, vastly imbued with the idea of his own overwhelming consequence—arrogant, dictatory, coarse and rude—just the man to inspire Cosella with a fixed and settled aversion. He had offered her his hand and heart and dry goods store, all of which Cosella had twice refused. But the persevering swain still hoped, and still visited the house in the hope of winning the "spunky Southern girl." Mrs. S—— used every argument within her reach, but in vain; and as her seamstress threatened to leave the house if she were persecuted on that subject, Mrs. S——, fearing that her sewing would suffer, yielded reluctantly, and ceased to urge the suit of the wealthy Helmerskop.

Cosella sewed and stitched from early morn till late at night, determined to earn her bread. She sewed so swiftly that soon there was scarcely anything left for her to do; for Mrs. S——, availing herself of so favorable an opportunity, *at so cheap a rate*, had provided herself and family with all the necessary garments for a long time to come. The seamstress was then informed that she might seek for employment elsewhere; and for a few weeks only she found it behind the counter of a trimming store.

One day, she saw an advertisement in the paper that an interpreter (a lady) was demanded by a family from Cuba. She applied for the situation, and was told by the swarthy and haughty señora that she required *a person* to assist in the charge of her little girl, do her shopping, interpret for her, and that person must submit to eat at the servants' table, and sleep in the same room with her child's black nurse.

Cosella told the lady she would submit to all the requirements of the labor, but not to any personal indignity. She would take her meals alone, and have her own bed; if the señora saw fit to engage her under those conditions, she was willing, not otherwise. The proud Creole reflected; she had advertised many times without result; all that had applied were women of coarse exteriors and uncultivated minds, or ladies so refined and fastidious they would not accept anything like a menial's post. But this girl wore the semblance of ladyhood; her speech was gentle and melodious, yet she was humble, too. The proud Cuban knew not that the last dollar rested in the young girl's pocket.

"You may come and make that arrangement you please," she said; and Cosella sped away with a lightened heart.

23

Toil and Suffering

Not in the laughing bowers,
Where, by green twining elms, a pleasant shade,
At summer's noon is made;
And where swift-footed hours
Steal the rich breath of the enamored flowers,
Dream I. Nor where the golden glories be,
At sunset, laying o'er the flowing sea;
And to pure eyes the faculty is given
To trace a smooth ascent from earth to Heaven.
But where the incessant din
Of iron hands, and roar of brazen throats,
Join their unmingled notes,
While the long summer day is pouring in,
Till the day is gone, and darkness does begin,
Dream I. As in the corner where I lie,
On wintry nights, just covered from the sky.
Such is my fate—and barren though it seem,
Yet, thou blind, soulless scorner, yet I dream!
And yet I dream—
Dream what, were men more just, I might have been.
　　　　　　—From A Volume Of "Poems By A Seamstress"

For three months of slavery, the young girl abode with the purse-proud task-mistress, submitting to all the varied humiliations that dependence imposes. She was employed as errand-girl, attendant, nursery maid, secretary and interpreter, all for the munificent sum of two dollars per week. But the labor and fatigue bore too heavily upon her, and she informed the señora of her intentions of seeking other employment. She was haughtily dismissed; and around the wide city she looked for the means of obtaining her subsistence, for the shelter of a home.

There lived in a fine house, with all the appliances of ease and comfort, an invalid old lady, with whom Cosella had become acquainted. Thither she repaired for a few days, until she should again obtain a situation. She was cordially welcomed by the helpless mistress of the house, but sternly scowled upon by the housekeeper, who feared every new-comer might prove her rival in the affections of her employer, although affection was not the bond that linked her to her service; she held much control over the purse strings of the old lady, and ruled the house at her own sovereign will.

She was a being low of moral stature, unrefined in soul, and odd of speech. A thorough worker as regards the vigorous use of broom and scrubbing brush; she delighted in the confusion of house cleaning, in the infliction of those minor deluges upon windows and pavements which form one of the cardinal doctrines of Philadelphia cleanliness. What stranger visiting that beautiful city but has gazed in wonder and alarm upon the torrents pouring from fourth story windows? Upon the winding streamlets underfoot? Immutable as the decrees of the Gods, as the "I have spoken," of the ancient Sachems, is the custom upheld: and woe to the uninitiated who foresee not the coming waterfall and cannot agilely spring from the daily inundation.

Miss Betsey Brian entertained a high opinion of her own literary acquirements, choice use of language, and elegance in dress and manner, no less than in her peculiar and thorough-going mode of housekeeping. The feather beds received not only their due amount of lawful shaking, but also sundry twists and punchings, as if an evil temper sought to wreak the malice it could not vent elsewhere upon the passive mass; pie boards and rolling pins, broom handles, and all things susceptible of the appliance of scrubbing brush and soap received such marvelous applications of what she refinedly termed "elbow grease" (that is strength) that their broad and fair proportions shrank visibly, and dwindled away from week to week. She was a wonderful cook, too; she prided herself upon the invention of various new and inexplicable dishes; she seasoned apples with vanilla, and put her favorite essence of peppermint into soups and sauces. She was peculiar in many ways; she sat down upon the floor to knead her bread and chop the mince-meat; suddenly recollecting some branch of her duties that had been neglected, she would run and leave the dough upon the board, the meat with its accessories upon the floor. At such times, puss would help himself, and Miss Betsey returning with flushed face and grey ringlets streaming, would vow to "kill and forever *experminate* that nuisance of an animal!" Then she would chase grimalkin through the house, and panting with excitement, "swow" that she would murder him at the first next opportunity.

Miss Brian wore spectacles, curls, collar and cuffs, in the afternoon when her work was done and she sat down to her sewing. Her morning toilet consisted of a short petticoat, a night gown, and a cap to correspond. Of course she was invisible to callers in this costume, therefore she managed to keep a "half-grown girl" to do her errands, attend to the door bell, and to bear with her outbreaks of ill-humor, for Miss Betsey indulged in a "tantrum" often, and the Irish girls she had hired could not stand its exhibition.

She disclaimed the "horrible vulgar idea" of Hibernian descent; and told long and contradictory stories of the glories of her ancestors, and the piety and wealth of her forefathers. On her wrinkled face there dwelt an expression of low cunning, and the daily cultivation of an avaricious spirit had tightly screwed up her mouth into an utter denial toward all charitable appeals. Affected, ignorant, professedly religious, and practically selfish and mercenary, this woman yet had redeeming traits. Toward the swarm of nephews and nieces that tormented her with visits and urgent demands for aid she was kind and benevolent. Her heart, closed to the duties of universal love, opened wide at the appeal of kindred; that voice of nature that was allied to her by the ties of consanguinity never pled in vain; many a freshly roasted fowl, fine dish of vegetables, or tempting tart found its way to the larder of her poor relations. From her own code of honesty, Miss Betsey reasoned thus—

"The old thing I live with, don't eat one half she makes me get; and it is a sin to waste wittals; my folks need it, and they shall have it, while the breath of life is in my nostrils!" and the emphatic individual enforced her resolve by a resolute up-and-down shake of the head and a stamp of the foot.

Her life's ambition rested upon the hope that the old lady would make a bountiful provision for her in her will. In view of attaining so great a boon, she was profuse of flattery and attentions, little deeming it possible that the sharp eyes of her world-wise employer saw clearly through her every artifice.

Her old lady had often requested Cosella to make her home there; a widow, her two sons living in another city, she found in the pale, reserved and silent girl that which touched her heart. Without an effort, the orphan would have won her love, and the rest of a quiet home. The helpless invalid, yearning for some responsive soul to cling to, felt her motherly affections going warmly toward the unprotected girl. But she imprudently expressed those thoughts before Miss Betsey, and that lady formed her plans accordingly. She received Cosella with a mixture of condescension and reserve, with an occasional frown darkening her face.

"Dear me! Miss Phillips; I should think you could have worried along with them Cuban folks a little longer. See what I have to put up with. Madam is calling, calling, all day long, and at night I don't close my eyelids; it's up and down, down and up, the blessed live-long night. I think sometimes I shall expire of heart-disease. And I have so much to do! There's pies to bake, and clothes to air, and sewing to get off, and general sweeping, and last week's ironing to do, and all the beds want shaking, and the tins scouring; the windows must be washed, quilting done, and the preserves overlooked. Do you know what a housekeeper's trial is? I swow, *you* don't! *I* have marketing to do, the dressmakers to hunt up—the desert to make, and that imp of a girl to look after. *Scat! Scat!* You beast," she cried, addressing the delinquent cat, who had mounted the table with a chicken wing in his mouth. "You abominably obnoxious critter! You vile cat! You villainous thief of a mischief! You salmagundian scamp! You scarawag! You scratching Lucifer! There, now, bite, scratch, if you dare!" and she applied in quick succession a number of heavy strokes with a brush and handle to the unfortunate cat.

"Now go out of doors, you incarcerated demon! You pestiferous, owlish, miserable scarecrow! If you dare to come into the house again today, I'll chop you up for mince-meat and sell you to the butcher—the Dutchman that buys up everything that crawls for sausages! *I swow!* If you come again in this blessed day I'll murder you, as sure as my name is Betsey Brian!"

"Please, please!" interposed Cosella, as taking the cat by the nape of the neck she was about to inflict a second series of strokes; the young girl's tender heart could not brook cruelty to animals. Miss Betsey took a few rapid strides toward the door, and with a parting kick dismissed poor puss. She returned looking flushed, weary, and excited.

"See here, Miss Phillips," she said, placing her arms akimbo, pulling off her spectacles, and speaking rapidly, "*you* and *I* must come to an understanding if you want to make *this* house your home. I wont bear no interference with my domestic and household arrangements. I'm second captain *here* and I wont give up no *furriner*. I hate furriners, anyhow, they're so tricky and intrigifying; and if there's a earthly thing *I* abhor, detest and abominate, it's intrigifying and manuverating! So don't *you* go to put on no airs; for I swow, *I* wont abide it. I say to the Madam, you can't get a living soul to do for you as I does, and if *you* mean to set anybody up over *me*, why, if *they* stay, *I'll* leave! That settles the Madam; she grows as soft as a new kid glove. *I'll* have no intermeddlers with *my* affairs; and the cat belongs to *us*. You may go upstairs now, and see the Madam; but don't stay long in the room, for it exhausts the Madam; and don't talk much to her—that excites her nerves, and *I'm* nervous enough myself. I'm ready to drop, with all the work before me. *You* can read to the Madam—that will keep you from gab. What a pity she likes those old, trashy novels, when she ought to be studying her prayers, and preparing for the great eternity!" And Miss Betsey cast up her eyes until the whites alone were visible and commenced singing vigorously—

"If I can read my title clear," &c.

Cosella sighed deeply, said not a word, but went upstairs, and to the "Madam's" chamber.

She was cordially received and indulged with conversation that did her good; nor did she notice that the old lady grew excited. On the contrary, she seemed to brighten visibly, and said she felt less of pain and weariness when in the presence of a congenial companion. She was pouring out some medicine, at the invalid's direction, when Miss Betsey entered the room. "What are *you* doing there?" she exclaimed, snatching the phial from Cosella's hand. "What makes *you* interfere? I always give the Madam her medicine; if she trusts to such as you, she'll get herself poisoned someday."

"I asked Miss Phillips to pour out my medicine," said Mrs. Rollins.

"*You did?* And what for, I should like to know, Madam? Haven't I served you on my bended knees and hands for four long years? And is this a return for my devotion and sacrifices of home and friends? Can't I make my living in the first houses in the lands? It's only for affection for you that I sacrifice my nights and days for *your* sake. I tell you *one* thing, Madam, if you are going to have any pets and favorites, and furriners, around *you*, why, if *they* stay, *I'll* leave, that's all! Let me give you your medicine; *she* would as soon give you hartshorn as anodyne. *I swow*, you are as faint as everything!"

"You excite me, Betsey, you talk so long and so loud," said the invalid.

"I do? And other folks talk soft and easy? Oh, my blessed Saviour! That I should live to have such monstriferous ingratitude thrown in my teeth!" and Miss Betsey burst into tears.

Pale and alarmed, Cosella ventured upon an explanation.

"*Be still*, be still! *You* excite the Madam! If she dies and leaves me in this dark, wicked, terrific, slanderous world, what will become of me? Oh, Madam, *dear, good* Madam! Let me give you some broth to revive you! Here is your medicine, just ten drops. *Dear* Madam, can Betsey do anything for you?"

"Help me to the bed," she whispered. Cosella's assistance was waved back, and Miss Betsey motioned to her to leave the room. In a state of bewilderment, she complied, and followed the housekeeper to dinner. Not a word was spoken during the meal. The dishes were pushed toward her, and Miss Betsey, leaning back in her chair and heaving deep sighs, did not touch a morsel; probably she had fortified herself with a substantial luncheon. That afternoon Cosella was advised not to return to the sick-room. Tea was disposed of in the same lugubrious manner as dinner. Only when alone in the silence of her chamber did she give vent to the feelings so long repressed. "Oh, my father!" she cried, "with *thee* what a different fate were mine!" She found that Mrs. Rollins, through sickness and helplessness, was completely at the mercy of the domineering Betsey, and that her home could not long prove a shelter.

She sought in the newspapers and among the "Wants" again; and finding that Miss Betsey took every opportunity to keep her from the old lady's room, and that she sought by every insinuation in her power to persuade her that "Miss Phillips was a lazy, proud and irreligious girl," and that Mrs. Rollins was fast yielding to the inroads of prejudice, she determined to submit to the unavoidable and seek employment in the world. Miss Betsey even took the trouble of seeking a situation for her; but Cosella indignantly scorned the offer of a place as waiting-maid in a wealthy family.

"While I have one remnant of health or strength I will *labor*, but I will not serve!" she said. "I find in this boasted land of liberty that servitude is as humiliating a badge as elsewhere. I cannot become a servant."

"Your pride and ignorance of household matters, and your want of religion, will make you come to trouble yet. *I swow!* Girls like you, that would be fine ladies and can't, ought to get married if they want to escape starvation. Why don't you marry the first fellow that comes and asks you?"

"Because I will not sell myself, body and soul, for money!" indignantly retorted Cosella.

She was fairly chased, by ingenious and petty torments, from the seclusion so dear and healing. Briefly as I may, I will place before you the records of her toilsome life. The only employment that offered itself, a little above a menial's station, was that of a seamstress. And thus it was she fared.

Mrs. Na——, a wealthy lady, one of the daughters of Israel, engaged her for three weeks. From seven in the morning until ten at night she served incessantly. As a favor, she was admitted to the table; as a mark of peculiar condescension, she had a bed allotted to herself. But she was never introduced to visitors, often admonished to sew faster, and told that "girls who made their living must not talk of exercise and such things—they had only to attend to their duties." The ill-bred children of the wealthy Mrs. Na—— tormented poor Cosella to the very utmost; and the sights and sounds that met her ear were repugnant to her mind and feelings. In that home of luxury, adorned with all that art could bestow of the beautiful—with pictures that lead the gazing eye and enraptured soul into the fairy grounds of the Ideal, with statuary that compelled the heart's tribute of admiration, with costly vases, silken curtains, marble, gold and velvet gorgeousness around—she felt that the souls of its inmates, the possessors of all that wealth and power, were devoid of the appreciation that makes the beautiful a source of joy. The revolting language of profanity was there indulged; vituperative epithets bestowed upon the handsome and fashionably dressed wife; scorn and reproaches cast upon the husband. The little boys swore, thinking it manly to ape their father's example; and the girls delighted in the repetition of words that caused Cosella to shudder as if in the presence of embodied and growing evils. They amused themselves, these princely dressed children of the rich, with calling Cosella "our hired girl."

"You is hired to sew, and that's the same as being hired to cook," said the rude Lucius; and his brother, Marcus, called her, "Old white face!" and little Olivia, when desired to be quiet, pertly replied, "You aint my mamma, and this is not *your* house"; and Sarah, the oldest, took a malicious pleasure in making the loudest noises whenever the poor seamstress's head ached. They threw books and papers, balls and tops at her, and to her imploring entreaties to desist, laughed mockingly; and in reply to her indignant remonstrances they threatened to "tell mamma."

Mrs. Na—— coming in, in the midst of the hubbub, would remark "that children would be children, and that Miss Phillips must learn to exercise patience, and control her temper."

Oh the little thorns, the prickly briars of daily life! How the soul is fretted and the thirsting heart is chafed by these petty cruelties! The daily amenities, the sweet, humble courtesies—how they cheer and strengthen! How wearisome the plodding daily labor that is unblessed by the sympathizing smile!

Cosella drew a grateful sigh of relief when the three weeks came to a close. Mrs. Na—— paid her for her unremitted labor, not as had been agreed upon, but deducted a quarter of a dollar from each week.

"You have made a mistake, madam," said Cosella, gently. "I agreed to sew for you for a dollar and a half a week, and though you offered me less, you at last agreed to my terms."

"There is your money," said the stately lady, in a quick, impatient voice. "I shall give you no more."

"Don't you pay any more than you bargained for," said the lordly and tyrannical husband, who was sitting beside her and leisurely enjoying the fragrance of a fresh Havana.

"There is your money; take your things and go," said Mrs. Na——.

"I agreed for—"

"I want no words upon the subject," interrupted the lady. "Here is your money and there is the door!"

She took the money with a trembling hand; she controlled her quivering nerves; she bade the loud, indignant throbbing of her heart be still. A flood of recollection rushed over her spirit; Shina's unfailing gentleness and goodness, the luxury and comfort with which Manasseh had surrounded her, the past life of travel—dreamy, poetically fraught with varied and sometimes pleasant incident—and now, the life of bitterest toil and deepest humiliation! All the inborn pride, the outraged dignity, asserted its sway. With deeply flushed cheek, kindling eye, and proudly erected figure, she confronted her oppressors and spoke:

"You may wrong the orphan and the stranger, but you will be none the richer, none the happier! To willfully defraud me of the proceeds of my hard-earned labor is becoming to such as you! But *never*, if I have to starve, will I touch a needle for *you* again—you pure-proud, vulgar, ignorant aristocrats! I feel myself your superior and your money cannot buy that consciousness! Your religion is a sham, your lives hypocrisy! I scorn, I shrink from association with such as you!"

She rushed from the room ere they recovered from their open-mouthed astonishment at such audacity. Out in the open air, she stopped and cried exultingly:

"I spoke my mind; I broke the slavish fetters of silence! I am *not* a slave; I will confront and confound these petty tyrants, though it cost me my life!"

The next day she sent for her things, and proceeded to fulfill an engagement with a shop-keeper whose principal gains were derived from the manufacture and sale of articles of female apparel. Cosella was employed at the rate of a quarter of a dollar per day in the making of silk mantillas of the style and workmanship known as "slop goods." To sew fast, not neatly, was the chief aim of those employed, and it is customary for "smart hands" to make as many as nine per day.

The owner of the establishment was a shrewd, life- and good-living loving son of Judah. His wife was a small, over dressed, fussy and novel-devouring lady; their daughter, Marianna, a spoilt, affected child, putting on many premature young-lady airs. Such souls could not peer into the sacredly veiled recesses of Cosella's heart or mind. But as in life, the ludicrous stands ever beside the gate of tears, and the heart pangs of a settled sorrow may be momentarily lightened by the amusing occurrences of the day; so Cosella was often drawn from deep and painful musings, by the profound reflections of Mrs. A—— upon historic characters, religious themes, and criticisms of the world.

"Oh, Miss Phillips," said the lady, one day, entering the back parlor where Cosella sat bowed over her work; "what a beautiful world it is that these novel writers tell about! I get carried out of myself when I read those glowing descriptions of duchesses, and queens, and royal princesses. I can fancy myself in the *boudoir* of Anne of Austria, and the fine figure of the Duke of Buckingham rises before me, all in velvet, and plumes, and diamonds! That blessed Alexander Dumas! To write so beautifully. I have read the 'Three Guardsmen,' and am going on with the whole series. Dear me! What scrapes those heroes and heroines get into! And at the end of the chapter, or the week's newspaper, they always leave off in the most interesting place— leave them hanging head foremost down a precipice, or in the power of robbers, or just escaping, or being caught, or something else that is heart-rending and terrible!"

"Nonsense, nonsense! stuff and tomfoolery!" good naturedly growled the husband, who had come in in time to hear a part of the address; "novels are good-for-nothing trash. I want the news in a paper, and the price current—none of your highfalutin love-sick twaddle. I'd rather eat a good beef steak any day than read a book."

"That's just like you men!" said the lady, with a sentimental sigh. "We, of more delicate and ethereal organizations, *we* understand the ideal life; and it is hard for such refined tendencies to meet the roughness of the world and the uncongenialities that surround us. I never wrote a line of poetry in my life, but oh, how I adore it! Delightful Shakspeare! gigantic Milton! beautiful Byron! How I worship their writings! I and my Marianna, we ought to live in a world of our own—not in this toilsome, plodding, mercenary world we live in."

"It's as good a world as you've ever been in," retorted Mr. A——, "and *I* wouldn't exchange it for the silly things you read about. What good do you get out of all that folderol?"

"What good? Oh Adolphus, you have but half a soul! Don't I learn of all the miseries that afflict humanity? Don't I learn how great griefs are borne in silence and resignation? Don't I learn how kings and queens and princes live, and how they come to poverty and nobly bear it? Don't I learn—"

"It's all a pack of trash!" interrupted her husband. "If you're in search for misery, there are plenty of beggars to see after; you can take a ride to the alms house, and see misery enough in one afternoon. You're not overfond of that sort of thing."

"I don't like *vulgar* misery," she lisped.

"Misery is misery, high or low, you romantic goose! And what have *we* to do with royalty? We sell dry-goods and mantillas, and go to the quarter-dollar place in the theatre."

"*I* don't!" said the lady, drawing herself up. "My motto is, 'the first place or none'; but it is useless to argue with you, Adolphus. I live in a paradise of my own—I soar away to the scenes of grandeur, I reach the stars, while you—"

"Stand behind the counter, or eat my dinner sensibly," replied the still smiling husband.

"Dinner!" she scornfully replied; "how can you dwell so everlastingly upon your animal propensities? When I become absorbed by the delicious descriptions of high life, I forget all about such vulgar things as eating!"

"See here, Sallie; don't young kings and highflyers, your queens and court damsels ever eat?"

"Oh, Adolphus, pray don't call me Sallie—that vulgar name! You know

I cannot bear it. Do call me Selinda! Why, of course the queens and princesses eat, but it is gossamer food, wrial dainties, nectared draughts."

"Is that Greek you are gabbling? Can any of those articles be found in market? Is it fish, fowl or vegetable?"

"You are incorrigible! Come here, Marianna, my love," she said to her daughter who had just entered. "Bless my beauty!" she continued, as she kissed the young girl on the cheek. "If the desire of her mother's heart were fulfilled, my daughter should marry a royal prince," she said.

With an amused smile, her husband responded: "How does that agree with your religious scruples, Selinda? There are no princes of the line of Judah, and would you have our child marry a Christian—say Selinda?"

"No, no; certainly not."

"You would not give our Marianna to an unbeliever, even if he was worth a hundred thousand dollars?"

"Sell my religious principles for a paltry hundred thousand dollars! No, indeed, *never!*"

"But consider, Selinda; supposing an English duke or a German count were to ask you for your daughter?"

"A count—a duke?" she said, hesitatingly. "No, I would not consent."

"Well, then, a Prince of the blood royal, an heir to the king's throne—what, then, Selinda?"

"An heir to the crown? And my daughter stand the chance of becoming a Queen? *Oh, he should have her!* I would not withhold my blessing," rapturously exclaimed the ambitious mother.

"But your religious scruples, wife?"

"I—I would submit to the will of Heaven, providing so glorious a destiny for my only child."

"But the sin of marrying a Christian? She would have to conform to the usages of the unbelievers."

"I would sacrifice my own feelings for the aggrandizement of my child. Yes; if a prince of the blood royal should seek my daughter's hand, he shall have it!"

"In spite of religion and prejudice? Eh, Selinda?"

"In spite of an opposing world!" she enthusiastically exclaimed.

"Yes, Marianna, my love; the crown-prince *shall* have you, whether your father consents or not!"

Mr. A—— left the room holding his sides. Marianna innocently inquired:

"Where is the prince you are talking about, mother?"

Cosella leaned back in her chair and indulged in a hearty outbreak of laughter. Mrs. A——, descending from the lofty and the regal, examined the work, praised Cosella's swiftness; and with her daughter returned to her room to commence the first chapter of a new novel.

From thence, after six weeks' constant and laborious toil, Cosella wandered to another transient home, still continuing the only available branch of labor that she felt competent to follow. She could not teach; her wandering life and desultory studies had unfitted her for that vocation. Her fine ear and soulful appreciation of music had never been cultivated; her knowledge of the languages was confined to an intuitive acceptivity that learnt easily, but could not impart its knowledge unto others.

Ever mindful of her ease and comfort, Shina, with mistaken indulgence, had kept her aloof from all culinary lore and household offices. Cosella could write poetry; and compose, as it were, without thought, prose-poems couched in choicest language and deep sentiment. She possessed enthusiasm, moral bravery, a tender heart, a soul o'erfilled with beatific visions of the beautiful. But what cares the working, gold-worshiping world for this? She was not rich; what cared the careless passers-by on life's high road for all the heart-wealth of her being? Once, her cheeks had glowed with the fresh roses of health and happiness; now they were paled by sorrow and hard toil. Once, the sunlight of prosperity, the joy of independence, the inner calm had spoken from her face, and made it lovely. Kind hands had twined the curls around her brow, and placed sweet flowers amid the shining tresses. Now, the light of soul seemed withdrawn from every lineament, and the care-mark stamped the brow; apathy and listlessness, distrust and hopelessness, rendered her almost insensible to praise or blame—stole the light from her eye, and the beauty of expression from her face. Her hair put plainly back revealed the sharpened outline; only momentary excitement could restore the rose flush to her cheek, the haughty self-possession to her manner. Yet she repelled all that savored of humiliation; she retorted to every insult; she allowed no doubt to linger on her name. Friendless, orphaned, solitary, she confronted the libertine who would avail himself of her helplessness with the thundering accusations of innocence—with the scathing rebuke of fearless virtue! She turned from the tempter with defiant horror; from a mercenary marriage with the shudderings of a virgin soul. The dying words of Shina returned to her in all their silver clearness. She oft awoke at midnight, and 'neath the pitying gaze of stars she heard the solemn thrilling words of the departed:

"Be ever true and pure, my child!"

And, "I will, so help me God!" replied the sufferer, feeling love and hope's renewal.

She went from house to house for many weary months, unappreciated, superciliously regarded, poorly paid. She dwelt awhile with those of minds of coarsest mould, with those of most unfeeling natures. She labored where refinement and politeness were as things unknown; she lived on miserable fare, and slept on wretched beds.

In the houses of the wealthy regarded as an inferior being; by the coarse and vulgar treated as a companion, sometimes as a mere hireling, with no settled home anywhere in that wide and hospitable city; was it to be wondered at that the heart of Cosella grew bitterly suspicious of its fellows? That she became moody and skeptical toward the highest intuitions of her soul?

The springtime came, and she who loved Nature with an undivided heart could not go abroad to cull the early violets and to sit beneath the leafing trees. She dared not leave the implement of torture that gave her bread even for a single hour. Oh, how she longed to gaze upon the sun's benignant face at early morn, to revel in his setting rays, to look once more upon the face of smiling earth abroad in the fair green fields!

Summer passed; and she could not gather the June roses, nor twine the abundant garland for her brow. With a wild, vain, speechless yearning, she stretched her arms toward the sea, and beholding not its azure mirror, hearing not its sweet and solemn murmur, she would cry in soul to God for *one* hour of freedom, for *one* ramble by the sea; for one glimpse of mountain and of plain! She was a captive, soul-bowed, chain forged, unto toil. So weary did she become when her week's tasks were over that the exertion that would have led her footsteps to the summer fields could not be taken. She threw herself upon her bed and slept, or indulged in the luxury of tears, from pride restrained during the laboring six days. Sometimes she visited the famous "squares," those miniature parks of Philadelphia, and beneath the tall trees there, and by the fountain in the "square" called by the name of "Franklin," she would sit and dream of the one waning hope of her solitary life.

Autumn came and passed; the Indian summer with its hazy mantle and balmy breath, lingered long and lovingly, and still the child of misfortune wept and toiled. She barely earned her subsistence; the last vestiges of her former condition were gone; the last dress and trinket sold. She could no longer be distinguished from the sisterhood of toil that abounds in cities. She had another offer of marriage, but her soul rebelled, and she cast aside the glittering chance.

Winter cast its snowy drapery o'er the earth; Cosella shivered 'neath its cutting blasts, and drooped before its long continued gloom. The winters of that city are proverbially mild and pleasant; but to the dweller of the Tropics, the spirit long unused to the sudden changes of a variable climate, it was uncongenial in the extreme. With scanty clothing, mechanically toiling fingers, almost breaking heart, she saw the seasons come and go; bringing to her aching frame no rest, to her soul no change. Thus four years passed; and she, once the admired of many, was known as "the cheap seamstress;" weaving life-dreams, soul-prophecies, and heaven-thoughts, queries and answers, in with the garments that her fingers wrought. And as time passed on, the hope that had cheered and brightened slowly died away; until she deemed that Manasseh had spoken falsely even in his dying hour. The future loomed before her dark and desolate; with clasped hands and eyes upraised she would faintly murmur: "I can but die!"

Thus it was that her youth was passed and lost.

24

The Mission of the Beautiful

I charm thee from the agony
Which others feel or feign—
From anger and from jealousy,
From doubt and from disdain.

—Hemans

"I consecrate thee to the service of humanity, to the healing of souls, as to the soothing of the body's pangs! Commissioned by the angel-world, go forth upon thy mission of beneficence; go, to upraise the fallen, and lead them gently to the sheltering retreats of safety; speak heavenly consolation to the mourner's heart; with inspired utterance dispel thou the looming shadows of skepticism, the utter darkness of bereavement; tell them of the encompassing glories of immortality, of the endless life joys, and the progressive unfoldments of the future. Go forth into the world thrice armed with the conscious strength of duty, the victory of self-sacrifice unto the universal good. Thou wilt live down opposition and incredulity, thou wilt gain thousands to the knowledge of their soul's divinity. Shrink not, sweet flower of the tropic solitudes, from the life work allotted thee. We will make thy mission glorious, and its compensations shall amply satisfy every yearning of thy love-full soul. Go into the busy walks of life, and tell the restless toiler and the scheming materialist of the heaven that may be theirs. Go to the lowly haunts, and to the world oppressed speak words of thrilling comfort. Take of thy soul's refinement there, and by the magic transmutation of love, change unto homes of neatness and beauty the hovels of the groveling poor. Teach men of the religious element that unawakened rests within; tell woman of the angel duties that devolve upon her; bid little children know the face of the ever-present Heavenly Father; and this, dear toiler, shall be thy soul's reward:

Ere the effacing hand of time shall plant one furrow on thy placid brow, ere the white threads of the human life-line shall mingle with the golden splendors of thy hair, while yet within thy bosom beat exultingly the joy-pulses of unfading youth, while thy heart is strong, thy intellect clear-seeing, and thy frame unbowed by one touch of earth's numerous ills, thou shalt be summoned to the heavenly land! Not rudely called, nor violently torn from this, thy birth-place, but invoked to come, with strains of welcoming delight, with outstretched arms of the loved and recognized, with the pearly gates of morning wide unclosed, the glory of eternity around thee! Thus, as the good and disciplined, the matured and willing soul should go, wilt thou, with smiling lips and willing feet, obey the Father's mandate. Thy mission to the earth fulfilled, the crowning of life's greatest joy will open for thee the heavenly portals. Joy, joy to thee, Solita, thou chosen and thou early blest!"

With his hand placed on her bowed head, with solemn thrilling utterance, Percival Wayne pronounced these words, and as the consciousness of their meaning flashed upon him, he bent before her, as to one already a denizen of the spirit-worlds. And on her heart there rested not the shadow of a single fear; resolve, enthusiasm, hope divine, were reflected in her every lineament; her heart throbbed joyously with the certainty of immortal blessedness, and she accepted humbly the duties that devolved upon her. Thenceforth she, too, became a wanderer from place to place; and her healing touch brought health and strength to the sickness-stricken, her inspired words sweet comfort to their saddened souls. The home of ease and luxury was abandoned in obedience to her guide's behest; she traveled through the land that gave her birth; she crossed the ocean, and landed on the bleak northern shores; she passed through cities, towns and hamlets, and everywhere the hearts that she benefited "arose and called her blessed." Without money or price she dispensed the heaven-gifts in her possession unto the clamoring multitude. At her soft touch, pain departed; at her spirit's invocation, the calm of better worlds descended upon mourning hearts. The evidences of immortality, at her bidding, aroused the skeptic from his apathy, the worldly plotter from his nefarious schemes. Fever and soul-fear, dangerous diseases of the body and the mind, departed at her earnest prayers, and strong temptations vanished from the weak one's path. The phantom horde of religious fanaticisms, the long train of maniac fancies, the sad throng of blighting memories—they all gave way at her approach. And though priests reviled and many scoffers jeered, she pressed on successfully, overcoming prejudice and suspicion, arousing thought, and challenging investigation, until her fame resounded over the land, and her appearance was hailed with the expected joy of relief by thousands of the suffering. She dispensed fortune's favor with a generous hand, making no provision for the earthly future, indulging in no selfish retrospections, but toiling nobly and unceasingly for the long uncared for masses. Only from the rich did she accept of compensation for her labors; to the toiling mother, the laboring man, the poor servant, she gave unasked of the love and wisdom messages of the beyond, adding often thereto her heart's prompted donation of benevolence.

She said not to the infirm, the soul hungry and the needy: "My price is so much; unless you pay my demand, I shall not cure your bodily infirmities, although the might of healing is in my hand. Nor can I oblige you with the evidences of your soul's immortality, the messages of departed loved ones, *unless you pay my stipulated price!*" Oh, no, Solita said not this. Freely, generously with unfailing love to heaven and self-devotion to the world, she pursued her mission; and angels guarded her securely from want and danger, from aught that would have rendered all too rugged her life path of use and goodness. Kind friends received her everywhere; hospitable homes admitted her, and loving human smiles beamed encouragingly upon her. She seemed fortified with unusual strength and endurance; her kindly labors for humanity affected not her health; the fatigues of traveling ensured the sweetest repose; the change of climate touched her not unpleasantly. The rose-tints of youth dwelt on her cheek; the rounded fullness of perfected womanhood rendered majestically beautiful her graceful form; the inspirations of the upper realms of light and poesy dwelt in the kindling glories of her large dark eyes; the living sunbeams sparkled from the braided and luxuriant hair. Still Psyche, Muse, and Grace, she was as wondrously lovely as in her earliest youth; and to the undimmed charms of yore were added rare mind treasures of thought and knowledge; to her heart, dove-winged peace now nestled; to her soul came visions of the beautiful vouchsafed unto but few of earth.

She met with Percival often, in cities, towns, and in the wayside villages; for he, too, wandered in obedience to the Master's will. And when for weeks and months they met not face to face, they yet communed in spirit, and the written messages of affection passed frequently between them.

The hope that his daughter lived on earth, that he should meet her and bless her as worthy of his earnest search, had grown and strengthened in the father's breast. The spirit messages of Lea promised that earthly reunion, and the soul imbued voice of Solita ever said—

"We shall find her soon, dear brother!"

In daily communion with the spirit realms, apart and unspotted by the world he lived in to bless and harmonize; the wisdom, love, and the sublimest teaching of those upper and enfolding spheres were graciously bestowed upon him. The secrets long sought by sages and philosophers were to his demanding soul revealed. Far past the then known boundaries of all human knowledge he sped unfearingly, and the world's wondering and admiring gaze brought astounding revelations from the distant bournes of soul-life. He saw in trance and vision the first chaotic mass of which the earth was formed, struggling for the birth of individualization, the beauty of expression. From the great central Source of all, he saw this infant world evolve; and with the spirit's gaze he saw the fine soul fibres of the divine life principle permeating its crude shape and striving for the light to which it was affined. Through the atom, rock and tree, through mineral grades and numberless degrees of vegetable life, he saw those fibers, golden fine and light enkindled, ascend. Coursing through the healthful veins of the wild animals, breathing from the rose's fragrant heart, leaping onward with the flow of waves, dwelling in the teeming earth, gleaming from the guarded mine, flashing from the rainbow tinted gem; in all-things life and spirit, soul and progress, ever tending onward and beyond.

Then from the untutored hearts of the earth's first human children he beheld the spontaneous gush of prayer arise and seek the Infinite! Ere language was established and the name of God was known, the heart was sanctified by his upsoaring power; the dimly burning spark of soul claimed kindred with the Beautiful, the all-Divine! Earth ever was the suppliant of Heaven; and what the heart demands, were it not for human misdirection, for the thwarting mundane influences that afflict and cripple, the Spirit realms would give, for all the soul conceives of, of its needful loves and laudable ambition, of its holy desires and blissful aspirations, your worlds contain in loving trust and boundless recompense for the toilers of the nether life. We will record a conversation that took place one day between the teacher, Percival, and the pupil of the Spirit-world, Solita.

"The conceptions of humanity have been gross and irreverent as regards the Deity," he said. "Lives of great and learned men have been expended on almost useless commentaries, while the great and ever unfolding book of Harmonial truth, as contained in nature, has been neglected. Far off and unattainable, they have enthroned the ever present God; fear and punishment are his attendant phantoms; and they, with myths and renovated fables of Paganism, have scourged the cringing and idolatrous world into a state of semi-obedience. Fear is the despot's watchword, the priesthood's insignia of power; over the forming mind of childhood it casts the superstitious shadows that pursue the man unto the very confines of Eternity! Fear and mystery in place of love and knowledge rule the earth; and they that wander there [in] moral darkness, war, enmities, and wrong! Why should they wander? The human soul is stripped of its inherent Godliness by this vile jargon of the priestcraft, who declare the subjection of the intellect, the humiliation of the seeking and aspiring reason, is necessary for man's salvation. Is he saved by dormant faculties, by blind obedience to mere outward forms, by the forced extinction of the soaring thought, the creed fetters that enslave and deny his right to investigate the holy mysteries of life and death? Is he free from sin, and fitted for happiness by this course? Do word prayers and churchly forms release his soul from bondage? Can man's forgiveness bid the soul atone unto itself for violations of His sacred laws? Where is the boasted salvation of the world?

"It can only come through knowledge, labored for and self-gained. No child of earth or heaven can save another from the inevitable consequences attendant upon transgression. Then only, when the divine predominates in the human, when earthliness is changed to heavenliness of thought and deed; then only can the attendant evils of the lower state retire; they cannot live in the angelic atmosphere of truth. Each step the soul gains is imparted to the feelings, the mind, aye, even to the physical body. Is there not a vast difference between the disfigured aspect of hatred or of anger, and the benign sweetness of love and peace? The noble inspirations that flow into the soul from a prayerful love of truth; they illumine not only the inner sanctuary, but the eye and brow; they give the majesty of conquest to the bearing, and a beautiful correspondence in strength and endurance to the body as to the mind. How sweet the calm delights that flow from cheerfulness! While tumultuous joy excites, and consequently enfeebles; while sorrow and repining bind the soul in chains, and render the frame unlovely—the happifying charm of an even flow of goodness, whose outer signs are beaming smiles and merry laughter, will brighten the encasement of the Godlike, and shed the fairest dreams upon the lowliest toiler's path.

"Angelic Charity! In the moistened eye and outstretched helping hand, the ministering spirit of advancement that shall lead the erring to seek once more their God! And, guided by thee, with thy sweet human accents, they will find the loving Father, not the inexorable Judge! Cradled in the arms of Divine Pity, they shall weep their griefs to rest, and know of life, and long for heaven. And in blessed reaction on the hearts that so exalt themselves and others thou wilt bring the Wisdom angels and the Love spirits of the brighter worlds to illumine the hearts and homes of those who, to the sufferer and the fallen, speak words of love and comfort. The eye of benevolence cannot hide itself beneath the drooping lash. The hand that gives to the needy is marked and known; not by the careless passer-by, mayhap, but by the soul readers of the present time. The trembling curve of sympathy on the lips of the world's benefactors is recognized; and by the conscious love light on their being, by the willing foot, the deep, melodious voice, we know them. They may be sad and sorrowing often, yet a happiness is theirs of which the worldling knows not.

"Would mankind be erect and noble in the consciousness of alliance with divine states of being? Would all be beautiful, free from care, and disease, and woe? The outward applications of earth's store of remedies has been applied and has often failed. The dogmas of the clashing creeds have failed to rob them of the fear of death, to reconcile them to the changes and the woes of earth, to save them from transgression, or to present the antidote against the poison-bite of sin. Would they know the secret of longevity, peaceful nights, and days of sunny heart's ease? Cultivate the soul; arouse, awaken, strengthen and unfold its manifold and divine capacities; overcome all acquired and inherited perversion by the Godlike force of Will. The fervor of *one* aspiration for the Truth will call to the battleground of life the ministering spirits, whose inspirational power shall chase the evil phantoms of the heart and brain. The power to know of the vast treasure realms of infinitude, to scale the planet heights, and drink of the celestial love tides; the power to ask of seraphs high and mighty, for the watchwords of Eternity; to unlock the secret avenues of thought, that in the soul-realm lead to hidden mines and sun born temples whence the true oracles of life proceed—all may be obtained for self and others, by the pure in heart, in life and in aim.

"Call into expression, life, and deed, every faculty that claims an origin with Good and Truth. The love of the beautiful, consecrated to divine use, will ultimate in glorious compensations in the inner, and in the gift of beauty to the outer sense and form. In banishing the evil shapes of envy, fear, distrust, anger and uncharitableness, the attendant physical ills will leave thy frame, in which thy mind, long brooding, has established them. In sunshine or in storm, repose thou sweetly in the omnipotent arms of Love; and fear not, though a world should totter, and the earth's foundations rock! Art thou not immortal, indestructible thy soul? Can earthquakes reach the imperishable, or mortal storms destroy that which is with and of God? Child of the Infinite! Cast aside, and forever, the silly fears that mock thy glorious destiny. Soul! Thou art young and beautiful forever, when thou hast gained thy freedom, and drank deep of love, be it on earth or in the spheres beyond. Dream not of health or beauty, power or wisdom, light or joy, while on the fervent sun-orb of thy spirit there rests one shadow of rebellion, one spot of sin or wrong. Cast out the rank, luxuriant weeds of worldliness; the upas plant of moral darkness—oh, uproot it from the sacred soil! Cast forth the vices all, and though the heart-stems bleed, and the frail frame be shaken by the purifying tempest, by the angel dictate of renunciation, pause not, falter not! Be strong, be noble, '*be pure as God!*' Harmonious, loving, all forgiving, what evil can assail, what ill afflict—thou who dwellest on the earth, with the heavens within and around thee?

"And now, I would question of the mysteries of love and life beyond thy intuitive and angel-visited soul! Speak, Solita, and cheer me with the messages of the supremely blest."

"I will speak my impressions as they come. Would that all could hear and understand these lofty truths," she said; and with uplifted eyes, and illumined brow and cheek, with a rapid flow of distinct and musical utterance, she spoke:

"Wouldst thou know of Love imperishable and divine, that, an attribute of Omnipotence, no more an earthly passion or a lower sense, ever nestles closely to the great heart of Infinitude? From thence it goeth forth in a thousand thought forms, royally invested with the ideal charms of beauty, power and persuasion. In the far-off seraph realms, in the sunland of the soul's central attainment, that attribute of the Most High is manifest in visible spiritual and divine realities. There, the hand of Love has beautified the heavens, calling into life the myriad worlds of song and music that revolve around the mighty fane. There, the joy-teeming earth joins in the chorus of the singing stars; the beacon-fires are fanned by the celestial airs of Paradise. There the Heart of Love has found the Wisdom that its vestal purity alone can win; there, from morn til night the incense of its tributary offerings ascends in winged and glorious shapes, gemmed aspirations, toward the Source of Life Eternal, toward the creative mind thrones of the vast unseen! There, on the bowed heads of the united worshipers descend the opal tinted shafts of inspiration, that afresh enkindle with diviner zeal and still holier enthusiasm, the eternally wedded souls of the ever young and glorified! The arcanas of the beautiful there guarded may be known to all of earth; but few are the initiated of the present; for no thought of grossness, not a tinge of lower earth may there intrude; only the pure in heart, the free in soul, may enter and behold, and learn to teach of the wondrous things they see.

"I behold there, dwelling in the bridal bowers and the sainted homes, the long-severed forms of those who loved and parted in this world below; ever true and faithful to the dictates of the inmost revelation, they bore their burdens bravely, and now reap the heavenly reward. Bound in unholy bondage, they yet were true and pure; guided by the soul-love that is of God, they sought for no other union; and now they wear the lilied crown of conquest, and live the realization that transcends their fairest hopes. I behold the tempted of the nether world to whom the serpent form of sin succumbed; the shield of innocence that kept unblemished the soul's virgin bloom; the crown of maidenhood, now lustrous with the added glow of stars; the wifely sceptre diamond shafted with the rays of holiness; and the won throne and trophies of the moral conqueror. I see them there; and I know that land is blessed, that it is nigh and dear to the creative source of power!"

"Yet there are those on earth, those even in our ranks, wearing the name of Reformers, claiming the holy gift of mediumship, who declare that love is dependent on the earthly senses; who dare to teach that the lower attractions are good and lawful, that all and every prompting of the undisciplined affections, and the wayward heart, is an urging of the motive power of God within the soul! Deeply have I grieved, often have I wept, for this!"

"It is not so, dear Percival," replied the pure recipient of truth. "Compare such happiness as ours to the so called enjoyments of the man of pleasure, the woman of the world. Bereft of kindred, home, and many friends, by my adoption of the new faith, who is happier than I? Yet no earthly love blesses me, save that which is universal. From every human heart I encounter, I gain a lesson; I borrow, or I give of truth and love; and the exchange of spiritual offerings is productive of good and joy; there is no need for the taught soul of other expressions. The caresses and endearments advocated by the sophistical followers of the lower attractions, are not needed by the advanced mind, the spiritualized affections; soul will respond to soul through distance and time; and the fraternal love, the sanctified affection, the holy and enduring friendship, need no outer token of their faith. By earthly means, the soul is led earthward; by heavenly aids, it mounts heavenward, even to the very gateways of celestial life. Few, very few, of this present age dare stand upon the pearly mount where all of Love is free and pure, because beyond the reach of the insidious serpent's trail. And to tell of this guarded mount of holiness to men enslaved by sense, to women bound by selfishness, is to tell them of the, to them, impossible and unreal. Because the few disciplined and life taught souls meet there, it is no fitting place for those as yet enveloped in their grossness. They would feel unsafe upon that towering summit; they would gaze bewildered on the yawning chasms opening wide before them; and awed by the enfolding nearness of the sun-bright heavens, the vivid glory of the noonday splendors there, they would veil their dazzled sight, and, blinded, stunned and dizzy, fall from the angel battlements down to the busy, jostling, sensuous world below.

"Only by a constant watchfulness of self that never wearies; a purification of the heart, life-lasting and accepted of Divinity; by purity most absolute, and moral power that the blended universes cannot combine to overthrow, can the soul of man or woman reach the pearly mountain whereon the Love that is all spiritual sits enthroned; the purity that is omnipotent for ever dwells; the peace that is of God abides, and the joy that is of truth illumines. There alone, and then, is freedom beautiful and holy; to teach of soul attractions, affectional liberty, and angelic law unto the masses bound in sensual ignorance is to teach what to their practice would ultimate in grossest immorality; in the casting aside of all the restraints of decency and order, in all the horrors, present and to come, of promiscuous sexual intercourse! No; woman must become to man a teacher and a guide, and by precept and example prove to him the beauty of true chastity. The maiden must be true to the ideal dream of her first youth; the wife must guard most sacredly the duties committed to her charge. Even though the bitter life-waves wash rudely o'er her shrinking spirit, she must be true and faithful still! Not to the world, with its false conventional rules and hollow morality; not from fear or by subjection, but for her soul's bright sake, and because her God enjoins it! Every soul must be freed from the despotic sway of sensualism ere the wisdom and the love of heaven can be known.

"The wife that is the sensual ideal or the legal slave, God will not hold her guiltless for the outrage on her woman honor! And the children born of lawless passions in the place of holiest love, they are the criminals that darken the fair earth with crime and anarchy; they are the avenging evils consequent on violated law; they are the demons and the vampires of this world!"

"Strange, bold and startling truths to utter to conventional and worldly ears! Yet they must be proclaimed, that stunted and deformed souls no more may be sent to the progressive worlds of spirit. Why should the curse of idiocy, of madness, and of foul diseases, rest upon the race that bears the Godlike impress of the Great Creator? They should be angels born, as angels live, and go hence as spirits disciplined and beautiful unto the summer lands. But we will not despair, my sister; we will teach them of the laws of purity and health; we will portray to the benighted masses the beauties of the pure love-heaven of our God, the horrors of the self-made hell of man!" said Percival.

"Thine is the mission to touch the heart and enkindle the soul," she replied. "Thou, who canst sway the multitude, thou wilt arouse the veriest skeptic to the investigation of his soul's destiny. Thine the gift, to bring bright glimpses of the fair beyond to mourning and long sorrowing hearts. Thy eloquence will charm, enrapture and convince; and thy career will be one of blessedness; and in its beauty and its usefulness our worthy brother, Almon Fairlie, will bear a part. He, too, is God commissioned and inspired."

"And thy blest sending to the earth is to pour healing balsam on the tortured frame, and sweet forgiveness on the burning soul. With charmed touch to call the white winged angel of slumber, and the smiling fairy host of dreams around the sufferer's couch. To heal, to bless, to purify and harmonize, how many gifts are blended in thy nature! Thou so like my sister, my own true friend!"

"I am greatly blest, and I am humbly grateful! To do good unto my fellow beings, to alleviate the manifold forms of sorrow, to wean poor souls from sin, and teach the darkened mind, of God, and law, and life eternal; it is a grand, a glorious destiny! That may not be fulfilled in the fleeting earth life," said Solita, with folded hands, and eyes o'erfilled with tears.

"The mission of the beautiful is eternal," was Percival's reply; "and through the countless ages it will be thine to upraise the fallen, to cheer, and bless and heal, the life of the disconsolate."

25

The Hour before Day

They who ne'er ate their bread with tears.
Nor passed the long night's sleepless hours
In bitter weeping for the past
They know ye not, ye heavenly powers!
—Freely Translated from the German

Winter, cold and pitiless in the world without, and in the darkened soul realm! The pitying stars look down into the cheerless room where in the relentless grasp of poverty sits, pale and shivering, the once tenderly shielded child of affluence. The room is cold; for the last flickering ember has expired, and the lights of heaven alone illuminate the darkness. By the window, with eyes upraised in solemn invocation, sits Cosella; the pallor of sickness and weariness upon her wasted face; her garments, loose and scanty, are damp, and whitened with the clinging snow; her hair has caught the falling shower, and her hands are blue with exposure to the storm.

Growing sadly faint and weary of the life of dependence and humiliation, she has rented a meanly furnished room, and has "taken in sewing," determined to be independent of others' caprices and commands, though she were to starve in the effort. At first, she succeeded in obtaining work; she sewed steadily from dawn till late at night, making shirts for six cents a piece in that vaunted and beneficent city—carrying home the heavy bundles, and enduring all the fault findings, tardy payments, and upstart commands of the illiterate petty tyrants that employed her. Not only is the seamstress cruelly wronged by starvation wages, but the language of courtesy is forgotten while dealing with her.

"Here, *you*!" is a usual form of address; and to find fault with the large stitches necessarily taken in the coarse garments is a common everyday occurrence. A seat is not offered to her; and "you must come for your money next week," is often repeated; then if the poor toiler urges her needs, she is gruffly answered with—"We can't help that; we have no change at present"; and perhaps, too, there will be no work cut out for the ensuing week. Oh God, that thy children should thus oppress each other! That power should lead to cruelty, and the sacred duties of humanity be thus forgotten in the busy marts of trade!

Poor Sambo! Toiling in the cotton field, be comforted; for know that delicate white fingers, all unused to labor, have fashioned the garment that protects thee; and tears, salt and bitter, wrung from gentle hearts, have fallen on the swiftly taken stitches. The curse of monopoly, the tortured wail of an enforced slavery clings to the work! For pride and selfishness, vanity and worldliness, have marked the toiler, and set her apart from the favored of this life.

There are exceptions, doubtless; honorable men, with the Christ love in their souls, who generously compensate, and mentally strive to elevate the laborer; there are women whom the glitter of gold and fashion has not led from the active duties of benevolence. Sometimes these ministering ones, with loving care and outstretched hand, save from the beckoning lures of desperation the weary and faint-hearted. But oftener, alas, are they left to perish—to die a moral death awhile, or to rest, heart-broken, in the grasp of necessity, until the invoked for death-angel comes!

Through all the various grades of discipline that poverty enforces has Cosella passed; for some weeks "companion to a lady," that misnomer for a ceaseless drudge; then assisting in the care of children; then laboring with the needle for the stores; then watching by the sick, deprived of weeks of rest, of night after night of sleep; then, in despair returning to the hated needle; and sometimes compelled to spend days of utter listlessness, when there was no work to be obtained and consequently no bread to eat. She would then go and offer her services at places where she had been employed before, in order to obtain a meal. Sometimes, with a few pennies saved, she would buy a loaf of bread and a draught of milk, and seek a lodging for the night. At last, she rented the small room in a retired part of the city, and for a while bore up bravely against the ills that beset her. She sold her few remaining books in order to obtain food; she lived for many days without a fire that inclement winter; and her scanty garments bore the marks of time, the shoes upon her feet were worn, the poetry, beauty, and refinement of life was gone.

"My God! Is there no help? What have I done to merit such a fate as this?" she cried, as shivering with cold she drew her faded shawl around her. "I do not live; and I cannot die!" she continued. "Oh, how long, my Father in Heaven! *How long?*"

She fell upon her knees, gazed tearfully up to the starlit winter sky, and from her soul, exalted by sorrow, burst one of those mighty heaven-reaching invocations, wherewith in its trial hours the human anguish approximates to inspirational fervor, and calls from love-lit home and lilied bower the ministering angels of the Father's will.

"Oh, take me home!" she cried. "Thou who hast immortality in store for all, oh, take me from this weary earth, this aimless life! But if there be in my soul one attribute of goodness, if ever I have thought nobly, acted well, and dreamed divinely, oh, my God, my Father, grant me *one* compensation *here*! Let me meet my father's smile; let me rest upon his bosom, hear his voice, and I will never, oh never more repine!"

Then loud and thrilling, so solemnly impressed with the momentary hope and desperate resolve that she deemed he must hear and answer, she cried unto the ear of night:

"My father come! I am cold and starving! My father, it is your child, Cosella, that calls! Come, come to me, quickly!"

Through the distance, over mountain, river, lake and plain, sped the spirit's plaintive call, until subdued and dreamy it reached the inner sense of him it sought. Starting from his sleep, the father stretched forth his yearning arms:

"My child, my child where art thou?"

"Peace, patience—we will guide thee," whispered the musical voice of the celestial life guardian, and Percival turned away his face and wept.

Again, through the far distance, borne upon the night-winds, floated dreamily that call for help, until it reached the kindred heart of the watching Solita. She started up and cried:

"A voice, familiar but indistinct—a woman's cry for aid and sympathy, is brought to my inner sense! Who is it that thus invokes the heavens, and the ministering aids of earth? With the strong attraction of the pure in heart, it calls me! Where, oh celestial monitors, shall I find that suffering one?"

"Peace, patience—we will guide thee!" was the silver toned reply; and, moved to the inmost, Solita bowed her face upon her hands and wept.

Over the couch of the dying bent Almon Fairlie on that memorable night; and there, too, the voice of sorrow reached him, starting him from his observant watchfulness of the beautiful process of transition. To his query, the celestial guides responded, even as unto the father and the maiden; but yielding to strong and irresistible emotion, he, too, the tried and loving friend, he turned aside his face, and wept the human tears of tenderest pity!

And Cosella slept with her head upon the window sill; and she dreamed that spirits re-visited the earth, and communed with men. She saw her mother, silver robed and radiant; and she touched the star illumined veil that floated on the aromatic breeze that warmly enfolded her. She saw the smiling face of Shina, beaming love upon her, from amid the thickly clustering branches of the clematis and the rose. She beheld Manasseh kneeling, with bowed head, entreating her to write forgiveness on the blank page which he held. And Cosella, wondering, dipped a golden pen in the clear waters of a singing stream, and wrote therewith, and lo! the page was illumined with a golden and an azure glow; and on the brow of the keeling man descended a chaplet of the myrtle entwined with jasmine stars. Then a delicious melody uprose and swelled in rhythmic grandeur 'neath the beauty of the summer's night; and a hand that caused her every life pulse to thrill with a sense of divine and most ecstatic love was laid upon her head. She saw the noble figure of a man, with a face of serenest majesty; the calm and holy eyes spoke to her soul, the pensive lips unclosed, the heart's tone of recognition called her "*daughter!*"

When she awoke from that blessed vision, the sun was streaming in, and its warmth enfolded her for a while. Slowly she returned to consciousness, to the memory of the present, and a deep sigh heralded the soul's return to the uncongenial daily toil and struggle. But what charm has been effected in the room? What good angel has banished the gaunt and threatening form of famine, at least for that day? A cheerful wood-fire has given warmth and an aspect of ruddy comfort to the bleak, cold room; a loaf of bread, a bowl of milk and some potatoes are neatly placed upon the table. The blessed sympathizing heart of poor Cosella's landlady, a weary toiler herself, a widow with four children, has arranged these little comforts for her sorrowful and uncomplaining guest. And Cosella thanked the good woman with tears, and enjoyed with grateful satisfaction the first food she had taken for two days.

Again the weary weeks and months sped on, and through clouds of skepticism, through conflict severe and internal, she emerged to the newly arisen glorious light of Truth, then pouring its first beams upon the startled inhabitants of the New World. With wonder, surprise and incredulity, she heard of the marvels of Spiritualism, of the return of the departed, of the established intercourse between the planet and the spirit-realms and our earth. At first timid, fearful, superstitious, she lingered long upon the verge of investigation; then followed skeptical inquiry, and at last came the restless desire for knowledge—that desire of the earnest and enthusiastic seeker, which becomes

——Blest or curst
As is the fount whereat 'tis slaked.

Her toilsome life afforded her but little opportunity for the investigation of subjects so profound. The incessant struggle for bread—the *curse* of labor as it is inflicted by man on man—deadens the finer sentiments, blunts the spiritual faculties, renders predominant the animal instincts, sometimes extinguishes the ideal enfoldings of affection, and leaves humanity alone with grossness, recklessness, and dishonest purpose. Labor, as instituted by God and nature, is the blessing of life; to it we owe all that the painter has made visible of the upper and inner realms of beauty; all that the poet has seen and felt of heaven; all that the architect has dreamed, the sculptor fashioned in his ideal trances. The actualization of the beautiful is the ministry of labor; as well fulfilled in the wayside walks of life as in its loftiest places; by the gentle housewife realized as by the grandest orator. But labor, to be thus nobly adapted to the soul's expansion, must be freed from the tyranny of the few, the monopoly of the wealthy, the despotic rule of compulsion.

As it was, Cosella found but little time for reading or investigation of this momentous subject; but what little she did read filled her heart with joy, and gave rise to winged aspirations, lofty hopes, heavenly anticipations. And when one day she laid aside her needle, and with a fervent and unuttered prayer invoked the coming light, it came and bathed her struggling soul in the sunrays of a diviner faith!

"Oh that some proof would come direct to sense and heart! some evidence of my soul's future destiny, some glimpses of the life beyond! Oh, for one word from the departed! For a spirit voice to tell me of my immortality! Oh, for help from heaven to lead me from this life of hardship to the sunshine of peace and love!"

The soft breeze that fanned her forehead in reply seemed to lull every doubt to rest; as if upborne on music's pinions, her soul's petition winged its heavenward flight, and the burden seemed uplifted from her aching heart!

A swift current of electricity passed from her elbow to the wrist, thence to her fingers; "*Write!*" whispered the soft tones of intuition. She took her pencil and wrote. In large, jagged, irregular letters appeared the spirit-written word, "*Immortality!*"

"I thank thee, oh my God!" burst from the grateful lips of Cosella. The over-laden heart found relief in a load of tears.

"*I love, and love thee still; angels watch over thy life-path; be patient, faint not—soon it will be dawn!*"

"God of love and mercy! It is Shina's hand—I recognize her writing!" cried Cosella, breathlessly.

"*Be calm, be hopeful,*" wrote the obedient fingers; "*I am thy second mother still, yes, my beloved, I am thy Shina!*"

Her eyes dilating with awe, her heart throbbing with joy for which earthly language can find no expression, she gazed upon the writings, formed by her hand, guided by spirit-powers; she knew that her mind could not have framed those communications, and she was satisfied and happy.

For weeks the consolations thus awarded cheered and brightened her lot; and, eager for more knowledge, she attended the public meetings, and listened to the first expounders of the spiritual faith. For the first time she heard the noblest truths advanced from woman's lips. A humble and unassuming laborer from the far West, a meek, Quaker-like woman, was the first speaker she ever listened to; and as her face grew beautiful in the transfigured glow of the trance, as the eloquent and thrilling sentences fell upon the hushed and wondering audience, Cosella felt that she who thus addressed them was indeed commissioned of the angel-world and inspired by spirit-hosts.

Oh, the storm of ridicule that poured upon the devoted head of Cosella when employers and self-styled friends found that she had accepted the new belief! Jew and Christian alike reviled and mocked and sneered; or solemnly reminded her of the danger to soul and body she was incurring by thus holding supposed communications with the dead.

"It is all of the Devil," said one, "and you'll peril your eternal salvation by meddling with forbidden subjects."

"Can the Devil elevate the soul, cheer the heart, brighten the intellect, and give us the desire for evidences of immortality?" queried Cosella of her opposers.

"Satan can transform himself into an angel of light. All you need to know of the future life, you can find in the Bible," was the reply of several.

"I cannot believe that a just and good God would suffer his children to be deluded when their aim is a search after truth. I have not been satisfied with the testimony of ancient Scriptures; and spiritualism *proves* immortality."

"You are deluded by evil spirits, and will suffer in everlasting hell for your infidelity! All you see and feel of spirits is nothing but a rank delusion."

"Can I doubt the evidence of my own senses—the intuitions of my own soul? Can I throw aside the overwhelming mass of evidence, the testimony of my own departed friends?"

"The senses are apt to mislead us; *all* visions are optical delusions. The departed are happy in heaven or suffering for their sins in hell. *Ghosts* never return; imagination makes you believe in these things; and if the dead *could* return, I would not want to speak with them."

"But reason—" continued Cosella.

"We have nothing to do with reason; reason is carnal, and should not be permitted to judge in religious matters. We have the Bible, and that is enough."

Such was the conclusion of some worthy Christians; and when Cosella inquired of them whether they had investigated the subject they condemned so fully, the reply was:

"No, I have not investigated, and I don't intend to. I *know* it's all a delusion, a trick of Satan, and I don't want to sit in their circles, nor go to their meeting."

"If I was to see my own mother, I would believe it was an evil spirit that had taken her form to delude me," said a lady, a church-member, to the remonstrating Cosella.

"You will go crazy if you believe in Spiritualism and become a medium," said another.

"What do you jump out of one humbug into another for?" asked an old materialist. "You cannot show *me* a spirit; it's all trickery and legerdemain. When we are dead, we remain dead; what should we do in another world?"

"Love and assist each other; do much that we have sadly neglected here," said Cosella.

"And sell dry goods, and go to market?"

She turned indignantly away, and wasted no more words in that quarter.

"I hear you have been bitten by a mad dog," said a young lady of the Jewish persuasion.

"I—bitten by a mad dog?" said Cosella, in astonishment.

"Yes; you acted as though you had; you go to the Spiritualists' meeting, don't you?"

A sudden light burst upon her. She laughed and said:

"Oh, Spiritualism is the mad dog, is it? Well, I prefer the peace and consolation it brings to me, to all the dogmas that were ever invented; to all the fables of Christianity and Judaism."

One acquaintance sent her a message that, as she had become a Spiritualist, she should no more darken her doors. Cosella poured out her full and indignant feelings in a letter to the lady; and when another offered her a home, on condition that she should renounce her new faith, she indignantly refused. A new born strength, hope and energy seemed infused into her soul.

"I will dare and brave them all!" she cried; "but I will be free to believe as I choose and feel, and if I die, I know that death is but a name, that life is eternal!"

So, struggling with toil and poverty, with foes and oppressions, the brave girl lived on; and few that looked upon her pale face and humble attire deemed her worthy of companionship, even in the crowded spiritual hall. A few humble ones spoke to her, invited her to their homes, and questioned her sympathizingly. It was not until she had won a name and a place that the great ones deigned to notice her. She was alone and unaided in the first initiatory phases of the new life; but she was not unaided by the great ones in the land of souls. Quiet and unobtrusive, she scorned to seek admittance to the houses of the wealthy; she would not ask for home and shelter, even of the new-founded brotherhood. So she toiled on, cheered only by the light above, the joy and rest within.

But clouds still overhung the present and the future; still the grim phantom of necessity lingered; still life was filled with cares and the human world was cold. By the aid of the inspiration showered upon her heart and mind, Cosella wrote, not only messages from the departed, but sweet poems, full of the plaintive energy of sorrow. These were published, and no doubt cheered many a like toiler's weary heart; but they brought no compensation in worldly returns. Still Cosella toiled at the needle, and wept and hungered often, and slept on a rude bed, and was clad in humble and scanty attire. The lone heart ever seeks to cling to something tangible. However enrapt in mysterious communion with the worlds of spirit; however deeply merged in the poetic sea, or loftily enthroned in the fairy realms of the ideal, it will in the actual life seek for an object that will respond, though it be only partially and feebly, to some demand of the affectional nature, to some outpouring of the deep heart's hoarded store of treasured love and sympathy.

Thus, in her utter loneliness, she cherished a sweet white rose, and tended carefully a fragrant mignionette. They seemed a part of her life, these floral beauties of our God; but being absent from home for some days, they drooped and dried up for want of moisture, and Cosella wept for them as for departed friends.

She had taken some sewing to do for a Jewish family. They owned a small white dog that was fancifully yclept Topaz. The little fellow formed a sincere attachment for her; he would frisk and run before her whenever she came; would lick her face and hands, and look up to her with his large, beseeching dark eyes, as if imploring her protection. She saw that he was neglected, harshly used, never petted; and the desire to possess the little animal grew strong within her.

"I promised you a present, Miss Phillips," said the lady of the house; you have done my daughter's things very neatly; and as she is going to be married, that is of some consequence. Now, say, what shall I give you? I am puzzled to think. Tell me what you want most; but mind, don't ask for anything expensive. I have so many things to get for Regina, I cannot spare much money. Shall it be a pair of shoes, or a calico frock?"

"Neither, I thank you, madam," said Cosella, a proud flush rising to her cheek. "But there is *one* thing I would ask for, if I thought you were willing." She was fondling little Topaz, who looked up into her face and barked.

"Anything I or Regina have worn? Is it a bonnet or a collar?"

"I do not desire any cast-off clothing," said Cosella, in a tone that caused the haughty and ignorant woman to blush and stammer forth, "Excuse me—I meant no offence."

"If you wish to give me a present, Mrs. L——, and think I have deserved one, let me take this dog home with me; give me Topaz." Her voice faltered and her eyes were full of tears.

"Why, you silly girl!" exclaimed the lady, totally forgetting her momentary prudence; "why you can scarce earn enough to buy victuals for yourself, and you want to be hampered with a dog! What do *you* want with that little beast?"

"I want him to love, for my experience teaches me there is but little love or sympathy in human hearts. My adopted mother had such a dog once; I cherish the memory."

The proud, resisting heart gave way; the tropical home, the patient Shina, the pet follower of their wanderings that had been faithful unto death! She bowed her head and wept, and the smooth, warm tongue of the dog lapped the streaming tears from her eyes. Mrs. L. looked on in silent wonderment. "Well," she said at length, "if you're so mighty taken with him, you may have him. I'm sure my husband doesn't care a straw about him, and Regina can't abide him. But maybe you'll think me unfair, for I promised you something useful."

"I desire nothing else. May I take Topaz home with me?"

"Yes, yes, and glad to get rid of him! Please sign this receipt, Miss Phillips, so I shall know I have paid you; and don't you blame anybody but yourself for a poor bargain, in taking live-stock instead of a gown or a good pair of shoes. Good-by, Topaz," and laughing at her own wit, the fortune-favored upstart left the room. Cosella walked home, with the dog in her arms, a child-like joy in her heart. Copious ablutions, a thorough combing, and the adornment of a blue ribbon, caused a rapid transformation in the looks of the hitherto neglected Topaz; and between them was established a life-long contract of affection and protection.

For many weeks and months he was the orphan's sole companion, her only grateful and responding friend. They suffered cold and hunger and privation together; together they took the few rambles stolen from the city's life of toil. Cosella shared with him the last crust and the last draught of milk, and often whispered in his ear, "This will not last forever, Topaz; one day we shall find my father, and then I shall be happy and you well fed." To this great crowning of life, the Spirit-messages ever pointed; but dark and lowering the clouds of adverse fortune yet encircled her.

I must go to the Spiritual meeting this evening," said Cosella, one day to her companion. "I must hear the famed and eloquent English speaker so loudly vaunted, though I lose my evening's work thereby. You must keep house, Topaz, and not howl for me while I am away." Topaz looked mournfully into her face, and wagged his tail in a pleading, deprecating manner.

"I feel strangely to night; some great joy or some great sorrow is about to come upon me. Have pity on me, gracious Father, for I cannot bear much more!" She said this as she tied on her bonnet to go; and kissing Topaz, she locked her door and wended her way to the Spiritualists' Hall.

26

Unrecognized

And ye, whose birthright is the glorious dower
Of eloquence, to thrill the immortal soul,
Use not unwisely the transcendent power
To waken, guide, restrain, direct, control
The heart's deep, deep emotions; let the goal
Of your ambition be, a name enshrined
By love and gratitude upon the scroll
Where generations yet unborn shall find
The deathless deeds of those who loved and blessed
  mankind.

—Sarah T. Bolton

The spacious hall was crowded, and expectant silence reigned in that varied multitude. In the front ranks sat the professed believers, the conspicuous members of the new faith, those whose wealth and social standing insured for them the respect of the community they dwelt in. The smiling daughters of fashion displayed their fresh and rich attire; old men and blooming maidens, staid Quaker matrons, and country damsels, investigators, scoffers, Jews and Christians, all assembled to hear for themselves of this much-talked-of Spiritualism; to judge for themselves of the merits of its doctrines. The learned of all professions there met and exchanged ideas; the stern materialist and the soaring transcendentalist there compared their views; the bigot and the infidel confronted each other; and the sea of agitation there invoked, wafted many a battling, storm-tossed soul to the safe haven of reconciliation, to the angel guarded shores of immortal certainty. From that place of true worship souls have gone forth converted to the belief of a God that heretofore had stumbled in the myth land of priestly teachings, or groped in the utter blindness of materialism. Mothers have gone home with a new-born joy in their bosom feeling that their children, transplanted to the spirit-climes, yet lived. Old men have bowed their heavy heads in reverence before the inspired expounders of the truths of eternal life; and the widowed and bereaved have blest them, and the stricken heart has murmured, "I know my God!" The lessons of purity, truth and wisdom given from that rostrum have spread a benign influence far and wide; darkened households and drooping hearts have been cheered by them; death and bereavement have lost their sting; and life, by those lessons, has been beautified and elevated into sanctified and prayerful uses.

When Cosella entered, the spacious hall was almost filled. The brilliant chandelier over the rostrum displayed its brightest light, and the numerous gas jets around illumined that pleasant meeting place. On the desk was placed a bouquet of choicest flowers; and the floral offerings held in fair hands that night exhaled their rare and rich perfume. Cosella breathed delightedly in that fragrant atmosphere, and leisurely surveyed the intelligent heads and smiling faces of the audience.

"Here, as elsewhere, I am alone and unheeded," she sighed. "But I can come here and drink in draughts of poetry and eloquence that beautify my life, strengthen my soul, that teach me love and forbearance. I too can appreciate intellect and goodness."

The hymn was sung. The speaker arose and anxious expectation sat enthroned on every countenance. Cosella started when the first clear musical tones of the gifted orator fell upon her ear. She started as if a voice dear and familiar from childhood had called to her. She half rose in her seat, bent eagerly forward, and as she beheld his noble face and tall commanding figure—as she caught the gleam of his eye, the radiant smile upon his lips, an involuntary exclamation escaped her. A confused whirl of thought swept over her brain, a flash of consciousness that thrilled to her very heart-depths seemed to illumine the inner sense; and joy unspeakable, rapture untranslatable, a bliss and mingled pain too deep for revelation, alternated in her being. To rush toward him, to fall in adoring worship at his feet, to pray to him with extended arms and uplifted soul for one token of recognition was the overwhelming impulse of the moment. To cling to him for safety and protection, to follow him through life, seemed in that hour all that life had of blessedness in store. With a magnetic attraction that was as irresistible as it was holy, a yearning of love as deep and high as it was passionless and pure, she longed for him!

All that the heart of woman holds within its angel-sounded depths of devotion and self- sacrifice; all that the soul contains of saintly adoration, and the mind of intellectual offering, she cast at his feet that hour! She longed with tears to tell him that no matter where she stood in life to him, he was all of life to her. It was not love, nor was it mind-homage only; it was not fraternal affection, nor was it the spiritual recognition of a kindred soul that thus strangely and deeply moved her. It was something mightier, holier still, for which earth could give no name. And thus entranced and worshipful she sat, shedding blissful tears, and smiling radiantly, as if the heaven of her imaginings was then unfolded to her gaze.

His soaring eloquence and unsurpassed powers of oratory delighted the charmed and silent multitude. Over that sea of upturned faces the softening influences of the better life seemed shed. They glowed as if transfigured by the innate might of soul. The sordid and the worldly forgot their plans and schemes, and dreamed awhile of heaven; the hardened and the irreligious listened with a throbbing pulse, a moistened eye; the coldly intellectual felt the heart's glow of affection; the doubter believed in God; the conscience-stricken wrong-doer veiled his eyes and communed with his own guilty soul.

Inspired and beautiful with the keeping of the wisdom-lore of the celestial lands, offering to the hungered children of a soul-starved world the gifts of knowledge, truth and genius, he stood before them in his regal and yet human angelhood. Involuntarily all hearts were charmed, and the admiring and reverential gaze of the many was riveted upon the serene beauty of his countenance, the noble bearing of his princely form. The deep, full tones of his musical voice appealed to the human heart's purest and holiest affections, to the soul's inmost thought, the mind's loftiest aspiration. The manifold fibers of the strange inner life, thrilled and questioned by that master spirit, responded in divinest language. Summoned from oblivion, worldliness and apathy, all the fine emotions and the sacred loves replied, as if unto the recording angel of that hour, "Here am I, Lord."

All noted the illumined face, the eye, enkindled by a fervid and divine enthusiasm. Those who sat near the speaker said that a low musical murmur, as of spirit voices, seemed to float on the air around him, as if in accompaniment to the poetry of his thought and the fervent beauty of his speech.

He spoke of the compensations of immortality; of the holy uses of adversity, the purifying influences of sorrow. He alluded to the past terrible bereavements of his youth, to the struggles of his manhood, whereby his soul had attained the heavenly knowledge that now blessed him. He stretched forth his arms in invocation to the beloved and living, from whom the barriers of sense alone did separate the soul. He blessed the All-wise Father for the darkness as for the light. He called the sorrow, *angel*, as well as the enraptured joy. He forgave his foes in love, and to the keeping of the pure wise spirits consigned the lowest and the vilest of God's children. He told of divine affections crowned by the hand of Deity, eternally beautiful as the source from whence they sprang. And then he spoke of the meeting of long severed hearts; of the welcome home of the waiting mother and the parted child; of the recognition of kindred souls; of the life warm clasp of the beatified; and a solemn sense of realization swayed that vast and differing assemblage. Men wiped their brimming eyes and women sobbed aloud.

As if an angel commissioned of the pitying God had spoken, the thrilling promise sank into their hearts, "Ye shall meet and love and live forever saith the immutable just and loving Father. And even now, though your eyes behold them not, the loved ones drawn to you by the divine chords of sympathy are nigh. Though you hear them not, the melodies of heaven sweep over the lyre strings of your spirit, and the prayer of your hearts is recorded on high."

When he ceased, the silence was unbroken save here and there by the uncontrollable bursts of emotion that brooked no concealment; but no one moved or attempted to depart. Spellbound, they gazed upon the speaker's face, as with uplifted eyes and hushed lips he stood upon the platform en-rapt in prayer or in thought.

"Good night, my friends!" spoke sweet and plaintively that voice of more than magical power. "I thank the Source of all Goodness for the great re-ward this night bestows upon me. In your tearful eyes, I read the sorrow and the rapture of your souls that by my words have been awakened. From the apathy of the life of worldliness ye have arisen; henceforth ye are toilers on the spiral pathways of eternal progress! We shall meet again—on earth or in the spirit spheres. Good night; God bless you one and all!"

A deep sigh burst from the strangely burdened heart of Cosella.

"He has blest me too!" she murmured; and she sat still in the same posi-tion, her hands tightly locked, her eyes riveted upon him, her heart beating wildly with its mingled sensations of blessedness and pain. Slowly the vast crowd departed; she saw the orator come forward, and speak with many; she saw him give the cordial hand clasp to the richly clad and to the poor alike. She could not muster courage to address him; she dared not approach him; but she lingered there until his tall figure disappeared from view; then outside the door she lingered still, until the carriage that contained him rolled away. She passed her hand over her brow, as if to collect her thoughts; a bitter pain gnawed at her heart.

"He is gone and I may never more behold him!" she exclaimed; and then with dread and wonderment, she vainly strove to analyze her own strangely mingling emotions, the sudden and irresistible attraction that drew her to that stranger's soul.

"You were mightily taken with the new speaker, Miss Phillips," said an elderly woman, whose acquaintance Cosella had formed in the hall. Well it's no wonder, *he is* beautiful! So eloquent, so poetical! There wasn't a soul there that didn't cry tonight; there, Miss Phillips, there's a white rose he held in his hand, and it dropped on the floor, and the janitor gave it to me; and seeing how mightily you are taken with the discourse, I thought I would give it to you."

"Thank you, thank you!" cried Cosella, eagerly, and she pressed the flower to her lips. "Tell me," she said, hesitating she knew not why, "what is the lecturer's name?"

"Is it possible you have been listening to him the whole evening without knowing his name?"

"I only heard by chance of the coming of an English speaker; I have not taken time to read the notices in the papers."

"Why, my dear, he is famed all over the land! He is one of the most talented, and was one of the first developed mediums; his name is Percival Wayne."

Again that delicious soul-absorbing thrill of delight, followed by the sense of utter loneliness. Cosella could not speak; a spell she could not fathom, an influence she could not define, was upon her. She could only pray with her heart's most fervent utterance: "Help me, my God! For I know not what this means."

She sat for several hours with Topaz in her arms that night, dreaming vaguely, wondering, and questioning her own soul. Then when she slept her dreams were broken and confused, and she awoke to the daily toil with a start and an exclamation of weariness. Hope, fear, doubt and unrest, alternated in her soul. Dreamy and abstracted, the compulsory toil she submitted to grew more and more distasteful; she did not obtain work for many days, and again she pined for food, and her little companion grew lean and silent. Despair came nigh to the bravely battling heart; the summer was waning fast; soon the autumn winds would chill her unprotected form, the snow-storm wrap her in its cold embrace.

"I cannot live through another winter," she said.

"If God does not send me relief, we must lie down and die, my Topaz, for I cannot earn wherewith to feed and warm us. My poor dog! I grieve for your fate, but I know of no one to whom I could leave you. We will die together, Topaz; and then I shall be with my mother, and perhaps the loving God will reward your fidelity with the compensations of immortality, for on earth there is no joy for us."

So the days sped on; and urged by the sharp pangs of hunger, thoughts wild and sinful crossed the bewildered brain of the long suffering girl, and she meditated a calm descent into the smoothly inviting river, there to end her earth life and its miseries. Then chasing hurriedly the fearful thought, she would cry aloud—

"No, no! I will not break thy laws, my Maker! I will die, unstained by the crime of suicide; I will abide my fate and fulfill thy will, for well I know this fleeting earth life is not all."

Not a morsel of bread to be obtained; not a hand upraised to aid in this her hour of sorest need. Her strength gave way, hope followed, and the expectation of death chased every other thought. She lay upon her rude couch, the hectic glow of fever on her cheek, the sharp pangs of hunger giving way to a deathly feebleness and a burning thirst.

"Thanks for the last of thy good gifts, my Heavenly Father!" she murmured, as she drank of the pure water by her side. The humane landlady knew not how utterly destitute was her unfortunate tenant; but Cosella knew that she too ate her scanty bread with tears, and she would not rob her children of their rightful share. Therefore, she pleaded only for a pitcher with water, and refused the kindly offered morsel. Curled up at her feet lay poor Topaz, almost as faint and inanimate as his mistress.

"I know there is a God, a spirit-world! There I too shall know happiness!" dreamily said Cosella, and she slept a while and dreamed that happiness had been awarded to her on earth; then awaking faint and weary, she stretched forth her hands imploringly and called on God to take her home.

That morning, led by her spirit guides, Solita Mendez for the first time visited the far-famed City of Brotherly Love. In the northern section of the city she engaged rooms, and proposed to give examinations to the sick and ailing as was her wont. She had not long rested from the fatigue of her journey, ere a gentleman was announced; and desiring him to be admitted, her sweet face glowed with pleasure on beholding Almon Fairlie, the efficient co-laborer of her brother Percival, the friend long known and prized.

"Happy to meet you again, dear friend and noble worker!" she said, extending her hand. "I had not hoped to meet with you so soon again."

"Nor should I have come here but for a persistent impression bidding me come to this city, I know not wherefore."

"For months a voice has called me—a wailing imploring voice. My spirit guides, who never have misled me, will now surely unravel the mystery," said Solita.

"We are here for some purpose." said Almon Fairlie; "there is a work of mercy to perform; you are to be the guide, the leader, and I your humble co-worker. That is my impression; have you aught more definite, Solita?"

"I have not," she replied; "but I have a definite and clear impression as regards myself. I have but few months or weeks of earth life left to me; soon I shall scale the spirit heights and rest in the blessed valleys; soon I shall dwell with my kindred in the fadeless realm; soon I shall be divested of the clogs of earthly sense, and float, heart and soul free, in the atmosphere of immortality! Oh, brother Fairlie, what joy and what rapture is in the thought! Emancipation from all clinging earthliness, mine the gained divinity of soul action; mine the sacred guardianship of souls!"

"Angel and prophetess!" he murmured, gazing reverentially upon her.

"I, with Lea, will be his guardian angel still," she continued. "Since my spirit has outgrown the earthly love that years ago bound me to his spirit—since I have exchanged the earthly hopes and fears for the fraternal, holy union, I behold the soul of Percival in all its beauty; and I hold that place within it that none other of earth or heaven can maintain. I have learned to know myself, and I yield the place once coveted to her to whom it belongs by sacred and immutable law. Through the eternal ages, soul-wed and heart-blended, the spirits of Percival and Lea shall ascend; and I, and one other, shall progress with them; for she is now my spirit-sister, and he has been a savior and a guide to me. And angels have told me that the crowning joy of his life shall be given through my ministering hand. And I know that his counterpart in spirit and in soul awaits me in the spirit-spheres; that a radiant star isle is his home; that I wear the betrothal token; and in the countless ages of the Hereafter, I shall be his blest and love crowned bride. Oh, brother Almon, how much of light and truth has dawned upon my heart and once desponding soul!"

"Thou art indeed thrice blessed!" he replied; "and of such indeed is the kingdom of our God. But, Solita, dearest sister, what can it be that has brought us hither thus suddenly?"

"We will be silent awhile; perhaps the wise and unseen ones will impress us," she replied.

They sat in silence with joined hands; Solita seemed to listen intently, and Almon too inclined his head as if in attentive attitude.

"Do you hear? Do you understand, my brother?" she whispered.

"I hear a voice—the same that startled me months ago! It is a human cry for help—it is a woman's voice!"

"It is the voice that clamors at my heart incessantly! It is one dear and near to us both, but as yet unrecognized and unfound. Almon, we must arise and seek that sufferer. Oh, wisdom guides! Oh, loving angels! Whither shall we bend our steps!"

"Someone we love is dying of necessity! No time is to be lost! Solita, tell me where to go. I hasten!"

"The impression comes to me. In the southern portion of the city, in a wide street—I cannot get the name—the railroad traverses it—a wide street, planted on each side with trees; in a small, dark-looking house, in the second story, in a back room—devoid of food and fuel, exhausted, helpless, almost dying, we shall find her who calls upon us. I know not who she is; but some great revelation awaits us both. Go, Almon; go and bring her here immediately! I would go with you, but some sufferers await my ministry; they have come from a distance, knowing I would be here this day. Listen, Almon: there is a park near the corner of the street; I cannot see the number. Do you think you can find the house?"

"God and the angels will direct me," he replied. "I know by your description that the street is in the district of Southwark; I have been there many times. Fear not but I shall find the way. I go at once, Solita; there is no time to be lost."

And he hastily left the room, walked rapidly the length of several streets, then hailed an omnibus and pursued his way down town. He stopped at the indicated street, and found the park; he surveyed the houses, and found the small, dark-looking one.

"This is the place," the impression whispered, and with his hand upon the doorbell he paused.

What should he say—who should he inquire for? He tried the door; it yielded to his touch, and he passed in; through the narrow and gloomy entry, up the crooked stairs, and with a beating heart he stood for a moment irresolute at the designated door.

He knocked; there was no answer. Again he knocked, and a low bark, or rather a whine, responded. He opened the door and passed within the bleak and scantily furnished room. In the furthest corner a woman's figure was discernable, kneeling and praying with uplifted hands. A feeble light was on the table beside a pitcher of water and a glass. Though the autumn day was chilly, there was not the last vestige of a fire.

The dog whined feebly at the intruder; the girl upon her knees seemed not to heed aught that was passing. She prayed aloud, and her words were interrupted by sobs, and the deep and uncontrollable emotion that weakness alone prevented from gaining the violence that would have broken forth in cries and groans.

"Take me hence, oh God! For I am weary of this struggle; I can no longer resist. Let me die this night, or in thy mercy, God of Love, send me help—oh, send me bread!"

"Father of the Universe! That voice—that petition—oh, it cannot, *cannot* be!—God has heard your prayers, lady; arise and greet a friend. I come to help you."

She arose from her supplicating posture with a wild cry and a bound.

"Who are you?" she cried, confronting him.

"A friend, a brother, sent by the loving hosts of heaven to relieve you!" he replied, and the tear-mist clouded his eyes.

"*Relief—bread—hope!*" she murmured. "Oh, God is good, and I shall not die the death of famine! Oh, angel, helper, friend, who—*who* are you?"

She had thrown back the veiling tresses that concealed her eyes and face; the sharpened outline, the careworn features were revealed.

"Father—God—oh, angels! It is—*it is herself!*" cried Almon, and he extended his arms and sobbed aloud.

"My brother, Almon Fairlie!"

With a loud shriek that startled the inmates of that retreat of poverty, she rushed toward him, fell on the broad breast so nobly offered as her resting place, and her senses closed to the outer world. Pale, still and lifeless, she lay upon his bosom, and the hand that smoothed back her tangled hair and magnetized her into sweet and healthful sleep was wet with the heart-wrung tears of truest manhood.

"To find her thus!—yet God be praised!" he cried.

27

Realization

Over thine orphan head
The storm hath swept as o'er a willow's bough
Come to thy father! It is finished now;
Thy tears have all been shed.

Cosella returned to consciousness as one awakening from a deep and dream-
less sleep; and as she looked around the spacious and lofty apartment, she
smiled and murmured faintly: "I am surely dreaming now."

Then she lay still awhile with closed eyes and meekly folded hands; large
tear drops stealing 'neath the veiled lashes, broken words escaping from
her lips. Over the couch bent Solita Mendez, and from her cheek, too, the
life tints had departed; expectation, anxiety, hope, a wild, vague feeling of
joy had whitened her lovely countenance unto the marble semblance that
it wore. On his knees, with that tender compassion depicted on his face
which the guardian angels of the race must feel, was Almon Fairlie; he had
whispered a few hurried words to Solita which had filled her breast with
a tumultuous joy! As she watched the rescued girl, a recollection, distant,
haunting and suggestive, came vividly before her. She placed her hand upon
Cosella's brow, and the wild and inquiring eyes flew open. They met the
angel face so lovingly bent above her; as if spellbound by the tender glory
of those eyes, the winning beauty of the pensive smile, the poor girl gazed
upon the vision, as she deemed it, and sobbed for fear that it would van-
ish from her sight.

"You are safe—safe with friends who will care for you. I will be thy
sister!" said Solita, fondly stroking the upturned brow.

She gazed around her in bewilderment; the ruddy fire-glow fell upon the
kneeling figure of a man, the shaded gaslight revealed the sylph like figure
of the lady—that golden hair, those lustrous eyes, Madonna-like in holiness, Oriental in their flashing light—where had she met with that wondrous embodiment of grace and thought?

The adornments of the room betokened ease and almost luxury; the downy
carpet, the marble chimney piece, the mirror and the pictures on the wall,
the velvet lounge on which her own poorly clad form reclined—where was
she? Was it all a dream, or a mocking cheat of the fever stricken senses?
Who was the man through whose closed fingers the tear-drops streamed?

"It is Almon Fairlie!" she almost screamed, and the memory of the past hours returned.

"I am here—I am with you! You are safe and sheltered"—he paused, and knew not by what name to call her.

"I remember!" and she raised herself and swept the tangled curls from off her brow, "you have saved me from the death of famine! God bless—but who is this? I know not—yet I remember—"

"We have met before, but we will not speak of that now. You need rest and nourishment; take this, my sister!" and Solita held a silver cup to her lips.

She drank of the sustaining beverage; she rose from the couch and threw aside the costly shawl which Solita had thrown around her. She tottered to the place where Almon Fairlie knelt, and with her thin hand resting on his bowed head, she spoke:

"You have been my saviour in my needful hour! Tell me why *you* weep thus, and what it is that agitates this lady? I cannot rest, nor eat or drink, until I know!"

Almon rose from his knees and led her gently to a seat. Kneeling before her there, he said in a voice that thrilled her soul:

"Life's compensations are being meted unto you; the goal is reached—the trial is withdrawn—a great joy is in store for you!"

"*Her name, her name!*" murmured Solita, clasping both hands to her wildly-beating heart. "It may be that we are mistaken."

"My name is Cosella"—she had heard the low spoken words.

"Father in Heaven, *it is*—and yet—" pale and trembling Solita sank upon the lounge, and almost wept again.

"My name is Cosella," she continued with rapid utterance, and her glances flew from one to the other, and her manner gathered unconscious energy, her eye new fire, her cheek the freshened glow of inspiration, or of strange resolve. "I know not my other name; for I have wandered over the world in storm and sunshine for these many years and names have been given me to which I have no right. I never knew my parents; but I know my mother is an angel in the courts of heaven; of my father—I know not if he lives on earth, but he is noble, true and just! I was stolen from his arms and heart, cast into the power of his most relentless foe, by fortune thrown upon the world's cold mercy; by adversity brought nigh unto the door of death. The only being who gave to me a mother's love and counsel—she sleeps beneath the willow shade in the far off tropical clime. He, who tore me from my father's arms, the cruel and revengeful Manasseh—"

She was interrupted—caught in uncontrollable emotion to the bosom of Solita, clasped again to the warm heart of Almon Fairlie, while tears and benedictions mingled with the sacred kisses showered on her brow. Not a word was uttered; but the attendant angels of that hour bore to spirit land the record framed of the soul's divinest thankfulness whose joy could not be given to this world!

"*It is*, it is his child!" softly spoke Solita. "Oh, dearest, do you not remember by the Virgin's shrine we met one morning? Away in the sunbright clime that gave me birth?"

"I know—I recollect—I never forgot you. And your name is?"

"Solita Mendez; and the angels have named me 'Guiding Star.'"

"You and he, then, are of the Spiritual faith?"

"We are the humble expounders of its new-brought light; and thou, Cosella? how sweet the name!"

"I believe in life eternal and progressive; in communion with the limitless worlds of soul; I trust in a God all love, and see no evil that is not of man's formation; no wrong that is not caused by human perversion of the holy immutable laws of Him who is all love and purity!"

She said this with upraised eyes, and hands close folded in the attitude of prayer. Solita murmured gratefully:

"I thank thee, Father!"

"I pray you," continued Cosella, and she knelt before the beautiful Solita and gazed imploringly into her rapt, illumined face. "Tell me what is it you know of me or mine? You know of the mystery that enshrouds my life! My name, my confessions have startled you. In your eyes and on your brow, I read the hallowed sign of knowledge—of mediumship. I have been led to you by the blessed angels! Tell me, in the name of God and Truth! *Where is my father!*"

And, as a weary and beseeching child, she laid her head upon the lady's lap and wept.

Struggling with the joy that deprived her for the time of speech, Solita bowed her golden head and mingled the sister's with the daughter's tears!

Raising his hand on high, the brave and noble Almon summoned from their love-lit homes the sympathizing spirits that yet loved the earth, their birthplace; and he called them thither to consecrate and bless the human hearts awaiting them.

"One glance of my father's face, one blessing from his lips, and I will go hence with joy to live the fate allotted me. Others may invoke of heaven the gifts of wealth and fame—I scorn them all! Of all that earth or vast eternity can give, I ask of God my father's smile! All love ephemeral and vain of life, all worldly honor, fleeting fame, and all of power and joy I would renounce for that divinest, holiest love my father's heart could give to me."

"Cosella, weep no more! Thy prayer is heard, thy filial love accepted, and the realization of thy hopes is nigh," spoke Almon Fairlie.

"Bless thee, thou friend and comforter; but tell me where, *where* dwells my father? Is he in poverty—is he a toiler, too?"

"He is a toiler in the ranks that wage eternal warfare against wrong. Crowned, regally, by spirit-hands, he walks among the titled and the lowly of the earth, a teacher and a friend to all. The hand of care and want has never reached him, as it has thee, his beloved, his idolized child."

"*You know him?*" With clasped hands and kindling eyes she stood before him.

"He has called me brother, often; together we have toiled and striven, suffered and endured, for the harmonization of man—for the world's adoption of a purer religion, a more Godlike standard of morality."

"And you—do *you*, too, know my father?" she questioned of Solita.

A rosy flush, luminous as the auroral glow of morning, overspread the perfect face. "He has called me sister, and by the very name you bear," she said.

Cosella, stooping, kissed her hands. "*His name*—tell me his name," she prayed.

"He is called Percival Wayne, my child."

A loud cry of joy, so loud and thrilling that it startled the listeners, burst from her lips. "*I have seen him!* I felt my heart go forth toward him, my life-chords entwine with his, my soul leap in devotion, my spirit thrill with love for him!—he, the great, noble, soul crowned, lofty being; he, who sways like a God the multitude; he, the commissioned teacher of eternal truths; *he, my father!*" and, in sweet and graceful humility, she bowed her head and thanked the loving God.

She told her friends how she had sat entranced and worshipful, listening to the inspired utterances that fell from his lips—of the strange and irresistible attraction that, magnet-like, drew her sad heart to his. "And I knew him not," she cried, "and I dared not approach him, and he felt not I was so near!"

Long after midnight they sat together, mingling their blissful tears; and Solita told her of the long sad years of pilgrimage endured for her sake; and she brought her father's miniature, and the daughter's holy tears and kisses rained upon the smiling pictured face. And Almon told her of her mother—of the glorious spiritual gifts the noble Percival had obtained by childlike obedience to the Creator's laws. Cosella wept and smiled by turns, and with a reverential gratitude she kissed the beneficent hand of Almon Fairlie, and the ever placid brow of her father's "Guiding Star."

Long after midnight, Solita led the weary wanderer to her chamber, arranged her disordered curls and put fresh, snowy night robes around her, filled a goblet with a strengthening draught, and with a fervent benediction and a good night kiss, she left her to repose. The next day, a letter freighted with the welcome tidings that his long-sought-for child was found was sent to Percival Wayne; and thenceforth, all three counted the days that would elapse ere the father would come to claim his child.

The sudden transition from despair to happiness, from abject wretchedness to joy and ease, had restored Cosella to almost her former bloom and strength. Once more attired in the becoming style of yore, tenderly cared for, lovingly administered unto, the traces of sickness and impress of sorrow departed. The soothing and magnetic touch of Solita charmed away all pain and weariness from her brain and heart, and the coming of the genial Almon was greeted as that of a beneficent and valued friend.

How swiftly, despite of their anxious expectations, sped away those autumn days! Slowly the fading leaves fell to the ground, and the hazy mantle that betokened the benign and royal presence of the Indian Summer cast its dream-folds o'er the busy city. But a summer joy dwelt in Cosella's world-tossed heart—a joy that was perennial, imperishable as the love of God. The rose tint deepened on her cheek, the soul-light kindled in her eye. Once more erect with conscious life power, she dared to greet the morn and welcome the soft twilight hour, fearing no more that jarring tones of discord would intrude, that oppression would overcome, or fear waylay her pleasant dreams. Once more the life of freedom was her own—the life of meditation, hope and aim. Again the glorious promises of youth returned, doubly freighted with fulfillment; the book, the dream, the reverie, the ramble by the water's side—she was free to choose them all; no iron chain of toil bound fast the fluttering heart, the soaring wish. She was released from bondage, and in deep and fervent humility her soul thanked God.

Thus passed three weeks, and she had learned to love Solita with all the yearning power of a soul long friendless. She indulged in rapturous anticipations of future happiness, in which Solita, the adopted sister of her father, was to share. With a rapt and pensive smile, that friend revealed to her that her stay on earth was short—that soon she knew she would be called to the spirit-realms. Cosella, tearful and wondering, hoped and prayed that the new-found sister would be left to earth for many happy years to come.

Resting a while from his labors, Almon Fairlie awaited the coming of Percival, and Solita dispensed unto the infirm and needy of the spiritual gifts of healing, the loving counsel and the sage rebuke.

One calm twilight eve, Cosella sat by the window in Solita's chamber dreaming sweetly of the future, and so absorbed in thought she did not heed the opening door. The now frisk and happy Topaz, who with his mistress had been rescued from the life of want, gave warning of the approach of an intruder, as he ignorantly deemed all who entered the room or house. His sharp, quick bark aroused Cosella from her vision of the cottage home by the sea-side, that favorite and long cherished hope of her life.

It was Solita, clad in white robes, who entered softly. "Come, my Cosella, come," she said, in the soft Spanish tongue wherewith she often addressed her; there was a tender tremulousness in her voice, and as she bent to kiss the upturned brow of the maiden, she left a falling tear-drop there.

A sympathetic tremor shook Cosella's frame—a sudden and delicious joy, followed by a vague apprehension, succeeded the first start of surprise. Her loudly throbbing heart, Solita's manner, the thronging intuitions whispering confusedly—revealed to her that the long prayed for hour had come that was to lead her to her father's love.

She gazed into Solita's face as they passed through the lighted entry. It was illuminated by a joy divine; a strange and solemn earnestness sat on her brow; the smile that wreathed her lips was one of mystic heavenly significance; the soul light in her eye was that of victory, saintly and achieved! The loosened golden showers of her hair fell in long ringlets over cheek and bosom; amid them she had twined a fresh and fragrant chaplet of white lilies, and at her girdle she wore the emblematic flowers she loved so well. Thus arrayed, in spotless white, thus radiantly beautiful and lily crowned, she appeared to Cosella's tear-filled eyes and adoring heart like some rare impersonation of a vestal queen, or bridal fay of heaven!

She knew not wherefore, but a vague, sad feeling stole timorously to her soul; she glanced at her own attire, arranged by Solita's graceful hand; her own white robes of a warmer texture were faced and embroidered with a rich roseate tinge, and the fresh blush roses of the guarded conservatory were twined amid her dark brown curls. Hand in hand, they descended the stairs and entered the sitting room. They were met at the door by Almon Fairlie, who greeted them silently.

Led on by Solita, the trembling girl advanced, never daring to uplift her eyes to where he stood, the noble and long-suffering man, the father of her thoughts and love!

"The Heavenly Father has supremely blest me, and the prophecy of years is now fulfilled!" spoke clear and thrilling the music voice of the "Guiding Star." "My life is crowned and blest! I bring to thee thy daughter, Percival!"

As in a dream, she felt his gaze upon her face, and her soul uprose in filial reverence and in holiest joy! One look into that pale and beautiful countenance, and with a cry of recognition, such as bursts from the lips of the blest and reunited in the spirit realms, she sprang into his outstretched arms!

"My wandering dove! My Lea's child!" he murmured; and the holy baptism of a father's love bedewed with sacred tears her upturned brow; his kisses, like the smiles of the All Beneficent, showered sunlight warmth upon the orphaned and long tortured heart.

Not with the calm of the ordinary filial relationship did Cosella return his love and tears. It was worship, adoration, the hoarded tenderness of life and soul that she with prayers and almost frantic joy gave to this long lost father of her dreams!

She kissed his hands, his hair, his very garments; she fell at his feet and kissed them, and in that worshipful attitude remained, gazing enwrapt into his face, until with gentle entreaty he called her from that lowly posture to his sheltering arms.

"My lamb! Long storm-tossed! Sorely disciplined! My pure, brave child! Rest safely on thy father's breast! There, nevermore the cruel world shall reach to harm thee; and hand in hand, linked with the inspiring angels, we two will work out the Father's will, and return the love of God for human hatred."

"With you, my father—with *you* I will dare and brave all of life and sorrow; but I could no more alone! My blessed father! Oh tell me that you love me, *once again*; me, the untutored girl—how can I stand by thee, the gifted and the mighty of intellect, heart and soul, nor feel my utter nothingness!"

"*Hush, hush, my daughter!* My beloved, long-sought for child! Do you know how I have mourned for you till my couch was wet with tears; and the night wind burdened with thy father's sighs? Have I not wandered far and wide to seek thee? And am I not grateful to find thee thus true to thy soul's intuitions, to thy God, and to my fervent hopes?"

"Say that you love me; tell me so again, *my father!*" she pleaded, dwelling prayerfully on the hallowed words.

"I love thee, child of my life's hope! Dearer than my own soul art thou to me. Of all the choicest gifts of God, thou art the most precious, my beloved child!"

"Oh forgive me!" she continued, with her tear-filled eyes fixed on his face. "I have been so long forsaken, so long alone, that I dare not trust my happiness. The holy name of affection is desecrated by the earth's abuse. I have lived to doubt the expressions, and disbelieve in the existence of all love, save that indissoluble tie of nature and of God that binds me to my father's soul! You, of all the earth's millions, are what my spirit craves and demands. With you I can pray and aspire, labor and achieve, trust and rest, now and in the hereafter!"

Again he pressed her to his heart, again he kissed her brow, and looked with paternal fondness in her radiant face.

A gentle sigh, mingled with the fragrant lily-breath, the soft night wafted toward them.

"Come hither, brother," he said to Almon Fairlie; and that true friend approached with beaming eyes that smiled through tears.

"And will not my sister Solita, too, come near? She, who with this our brother has prepared this great joy for a father's heart? Will she not share the joy, as she has shared the sorrow?"

But Solita replied not. She sat in her accustomed place by the window, in the crimson velvet and antique chair that was her favorite seat. Her hands clasped on her bosom, her head thrown back, her golden ringlets floating over neck and cheek, she moved not at his call,

With his daughter clinging to his arm, Percival approached her, and called her by her spirit name. There was no reply; and bending down, he laid his hand upon the pure white forehead—it was cold and still; the dark eyes, veiled by the soft golden lashes, would flash no more their love-beams on this world. In an attitude of rapt repose, calm, happy, peaceful, she had heard the angels' call, and with a child's submission and a seraph's joy, had passed unfearingly, the morning portals of another life!

"*Thy will be done!*" said Percival, in the low and solemn tone of fervent acceptance. Weep not, my child, she is not dead! To our outer sense she is no longer visible, yet will she be with us often, and be the "Guiding Star" unto a host of souls. Thy restoration to my arms was the signal of her fulfilled earth-mission. Joy, joy, to thee Solita! Thou favored and blest of God!"

With her head upon her father's shoulder, Cosella wept for the beautiful one just departed; and Almon Fairlie, gazing through a mist of tears upon the serene and sleeping countenance, said in a low and trembling voice:

"Of such is the Kingdom of Heaven!"

28

The River of Death,
and the Waters of Life

Thy current makes no music—
A hollow sound we hear,
A muffled voice of mystery,
And know that thou art near.

—Hemans

If there be but one spot upon thy name,
One eye thou fear'st to meet, one human voice
Whose tones thou shrink'st from—woman, veil thy face,
And bow thy head—and die!

The cold wind sighed amid the denuded branches and swayed the leafless city trees; the summoning storm clouds sped across the starless sky, and hung their pall like drapery athwart the moon's pallid face. Many a gay chandelier illumined the scene of revelry in that midnight hour; young feet beat time to inspiring music, and young hearts throbbed elate with love and beauty's victories. Upon his humble bed the toiler slept, and dreamt of rest in heaven; in her solitary garret the wasting seamstress stitched and pined; and beneath the city lamps, attired in the vain mockeries of dress, in the alluring glitter that bespoke their unfortunate calling, wandered, with hungry eyes, and souls transfixed with anguish, those wretched children of the world, the doomed Magdalenes of the town! Ah, superficial observer, stern, uncompromising moralist, judging only by the artificial rose-tints on those death-like cheeks, the assumed demeanor and the shameless air, you know not of the anthem peals of sorrow, uprising in divinest strains of music from those fettered hearts—arising from amid the daily grossness and the hourly outraged womanhood—the pure, meek, fervent invocations, reaching through the ascending angel link unto the pitying heart of the Infinite, whose answering grace is given through the release of the death angel! Oh, man, absorbed in worldly honor, enwrapped in the immaculateness of thy world-untainted position, pass not the outcast thus, with frowning brow and sneering lip! She is thy sister, all deep and womanly, and sweet emotions once nestled to that tortured heart! They linger still, sweet, sorrowing spirits of departed innocence and joy; they uprise, wild and accusing phantoms—eager for yet dreading the earthly end of all this tumult and bewilderment of soul and brain. The strong, self-conscious spirit learns to look with fear and horror on the desecrated temple, and the divinity in woman asserts its retributive power by a weight of woe unspeakable, untranslatable—so far reaching in its agony, so heaven piercing in its poignancy, that the love angels start from paradisean dreams, and the wisdom spirits cry aloud to God! And those whom the ministering hosts of heaven come nigh unto, wouldst thou, weak man, pass by with scornful mien and Pharisaical assumption of superior holiness—*thou*, untried, untempted, the favored son of fortune, and the pampered child of destiny?

Dainty lady, stepping over flower enameled life-plains, dwelling amid the enervating influences of unshared wealth and heart deadening luxury, can *you, dare you*, judge the child of a thousand privations? The aristocratic pride of earth has strung the soul, once as finely attuned to the sublime melodies of truth and love as is thine own; the coldness of deceit has frozen a heart once as responsive and thrice as warm as thine. Fenced in by man-made laws, *thou* dwellest safely in the home shelter, and the sanctities of a thousand conventional barriers to sin suffice to keep thee "pure and unspotted from the world." Have you measured with the line and plummet of experience that fallen sister's untold capacities, that, cherished, nurtured and cultivated as *thy* gifts have been, would have eventuated in glorious fulfillment of the promises of truth and goodness? Oh, judge not, undisciplined heart, untried powers—condemn not her whom the pure Jesus so lovingly forgave!

Enfolded in the guardian sanctities of home, the cherished wife may not sit in judgment on the sinning sister. The rich man knows not of the gnawing pangs of poverty; the joy blest dream not of the incoming of a morn of sorrow; the loved know not of the heart hunger of the desolate, nor the trusting and the happy of the utter change that sears and blights the soul of the betrayed. They know not of the lava surgings of lost hope and wrecked love, of the utter agony of friendlessness; they know not of the more than death struggle that virtue holds with cold and hunger, of the impotent resistance of the virginal soul of woman to the tyrant invasions of force and famine. Oh, mothers, sister, daughters, children of the same God of love and mercy, I beseech you ponder on these things, and with the angels of redemption link yourselves in life lasting bond for the upraising of the fallen, the erring and the world abandoned. Join with the spiritual hosts in the great work of moral emancipation, and with the human aids at your command lead erring souls unto the opening portals of a better life.

That stormy night a young and lovely girl, watching her opportunity, stole silently away from her boisterous and drunken companions, and with rapid footsteps sped toward the darkly flowing Delaware. Very young and very beautiful was that poor victim of worldly cruelty and circumstances, and once the golden smiles of fortune had illumined the path of life for her. Deprived in childhood of a mother's love, dreaming away her youth in frivolous pursuits and occupations, beneath the world wise guidance of a father who never thought of God, this girl of seventeen summers was cast upon the world by his sudden death, and, after a few ineffectual efforts to seek and obtain an honest livelihood, she joined the wretched sisterhood; and with shudderings of terror such as the innately good must ever experience she plunged into the whirlpool, and in the brimming wine cup drowned reflection, peace, hope, all of a woman's faith and honor! And yet she was not lost; for the angel within strove mightily, and not in vain. In nightly vision the mother, fondly cherished, and vaguely remembered, stood before her, with beseeching eyes and prayerful lips. As her once bright eyes lost all their youthful lustre, as the paled lips told, in their mournful compression, of the bitter strife within, as the care-lines marked the once fair and placid brow, a terror undefinable, a fear that should not frame intelligibly, seemed to pursue her by night and by day. She awoke from haunted dreams with screams of terror that alarmed her companions; and the restlessness of her spirit urged her ever on toward some dark and indefinite goal.

On that night her purpose grew clear, and she acted deliberately, if deliberation can result from the fixed madness of the brain and heart. She felt that her frail strength was giving way; that the artificial bloom upon her cheek could not conceal the fearful ravages of disease and remorse, and that the poisoned draught failed in its efficacy of imparting lustre to the sunken eyes, or forgetfulness to the accusing soul. She could not find oblivion in the usual haunts; she now would seek it, where she deemed it dwelt—beneath the river's raging tide!

On, on, with flying footsteps, hair unbound and searching eyes, she sped, until she reached the deserted bank, and for awhile she rested on the cold, damp ground, joyless and fearless alike in view of the coming deliverance, knowing not that the tempter and the saviour alike were on her path.

For one who had pursued her long, and from whom since her soul's awakening she had turned in utter horror and disgust—had that night followed her maddened flight, and now stood with his mantle closely drawn around him, eager, certain, and triumphant in his prey!

Led on by the guiding invisible intelligences, Almon Fairlie, the strong, brave, lion hearted man, had obeyed the mandates of the whispered voice that bade him hasten to the rescue of a human soul. And he, too, stood within the darkness, watching the young girl's movements, and those of her sinister follower.

"*No more! No more!*" he heard her say, in tones that rose shrill and piercing above the howling of the precursing storm. "I shall feel no more, *there*; I shall rest; and if there is a Heaven and a God, *I* too, shall be forgiven; for I repent me of my sins! Forgive me, oh, my God, forgive! Sweet Jesus forgave the Magdalen, and I am fallen as she was who wiped his feet and bathed them in her tears. Forgiveness! Oh, my God, forgiveness!"

Something musical and pure in that young invoking voice thrilled to the pure man's soul, and aroused its deepest feelings of pity and veneration. The watching sensualist heard not the soul ring of that petition, its earthly melody alone could touch his senses; and he reached her with a bound, and endeavored to clasp her in his arms.

To her scream and start of surprise, he said:

"Do you not know me, Sybil? It is I; and what are you doing here, so sorrowful and alone?"

"I am about to end my miseries; to bury this beauty that has been my ruin, these graces that have been my destruction! To take my soul into annihilation, or before God, I know not which—I cannot live so any longer!"

"But, you foolish girl," replied the man, "have I not offered to take you out of the life you are leading, and to provide for you in comfort, ease, and luxury? What hinders you from leaving your low course of life—"

"And exchanging it for a higher form of infamy? Do you propose to give me honorable shelter, peace, rest? *Not you.* You would keep me in splendor until my youth was gone; with the first wrinkles and the first grey hair, I should be cast from your gates, and a fairer victim installed in my place. Go, leave me!"

"But Sybil, you are mad to refuse such an offer! I will furnish a house; you shall have servants, jewels, books, dresses, pictures, all your heart can desire. Come, do you yet refuse?"

"A week ago, I should have listened—*now* I am resolved. Go home to your wife and children—" she called him by name, and Almon Fairlie started with surprise.

"Go fulfill your duty, and leave me to mine."

"Are you in earnest, girl?" he demanded, and he flashed full upon her the lantern he carried beneath his cloak.

It was indeed as if the embodied vision of the beautiful and sorrowing Magdalen of old had been revealed. A face colorless as marble, pure and fine and classical, in its grief sharpened outlines, colored fitfully for a moment beneath the searching light. The waved and silken hair hung in loosened braids around the wide, vein traversed brow. Those tresses bore the rare golden hue, that deepest tinge of sunset glory, that is evolved from the crimson hangings of the Western sky, imbued with splendor, warmth, and glory such as marks the sun orb's attribute. The hazel eyes divested of their baleful fires, gleamed mournfully and appealingly pure as in life's first awakening from amid the saving mist of tears. The sweet mouth kept its rigid impress of determination; the little hands, so white and smooth, were folded resolutely over the heaving breast. Sorrow and humiliation had bent the queenly, sylph like form, and bowed the once erect and fearless head. Deep hollows marked the places where the laughter loving dimples once had nestled; she had wiped the false hues from off her cheek; she had cast the gaudy ribbons and the faded flowers from her dress. With an impulse of true womanly modesty, she had covered her bare arms and shrinking shoulders with the crimson shawl she had brought with her; she had drawn one end of it over her head, and her pallid face shone whitely luminous from amid its lurid folds. In strange contrast with her manner appeared the tattered flounces of her voluminous robe—its striped and gaudy colors.

"*I am in earnest!*" she said, gazing the tempter in the eye.

He read there an irrevocable purpose; he glanced at the midnight sky; he shivered as the cold blast whirled around him. One more effort, and he would leave the girl to her fate.

He drew from his pocket a silken purse, well filled with shining gold pieces. Again he flashed the lantern full upon the face of the unfortunate, and displayed the glistening treasure to her tear filled sight. With a sudden motion she flung aside his outstretched arm; the price of sin fell from his hand, and he staggered back; in his haste and confusion overturning the lantern and extinguishing the light. With a loud curse he sought for his money; but there were no cheering moonbeams, nor friendly stars, to aid him in the search. Baffled, disappointed, furious and alarmed, he retraced his steps toward the inhabited portion of the city, and regained his sumptuous mansion.

On sped the desperate girl; and, spirit guided, the unseen friend followed, led on by the whispering voices, and occasionally by the gleams of something white in her vestments, like faint glimmers of light, these tokens led him on until nigh to the very brink where the wind tossed waves already laved her feet, he caught her fluttering robes, and saved her from the fate of the suicide!

She struggled madly in his grasp, but he soothed her into quiet by the language of respect and pity; he spoke to her of a God of love; of a new faith abounding in promise and fulfillment to all mankind. He told her of the spirit-worlds, and the messengers they sent forth for earth's redemption. With the persuasive power of truth, he won her soul from the sin she contemplated. Trembling, shuddering, weeping, she clung to his protecting arm, and in faltering tones she said:

"You are the only man who has ever spoken to me thus. *You* do not taunt, revile, accuse, or condemn me; and yet you speak the language of religion; you mention God and Heaven, and you threaten not nor denounce. And you tell me of Heaven upon earth. Kind sir, the world disowns such as I. I dare not kneel in their churches; I cannot be admitted to their Christian homes. I cannot return to the life I have left; and the virtuous look in scorn upon me. Oh, why did you save me from the river?" she cried, and entreatingly clasped her hands.

"Because it would be wrong for thee to fling away the precious boon of life," he said impressively; "and because the earth life's mission is not yet accomplished for thee. Child of misfortune, thou hast lived to suffer; now live to enjoy—not the mere material blessings of this life; not its vain and evanescent pleasures; but the supreme and sacred blessedness of living, acting, and fulfilling the divine requirements of thy God."

"Can I return to life, to hope, to peace and honor?" she faltered.

"To all of these; from the ruin and the degradation thou may'st arise, strong, womanly and pure; angels will guide and aid thee, and the Father shower his most benignant blessing on thy head."

"But the world—?"

"With the cold, heartless, shallow mass thou hast naught to do; there are a thousand worlds to live for; an endless progression awaits thee; and *here,* by purity for example, thou canst teach and reprove those who would scorn thee. Hast thou not aspirations toward the Infinite yearnings for the beyond, intuitions of a higher life? I am not speaking to one who comprehends me not. My words are felt by thee, my child."

"Oh, God! That *one* man would have spoken to me thus, ere I fell into the lowest depth! Oh, unknown friend, they jeered at all religion, and scoffed at all morality; *all,* even the highest, most influential in the land; and as a reed I bent beneath the storm, and thought it my destiny to suffer, sin, and die eternally."

"Perverted religious teachings, and a world's false morality, brought thee such thoughts. Happiness, though born of toil and sorrow, is the destiny of all God's children. They mistake the mandates of his love who cling to mere externals. Come, *sister,* I will provide thee with a home and friends; and thou shalt no more barter thy womanhood for bread."

Wildly swept the late autumnal blast; loudly moaned the darkly flowing river, beneath whose turbid waves so many an unfortunate outcast had sought for refuge. Almon Fairlie, the true disciple of the loving Jesus, wrapt his mantle around the shivering form of the rescued girl; and, leaning on his arm, she passed those gloomy precincts, and bade adieu forever to the life of sin and shame.

He led her, weeping, abashed, and trembling, with the newly awakened emotions of her soul, along the deserted streets; and ere the long gathering rain storm burst, they stood within the hospitable home that sheltered Percival Wayne and his new found daughter. With tender and sisterly care, Cosella folded her protecting arms around the rescued one; and her father, smiling that triumphant smile of joy and love, fervently blessed his child; blessed the strong heart, the Christlike soul; that brave, and true, and faithful, in prosperity and in adverse fate, clove to its own highest intuitions, nor scorned the image of her God.

And Almon Fairlie, blest in the consciousness of duty well fulfilled, saw visions of Heaven's compensating glories that eventful night.

Sybil Ray, the child of misfortune: the scorned and world aparted outcast, from friends and home, new life, and aims and joy. Not a trace of impurity rested in after years upon that childlike spirit; poverty, misdirection, the world's coldness, heartlessness and desertion, had driven an impetuous, inexperienced soul to guilt; with many tears and daily efforts for the good of all; with many prayers that were followed by the sweetest offices of self-denying charity, she sought to atone for the past. She offered to become the servant of Cosella, but that life-experienced one gave to the humble penitent her fitting place; the naturally fine mind was cultivated, the latent gifts called into being; the laudable ambition aroused; hope, love and encouragement awarded. With eager attention the young Sybil sat at Almon's feet, and drank of the crystal waters of eternal life, offered by his teaching hand. Beneath such guardianship the rose tints of health revisited the cheek, and decked afresh with coral hues the pensive lips. Once more erect and spirit-conscious, she walked amid the more favored ones of earth; and each fresh outburst of regret and sorrow for the past, was met by the soothing ministrations, the guiding counsels of her life-long friends. She was the friend of Cosella; the pupil of Almon Fairlie and his brother Percival.

29

Fraternal and Heavenly Union

I will unto the untaught souls declare,
How angels dwell in soul-minds free and fair,
How vestal brows Love's lilied chaplet wear.

—A Spirit

Dear readers of this life record! Methinks I hear the numerous queries from all sides—"Is there to be no marriage in this story? Is not a wedding the accepted finale of all novels and heart histories? Shall not Cosella, the weary wanderer and long tried one, pass from her father's sheltering arms to the holy keeping of a still higher and more sacred love? Shall Almon Fairlie, the favored of spirits, wend his earthly pilgrimage alone, uncheered by the household smiles and sweet home-'ies?" For the beautiful and angel-like Solita, we had hoped for the fullness of earth's blessedness, and behold! We were sadly disappointed; she passed beyond our mortal vision, and we shall hear from her no more. And now in eager expectation that the last chapter shall bring the myrtle wreath and the bridal orange blossoms for the brow of Cosella, shall we be disappointed again, and the story close without the attainment of that legitimate and rigidly observed rule?"

My friends; I have written for you all in loving effort, trust and faith. But to the understanding few whose spiritual perceptions have awakened to a higher knowledge of life's uses; to the intuitive soul, the far-reaching psychometrist; the enthusiast for Truth; the recipient of the yet rare lore of the enfolding life; to the high priests of purity among us; to the apostles, meek and lowly, of the new gospel of Love's sacredness; to the prophetesses of the future; the vestalic hearts allied to angels—to these, where-ever they dwell, this history will be acceptable, and its departure from the worldly rules will be forgiven. To those I can speak of love, fraternal and abiding; of love, conjugal and eternal. *They* will not smile in derision of the imperfect portraitures that seek to convey to earthly homes the teachings of angelic love; of passionless, divine, exalted companionship between the toiling, battling, struggling souls of earth, and the beatified of Heaven.

I have two marriages to offer you. One on the self-sacrificing, broad, fraternal and divinely abnegating plane; the other on the highest summit of the spiritual and divinely Real. One was sanctified on earth; the other by the angel witnesses—and both were blest of God.

From all dread of the future, from past regrets and a world's accusations, the noble Almon Fairlie took to his protecting arms the trembling dove that nestled there in peace, security and love. He would have been content to have called her sister before the world, as she was to his spirit consciousness; but he feared its misconceptions, not for himself, but for her, who trembled as the aspen at the remotest allusion to the great wrongs she had escaped from. Therefore a worldly formula pronounced Sybil Ray and Almon Fairlie man and wife; but in the Father's and the angels' sight, they lived and loved fraternally. And no regret ever escaped the lips of Almon; no thought of other ties or more remote desires ever invaded the peaceful sanctuary of young Sybil's rescued soul. With modest grace, and true womanly dignity, she fulfilled her duties; and when her heart was purified from the sin stains of the past, she, too, felt the nearness of the heavenly messengers; and on her spiritual sight dawned the holy visions of the upper life, and she shared in the manifold blessings awarded to the "pure in heart."

As Cosella Wayne lived, grew and strengthened in the heaven light emanating from the spirit realms, and her worshiped father's soul revealed to her its unfathomed depths of tenderness, its heights of intellectual and moral grandeur—as in that hallowed atmosphere of love, her being rapidly unfolded, and her soul expanded, bright and fragrant and musically triumphant; a new and unexpected joy was added to her list of blessings. From her father's lips she learnt of the exalted spirit whose star soul mingled with her own; whose lofty inspirations gave to her penned ideas their eloquence and power; whose impressive touch enkindled nature's beauty with the divine significance of love; whose voice at morn and even whispered strangely of the mystic spirit laws of supreme attraction, inviolate faith; of love, God like, vestal-pure and holy as the heart chaunt of the seraphim! She knew, then, that oft in danger, and in sorrow, that loved and loving one had been nigh with whispered cheer and all protecting care. In him the angel, the almost seraph, she recognized the high and bright ideal of her youth; and ever the lustre on his kingly brow grew luminous with thoughts sublime; ever the sapphire glory of those light-enkindled eyes beamed with the love of heaven; ever the smile upon his lip transformed the wintery world into a realm of summer joy; ever there was enchantment, wisdom, joy and peace in his coming—deepening and eternal love within his soul, for her alone of all on earth, or in the boundless worlds beyond!

Enwrapt in this beautiful reality, she sought only for the perfection of her spirit; the subjugation of all earthliness, the overcoming of all evil. And she turned with soul-abhorrence from the proffered loves of earth; from all that bore the stamp of earth's desire; from all that shared its conventional mockery, its mercenary calculations, its worldly aspects.

Secure, content in the possession of her father's love, and in that heaven abiding affection, consecrated by the soul laws of eternity, Cosella passes through the earth life, smiling, happy and greatly blest! The fettered heart is freed, and the gloom clouds of her destiny have dispersed beneath the sun rays of divine compensation. The glorified face of Lea beams upon her musing and invoking hour; the smiling, radiant countenance of Shina meets her in her contemplative moods. Manasseh, the dark spirit, has been to her for guidance on the upward path of life, and to her father for forgiveness. She feels his spirit-touch upon her garments, and at such times her lips say sweetly forgiving, "God bless thee, Manasseh!"

The gift of inspiration has fallen on the long weary wanderer. She, too, addresses the multitude in persuasive tones of loving fervor, entreating them to come to God and Truth; to forsake the grossness and the darkness of ignorance, and embrace the glorious revelations of knowledge showered upon each receptive child of God.

From place to place they wander, father and daughter, in obedience to the angel mandates; and everywhere they sow the seeds of everlasting life, and plant the undying flowers, and leave the gems of truth. And worldly triumphs, too, have been awarded to the once poor and despised Cosella; the unheeded stranger, the superciliously regarded seamstress, is now the inspired speaker, the admired and applauded exponent of the beautiful and the spiritual. In the same city that witnessed her poverty and her friendlessness, she had reaped the highest meed of fame and honor. In the same place where once she sat a silent and neglected stranger, listening to the inspired utterances that fell from her own dear father's lips, she now stands by his side; and he presents her to that vast assemblage; and her words of truthful beauty and powerful eloquence melt the human hearts there throbbing, and the tears of a heartfelt appreciation moisten the eyes of young and old.

They roam from place to place, and everywhere they lead souls unto the Kingdom of Rest that begins within; they pass through hamlets, towns and villages, fearlessly rebuking evils and opposing conventional crimes. Cosella teaches woman of the laws of life and soul health; and enjoins upon mothers and children the sacred observance of the laws of purity. And Almon Fairlie and his sister, Sybil Ray, wander also from place to place, healing the heart wounds of humanity, and teaching to all the law of love they practice. They often meet, these loving four; and Cosella greets her brother Almon with the radiant smile and outstretched hand of an abiding sisterly affection, and Percival names him ever as the brother of his eternal love.

And Topaz, the humble favorite, the sharer of her utter loneliness and privation, he is with her still, the same indefatigable guardian as of yore; and though many friends throng around her, though fame and happiness are hers, the grateful heart of Cosella cannot discard the faithful friend that once filled its need of companionship; therefore, privileged and petted, Topaz is the companion of her wanderings still.

Beneath New England's sky, where the sea-waves beat upon as fair a shore as ever gladdened poet or painter's beauty-seeking sight, where towering cliffs enclose the forest and the woodland range; where the storms beat grandly in the winter time, and the enchanted summer world is calm 'neath the golden and azure glories of the heavens; a cottage, flower environed, almost wood embosomed, meets the admiring traveler's sight. It is the chosen home of Percival Wayne and his daughter Cosella; and to its rural shelter they will retire when their public duties shall have been fulfilled. Not far distant from a thriving city, and in the immediate neighborhood of several pleasant villages, it is just such a residence as the lover of Nature could desire. From thence to the spirit home their transition will be painless, beautiful, and consciously achieved.

Letters from Santa Lucia informed Cosella that the Señora Teresa de Almiva, after the death of her husband, sank lower still into the depths of degradation; the once refined and gentle lady became a known and stigmatized outcast; she drank deeply of the intoxicating draught, and was often seen reeling in the streets. Her sons, bitterly ashamed of her conduct, had left the country, it was presumed never to return. Cosella and her father intend a visit to those tropic shores; they will carry with them the new Gospel of Universal Freedom, and Cosella longs to revisit the scenes where she took the first initiatory lessons of life. She corresponds with the faithful Clara and her family, and sends many a token of remembrance to the old Panchita.

One day a spirit demanded in piteous accents and imploring prayer for pardon of Cosella. He came through the chosen mediumship of her brother, Almon Fairlie. With pity and surprise she recognized the misguided Salvador del Monte. He had become the victim of intemperance, and his favorite sin had prematurely terminated his earthly existence. How elevating and consoling it was to turn from that illusion of the past to the glowing and hallowed realities of the present; from the doubt-clouded, trembling love of earth, to the blest and confiding sacred love of Heaven!

The good Mrs. Rollins long since has departed to the spirit home. Miss Betsey Brian has not risen above her former condition, socially or spiritually. She ventured to call on the famed Miss Cosella Wayne, and was kindly received. She ever after boasted of the acquaintance, and of the "super elegant manner with which the noble looking, beautiful Mr. Percival Wayne,

Esq., offered her a chair and bade her welcome." Some of the children of the Covenant yet keep aloof from them, but many deem it good policy and good breeding to acknowledge as acquaintances the talented Spiritual lecturer and his daughter. Have they, or can we, forget Solita, the star guide of Percival, the beautiful intuitive soul, that so early learnt of life above the clouds of earth? Can such spirits ever be forgotten? They live in the home, in the heart and memory.

But Solita also came visibly and tangibly before her friends, and the odor of her vestalic lily crown perfumed the earthly air that was all tremulous with spirit sounds of joy. She came with revelations from the mount and fane; with heart hymns of devotion and love-songs of the beautiful. She described the enchanting wonders of the upper lands, and told of its innumerable blessings. She sang to ear and heart the melodies of Heaven, and brought to earth the love and wisdom lessons of the inner life. Re-united with that seraphic soul, with the mother of her dreams, the guardian of her childhood, blest with angelic ministry and crowned by celestial love, Cosella ranks among the blessed and the ransomed of this world. She has fulfilled the destiny that out of seeming evil brought incalculable good; and by the exercise of the Godlike faculty of will, she overcame the earthly obstacles and gained the spiritual summit of her loftiest aspirations.

"Through darkness to the light;" through purifying sorrow to sublimest and imperishable joys; through the clouding mists of fanaticism to the sunlit valleys of truth; through the tempestuous ocean to the silver lake of spiritual serenity; from the storms of human passion and the agony of discipline, to the summer lands of peace, the soul's repose of perfect trust and love. The angel band has won; victoriously enthroned above all earthliness and fear, Cosella Wayne reviews the past with smiling lips and grateful heart, beholding in the gemmed glories of the present, the ultimated beauty of the past.

Perhaps some lonely heart, toiling sadly in the valley shadows, may have been strengthened and encouraged by the perusal of this record. God bless and angels cheer that heart! Perhaps some world aparted, thirsting soul has gathered one stray gleam of truth from these imperfect portaitures of life above and within. May pitying, teaching and saving angels come to us all! To the eyes that have moistened above these pages, to the hearts that have throbbed in kindred sympathy, to one and all, my spirit's greetings and my soul's return of gratitude is uttered in the earthly word—Farewell!

Notes to *Cosella Wayne*

p. 3 Barry Cornwall was the pseudonym of the English poet Bryan Waller Procter (1787–1874). His "History of a Life," from which this verse is drawn, was widely anthologized.

p. 6 "the watchers"—Jewish tradition holds that a body must be watched ("guarded") from the time of death until burial. Watchers, known in Hebrew as "*shomrim,*" prevent desecration of the body prior to burial.

p. 10 "Gaze on, 'tis lovely!"—From Felicia Hemans, "Evening Prayer at a Girl's School," in *The Poetical Works of Mrs. Felicia Hemans* (Philadelphia: Grigg, Elliot, 1847), 289. Felicia Dorothea Browne Hemans (1793–1835) was a prolific and popular English poet as well as a role model for women writers, since she lived apart from her husband and supported herself and her five sons through her pen. Cora Wilburn quoted her poetry frequently.

p. 13 "The heart of the true Israelite"—In arguing that "true Israelites" were no different from "pious followers of the loving Nazarene," Wilburn set herself apart from most Jewish and Christian writers of her time, who portrayed their own faith as superior to others. Her apologetic, addressed to non-Jewish readers of the *Banner of Light,* sought to defend the Jewish people, even as it painted a devastating portrait of Manasseh, the Jewish father who raised her.

p. 14 "the eve of the Jewish Sabbath"—A rare thick description of the Jewish Sabbath from an early nineteenth-century woman's perspective, focusing on dress and domesticity.

p. 17 "Come, my beloved! To meet the bride"—This much-beloved hymn of welcome for the Sabbath, known in Hebrew as *Lekhah Dodi,* was composed in sixteenth century Safed by the mystic and poet Solomon ben Moses Ha-Levi Alkabeẓ. Here and elsewhere in *Cosella Wayne,* Wilburn borrows her translations of Jewish prayers from Isaac Leeser's prayer books, in this case *The Book of Daily Prayers for Every Day in the Year: According to the Custom of the German and Polish Jews,* edited by Isaac Leeser (Philadelphia: C. Sherman, 1848), 82.

p. 19 "land of souls"—Spiritualists hold that the human soul exits the body upon death and settles in the "spirit world" ("land of souls"), where the spirits of the deceased live on, and, via mediums, may communicate with human beings on earth.

p. 27 "Genadin"—Western Yiddish for the Garden of Eden (in Hebrew, *Gan Eden*), meaning Paradise.

p. 27 "I have changed my name"—Name changing is a recurrent theme in *Cosella Wayne*, and likewise in the life of Cora Wilburn. She arrived in America under the name "Henrietta Jackson," and her father's original last name was "Pulfermacher." It was (and remains) common for immigrants to change their personal and family names so as to better accommodate to their surroundings—a form of "self-fashioning." In *Cosella Wayne*, and in the real-life case of Cora Wilburn's father, name changing also functioned as a cover for crime and a means of escaping detection.

p. 27 "you must be submissive"—The Spiritualist movement, Cora Wilburn in particular, championed women's rights and opposed traditional male dominance within marriage.

p. 31 "Mrs. Taylor"—"The White Dove" was actually composed by the American woman poet Elizabeth Akers Allen (1832–1911). Her first husband, who later abandoned her, was Marshall S. M. Taylor. The poem was published under a pseudonym ("Florence Percy") in *Forest Buds from the Woods of Maine* (Boston: 1856), 74.

p. 31 "the habiliments of the grave . . . the conical cap upon their heads"—The custom of wearing shrouds, also known as *sargenes* or a *kittel*, dates back to Talmudic times. Described as a "white linen over-garment reaching the feet with voluminous sleeves," it is customarily worn by males in the synagogue on the high holidays, by a groom at his wedding, and by the celebrant at the Passover seder. The conical or pointed hat (*Judenhut*) was one of many special hats prescribed for Jews to wear, some of which Jews later took on as markers of identity. For discussion and illustrations, see Albert Rubens, *A History of Jewish Costume* (London: Vallentine, Mitchell, 1967), esp. 99, 106, 124, 152.

p. 39 Solita—Cora Wilburn's diary reveals her own brief infatuation with a woman named "Solita"—named for Our Lady of Solitude, the Virgin Mary—in 1847/1848 in La Guaira, Venezuela. Her love went unrequited. In the novel, Solita's love for Percival likewise goes unrequited.

p. 40 "New Granada"—The Republic of New Granada (1831–1858) consisted primarily of present-day Colombia and Panama.

p. 40 "Santa Marea"—Probably a reference to the town of Santa María in the state of Barinas, Venezuela. For an illustration of its beauty, see "Landscape of Santa María, Barinas, Venezuela, *International Cooperation and Development, European Commission*, https://ec.europa.eu/europeaid/landscape-santa-maria-barinas-venezuela_en.

p. 44 "City of Palaces"—Kolkata (Calcutta), in West Bengal, India, is known for its British Raj palaces. The city's Jewish community arose in the eighteenth century and was largely composed of Jewish traders from Aleppo, Iraq, and elsewhere in the Ottoman Empire, whom locals called Baghdadi Jews. In the 1840s there were about six hundred total Jews in the city.

p. 44 "a snowy bearded, crimson turbaned and richly attired Israelite"—This may be a reference to David Joseph Ezra, the community's leading Jewish merchant. For a surviving portrait that matches this description, see *Recalling Jewish Calcutta*, http://www.jewishcalcutta.in/items/show/1126. I am grateful to Prof. Elizabeth Imber for this reference.

p. 45 "He married again, and with his first wife's free consent"—Polygamy among Baghdadi Jews in India was rare, albeit permissible. See Dalia Ray, *The*

Jewish Heritage of Calcutta (Calcutta: Minerva Associates, 2001), 37: "Calcutta Jewry followed the Mosaic law which sanctioned polygamy and divorce by mutual consent."

p. 45 On the clothing of Baghdadi Jews in Kolkata, see Orpa Slapak, ed., *The Jews of India: A Story of Three Communities* (Jerusalem: Israel Museum, 1995), 138–39.

p. 45 "That makes the maids"—A slight paraphrase from Sir Thomas Moore; see *The Poetical Works of Thomas Moore* (Paris, 1842), I:333.

p. 46 "Hindostanee"—Baghdadi Jews actually spoke Judeo-Arabic among themselves.

p. 47 "They brought me a pipe"—Among Baghdadi Jews in Kolkata it was "customary, among both men and women, to smoke a hookah or take snuff." Slapak, ed., *The Jews of India.*

p. 47 "'I had a piece o' pork'"—On this well-known antisemitic children's ditty, found throughout the English-speaking world, see Jonathan D. Sarna, "The Pork on the Fork: A Nineteenth Century Anti-Jewish Ditty," *Jewish Social Studies* 44 (Spring 1982): 169–72.

p. 47 "Cosella, a child of nine years, was betrothed to the young Asaph"—According to Prof. Elizabeth Imber, "while child betrothal was not uncommon, 'intermarriage' between a Baghdadi Jew and a Jew of another background (including Ashkenazi) was extremely unusual and considered undesirable. Wealthy Baghdadi Jews were highly endogamous and often married cousins to keep the family fortune intact" (email to editor, January 16, 2018).

p. 53 "C. W."—Cora Wilburn.

p. 57 "like the Miriam of old"—see Exodus 15:20. There is no mention that the Jewish travelers continued north into Palestine, probably because it was too dangerous to do so in the late 1830s/40s, when the novel is set. Wilburn traveled the world as a young woman but never appears to have visited Jerusalem.

p. 58 "many of them had been sent from the land of their birth for theft and plunder"—see J. S. Levi and G. F. J. Bergman, *Australian Genesis: Jewish Convicts and Settlers, 1788–1850* (London: Robert Hale, 1974).

p. 60 "the synagogue"—Australia's only Jewish congregation was in Sydney; its members rented quarters until they built Australia's first synagogue, on York Street, in 1844. Sydney's 462 Jews in 1841 included some free settlers in addition to convicts and former convicts. Men far outnumbered women, making it easy for visiting single women to find husbands. See Levi and Bergman, *Australian Genesis,* 217–35.

p. 60 "Santa Lucia"—Saint Lucia, part of the British Windward Islands, is an island country rather than a "rural town." Cora Wilburn appropriated its name, in the novel, for what was really La Guaira, Venezuela. Perhaps she chose this appellation knowing that Saint Lucia was named for a woman.

p. 62 "Enthusiast! Dreamer!"—From "To a Reformer," in Grace Greenwood, *Poems* (Boston: Ticknor, Reed & Fields, 1851), 113. Greenwood, pen name of Sarah Jane Clarke (1823–1904), was a poet, journalist, and activist, remembered for being the first female writer for the *New York Times.*

p. 65 "This method of communicating is tedious"—Spiritualists believe that souls in the spirit world can communicate with human beings through "rappings" —akin to Morse code—or, more efficiently, through a trance medium who transmits the spirits' messages via speech.

p. 65 "A few years more"—The sustaining Spiritualist belief in future triumph, when they anticipated that "the new light will dawn."

p. 68 "the discipline of life is good for the expanding soul"—Frequently in her writings, Cora Wilburn explained adversity in terms of "discipline." See especially her novel *Jasmine, or the Discipline of Life*, where a character named Miss Vane proclaims, "I look upon every trial as a means of discipline, as upon some healthful, though bitter medicine, necessary for the cure of the soul" (*Banner of Light*, October 17, 1863).

p. 70 "Marah waters"—bitter waters; see Exodus 15:23.

p. 70 "the cross had been meekly, lovingly pressed to the quivering lips"—a christological reference.

p. 72 "I called on dreams and visions to disclose"—see William Wordsworth, "Despondency," in *The Collected Poems of William Wordsworth* (London: Wordsworth Editions, 2006), 944. Wordsworth (1770–1850), an orphan like Cora Wilburn herself, was a major English romantic poet.

p. 78 "Gehenim"—Gehenna; in Hebrew, *Gei Ben-Hinnom*. A small valley in Jerusalem where children were allegedly sacrificed (Jeremiah 7:31), the term in later Jewish and Christian tradition meant "hell."

p. 86 "*Shemang*"—Known as the "watchword" of the Jewish faith, the *Shema* (Deuteronomy 6:4–9), or *Shemang* (the latter a Sephardic pronunciation that preserves the guttural form of the final letter *'ayin*), testifies to God's oneness. Jews traditionally recite these words twice a day in prayer, at night upon retiring, and for a final time when approaching death.

p. 87 "by the assembled ten"—A prayer quorum consisting of ten men, known as a *minyan*, that is required for Jewish communal prayer.

p. 88 "not the custom of the country for women to attend funerals"—This misogynistic custom is attested in the Code of Jewish Law (*Shulhan Aruch Yoreh Deah* 359:1–2). For additional sources and a critical analysis, see David Golinkin, *The Status of Women in Jewish Law: Responsa* (Jerusalem: Schechter Institute of Jewish Studies, 2001), 109–22 [in Hebrew, with English summary, pp. xxxii–xxxiv].

p. 90 "Oh, I envy those / Whose hearts on hearts as faithful can repose"—From "The Corsair," by the English romantic poet known as Lord Byron (George Gordon Byron, 1788–1824). See *The Works of Lord Byron: Complete in One Volume* (London: 1840), 100.

p. 90 "Love covered all with rose-like flowers"—From "The Renegade's Daughter," by the British poet Thomas Kibble Hervey (1799–1859). The poem begins "She sitteth there, this summer eve / That lonely thing, an orphan girl," which may explain why Wilburn, an orphan, was drawn to it. See *Friendship's Offering and Winter's Wreath* (London: Smith, Elder and Cornhill, 1840), 214. The poem was not included in *The Poems of Thomas Kibble Hervey* (Boston: Ticknor & Fields, 1866), but the stanza Wilburn quoted did appear (albeit wrongly attributed) in *The Prose and Poetry of Europe and America*, ed. G. P. Morris and N. P. Willis (New York: Leavitt & Allen, 1845), 350.

p. 92 "Carmela, the mulatto woman"—Significantly, it is a "mulatto woman" who entices Cosella to "love one of another race," p. 94. Spiritualists, anticipating later ideas concerning love and marriage, argued that love, rather than "race," should determine whom a woman marries.

p. 96 "Canida"—Spanish for a type of female parrot found in the West Indies.

A thinly veiled reference to the island of Curaçao, across the water from Venezuela, whose Jewish community dates to the seventeenth century. See Isaac S. Emmanuel and Suzanne A. Emmanuel, *History of the Jews of the Netherlands Antilles*, 2 vols. (Cincinnati: American Jewish Archives, 1970); and Isidoro Aisenberg, "Efforts to Establish a Jewish Cemetery in Nineteenth Century Caracas," *American Jewish Historical Quarterly* 67 (March 1978): 224–32.

p. 96 "Jeshurun Lopez"—Wilburn likely bases this character upon Jacob Abraham Jesurun (1806–1875), known as "The Curaçaoan Rothschild." There are references to Jesurun in Wilburn's diary. The name Jesurun, a synonym for Israel (see Deuteronomy 33:5; Isaiah 44:2), was sometimes adopted by *conversos* when they returned to Judaism. A photo of Lopez, as well as biographical information, may be found in Emmanuel, *History of the Jews of the Netherlands Antilles*, see especially illustration 105 (following p. 176); see also Robert D. Leonard Jr. "Tokens of Jewish Merchants of the Caribbean before 1920," *Money of the Caribbean*, ed. Richard G. Doty and John M. Kleeberg (New York: American Numismatic Society, 2006), 224–25.

p. 97 "*never*, NEVER"—Cora Wilburn never married. For the mandate within Jewish law to marry and procreate, see Code of Jewish Law (*Shulhan Aruch, Even ha-Ezer* 1:1–2).

p. 101 "Scratch the green rind of a sapling"—This line, sometimes attributed to others, is found in the popular *Proverbial Philosophy* (1838) of the British writer and poet Martin Farquhar Tupper (1810–1889). See Martin F. Tupper, *Tupper's Complete Poetical Works* (Boston: Crosby, Nichols, Lee, 1860), 108.

p. 101 "Oh! Fair as the sea-flower close to thee growing"—From Sir Thomas Moore, "Lalla Rookh," *The Poetical Works of Thomas Moore*, ed. Charles Kent (London: Routledge, 1883), 290.

p. 102 "She had heard the history of Jesus"—An apparent reference to the anti-Christian text known as *Toledot Yeshu* ("The Life Story of Jesus"), which circulated in different recensions, beginning in the Middle Ages, across the Jewish world. For recent scholarship, see Michael Meerson and Peter Schäfer, *Toledot Yeshu = The Life Story of Jesus*, 2 vols. (Tübingen: Mohr Siebeck, 2014); and Peter Schäfer, Michael Meerson, and Jaacov Deutsch, *Toledot Yeshu ("The Life Story of Jesus") Revisited : A Princeton Conference* (Tübingen: Mohr Siebeck. 2011).

p. 107 "I thank my Creator, who has not made me a woman"—Traditional Jewish liturgy includes a blessing that reads "Blessed art thou, O Lord, our God! King of the universe, who hast not made me a woman." *The Book of Daily Prayers for Every Day in the Year. According to the Custom of the German and Polish Jews*, edited by Isaac Leeser (Philadelphia: C. Sherman, 1848), 7.

p. 109 "MAX."—The poem and the poet are unidentified. Could this be a translation from the German Jewish poet, Max Ring (1817–1901)?

p. 109 "But thy deep peace doth on me fall"—A stanza from a longer anonymous poem entitled "In the Night-Time" that appeared in *Sharpe's London Magazine of Entertainment and Instruction for General Reading* 16 (1852): 361.

p. 110 "Oh, give thanks unto the Lord"—Selections from Psalm 136; see *The Book of Daily Prayers for Every Day in the Year*, ed. Leeser, pp. 19–20.

p. 110 "The soul of all living bless thy name"—Selections from the prayer known in Hebrew as *Nishmat*; see *The Book of Daily Prayers for Every Day in the Year*, ed. Leeser, pp. 94–95.

p. 119 "Say not the law divine / Is hidden far from thee"—These lines are usually attributed to Bernard Barton (1784–1849), known as "the Quaker poet" (see *Hymnary*, https://hymnary.org/text/say_not_the_law_divine). Wilburn apparently knew them from John Stowell Adams, *The Psalms of Life: A Compilation of Psalms, Hymns, Chants, Anthems &c. Embodying the Spiritual, Progressive and Reformatory Sentiment of the Present Age* (Boston: Bela Marsh, 1857), 99 (#223).

p. 121 "Proverbs of the Fathers"—This is the term employed by Isaac Leeser in his *The Book of Daily Prayers for Every Day in the Year*, 131–49, for the Hebrew *Pirke Avot* (literally, "Chapters of the Fathers"), today commonly translated as "Ethics of the Fathers." The *Encyclopaedia Judaica* describes this tractate of the Mishna as "the most popular rabbinic composition of all time." For an explanation of why these chapters from the Mishna became known as "Ethics of the Fathers," see *Mosaic Magazine*, https://mosaicmagazine.com/observation/2017/01/how-do-you-say-pirkey-avot-in-english/?print. However, the pseudonymous author there is incorrect in ascribing the earliest English translation of the work to Charles Taylor in 1897. Isaac Leeser's translation appeared almost half a century earlier, and Cora Wilburn, who borrowed selections from Leeser's translation for her novel, helped to introduce these popular rabbinic teachings to a broader non-Jewish audience.

p. 122 "All Israel are entitled to a portion of future happiness"—While Leeser included this in his text of the "Proverbs of the Fathers," it is actually a teaching from Tractate Sanhedrin 90a that is customarily recited *before* each chapter is studied during the Sabbath afternoons following Passover.

p. 127 "Rabbi Chananya, the son of Akashya, saith"—While Leeser included this in his text of the "Proverbs of the Fathers," it is actually a teaching from Tractate Makkot 23b that is customarily recited *after* each chapter is studied during the Sabbath afternoons following Passover.

p. 128 "Yet was there light around her brow"—From Sir Thomas Moore's *Lalla Rookh*, in *The Poetical Works of Thomas Moore*, ed. Charles Kent (London: Routledge, 1883), 277.

p. 128 "Come to me, thoughts of heaven!"—Felicia Hemans, "Thoughts of Heaven," as quoted in John Stowell Adams, *The Psalms of Life: A Compilation of Psalms, Hymns, Chants, Anthems &c. Embodying the Spiritual, Progressive and Reformatory Sentiment of the Present Age* (Boston: Bela Marsh, 1857), 100 (#225).

p. 136 "A sound, as if a spirit's wing"—From a poem entitled "The Renegade's Daughter," by the British poet Thomas Kibble Hervey; see note to p. 90 above.

p. 138 "In the deep hour of dreams"—From Felicia Hemans, "Italian Girl's Hymn to the Virgin," in The *Poetical Works of Mrs. Felicia Hemans*, 232.

p. 138 "shrine of the 'Virgin of Solitude'"—Worship of the Virgin Mary has long been commonplace in Latin America. An important shrine to Señora de la Soledad is found in Caracas, at the Temple of San Francisco (*el templo de San Francisco*), which Wilburn likely visited; a similar shrine is located in Oaxaca, Mexico.

p. 146 "Grows dark thy path before thee?"—An anonymous hymn (see *Hymnary*, https://hymnary.org/text/grows_dark_thy_path_before_thee), which Wilburn knew from Adams, *The Psalms of Life*, 158 (#348).

p. 148 "I shall never sin for bread"—See the September 3, 1848, entry in Wilburn's diary: "Mr D came up and after talking for some time on indifferent matters, made me a proposition no honourable man ought to make to a virtuous woman! Answered *as I ought* and he left me, the low-minded villain."

p. 151 "wilt thou accept the Virgin Mother's love, the church's saving grace?"— On young nineteenth-century Jewish women who ran away from forced marriages and molesting fathers into the hands of the church, see, for example, Rachel Manekin, "Agnon's Tehillah and Michalina Araten," *Ha'aretz*, June 27, 2003, online at https:// www.academia.edu/10113268/Agnons_Tehillah_and_Michalina_Araten_Haaretz _Hebrew_.

p. 153 "How pure in heart and sound in head"—From Alfred, Lord Tennyson (1809–1892), "The Angel Guest"; see Adams, *The Psalms of Life*, 53 (#106). These lines were particularly beloved by Spiritualists; see, for example, James Robertson, *Spiritualism: The Open Door to the Unseen Universe* (London: Fowler, 1908), 221.

p. 157 "The emerald's deepest lustre tints the unfading leaves"—This discussion of the spiritual significance of gems anticipated Wilburn's poetic work on this same subject entitled, appropriately, *The Spiritual Significance of Gems* (1868). Where her father used precious stones to profit and deceive, she looked upon them as spiritual preceptors, each imbuing its wearer with a moral lesson.

p. 160 "Be still, oh soul undisciplined"—See, on this theme, note to p. 68 above.

p. 161 "The spiritual ministry of Night"—See Thomas Lake Harris, *A Lyric of the Morning Land* (New York: Partridge and Brittan, 1855), 39. Harris (1823–1906), a devout Spiritualist, claimed that his poetry was "wrought by spiritual agency into the inmost mind of the Medium (p. 254)."

p. 161 "a whispered discord that caused her heart to flutter with a conscientious fear"—Nineteenth-century accounts of Jewish conversion to Christianity often reverberated with triumphalistic religious fervor. By contrast, Wilburn's diary reveals that her conversion on June 24, 1846, was a "sacrifice," and that she "had repented before it began." She subsequently returned to Judaism.

p. 163 "Upon the walls they rapped again and again"—Spiritualists traced the beginnings of their faith to the mysterious "rappings" heard in 1848 at the home of the Fox sisters in Hydesville, New York. For a popular account based on scholarly sources, see Karen Abbott, "The Fox Sisters and the Rap on Spiritualism," *Smithsonian Magazine*, October 30, 2012, https://www.smithsonianmag.com/history/the -fox-sisters-and-the-rap-on-spiritualism-99663697/.

p. 165 "Cosella offered fraternal and universal love, in place of exclusive dedication"—Wilburn associated herself with the Spiritualist critique of nineteenth-century forms of marriage. See introduction to *Cosella Wayne*, above, pp. xxiii–xxiv.

p. 166 "false to woman's truth, to her marriage vows, to God and purity!" See Cora Wilburn's diary, June 24, 1847: "She whom I had loved & idolized as a mother, she whom I believed my truest friend, whom I had worshipped as a paragon of virtue and modesty is a false dissembler, an adultress!!"

p. 167 "black slave Panchita"—Slavery was officially abolished in Venezuela on March 24, 1854. Having witnessed slavery close-up in La Guaira, Cora Wilburn firmly sided with radical abolitionists in America, and published a well-received poem, "The Slave-Mother's Lament," in William Lloyd Garrison's newspaper, the *Liberator* (November 2, 1860). She justified the Civil War, in the *Banner of Light* (December 19, 1863), as expiation for slavery: "It is because God's retributive justice has decreed that slavery shall no longer be endured by his black children, that we, who have been the guilty participators and abettors of that foulest wrong against humanity, should now be called upon to expiate it by the sacrifice of blood." Note that in her diary entry of April 16, 1844, Wilburn mentioned a white woman named Panchita Lazard who "louses the little black slave, Victoria." In her novel, Wilburn transformed Panchita herself into a slave.

p. 170 "Beware, Jewess"—Jewish converts to Christianity, as Cora Wilburn discovered in her own life, could never fully escape their past.

p. 171 "Silently, strangely the darkness / Has fallen upon thy way"—See Warren Chase, *The Life-Line of the Lone One* (Boston: B. Marsh, 1857), 10. The book advertised itself [p. 225] as a "true and literal history of the struggles of an ardent and ambitious mind to rise from a dishonorable birth, and the lowest condition of poverty and New England slavery (p. iii)."

p. 175 "a malady peculiar to our climate"—Venezuela, in the nineteenth century, suffered pandemics of yellow fever.

p. 175 "Don Jorge de Mas"—In her diary entry of January 4, 1846, Cora Wilburn identified "Dr. Damas" as the man who robbed her of her father's estate and, according to rumor, "caused my father's death."

p. 177 "Wherefore so sad and faint, my heart?"—Felicia Hemans, "Swiss Homesickness," in *Poetical Works of Mrs. Felicia Hemans*, 432.

p. 178 "Tulic"—There is no such island. Could this be a veiled reference to the island of Saint Thomas, in the Virgin Islands?

p. 186 "Eye hath not seen it"—Felicia Hemans, "The Better Land," in *Poetical Works of Mrs. Felicia Hemans*, 332. Note that Wilburn deleted Hemans's reference to the male subject in this stanza ("my gentle boy").

p. 186 "come in spirit to the heavenly land"—A remarkable poetic depiction of "the land of souls" that Spiritualists like Cora Wilburn believed existed. The centrality of women angels in this chapter is particularly notable. Spiritualists promoted women's equality not only on earth but in their visions of heaven as well.

p. 196 "And ye, who sit aloft in earth's high places"—From Sarah T. Bolton, "Awake to Effort," *The Life and Poems of Sarah T. Bolton*, ed. John Clarke Ridpath (Indianapolis: Horton, 1880), 55. Bolton (1814–1893) was a poet and women's rights activist in Indiana.

p. 196 "City of Brotherly Love"—Philadelphia. According to her diary, Cora Wilburn arrived there on September 30, 1848.

p. 197 "Those of her mother's race"—Philadelphia's Jewish population was estimated at between 1,500 and 4,000 in 1848; see Jacob R. Marcus, *To Count a People: American Jewish Population Data, 1585–1984* (Lanham, MD: University Press of America, 1990), 193.

p. 197 "I will briefly sketch *from life* some of the young girl's experiences"—Rabbi M. M. Eichler quoted the noted book dealer A. S. W. Rosenbach of Philadelphia "that Cora Wilburn was a servant in the home of . . . Mrs. Abraham S. Wolf of Philadelphia, about 1850, and was known by the [family] name of Jackson" [*Jewish Advocate*, February 23, 1912, 6]. For background on this period in Cora Wilburn's life, see Jonathan D. Sarna, "Jewish Women without Money: The Case of Cora Wilburn (1824–1906)," *Nashim* no. 32 (2018): 23–37.

p. 204 "Not in the laughing bowers"—From an anonymous poem entitled "The Toiler's Dream," reprinted in Peter Scheckner, *An Anthology of Chartist Poetry: Po-*

etry of the British Working Class 1830s–1850s (Rutherford: Associated University Presses, 1988), 80.

p. 209 "Mrs. Na—, a wealthy lady, one of the daughters of Israel"—Likely a reference to one of the various Jews named Nathan or Nathans in Philadelphia; see many references in Henry S. Morais, *The Jews of Philadelphia* (Philadelphia: Levytype, 1894).

p. 211 "Alexander Dumas"—Alexandre Dumas (1802–1870), whose father was of mixed race and whose grandparents were slaves in Haiti, was a popular French author of historical novels. Many became translated into English and were serialized in newspapers, including *The Count of Monte Cristo* (1846), and *The Three Musketeers or The Three Guardsmen* (1847), which is referenced here.

p. 215 "the famous 'squares'"—William Penn planned five open-space parks when he laid out the plan for Philadelphia in 1682. He believed that well-ordered public spaces, in addition to firm laws and responsible government, would ensure virtuous behavior. North East Publick Square was renamed in honor of Benjamin Franklin in 1825. See Elizabeth Milroy, "Repairing the Myth and the Reality of Philadelphia's Public Squares: 1800–1850," *Change over Time* 1 (Spring 2011): 52–78.

p. 217 "I charm thee from the agony"—From Felicia Hemans, "The Childe's Destiny," in *Poetical Works of Mrs. Felicia Hemans*, 439.

p. 218 "She said not to the infirm"—Wilburn sharply criticized Spiritualists who labored only for the wealthy, from whom they received high fees, while refusing to serve the poor, the ignorant and the infirm; see, for example, her "My Religion," *Agitator,* January 1, 1860, 54, and February 1, 1860, 70–71.

p. 227 "They who ne'er ate their bread with tears"—a translation from one of the best-known lines in Johann Wolfgang von Goethe, *Wilhelm Meister's Lehrjahre [Apprenticeship]* (1795–1796): "Wer nie sein Brod mit Thränen ass, / Wer nie die kummervollen Nächte/ Auf seinem Bette weinend sas, / Der kennt euch nicht, ihr himmlischen Mächte. See *Goethe's Werke.* Vollständige Ausgabe letzter Hand. Zweyter Band. S. 118 and the discussion of the German Lieder based on these lines online at https://www.liederabend.cat/en/bloc/2-bloc/178-bread-with-tears. Many a *Bildungsroman* (novel of formation), including *Cosella Wayne*, was clearly influenced by Goethe's novel. Wilburn read German fluently and translated novels from the German for the *Banner of Light.*

p. 227 "Poor Sambo!"—By 1860, the word "Sambo" had already become "a nickname for a black person . . . especially with reference to the appearance or subservient attitude held to be typical of the black American slave" (*OED Online*, Oxford University Press, June 2018, www.oed.com/view/Entry/170350. Accessed 2 July 2018). However, the children's book *The Story of Little Black Sambo*, by Helen Bannerman, only appeared in 1899. On the rough, poorly made clothing worn by African American slaves in the South and produced in northern factories (many of them owned by Jews), see Adam Mendelsohn, *The Rag Race: How Jews Sewed Their Way to Success in America and the British Empire* (New York: NYU Press, 2015), 55, 136–41.

p. 233 "on condition that she should renounce her new faith"—Spiritualists did not demand any form of conversion or ritual in order to join their ranks, so the question of whether Spiritualism should be classified as a separate faith, incompatible with existing ones, remained open for debate—anticipating parallel debates concerning Unitarianism, Ethical Culture, Christian Science, and Buddhism. Wilburn indicates that some Jews did consider Spiritualism incompatible with Judaism and offered incentives to her to remain squarely within the Jewish fold. For Isaac Leeser's views on Spiritualism and Judaism in Philadelphia, see "Superstition," *Occident* (May 1, 1853), 37.

p. 237 "And ye, whose birthright is the glorious dower"—From Sarah T. Bolton, "Awake to Effort," in Ridpath, *Life and Poems of Sarah T. Bolton*, 54–55.

p. 239 "Here am I, Lord"—See I Samuel 3:4–8.

p. 244 "The district of Southwark"—originally a municipality south of Philadelphia, it bore the same relationship to Philadelphia as the Borough of Southwark did to London. Southwark was incorporated into the city of Philadelphia in 1854 and comprised the area bounded on the north by South Street, on the west by Passyunk Avenue from Fifth and South to Tenth and Reed; it then ran along Reed Street, down Seventh, and along Mifflin Street to the river—see Wikipedia, https://en.wikipedia.org/wiki/Southwark,_Philadelphia.

p. 246 "Over thine orphan head / The storm hath swept as o'er a willow's bough" —From Felicia Hemans, "The Angels' Call," in *Poetical Works of Mrs. Felicia Hemans*, 406.

p. 253 "Of such is the Kingdom of Heaven!"—See Matthew 19:14. Cora Wilburn may originally have intended *Cosella Wayne* to end with these words. Significantly, the June 30, 1860, issue of *Banner of Light* containing this chapter did *not* conclude with the phrase "to be continued" as all previous issues did. The following chapter (chapter 28), published a week later, seems like a hastily produced addition to the novel.

p. 254 "Thy current makes no music—A hollow sound we hear"—From Felicia Hemans, "The Subterranean Stream," in *Poetical Works of Mrs. Felicia Hemans*, 285.

p. 254 "If there be but one spot upon thy name"—From Felicia Hemans, "The Lady of the Castle," in *Poetical Works of Mrs. Felicia Hemans*, 145.

p. 254 "the doomed Magdalenes of the town"—Mary Magdalene, a follower of Jesus (John 20:1–18), is identified in Christian tradition with the prostitute mentioned in Luke 7:37. The term eventually came to mean "prostitute," especially one who had reformed. Around the same time that this chapter appeared, on May 29, 1860, Wilburn sent a letter to the Pennsylvania Yearly Meeting of Progressive Friends promoting a plan "to rescue our sister Magdalen from degradation, shame and ruin"—see *Proceedings of the Pennsylvania Yearly Meeting of Progressive Friends Held at Longwood, Chester County 1860* (New York: Oliver Johnson, 1860), 61–62.

Selections from the Diary
of Cora Wilburn, 1844–1848

Journal La Guayra [Guaira], 1844

Friday 1st of March.—The weather continues rainy. I had not been home long yesterday but it began anew. I know nothing very particular to note down.

Saturday 2nd. The day of rest, but always a dull day for me. Passed it reading Schiller,[1] playing with Cidelle and Lora.

Friday 8th. Last night about midnight or one o'clock we had again a most tremendous row, as usual for nothing, about going out to give some person a water. The brandy bottle was applied and so began his cursing and bellowing; it continued till near morning. I was up late for at 2 o'clock we made tea in the kitchen, another rare row this morning with me. Now all is quiet 4 o'clock. Had our usual visit this evening.

Friday [March 22]. Today a year ago we left Singapore for Bremen. This evening we went to Miss Ely's, her husband being in Caracas. They live in a very large house beautifully furnished. Miss E's name is also Henrietta.[2] Went up to her sleeping baby and she also showed me and mother through the rooms and in the top of the house, which excursion had bad consequences for me. The house is painted lately and I blackened all my arm which was without a long sleeve. As E washed the paint off for me, her little Lizzy was very rude and pulled me about more than was necessary. Mr. Ely came from Caracas while we were there. Our Therese has like me not been bred in the best school of manners, but [in her] I miss everything like the least glimpse of education or manners.

Saturday 23. The holy day of Rest! Passed it as usual it is always a dull day for me.

Saturday 6th [April]. Alas! A word to the wise is enough. I read the rest of Ivanhoe[3] today. This evening our Therese got us the key of a nice house in a good neighborhood. Tomorrow it will be inspected. My three wishes now are to have peace and quietness about ???, to learn Embroidery, and to have a House.

Monday 15. Two months on shore today! Went to the Lemains to embroider. My harp has not come home yet. The chords were not yet all in order. They say there was a slight earthquake last night about 9, just at the time we were coming home. They say it was in the air so not a real earthquake.

Tuesday 16. This day 2 years I arrived in Sydney! This morning my harp came in order and in time.

Panchita Lazard, Mrs. L sister, was here all the time and remained till near 12. We then went together at 2 oclock. Mrs. L. went to see my mother and I remained. Panchita has made me her confident, has told me the history of her love &c. She seems a good tempered being and is accomplished as much as any female need be in all kinds of embroidery needle work &c. but she is somewhat of a stutterer, wears dresses all in holes about the house, and louses the little black slave Victoria. So while I try to copy all her virtues, and as far as my poor abilities allow her accomplishments too, I can see myself superior to her in many other littler virtues in the "small sweet courtesies of life."[4] My mother fetched me home.

Wednesday 17th. This morning before 6 Mr and Mrs. Lemain were at the door. Mrs. Lemain's black negro, the husband of the cook, ran away some 8 or 10 days ago. This morning or in the night the whole family has decamped.

Thursday 25. Raining again, though not such showers as yesterday. Dolore came about 12 oclock. I think there is a chance of getting Mr. Groseos' small house after all. Mr Lemain's slaves are caught and are in prison at Caracas. There is a rumour that all European inhabitants at St. Domingo have been murdered by the Negroes.[5] They will have to pay for this. At St. Thomas, 1600 people have died of small pox in the last 4 or 5 months. My earache was very bad indeed causing me to be quite feverish. I had it very bad last night.

Thursday 2nd [May]. Do I not say Friday is one unlucky day to enter a new house? Well I am right. I have been so maltreated and beaten that I went to Lemains with my hair about me all in disorder—all for nothing again. I will not put down more as I remember well all I wish. I screamed murder and Mr. Starel [?] coming up the street entered to see what was the matter and a black woman from opposite came to my help. In four minutes I would have fainted under his hands. But God will surely deliver me out of the hands of the Philistine.[6] Rain nearly all night but I slept and heard it not.

Friday 3rd. Ordered me out of the house and I went up to Lemains. Afterward, my poor mother came to fetch me and Mrs. Lemain went with us to reestablish peace. As soon as she was gone, he began with my mother and Mr. H——so that we were both ready to drop with the noise and scandal. Yesterday the looking glass was broken, today after 15 glasses butter glasses were broken. Mr. L called in and took dinner with us, he began to take a knife up to my mother so we both left the house intending *not* to return however as we could see Mrs. A—— [?]did not seem to like our staying for the night my mother thought it would be best to go home which we did. Mr. H and Mr Groseos were there. They got in slyly, and afterwards my mother sent in word to excuse her as I was very unwell, which was true. I nearly dropt for fatigue. They quarreled till near 2 but I slept till at last he was silenced. My harp I had sent to Mrs. Lemain as he would have broken it.

Sunday 5th. This afternoon took a walk with my mother and Mr and Mrs L and Panchita up to Guanapa . . . Met several Europeans, Mrs. Schimmele [?] and the old Mrs. Pardo[7]—a Jewess who lives right opposite to Mrs. L with her sons.

Tuesday 14th. . . . . . Some weeks ago I heard that all or almost all of the European inhabitants of St Domingo had been murdered by the blacks with wives and children. I believe it is about 2 months ago this occurred. The mulattos also they say have been murdered. The newspapers now say the French are going to take possession of St. Domingo and men of war are going there to take revenge on the negroes. Mrs. Lemains slaves are in Caracas in prison so they say and Mrs. L has employed a lawyer. She is willing to take them back, I believe, if only for the sake of her Lone, her cook, that she may get her favorite dishes and caress little Victoria.

Sunday 19. Almost half past 5 it began pouring of rain but in such a manner as I had seldom seen it before. To see the river, dark and muddy, raised to twice its height is really terrible. It reminded me of the infernal regions. The look [?] of it was terrible. The darker it grew the stronger it rained. Mr. Pardo from opposite came out of the house in a great hurry and wet to the ancles, the rain was pouring in at the back of the house and they thought the river or stream of water from the mountain was coming into the houses. The poor old lady was at her door and seemed in great trouble. Mrs. Lemain and my mother ran over. I, acting on the impulse, followed, glad of an opportunity to form the acquaintance with one of my religion, which I had often sincerely wished for. There was no damage done and in the parlour all is dry. She is a venerable old lady. She was very much pleased when she heard me speak German. She took my hand and begged of me to come and see her as she had no one to speak to. How these words touched me! I answered that I too had no one here and begged her to visit us too. She is like myself a solitary being but she has three [Dalte?] sons and a married daughter in Caracas, and a son who is deprived of speech the effect of a cold and who has come to this country for his health, also in Caracas. Mrs. L. also offered her her house etc. She has been once or twice before for a few moments at Mrs. L. The house is right opposite. I noticed a picture of וואילעה רעבייזס [many rabbis?] giving the law on Mount Sinai.

Thursday 30th May. A long lapse since my last written lines. Since last Thursday I have been ill. Today thank God I may say I am well though not yet as strong as before. I felt indisposed last Thursday morning already and did not go out that day. Friday I was worse and I believe it was on Saturday the Doctor was called. I felt no pain only great heat. He ordered me a foot bath at night with salt and ashes. Mrs. L, Mrs Mavou and her mother were here Friday morning. My Mother is ill now but is getting better, she has an attack of the dysentery. Yesterday, Wednesday, Panchita with another lady were here, the latter bought 2 pieces silk. She is a modiste[8] from Caracas. Panchita too had been indisposed and besides she is the slave of her sisters caprices which hindered her coming to see me. Mrs L had been here this week. She ill treats poor Franzel terribly and in fact is an infernal spirit assuming a woman's form, speaking of duty and charity and practicing cruelty.

Friday 31st. This evening Mrs. Lemain came. She has been here this morning the meddling creature and nearly turned the whole house topsy turvy. I gave her a bit of my mind, as she said my mother ought to have a certain woman who lives close by to tend her, which in itself was no harm but Mrs, L. has already often insulted me and I am determined no more to brook it quietly. My spirit is not so broken down that I need stand insults from one like her. This evening Old Mrs. Pardo and her son came to see us. My mother is still unwell. Mr. Lawrence the partner of Mr. Gill of Caracas who with his wife and little girl were wrecked some distance from here was here this evening also; his account of the disaster is terrible. What that poor lady must have suffered being pregnant too!

Sunday June 2nd. A miserable day nothing but noise. That creature Mrs. Lemain here to witness it. Poor poll[9] got his wing broken. Oh when will the good genie above me turn for me a bright page in the sorrowful book of my young sad life? Oh when!

Monday 3rd. My Mother still continues unwell she has had leeches last week but the doctor treats her illness light and thinks it of no consequence. We got the book Mr Dalte[?] promised us this evening. He often comes here poor good old man. The last few days I have been the cook of which but I have had a slight acquaintance with, but Mariela shall teach me.

Wednesday 5th. Today Mrs Lemain, her husband and sister left for Caracas having received some news on account of their slaves. She sent her servant to ask us to lend her our cloaks which was politely put off with an excuse. She went past the door with Panchita and her husband but did not in her hurry come in and bid us adieu.

Sunday 9. Nothing particular only it is an ill wind that blows no body any good.

Friday 14th. Dolore has been here and tuned my harp. I cannot yet play. My mother has taken a vomitive, but now seems better.

Saturday. Today was the 29th June. Sunday morning at 3 oclock my beloved mother departed this life for a better. God gave her a calm and peaceful end. Sunday 30th at 6 oclock she was taken from me and sleeps her last sleep amid the calm beauties of nature in the garden of Mr. Lyes at Guanapa. This gentleman kindly gave his permission for her remains to be deposited there. I feel no wish to continue my journal perhaps at a later period I may. I am alone in the world but still do I hope, unworthy as I am, that God the just and forgiving is with me and will guide my steps to right and forgive me my trespasses.

Tuesday 16 July [1844]—By fine weather clear sunshine about ¼ past 8 this morning was felt a strong shock of an earthquake. It did not last long but was distinctly felt.

Tuesday 13 [August]—I have been to Mrs. Jesurun a Jewish family her daughter Estela is the handsomest lady I have seen in this country.[10]

Monday 19. This evening we were invited to a splendid dinner at the Jesuruns There was there Mr. Samurnne [?], a Frenchman, Doctor Morton, another Doctor and Mr. Laurence. A splendid dessert was afterward served up, but what is all this to a being who is "love at heart"?

Thursday 5th [September] had a small dinner party this evening. . . This evening has been a memorable evening to me. Alas I am beset by troubles.

Wednesday 11th September. Left Delfinos Hotel for two rooms in a house opposite and belonging to the Hotel De Vapane. The steamer for La Margarita which was to sail this evening after five and in which my father had already taken his passage sailed without him in consequence of his having bought a lot of pearls today so he changed his mind. It had been agreed on that I should live with Mrs. Bernard during his absence which would be for about 10 or 15 days. Another disappointed hope!

Thursday 12. Went home and had a glass thrown at me in the stead of an evening blessing.

Monday 23 September. Today has been Yom Kippur, what a day! Such a noise nearly all night and all the morning. I left for Mrs, Bernards quite desperate. Oh what have I suffered since I came back from Caracas.

Sunday 5th October. All is settled—tomorrow we go on board the Caraquena for Bordeaux. What have I not undergone since the 23 of last month, but now I am though still unhappy, full of hope confiding and trusting and putting my faith in God. Received the day before yesterday a letter from Mrs. Pardo, her daughter has presented her with a little girl. Mrs. Lawrence has given birth to a boy. Oh La Guayra how can I leave thee now!—

Tuesday 7th. This morning I took leave of all my acquaintances, having done the same partly yesterday. Oh my dear good motherly Mrs. Bernard! how thou wept when I took leave. She had sent me a note to say she could not accompany me on the way as her feelings at our separation were too strong. . . . Farewell beloved La Guayra—farewell!

1845

Monday June 16, 1845. To remember that morning five years hence![11]

2 November This evening went to several churches which were all illuminated. The services for the dead affected me exceedingly.

1 December [1845]. Sunday. My nineteenth[12] birthday, a fine glorious sunny day, but my heart was sad and alas so strangely changed am I since then that I long for the tidings of that day which seems joy when compared to the deeper degrading melancholy, the utter absence of hope I now endure! They danced this evening, Mr Calmenore, a young physician who had been in attendance in Tomas [?] was also there.

24 December. Christmas night . . . Mrs. B was out of humour with me, which is often the case now; am I ever happy? Am I ever really merry?— Had been to the midnight mass.

1846

1st of January. A rainy day. Went out with Isabel my tormentor to buy some things.

4 of January. Returned to La Guayra at 9 oclock in the morning. I have suffered greatly in Caracas! Mrs. B has made me suffer with her wayward and capricious temper. Isabel the mulatto girl governs and chides me. I suffer in silence, weep & complain not. The doctor Damas[13] [?] promised to come in November to settle accounts with me. Mr. B went to Margarita to secure my father's trunks and property. Before leaving Caracas he returned

with the news that only 8 hundred dollars were left to me which the Dr D would deliver to me in person. Another disappointed hope. I had built so many castles in the air, with the little property I expected to receive, had made so many plans of doing good, and had called up so many fairy visions never meant to be realized. Alas I am a being doomed to misfortune.

Doctor Damas never came! Mr B brought me my father's trunks & some jewelry, my little fortune is irrevocably lost! No one knows where Dr D is gone. The public rumour says he caused my father's death. God alone knows all I have suffered, the pangs my heart endures.

Nothing particular occurred in the months of February, March or April.

24 May. Went to pass the day at the Tower in company with a lady from Alto Cabello, Merced Mendes and her husband . . . altogether passed as agreeable a day as might be expected from a suffering and broken spirit like mine.

Alas, I have now to note down an event that fills me with reproach and repentance, an event that has called upon me the just anger of a most just God! An event that I long oh how sincerely, how fervently! to atone for, to win the pardon of my offended, my just and Benevolent father! Alas, misled by a fake enthusiasm which I mistook for conviction in a strange country amid stranger[s] my weak and hope forsaken spirit forsook its God!! Forsook the God of Abraham, of Isaac & of Jacob, the Only true God of Israel, for the false one of Nazareth! Bowed these knees in worship to the idols! And since that day of evil memory, a heavy & severe chastisement has fallen upon my guilty head. Had I not forsaken the God who till that day had supported and comforted me in all my troubles, he would not have forsaken me. I forgot what a brother had enjoined me, forgot my God, and as an accusation, a bitter & stern remembrance, do I note down the fatal day & hour now awake to my error repentant and afflicted. I pray for pardon and forgiveness from the only God and curse the Idols I once had the weakness to have faith in. Pardon me my God! Oh pity and pardon thy repentant, thy broken-hearted daughter, thy Marah!

Wednesday 24 June at 6 oclock in the morning [1846] was consummated my sacrifice. I had repented before it began but it was now too late, my word had been given. Mr B became my godfather, Mrs B. my godmother. This evening there was a table laid with refreshments, and the invited danced till 12 oclock.

Nothing particular occurred in July nor in August. I had left off mourning the fatal day I changed my pure and holy religion for a false one. Suffice it to say I suffered day by day unheard of torments: my godmother's icy cruelty, her ironical manner towards me, the over bearing behaviour of her Isabelle were breaking my too sensible heart, I became almost like an idiot. I would sit on the step of the door that leads to the yard and dream or weep. Strange infatuation! I still prayed to saints that could neither hear nor help me and forgot the God of our ancestors!

In September nothing particular occurred.

Three days after my arrival at this house I asked my letters back from _____ and began to forget that first serious folly.

5th of October. Today a year my new tormentor Isabel lives beneath one roof with me. That proud & vain girl vulgar and uneducated as she is makes me suffer. God knows how much!

Nothing particular occurred nor in November, my days pass in the dull monotony of sorrow and heart anguish, each day finds me more miserable, more desponding than the last!

1st of December. My 19th [actually 22nd] birthday. How time flies. Last year I was unhappy but not without hope, now I am of Earth's creatures the most forlorn, an "orphan of the soul," a spirit tired wo[be]gone being, deserted by all and unbeloved. About three days after my arrival at this cursed house, my ever beloved and respected friend & brother Mr Hohnert bade me farewell, a cold and indifferent farewell! He has gone to Hamburg taking with him an ill-formed opinion of one he once called sister! He too has partly believed my calumniators; he too thinks me unworthy his friendship; he too hates me perhaps! alas! What a dark & evil destiny is mine!

1847

1st of January 1847. Nothing particular occurred. The 23 of December died Aquales Badarrasco [?] after an illness of a week. I had been for three days in the house during which time all attended and nursed him. I did not sleep for 3 nights. At midnight of the second night went with Isabel to get some leeches. In January the President Monagas[14] arrived; the wharf & customs house illuminated.

In February nothing particular occurred that I remember. In March wrote to Caracas to the Señoras Guidos who keep a young ladies seminary to enquire whether they would receive me. Have destined for that use 250 dollars, which money Adolfo brought me for jewels sold for me and some few dollars of jewelry that I had sold, in all, 295 dollars. After waiting for more than a month received the ladys answer, they ask 15 dollars per month.

24 June. This fatal anniversary [of conversion] passed by without fete, my tormentors being indisposed. About the end of this month was revealed to me by Isabella a most awful secret! Of its truth I afterward convinced myself. She whom I had loved & idolized as a mother, she whom I believed my

truest friend, whom I had worshipped as a paragon of virtue and modesty is a false dissembler, an adultress!! And with that immoral woman, that essence of impurity and vice, all—have I lived beneath one roof! Poor old B now lives entirely in the house. And that evil woman has illtreated me and wrung my heart with anguish. Each moment that I remain in this house seems an age to me. I wait for Mr B's leisure to take me to Caracas.

13 August. Another ball at Chaquerts. Mrs. Hippolita's Chaquert's saints day. The saloon was very full. Retired at 4 in the morning. I have got very friendly with the Chaquert family, especially with the daughters Carlotta and Dolores . Mrs C is the mother of 10 children, all alive, has a son twenty years old, but she looks as young as her daughters and dresses with great taste.

Have seen Sarah Jesurun. Estela is married and lives at St. Thomas. Sarah & Delia are very friendly to me but their father is not. Has he no right to be offended with me?

17 September The old Salone's saints day. Had a reunion in the house, the second they have had since my arrival. Danced till near 4, I am embroidering a *franela* [flannel] for my godmother, who although I pray God never to let me return to her house, I am obliged to write to her and answer her letters, although I most sincerely despise her!

Nothing particular recurred in the remainder of this month. . . . In this month I sold my four remaining diamond rings, and the pair of diamond earrings, and the watch, in all 225 dollars, to the father of the Palacios, who keeps the money for me and pays me the interest of 1 per cent. In October nothing particular occurred. I pass the day sewing etc. and the evening I go to Chaquert or stay with my companions, reading or conversing. I am tired of balls and visits, and long for a quiet retired life.

In November nothing particular occurred.

In December wrote to my godfather to come and fetch me to spend Christmas in La Guayra. . . . My greatest trouble consisted in my being obliged to return to that house. I fervently prayed with such agony of spirit to be delivered out of the hands of those wretches!

My object in spending Christmas time in La Guayra is this. These are days of festivity and dressing and my poor means do not allow me to buy new dresses etc and my *pride* does not permit me to present myself ill dressed and poorly arrayed. I am too heartily tired of balls and visits, and to avoid all this determined to go to La Guayra.

Monday, the 22 December. My godfather arrived at 12 oclock My birthday was passed over. I am 20 years old [actually 23]!

Tuesday the 23rd. Walked out with Mr. B and returned home at 4 in the afternoon. Solita has offered me to live with her. She is going to live with her two brothers in a delicious country house in the Cuadra de Bolivar. Her offer has filled me with pleasure. To live with so kind a friend, so talented, so lovely a girl! thought I then.

For some time past, my heart has begun to awake to the truth, and miss its old pure and holy customs. My forgotten prayers obtrude themselves on my mind, a feeling of despair overcomes me, to think that I am separated oh so far from *my people*, from my old loved habits! I had taken a desperate resolution of going to Curacao, of returning although alone, friendless and penniless to my religion, to my God! But now the promised friendship of Solita, the asylum she offers me, has anew tempted me to remain among Christians, although my heart has repented, and it is my firm resolve to return to my religion when I can.

This afternoon at 9 oclock went to the Posada Leon de Oro with my godfather, my poor good godfather! I had a room given to me. By a strange coincidence it was the same room we breakfasted in three years ago when first arrived in Caracas. My father, Mr. Hohnert and Mr. Dalte, and I. Of these three persons, one sleeps the calm sleep of death, the other has forgotten my existence and lives the creature of folly, vice and interests too vile to be mentioned! And he, the pure, the noble minded one, who called me sister and swore to me through life a brother's love has he too forgotten his orphan sister? Alas, calumniated by the snide and calumniating world he too has forgotten me as unworthy his ~~marriage~~[15] embrace. I have written to him. Will he ever answer me?

Many memories pleasing and sad assailed me as I sat in that silent chamber and brought the tears into my eyes. Poor forlorn orphan! How am I changed. What sorrows, what bitter anguish has wrung my bosom, since the morning we three were here assembled! If I say we *three* for the fourth exists not in my memory!

Took my silent supper, my cup of chocolate *alone* and retired to rest at past 10 oclock. At 5 we started, and after having breakfasted, "desayunado,"[16] in Guaracarumbo, arrived at breakfast home at La Guayra.

Saturday 27. Went to see Clarita who received me very friendly; she too knows who *that woman* is.

1848

1st of January 1848—This evening went to a small party, returned at 10.

7 of January Mr. Bernard went to Caracas. I did not return with him as I wish to remain some days more. I have not yet been to Guanapa. My godmother has returned to her old ways with me. She did not wish me to go to Clara's house and I passed a fortnight without going for fear of her!! But at last went since that day her friendship to me was gone and she returned

to her old way of tormenting & mortifying me, not speaking to me etc. I went to see Clara another day . . . I went to Sue's another day, to Carmelita Elster . . . and so contrived to pass my time till my godfather's return, that he might take me to Caracas. At last not being able to bear my torments & that woman and her Isabel's irony, went to Clara to remain there. Have suffered greatly since my return here.

For some time past there has been rumors of an expected revolution.[17] The 24 of this month at 6 oclock in the evening, Meynadier told us to shut the doors and windows as the expected revolution had taken place in Caracas and was expected here. It would be needless to describe the fear & alarm we were in.

25 January—This afternoon 9 persons were killed in the Congress chambers of San Francisco. Caracas was in a state of consternation. They have prevented the ships from leaving the port but afterwards revoked the order. We were for many days in a state of the utmost alarm. My godfather has returned but will not take me to Caracas.

February 12th Saturday returned to Caracas. Meynadier accompanied me. Had received many affectionate letters from my beloved Solita. I had for her a deep, sincere and enthusiastic affection, and thought to have found in her the friend of my bosom and the confident of my secret thoughts. Alas! I was doomed to be disappointed anew!

Arrived at 9 oclock. I would not have returned to Caracas in such haste had it not been for Solita whom I loved and idolized with a most besotted affection. The country is in a very unsettled state. I would have remained in La Guayra yet for some time did I not wish to return to one who in her letters full of the sincerest and warmest expressions of friendship, called me her sister and companion!

All this week passed away in sadness and hope deferred. Solita came not, though she sent me several notes.

Friday 15 This evening went out with the old ladies and the young ones and on our return found my idol, who passed the night here, but had not come to stay altogether as I thought she would.

Politics are in a bad state, the country involved in civil war. All is very sad. My life passes in cold monotony.

May. Day by day brings me more doubts of the sincerity of Solita's friendship, though the thought seems a profanation [?] to me! I am in a sad [?]. I have settled the accounts with all the witches and by *their reckoning* cannot stay here longer than June, so what will become of me? Solita answers me that she is always of the same intention regarding me but cannot provide me the exact time when she will be in her own house and so secure me a house.

21 May. Wrote a letter to Solita in which I spoke to her sadly and sin-

cerely, telling her how much I had felt her apparent indifference. This same day Solita came to pass a few days with us, in order that the old Dolores might take her to have her picture taken in Daguerreotype. Staid two days in which she treated me as before. My illusions are gradually dispersing, my dreams of real friendship awaking to a dreary reality. Solita replied to my letter of the 20 in a somewhat ironical way.

"Solita is an egoist who was for and loves but self." Bitter is that truth that gradually has been revealing itself to me.

In June wrote again to my ungrateful friend. Not once has she asked me to visit her, or indeed given me any proof of *true* friendship. She answered me rather sharply and I replied that I confessed I did not [intend?] to return to Caracas as I saw she did not love and esteem me as I thought and therefore thought of remaining in La Guayra. Wrote to C. with whom I had kept up a regular correspondence and had made for her several little things for her expected baby. Wrote to her but without mentioning what has occurred between me and Solita, only telling her I meant to spend a few weeks with her. If I had not that house to go to what would become of me? I have no hopes that my selfish friend wants me here! So much suffering so much trouble, so many emotions had had their dire effect upon my spirits. I have become very morose & low spirited, almost heart broken! At times, a silent and dread despair seizes upon my heart.

I have formed anew my old plan of going to Curacao, alone and penniless, to throw myself upon the mercy of *my people*, go to the synagogue and implore help of *my God* or die of despair if denied me within its sacred walls. Thought of going with Mr. Annilo Lopather [?].

Wed 14 June. This evening at 9 oclock M's baby was born, a little girl. Had spoken to C about my staying here and told her all that had happened between me and my false friend, who before my leaving Caracas had sent me a very sharp unfriendly and ironical letter.

This month passed with[out] any thing particular occurring.

M had told me that a German captain had something to communicate to me. My heart leapt with joy at the thought that it must be from my brother, Mr. H. or as I call him when I bid him good night each day my brother "Adolf." Have waited day by day and my wounded heart has bled afresh for hope deferred. The Marcanos have been here to see me. Have been to see Mrs. Hill; poor Linda knew me!

19 July Wednesday. Wrote to Francesco Badarraco [?] to get some notice about the captain. He came to see me and in the forenoon called with Captain Smith, the ship's name is "Echard." My friend & brother has told the Captain to come & see me and take information respecting my circumstances, and that he would have told him more but that the captain did not

again see him. Felt mortified at the thought of not having a letter in answer to mine, but was most joyful to think that one being remembers with affection the poor forlorn orphan! Could not speak freely with the captain because A.B was present, but told him I would give him a letter. He will not sail yet as Hamburgh is occupied by the Danes, the country in war, therefore he cannot return. I have written to Bordeaux to my friends the Mipes [?], a long supplicating and despairing letter confessing to them my remorse at having left my religion and my earnest desire to return to it, entreating of them their Father's permission to reside with them or to find me a home with some Jewish family. These letters went by the Abeille [?] at the beginning of this month. My health is not in a good state. The doctor has ordered me to bathe early in the morning and to take some drops. My head feels at time as if reason would forsake her seat and the dream palpitation and nervousness render me unhappy, and my hapless lot and cruel sufferings oppress my heart with unspeakable anguish!

Thursday 27 Wrote to Caracas to Mr. & Mrs J[esurun], a last and desperate effort to see if that gentleman would receive me in his family who are now in Curacao. I *cannot* remain here! Received a long and insulting letter from Solita, in answer to my last. Have written her a short note and returned her letters as she desired.

Friday 28th—Passed a miserable dull day as all my days are! Have been doing nothing but reading. Mr. Annilo [?] thinks of sailing tomorrow. Tomorrow is "Shabbas," my own holy beloved day of rest. Will Mr. J[esurun] do me the favor I ask him or shall I forever live on as I do?

Monday 31st—Passed as usual. No answers yet from Curacao. Each day my longing to be among mine own people! becomes more strongly.

Tues, 1st of August—What a terrible day! The squadron of Paes[18] presented itself and of course caused great disturbance in the minds of the inhabitants. All were called to arms, the can[n]ons mounted on the Esplanade, etc. This evening the ships were in sight and it was doubtful where they would proceed or come attack La Guayra. What a day!

Wed 2nd—The squadron is out of sight, they say gone to Margarita.[19] How good is the great God of Israel! He has taken from me the fear that I labored under yesterday. And if I had gone to Margarita as I had thought to have done to be out of this hateful place, I should probably find myself witness of a revolution. How inscrutable are the ways of Divine Providence! I know and feel that though unworthy of His protection that the God of our Ancestors watches over me. Oh my God, bring me but among mine own!

Thursday 3rd—This morning a Hamburgh ship entered the port. I had hoped to receive a letter by her, but was doomed to be disappointed. The place here is very unsettled. They say the Squadron is cruising about the port.

Friday 4th—Nothing particular occurred. Have felt rather unwell and went to lay down a little. When shall I be mid my own people. When oh when?

Friday is "Ereb Shabas" ערב שאבאס[20]

Saturday 5th—Passed as usual. I have fully determined not to work this holy day. Last "shabas" went to Tue's. Today spent my time reading.

Tuesday the 8th—Received Mr. Jesurun's answer. A negative but conveyed friendly and kindly, and after all I feel my heart somewhat relieved. God will surely not forsake me & will return me to mine own & to a home at last.

Thursday 17th, A memorable day! Marie, Mrs. Paulsen's adopted daughter comes often here. They intend to go to New Orleans and are waiting for an opportunity. Took a sudden resolution of going with them, and something within me told me I should go, that my lot would be fairer and my hopes return & above all I might return to mine own people, to my own God. After breakfast, went to Mrs. Paulsen and spoke to her; made the resolution of going with them.

Friday 18th. Went to Ine's and to Mrs. Belen. This evening told Clarita what I had made my mind up to.

Saturday 19th Made to hear a rather long tirade about my intended voyage.

Tuesday 22

אשע ייהוזחט וכך לייסזן סעפליך צברץ

ליבער פאטטער פאן ייסראאל ברינגר מיט באלד אונזער

ריטפן אמיט איך וייז היילאגען לאבא אונד יום טאו

הלטען כאן אמיין סעלאה[21]

Thursday 31st Mrs. Paulsen & daughter went on board the Danish schooner "Otto" to see if we could find passage to New Orleans and lost 20 dollars, which she had taken with her in a purse and which fell into the sea as Maria was going up the vessel's ladder; 15 were mine!

Friday 1st of September. Cannot go with the "Otto." The "Venezuela" has arrived and we think of going by her if they will lessen the price. I wrote an entreating letter to Mr. Dallet one of the owners who sent us word we should have the answer on Sunday when Mr Baultor [?] the chief owner would be down from Caracas.

Sunday 3rd. Mrs. Paulsen went out after breakfast and I remained waiting for Mr C who was to give me a definitive answer. This morning has been of the most severe days I have yet undergone. Mr D came up and after talking for some time on indifferent matters, made me a proposition no honourable man ought to make to a virtuous woman! Answered *as I ought* and he left me, the low-minded villain.

Monday 4th. I went to get our passports, went thrice to the Governor's house. Went to the Casa de Gobrena, to the Gobernacion and to the Casa de Sensas Municipales, and half dead with so much walking about in the hot sun—the mornings only are very cool. On Sunday morning spoke with Mr. Bandloir [?] who came up to our room in the inn upon leaving for La Guayra and told us the lowest possible price he could let us go for in the Venezuela were 50 round dollars each. I believe we shall not be able to get so much money together.

Wednesday 6th. This morning at 6 went with Mrs. P to Old P's house, gave me a check on Mr. Gaspari [?] and spoke very rudely, unfeelingly and harsh towards me and last not least denied me 10 ps and gave me the check only for 100 ps The bitch! So rich and so low minded to rob an orphan. Ah Venezuela you have made me suffer . . . made me suffer in four long endless years.

At 2 oclock the coach came to the door for me, drove off, took a glass of sugar water in Guaracarumbo. Had [?] for fellow passengers. Arrived at 6 o'clock. Went to [??] and staid the night. Took footbath, some tea, felt very ill, and slept very soundly and in quiet. Who knows if I shall get out of this country yet?

Thursday 7. Went to Clara's after breakfast. We cannot go with the Venezuela, but may if God helps us go with the schooner "Euphemia" who goes to New York and who asks 40 round dollars a head. Went with Mrs P. this morning to Patrick McClarens and there saw the captain also got my money from Gaspari [?] and told the captain he should have the answer tomorrow. This evening went to bed early. I was ill and unquiet [?]. Took a footbath and some aqua de nance.[22]

Friday the 8th. We think to go with the schooner not quite sure though.

Saturday 9. All settled we shall go with the Euphemia . . . Bid good bye to all my acquaintances & friends.

There was a nice breeze and sunshine. Came on board at 4 oclock in the afternoon. Was astonished at the size of the cabin; they say its larger than the cabins in the Venezuela; we have got a state room . . . very roomy & agreeable. Patrick also came on board and Mr. Jackson a passenger by the Venezuela, a very agreeable gentleman. They staid about an hour eating and drinking. Patrick playing quite a comedy. We are already under weigh [way]. I slept as well as the severe cough I got in Caracas would allow me.

Monday 11th—The captain has been kind enough to give me something for my cough & I feel a little better though I coughed at night and in the morning as if I would choke. The captain is very kind and obliging to his passengers.

I shall soon get into a new part of the world, and among mine own nation!! God of Mercies, grant us a fair and speedy passage and a good welcome from *my brethren.* N.B. Have bought a paraquite [parakeet].

At 12 were at sea.

Friday 15 Saw the land nearly all day. Do not feel at all seasick.

Saturday 16 Passed the day reading, Fine weather, rather squally.

Sunday 17 We have passed the Mona Passage,[23] and have fair strong wind and a squall now and then.

Monday 18 Passed Porto Rico; and see the land.

Tuesday 19 Am making a dress to put on when I get to Philadelphia, Please God.

Wednesday 20th Saw another schooner going the same way. Sat on deck this evening.

Saturday 23 A very rough day. The sea running mountains high.

Sunday 24 The same as yesterday, I am half sea-sick.

Monday 25 We are near Bermuda. Today it is smoother.

Tuesday 26. Fine weather . . . We might get to New York the day after tomorrow.

Wednesday 27 Fine weather till 11 oclock when a squall came on and increased to a gale; at 6 blew like fury and we went under reduced sails. Today is Ereb roshashonah.[24]

Thursday 28 Blew a storm all night. Breakfasted in my berth and got up at 1 oclock. It is a dry NorthEaster we have got and the wind blows. . . . The weather is clear and the sun shines. It is *very* cold since last Monday. There has been a considerable change of climate. The gale abated about 4 o'clock, thanks be to God. We are in soundings.

Friday 29th Yesterday my paraquite died! Fine, cool sunshine weather! At 8 oclock saw the first light house and soon after "Barny Gap" (I believe they call it so). At 2 were close to the land, plenty of vessels about. At 5 got up to "Staten Island"—the Doctor etc came on board. We have been put into quarantine till tomorrow morning because we have hides on board. Beautiful European scenery around. We are anchored close by the land.

Saturday 30 Got leave to go. Arrived at New York at 10 oclock. The captain went on shore, came back at 3 telling us we could go to Philadelphia in the railway at 4 oclock. The porter sent us a dragoman who took our things in his cart as the [??] lay close to the dock. We had only to pass over one vessel to gain the shore. Followed the baggage to the ticket office. After waiting for an hour got our tickets. At half past 4 were ferried over the Jersey river on the opposite shore, got into the railway train and started off. Passed through many towns, whose names I did not know, at the last town got into a steam boat again and after about half an hour's sail arrived at Philadelphia, it must have been about half past 9. Went to Penn Street to Mr. Kraus [?] where Mrs. P was addressed to and was astounded to find it a sailors boarding house! Had no room for us. Went to Mr. F -([?] and got beds there . . . bed at 12.

Tuesday 3rd Went to Townsend place to see Mr. Rabe [?] It was raining fast and the streets muddy and full of pools of water. I went out with Mr. Rabe and went to the houses of my brethren, was but ill received alas! & told at a certain Mrs Steins to return on Sunday, they only want *me* as a *servant*! & could not even let me remain until Saturday, which is "Yom Kipur."[25] Alas! Alas! Returned at 7 oclock in the evening soaked through by the rain! O what a sad and evil destiny is mine!

Thursday 5th Went to see Mdme Baullie [?] Marie has entered service here in the house. How sad and depressing are my future prospects, to become little less than a servant. I the great, the delicate minded one that once aspired to the loveliest dreams of poetry & imagination, the being who lived in a world of fancy & flowers & celestial sunshine now shrunk to so dreary and dire a reality! Where are all my illusions, all my dreams & hopes of a fairer lot beyond the wide waters? And not a being that can discover the kindest heart & mind, not an eye to read the hidden treasures & deep affectionate feeling hid neath the garb of this desponding brain & downcast eye? Will it be believed that I have wished myself back to the land of my sorrows to Venezuela? And ye my cold hearted brethren, Ye who worship the God my soul adores, the High & Holy One of Israel, wherefore meet me with the cold look of indifference, and the haughtiness of superior wealth? Does no voice tell ye that within that orphan's breast lie hid the purest hopes and ambition the most Holy? Does no inward voice plead in behalf of my suffering youth & orphan life? I tell ye to be as a mother and ye as brother toward a lonely and world forsaken daughter of Israel? And ye wish to humble me, you can reduce me to a menial station?

Friday 6 Went this morning to a fortune teller's who told me among other things that my father was alive, and that I had a brother in Europe! I am growing superstitious. Oh! If it were true that I might yet find a brother's arm to cling to, a brother's heart to cherish me, what more could I wish in this world of sorrow? Oh! For a brothers pure affection for a brothers close holy love!

Saturday 7th Today is "Yom Kipur." Fasted well, have dreamt today of *my brother*.

Notes

1. Johann Christoph Friedrich von Schiller (1759–1805) was a German poet, dramatist, historian, and philosopher.

2. This confirms that Cora Wilburn's first name was originally Henrietta.

3. Sir Walter Scott's historical novel *Ivanhoe: A Romance* was first published in 1820.

4. Laurence Sterne, *The Pulse, Paris.—A Sentimental Journey through France and Italy* (1768), reprinted in Sterne, *The Beauties of Sterne* (London: [C. Etherington], 1782), 23.

5. Presumably a reference to the Dominican War of Independence, which began on February 27, 1844.

6. See I Samuel 17:37.

7. On Pardos in La Guaira, see Isaac S. and Suzanne A. Emmanuel, *History of the Jews of the Netherlands Antilles* (Cincinnati: American Jewish Archives, 1950), 831, cf. 964–65.

8. French for "milliner."

9. Her parrot.

10. Probably the family of Jacob Abraham Jesurun (1806–1875), known as "the Curacaoan Rothschild." See Emmanuel and Emmanuel, *History of the Jews of the Netherlands Antilles*, illustration 105 (following p. 176), and 917.

11. Internal evidence suggests that this was the date of her father's death.

12. The word "nineteenth" is crossed through in the original. Cora Wilburn was actually born on December 1, 1824, so it was her twenty-first birthday.

13. In *Cosella Wayne*, she identifies him as "Don Jorge de Mas."

14. José Tadeo Monagas (1784–1868) was president of Venezuela from 1847 to 1851 and from 1855 to 1858.

15. Crossed through in the original.

16. Spanish for "breakfasted"; the implication is "Spanish-style."

17. Conservative pro-clerical elements led by the former Venezuelan president Jose Antonio Páez (1790–1873) rebelled against his more liberal successor, José Tadeo Monagas, in 1848. The revolt was put down in 1849, and in 1850 Paez settled in the United States; see Francis James Dallett, "Páez in Philadelphia," *Hispanic American Historical Review* 40, no. 1 (February 1960): 98–106.

18. Jose Antonio Páez see n. 17 above.

19. Margarita Island in the Venezuelan state of Nueva Esparta.

20. "Sabbath Eve"—the use of Yiddish orthography signals Wilburn's heightened desire to return to Judaism.

21. The orthography of Wilburn's halting Yiddish is difficult. The sense seems to be that this is the cry of a Jewish woman—Dear Father of Israel, bring me back to our [people]. Secure me in thy sacred ways and holy observances. Amen Selah.

22. Nance is a sweet yellow tropical fruit produced by the *Byrsonima crassifolia*.

23. A strait that separates the islands of Hispaniola from Puerto Rico, connecting the Caribbean to the Atlantic.

24. Eve of Rosh Hashanah, the Jewish New Year.

25. Yom Kippur, Day of Atonement.